flint's code

Also by Paul Eddy

Flint
Flint's Law

flint's code

Paul Eddy

This edition published 2006
by BCA
by arrangement with HEADLINE BOOK PUBLISHING
A division of Hodder Headline

CN 146134

Typeset in Sabon by Avon DataSet Ltd,
Bidford-on-Avon, Warwickshire

Printed and bound in Great Britain by
Mackays of Chatham plc, Chatham, Kent

In memory of Robert Ducas
and for Annoushka and Louise

Kissimmee
Central Florida

One

Grace Flint is bent like a question mark, up to her ankles in cloying mud, pulling on the crank handle of a rusted John Deere, only too aware that the chances are better than even that if the engine catches it's going to backfire and the crank will kick with enough strength to break her arm, and she's not paying the slightest attention to what Special Agent Jarrett Crawford is saying.

'DD!' Crawford demands, irritation in his voice.

'What?'

'I *said*, we could just kick down the friggin' door.'

Flint grunts. 'Not if Gröber's people have been here,' she replies, referring to Karl Martin Gröber, who occupies a place on the FBI's Ten Most Wanted list, though not with the prominence that Flint and all of her agents in the Financial Strike Force would accord him. She lets go of the crank handle and straightens her back and pushes her hands through sodden hair that clings like a skullcap. 'Because if this is Karl's work, you know he'll have told them to rig a little surprise for us.'

Now it's Crawford who grunts, as if he doesn't share the deputy director's certainty. 'You know something, DD? You need to be careful because that tractor you're messing with is what they call a Poppin' Johnny, and a Poppin' Johnny's got a kick like a mule.'

But Crawford doesn't volunteer to emerge from the shelter of the slash pines and the four state troopers who are providing back-up show no inclination to leave their vehicles while this sudden summer deluge lasts. Of course Flint could order Crawford to take a turn with the crank but delegation is not one of her strong points.

She stalls for time, running an eye over the bowline knot she has tied to attach a towrope to the tractor's drawbar. She has tied the other end of the rope to a security grille that guards the only window of a sprawling cinderblock barn and Flint reckons that if her knots hold, if the rope doesn't break, if she ever gets the bloody engine started, then the John Deere will pop that grille like a cork – and, as likely as not, bring down half the wall with it.

Listen, I did what you wanted and now I'm shitting myself, Vincent Regal had said in the message he'd left on Flint's voicemail, sounding like she'd never heard him: not the usual cocky, strutting Vincent – fraudster, facilitator to money launderers, and, when it suits his purposes, Grace Flint's grade A informant on matters apropos of Karl Gröber – but deeply scared. *You need to get there fast . . . You've got to get to me before they do. You owe me, Flint.*

True enough. Which is why Flint and Crawford, and their modest back-up of state troopers – all they could arrange for in the time – are now assembled at the end of a two-mile dirt track observing Vincent's hideout or, if they have arrived too late, his last resting place. There was no response when they'd banged on the door, called out his name.

Flint reaches under her parka to dry her hands on the Kevlar vest she has borrowed from the troopers and then she stoops once more to take hold of the crank. To give herself a boost of adrenaline she focuses her mind on just one of Karl Gröber's many crimes, and feels her rage swell.

'Hey, DD.'

This is Crawford, still nagging at her from the shelter of the pines. 'Think about it. If Gröber's hoods have been here, maybe they also booby-trapped the window.'

The tractor's engine coughs into life.

'Then, Crawdaddy,' says Flint, heading for the driver's seat, 'maybe you should duck.'

'Roger that,' replies Crawford, unabashed.

Unbidden, a searing memory from Flint's childhood is demanding her attention: the ghostly, porcelain-white face of a young man – no more than a boy, really – who lies crushed under an upturned tractor, her father coming late onto the scene, pulling her away, hiding her eyes in the folds of his coat.

To minimise the risk of back-flipping she has lowered the drawbar but the big rear tyres are excavating trenches in the mud and the John Deere bucks like a skittish colt, the front rearing up as the rope takes the strain. Crawford is calling to her, offering what Flint assumes to be critical advice, but he's wasting his breath because she can't make out what he's saying above the popping of the exhaust. Ignoring Crawford and the voice inside her head – that carping, whining side to her subconscious that she so despises; the voice that nevertheless wishes to point out the cab is *open*, that there is no top, *nothing whatsoever* to protect her in the event of a roll-over – she opens the throttle wide.

Pressed into the seat, feeling the metal struts digging into her back, she would be looking at the stars if there were any stars to see.

'*Jesus!*' – a piercing cry of alarm she hears above the racket of the engine, coming from the track to her left where the patrol cars are parked. She guesses that the troopers have finally abandoned the shelter of their vehicles, finally decided they'd better do something before the nose of the tractor rises towards the perpendicular.

About bloody time!

But not soon enough. Without warning, the John Deere shudders and lurches forward, the front end sags, the sudden momentum lifting Flint into the air. She's hanging on to the steering wheel, hanging on for dear life, when the engine dies with a single cough and for a moment there is a startling silence, until the security grille smashes into the back of Flint's seat with the force of ordnance.

Instinctively she ducks her chin into her chest and plunges to her right, letting go of the steering wheel and falling into a parachutist's roll. Even so, the ricocheting grille catches her on the shoulder with a stunning blow, sending her sprawling.

She lies in the mud waiting for the shock to subside, waiting for the pain to come, and part of her registers Crawford's fleeting inquiry.

'You all right, Grace?'

'Jerry, move it. Make a hard entry. Just in case . . . And, be careful in there.'

Then, no need of further instructions, he is no longer beside her but running in a crouch towards the gaping hole in the cinder block wall, his gun arm extended, the troopers following behind, passing by Flint as though she isn't even there.

She hears the shunting of multiple firearm mechanisms and a babble of commands and confirmations.

'Cover me!'

'Copy that.'

'Okay, come ahead . . . Go left, go left! Nine o'clock . . . Hold it there.'

'Set.'

Now there is silence and Flint cranes her neck trying to see what is happening. To her right, maybe fifteen feet away, she can just make out one of the troopers lying prone in the mud, aiming his shotgun like a sniper's rifle at the gaping hole in the cinderblock, covering the killing zone if that's what it becomes. Ten feet beyond him, Crawford and the remaining three troopers are set in a classic two-by-two split stack formation, their backs pressed against the wall, two on either side of the hole, preparing what the instructors at the Quantico training academy call a cold entry. In case there are opposition forces inside, Crawford has switched to non-verbal signals, trying to regain some element of surprise. He's pointing to himself to say he'll be the point man, the first one in, and then he points to each of the troopers in turn to indicate who's second, who's third, who's fourth. Now he's using his right arm to describe the type of entries he wants. His will be straight and fifteen feet into the barn, then he wants a button hook, then a cross entry, then a limited straight penetration from the last man in.

So it's a combination entry going by the book, as you would expect when Crawford's in command. But in Quantico's terms there are 'good' entry points and 'bad' entry points and Crawford doesn't have a clue what lies beyond the breach in the wall. Is the barn an open space or a cluster of rooms and corridors where any number of Karl Gröber's hoods could be hiding? And, if it's the latter, will Crawford find himself in a hallway – which is considered 'good' – or in a confined space facing an open door-way – which is definitely 'bad' because the point man becomes a sitting target long before he has a chance to visually clear the room and, as the training manual drily observes, 'this may cost you your life'.

Flint would join the raiding party, would if she could, but her shoulder has gone numb and she can't get any purchase on her arms, can't lift herself beyond the point where she is propped up on her elbows, supporting her head with her hands, staring at the hole in the cinder block and trying to penetrate its charcoal blackness, trying not to giggle at her absurd thought that since the breach she has made is called a 'mousehole' in Quantico-speak, what she has allowed for is one gigantic rodent.

Now Crawford is counting down the seconds with his fingers – five, four, three, two – then he spins from the wall and into the darkness, and now Flint is the one doing the counting – one, two, three – waiting for an eruption of gunfire. As she reaches five she hears a shout, 'Harper, coming in!' – the by-the-book warning that reduces the chances he will be shot by the point man – and the first of the troopers spins away from the protection of the wall and into the darkness. As he vanishes from Flint's view, the second trooper calls, 'Connelly, coming in!' and then she hears, 'Kowalski, coming in!' and both of them disappear, and now she is alone with the cover man who still lies frozen like a fallen statue, guarding the killing zone.

Eight, nine, ten . . . and another useless thought flits into her mind.

It's like being on an airliner racing down a runway, counting off the seconds between the moments when the nose lifts to when the plane can remain airborne even if an engine fails, and if you think about all the things that can go wrong in that envelope of potential disaster – if you *know* about all the things that can go wrong – your breathing shallows and your heart pumps harder to replace the missing oxygen.

She pushes the thought away and concentrates on her count. She's got to thirteen when she hears a bang that makes her heart shudder, then a second bang – but this time she thinks she also detects the sound of splintering wood and she figures that what she's heard is two mule kicks against a door, or maybe two doors. So, Flint decides, the chances are that they're in some kind of corridor and she imagines Crawford, the point man, moving fast, but not too fast for the others to keep up, and the second man peeling away at the first door they've come to, peeling away to kick it down and search and secure the space that lies behind it.

The numbness is leaving her shoulder, making way for the arrival of throbbing pain, but at least the strength is seeping back into her arms and she pushes herself to her feet. She stands unsteadily, giving herself a moment while she fumbles under her parka and the Kevlar vest to free her weapon from its holster, and now she's moving fast towards the black hole, calling a warning to the cover man, 'Flint, coming in!'

She doesn't make it. In an instant, in a process faster than her retinas can register, the impenetrable blackness of her mousehole transmutes into brilliant, blinding white. She hears a roar of wind and then she feels its intense heat on her skin, feels it sucking the breath out of her lungs, feels it lifting her from her feet as though she weighs nothing, hurling her backwards.

Now she's on the ground, rolling in the cloying mud, rolling over and over and over, slapping at her hair with her hands, trying to douse the fires that seem to have engulfed her.

Two

She feels cold, so terribly bloody cold. The paramedics have wrapped her in a blanket that seems to Flint to be made out of tinfoil, which retains body heat, they'd said. But there is no heat in her body, none that she can detect, only frost in her veins, or that's how it feels. They've got her lying in the back of their wagon, hooked up to a heart monitor and an intravenous drip that's feeding her glucose and salt solutions to kick-start her circulation. She's refused a sedative because she needs to make a call – correction, should *already* have made a call. She needs to tell Director Cutter what's happened before he hears it from somebody else. That, once again, people have died on her watch.

This is getting to be a habit, Flint.

That's not fair, Mr Cutter.

Not fair? Flint, you took a raiding party backassward into a building you knew nothing about, but which you knew was likely booby-trapped . . .

Crawford took them in.

You were in command.

I was lying on my belly in the mud trying to get my shoulder to work.

Grace, tell me, what were you thinking when you turned up there, what was the plan?

What I hoped—

Hoped? What you hoped? Hope is not a plan, Flint, not in my book.

That's what Aldus Cutter will say, something like that, and he'll be right and he'll make her feel even worse than she's feeling now, but she's still got to call him. Just as soon as her hands stop shaking so she can dial the number. When her teeth stop chattering, when she can string some words together that might make sense.

The rear doors of the wagon are open and she can see part of the posse of vehicles that has arrived. There are patrol cars with their strobe lights still flashing and unmarked saloons of the FBI, fire tenders and ambulances and a mobile lab from the ATF and, closest to where Flint lies, a huge white truck from the bomb disposal unit, and its looming presence strikes Flint as more than a little ironic for there is no bomb to dispose of, not any more.

It disposed of itself, spraying troopers Harper, Connelly and Kowalski with toxic smoke and globules of white phosphorous – phosphorous burning at more than two thousand degrees centigrade, beyond the melting point of steel – coating them, immolating them. Even in shock, Flint can still hear their screams.

Jerry Crawford wasn't killed because, being the point man, going by the book, he was further down the corridor, further away from the blast, and it's only the back of him, from his neck to his ankles, that is laced with third-degree burns.

They've told Flint little of this but she's seen three body bags being loaded into a truck, seen Jerry lifted gingerly into the helicopter that is taking him to the nearest burns unit. She'd wanted to get to him, to hold his hand, to tell him just how damn sorry she was, but the paramedics wouldn't let her move.

By comparison, Flint's injuries are minor. She was singed more than burned and they've hurried to assure her that it will all regenerate: her hair, the eyebrows, the eyelashes, the soft down on her neck and arms. She hasn't asked for a mirror because she doesn't care what she looks like. All she wants for now is to be warm.

She must have fallen asleep or, more likely, passed out because she doesn't see or hear him coming. The first she knows he's leaning over her, a barrel-chested man with a shaven head and small, pale eyes the colour of cardboard. He's wearing combat fatigues and there is a large name tag sewn on the jacket above his heart that says 'CHARLIS, FDLE'.

'Florida Department of Law Enforcement,' he tells her, as if she didn't know. 'I need to ask you something.'

The spittle on her lips has dried, gluing them shut, so all she can do for now is nod.

'We've found another body, but this one didn't die in the blast. We found him in a box, a TV carton, and I'm not talking wide screen. He was folded up like the India-rubber man. We need to know who he was.'

'Cribe im,' says Flint.

'Excuse me?'

She works her mouth to produce some saliva and tries again.

'Describe 'im.'

'That's not so easy, ma'am. His throat was cut, and the veins in his wrists, and it looks like he was drained. Then they broke his back, his ribcage, his legs, his ankle bones, his arms, his wrists – or maybe they did it the other way round. Anyway, that's how they folded him, you see. That's how they got him into the box.'

'Age?'

Charlis shrugs. 'Forty plus? Could be fifty.'

'Ow all?' asks Flint.

'How tall? Difficult to say in his condition but pretty short. Guessing, I'd say five five, maybe five six.'

'Build?'

'Folded out, he looks like he's been flattened with a roller, but from his bone structure I'd say on the heavy side.'

'Eyes.'

'That's another thing, Agent Flint. He doesn't have any eyes, not any more.'

Jesus Christ!

'Air,' Flint says, and then she repeats herself to make it clear she's asking a question, not appealing for help. 'Hair? The colour of his hair?'

'That he still has. Black, mainly. Streaks of grey, could be natural, could be highlights. Longish, over the ears, layered cut. I'd say he spent money on his hair.'

'Marks?' she asks. She means 'distinguishing marks' but that's more than she can manage.

Charlis understands. 'Listen, given the state of the body, I really couldn't say what was there before and what was inflicted pre- or post-mortem, and we're not going to know that until the autopsy's done. But I can tell you one thing: he was a hairy sonofabitch. A lot of body hair. I shouldn't say this of the dead, but he looks like a gorilla.'

Flint has gone to another place.

It's almost two and a half years ago, an hour after midnight, and she's in the parking lot of the River Café in Water Street, Brooklyn, sitting in her car, alongside her best CI, her most productive confidential informant, listening to him describe how easily Karl Gröber launders hundreds of millions of dollars for the crime syndicates from Eastern Europe through anonymous Delaware corporations.

Because in Delaware they don't want to know a damn thing. Who are the principals? They don't give a shit. What's their nationality? Who cares? Where are they based? Fuck knows. All the client needs is a registered address in Delaware that I can rent for fifty bucks a month.

And sitting in the back of the car listening to this is young Ruth Apple, newly recruited to the Financial Strike Force, newly recruited by Flint; about to become the undercover operator who will penetrate Gröber's organisation, skilfully directed by Flint. Ruth will eventually die by Gröber's hand, and it will be Flint's fault, in her opinion.

But what grips Flint now is the memory of her confidential informant reaching out to touch her arm with his hand, a hand matted on the back with black hair.

Her mouth is no longer dry and the trembling has stopped. Heated by her anger, she no longer feels cold.

'His name is – was – Regal, Vincent Regal,' she tells Charlis. 'He was one of our CIs and he's the reason we're here. Regal had been working for me trying to locate the whereabouts of a major perpetrator named Karl Gröber who's one of the Bureau's Most Wanted and subject to an Interpol Red alert and he's a grade A, world-class asshole and our number one priority, not least because—'

She is beginning to gabble and Charlis says, 'Ma'am, you need to slow down.'

Flint swallows to clear her throat. 'Mr Charlis, about two years ago Karl Gröber killed one of my agents . . . He threw her out of a helicopter while the rest of us watched.'

'In New York, right?'

'Yes, sir . . . Well, actually about six hundred feet *above* that particular part of New York . . . I tried to catch her, break her fall.'

Charlis says he recalls seeing the pictures on the TV news.

'Ever since then Karl Gröber has been our number-one priority
and there's almost nowhere in the world we haven't looked for
him; not a strike force resource we haven't used – including
Vincent Regal . . .'

She has to break off her account for a moment because her head
feels as if it's about to split in two.

'Take it easy,' says Charlis, seeing the pain in her eyes.

'I'm okay.' Not true but she has to press on. 'Vincent Regal is –
was – a facilitator for people like Gröber; people who need a
thousand dummy companies and the bank accounts to go with
them. But he was also our informant, because we had enough on
him to put him away for thirty years, so Regal walked on both sides
of the line. He was a devious, greedy little shit but he was our shit,
at least part of the time, and he wasn't entirely without merit. For
one thing, he had the guts to inform on Gröber even though he was
terrified of him . . . Even though he knew that if Gröber ever found
out he was informing, he'd end up in a box.'

'In a TV carton?'

Flint shivers inside, tries to mask her feelings behind a wan
smile. 'No, I don't think so. But he sure as hell knew that Gröber
was unforgiving and utterly ruthless . . .' *And he knew that I was,
too* – but that part she doesn't say.

'Anyway, about a month ago I hauled Regal in and made him an
offer: if he could come up with Gröber's precise location – a specific
place on a specific date and time, and it turned out to be real – we'd
wipe his slate clean *and* we'd pay him a reward of one million
dollars. Otherwise . . .'

Charlis whistles through his teeth. 'Hell, did you win the lottery
or something? And what was the otherwise?'

'That's way and beyond the largest reward we've ever offered,
which tells you the importance we attach to Gröber. The otherwise
was he'd lose his protection. I told Regal that if he couldn't or
wouldn't deliver we'd walk away from him; not try to intervene the
next time the Bureau or IRS or any other agency wanted to indict
him. What I didn't say – what I didn't need to say, because Regal
already knew – was that if he was indicted, and Gröber got to hear
about it, it was very likely he would never make it to trial. Gröber
doesn't like loose ends, you see.'

'You folks play hardball, don't you?' It's not really a question.

Charlis's tone, like the expression on his face, is entirely neutral; nothing to tell her what he's thinking.

'For the first couple of weeks Regal called me on a daily basis, more or less; mainly bitching about the impossibility of what I'd asked him to do. Then he called again, on a Sunday, and left a message on my voicemail – and this was the cocky Vincent of old. He said he had a lead, that he was taking a trip, that he might be sending me a postcard from "somewhere warm". I heard nothing more from him, until yesterday; another message on my voicemail.'

It's me. Listen, I did it! I know where he is, I found the fuckhead. But he knows that I know, and he's not a happy man, and I've been running for the last forty-eight hours and I'm almost out of gas. His people were waiting for me at the airport, Orlando, and I only got away from them by the width of a gnat's dick. Right now, I'm heading for my sister's place – kiss my ass, remember? You need to get there fast. Listen, I did what you wanted and now I'm shitting myself. You've got to get to me before they do. You owe me, Flint.

'Kiss my ass?'

'Kissimmee. Here . . . Regal's sister's husband owns this place.'

'Well,' says Charlis laconically, 'I guess you didn't get here in time. Are you up for making the formal ID?'

Not really but she nods her head to say yes.

'Is Jerry Crawford going to make it?'

'Touch and go.' Charlis adds something else but it's Cutter's voice she hears.

What were you thinking, Flint? What did you hope?

Three

Director Cutter's voice on the telephone, this time for real. His tone is soft and concerned. Nothing he says meets Flint's expectations of their conversation.

'No point in beating up on yourself, Grace. Wouldn't have mattered how you ran it or how Crawford went in. It wasn't a pressure switch or a wire or a fuse. The creeps who did this rigged a remote control detonator attached to a cell phone – or that's the way the crime scene folks are reading it. Likely as not, they had a button man on a hilltop half a mile away watching through a night scope, waiting for his moment. When your guys went in, all he had to do was call the cell phone to complete the circuit. Nothing you did different would have stopped him.'

'There are no hills around Kissimmee, Mr Cutter,' says Flint. Expecting to be blamed and half ready to defend herself she's confused, not yet ready to accept that he's letting her off the hook.

'From wherever,' Cutter replies, not missing a beat. 'He was watching you – or listening. It could be they stashed a mike and a transmitter somewhere in the barn so they'd hear you going in. The button man could still have been half a mile away, maybe more. Whatever they used, there was no way to spot it, nothing you could have done.'

'I could have sent in a bomb unit. To check for traps.'

'Sure you could – and those are the guys who would have gotten killed. Grace, listen up. It didn't matter who went in first or what their expertise was, the minute they went through your breach they were as good as dead. Whatever else they are, Gröber's people are pros and when you go up against psychopaths with tactical skills you've got to assume you're going to take casualties. Just count yourself lucky you were out of it.'

'Jerry wasn't lucky,' Flint says quietly. Cutter's equanimity is beginning to get on her nerves.

'Maybe luckier than you think. I spoke with the head of the burns unit in Orlando ten minutes ago and he said Jerry's got a fighting chance, maybe more than a fighting chance. Now' – Cutter pressing on without a pause, the timbre of his voice changing as he turns to business – 'I've sent Rocco Morales and the Go Team down there on a Gulfstream and cleared it with Supervisor Charlis. They should be at the scene any time about now.'

It wasn't Flint who broke the news. Long before she was in a fit state to call Cutter in New York – after Charlis had told her that she would either go to the hospital voluntarily or he'd have her arrested on whatever charge occurred to him and taken there anyway – the first sparse accounts of the Kissimmee massacre were on the wires, leading the evening news bulletins. The night-watch supervisor at the headquarters of the Financial Strike Force had put two and two together and called Cutter on his car phone, and Cutter had abandoned his dinner date and turned the car around and returned to the Marscheider Building to take command of the Ops Room. Within ninety minutes of the explosion, Cutter had established the outlines of what had happened, called in a favour to borrow a Gulfstream jet from the FBI, scrambled the Go Team, called Supervisor Charlis of the FDLE to tell him a simple truth: that when it comes to know-how about rigging bombs, Rocco Morales is right up there with the best, on account of his previous service with Delta Force. Then Cutter had called the burns unit where Jerry Crawford was not really expected to live, called Jerry's wife to tell her otherwise.

Lying on her hospital bed, partially covered by a thin cotton towel which is all the weight she can tolerate, feeling the soothing breeze of an electric fan that is cooling her skin, Flint lets her mind drift to imagine the half-truths, the almost-lies, that Cutter has been telling Crawford's wife.

He's going to be fine, Christie. The doctors say he's got more than a fighting chance, and we both know he's going to fight because that's who he is, right? Believe it, Christie, you'll have him home before you know it.

Something like that.

Christie Crawford won't be fooled, not for long. She's as bright as a button and she trained as a nurse, and when the shock wears off, it will quickly dawn on her that a husband who's been sprayed with burning phosphorous is not going to be home anytime soon, if at all, and Christie will be on the first plane to Orlando. But by then Cutter will have minders from the strike force in place, people to accompany her, hold her hand and deal with the doctors, the media, shield her from the worst of the truths. Director Cutter is scrupulous about that: about dealing with the collateral damage when one of his pilgrims gets hurt.

On the phone Cutter is saying, '. . . find yourself a mousehole, find a way into his organisation.' Flint has lost the thread and she doesn't respond and suddenly there's a sharp edge to Cutter's tone: 'Flint? Am I talking to myself?'

'Sorry, Mr Cutter, say again. The connection isn't too good.'

'I said I need you back here ASAP. Your operation, it's a shambles. With Regal dead you don't have any way of finding Gröber and—'

'Maybe not,' she interrupts. 'And maybe I do.'

'Really? You think so? Tell me how.'

'Regal flew into Orlando yesterday from *somewhere* and even if he was using fake ID we can probably trace the flight – even if we have to go through every single manifest, check the passengers one by one. Then there's Gröber's goons who were waiting at the airport. It's unlikely they were local talent so the chances are they also flew in from somewhere and maybe we can backtrack their flight. There will be CCTV footage we can look at and—'

'*Grace!*' Cutter cutting her off. 'You're talking utter bullshit. A thousand to one shot, at best. And even if it comes off, even if you can find Gröber, you're missing the point. The point is, he's taken out Regal, and Regal was the only breathing witness you had who could identify Gröber, point to him in court. The rest of what you've got is circumstantial: bankers and accountants who've never seen Gröber, wouldn't know him if they fell over him; scumbag lawyers who are going to fight and scream all the way to court – and even if they're forced to testify, no jury's going to believe a frigging word they say. That's all you've got, except for flow charts and timelines and analyses that are going to send the judge to sleep. The way I see it, without Regal to stand up for you, you don't have a case you can win, and that's the message Gröber was sending you tonight. And, I'll tell you something else: the one thing that surprises me is that he didn't put a goddamn ribbon around the box.'

Flint is silent for a while and then she says quietly, 'Gröber crossed the line tonight, Mr Cutter.'

'He surely did.'

'And not for the first time.'

'You've got that right.'

'And taking him to court is not the only option ... not if he resists arrest.'

Now it's Cutter's turn to pause. Then, 'Only if you find him, Grace.'

'I'll find him, Mr Cutter. I'll find the mousehole, get inside.'

'Amen to that,' says Cutter.

There are blisters erupting on Flint's skull and neck, indicating that some of her burns are second degree but, she tells Cutter, she will be back in New York by the weekend, back in the Marscheider Building first thing on Monday morning, whatever the doctors may say.

After the phone call she drifts into shallow sleep that is too often disturbed by thoughts of Jerry Crawford and the memory of screaming troopers, until the night nurse insists on injecting a sedative.

Under the influence of a powerful narcotic, what Flint hears now, what she imagines in her dreams, are the screams of her child.

Washington DC

Four

To the Senate Permanent Subcommittee on Investigations Flint says, 'Karl Gröber launders funds that are the proceeds of criminal activity. His principal client is one Alexander Çarçani – Sasha to his friends – an Albanian national with a similar background to Gröber in that they were both apparatchiks of the old school who served their respective communist regimes with ruthless devotion, until those regimes imploded. Then, overnight, they each embraced capitalism as though they had been born to it – the very worst aspects of capitalism. Çarçani makes his money out of some of the worst crimes imaginable.'

'Could you be more specific, please?' asks Senator Coleman, chairman of the committee, an air of weariness about him, as though he is growing tired of indulging the reticence of yet another recalcitrant witness.

Flint hesitates, unsure how far to go, her copper's innate distrust of all politicians showing like a badge.

Senator Coleman sighs. 'Very well, I'll say it again. This a closed hearing, Miss Flint, which I have called so that this committee can learn the background to the Kissimmee massacre. Your testimony is confidential, meaning for our ears only, for, whatever you may believe, this is one committee that does not leak' – and he glances left and right to receive righteous nods of confirmation from his fourteen fellow senators. 'Nothing that you say in this room will be repeated outside of it; not one word. Are we clear on that, Miss Flint?'

Still she hesitates until, under the table, she feels a commanding nudge from Aldus Cutter's plump thigh.

Another beat or two of silence and then, 'Since late nineteen ninety,' she begins, 'and ever since, Alexander Çarçani has sold women from the old Eastern bloc into prostitution in the West, and Karl Gröber has laundered the funds the trade generates. Let me be clear about the scale of this trade. I'm talking about *thousands* of women every year, many of them little more than children, and hundreds of millions of dollars in revenues. According to our information, Çarçani now controls prostitution, or is the prime source of its fodder, in many cities around the world.'

'Specifically?' Coleman reminds her. 'Can you help us with specifics?'

'In Milan and Rome, London and Manchester, Madrid and Barcelona, Amsterdam and Rotterdam, Hamburg and Frankfurt and Berlin, and' – Flint pauses a moment for effect – 'New York, New Jersey, Chicago, Miami, Los Angeles. That's just a sample list,' she adds. 'Anywhere in the West where prostitution is flourishing – prostitution and the production of pornography – Çarçani has his fingers in the pie. Shall I go on?'

'You have our full attention,' says Senator Coleman.

'Senators, this is the scrag end of the trade, where Çarçani operates. The women he enslaves are lured to the West with promises of lucrative work, usually in nightclubs; they think they're going to be waitresses, hostesses, working behind the bar, that sort of thing. If they want to make extra money they can be strippers, they're told. If they want to make in a single night what it would take them six months to earn in Tirana or Bucharest or Sofia, then they can be table dancers, or maybe lap dancers – or, again, that's what they're told. The reality, when they get to the West, is very, very different. Most of them, almost all of them, never see the inside of a nightclub. If they're lucky, they end up imprisoned in a room above the club, where they are repeatedly gang-raped by their minders until sex becomes meaningless. Then, when they are sufficiently submissive, when they no longer care what a man does to them, they are put to work, expected to service fifteen to twenty clients a day, every day. They are in demand because they're young, usually attractive, and Çarçani's women are always priced below the local competition – that's the key to his success, he undercuts the competition. Not that it matters to the women what the punters pay because they don't receive a cent of it. They're fed and housed and clothed, and given cosmetics and cigarettes, and that's about all. If they complain about their treatment, or the demands of the punters, they're beaten. If the punters complain, they're beaten. Sometimes the girls are beaten anyway, just for the hell of it. If they get pregnant – and most of them do, because protected sex is not an option – they're forced to have abortions. Usually,' Flint adds and then she pauses again, and this time it isn't for effect.

Senator Coleman waits a decent interval before urging, 'Go ahead, Miss Flint.'

'We – and by we I mean law enforcement, here in the US and in Europe – we have documented hundreds of women who were enslaved by the Çarçani organisation, who say they were forced to undergo abortions. These are women who were either arrested in the course of police raids and who volunteered to talk, or women who escaped from their minders and sought help from sanctuaries, refuges, social workers. But, recently and increasingly, we've seen a new pattern: women who got pregnant and were forced to go to term. In the last year, we have sixty-eight documented accounts, more or less identical, of Çarçani women – if I can use that phrase – who were forced to go to term only to see their babies taken away from them, either immediately after birth or within a few days. They never saw their babies or heard of them again. That is because, we have good reason to believe, Çarçani has developed two small but very profitable sidelines: he sells the babies to the illegal adoption trade, or . . .'

This time Flint does not pause but the rest of what she says comes out like an expulsion of breath, as though she's been punched in the stomach, and the senators cannot grasp her meaning.

'Or what? We can't hear you, Agent Flint. You need to keep your voice up.'

'I said, Senator' – her voice now stridently loud – 'or the babies are sold for body farming.'

'Farming?'

'Farming for transplants. Hearts, lungs, livers, kidneys . . . The butchers that Çarçani deals with, they harvest from the babies whatever organs they can sell.'

Then her voice fades again and whatever it is she whispers is lost in the stunned silence of the room.

'Ruthlessness is a term we use all the time to describe perpetrators, and we devalue it,' Flint says. 'Compared to these two, compared to Karl Gröber and Alexander Çarçani, most of the organised criminals we're up against don't know what ruthlessness is. Oh, we can say, often do say, that this villain or that would kill their own mothers – but that's *exactly* what Gröber did. He killed his mother *and* his father, by betraying them to the East German authorities, by *ensuring* they were shot by border guards while attempting to escape to the West. He was just eighteen years old at the time.'

The dam seems to have been breached; Flint is transformed from a reluctant witness into one who can't say enough. Why, exactly, she doesn't know but she has found something reassuring, even seductive, in Senator Coleman's air of quiet authority and his grave politeness. What the hell, she has decided, she will tell it all, and the only thing she fears now is that she will run out of time; that before she can give the committee much more than an inkling of what she knows about Gröber and Çarçani, the senator will call an end to the hearing.

She is hurrying to continue when he interrupts.

'Miss Flint, if you could just—'

'I'm sorry?'

'If you could just slow down a little. If you could just take us back to the genesis, tell us for the record who these people are.'

She would have said, 'It's in the file, Senator,' if Cutter hadn't nudged her thigh.

But, come on, Mr Cutter, why did I have the terriers working all hours preparing an A-to-Z on the case if these people won't even look at it?

The terriers are the analysts of the Financial Strike Force, hand-picked by Cutter from a small number of universities; therefore young, mostly irreverent and, without exception, exceptionally bright. Their raison d'être is to reduce thousands of pages of evidence and intelligence – sometimes tens of thousands of pages – into comprehensible 'case narratives' that even the most jaded investigator or prosecutor will find compelling. For practice and their own amusement they have reduced *War and Peace* to a narrative of thirty-eight pages that still retains every one of the novel's characters, and describes every major event.

On the desk in front of Flint there is a copy of the terriers' file on what Cutter has christened Operation Payback but she has no need to consult it.

'Karl Martin Gröber,' she says flatly as though she is reciting, 'born in Leipzig, in what was then East Germany, in June nineteen fifty-one. Çarçani, Alexander George Çarçani, he's older; born in Vlorë on the Adriatic coast in either November nineteen forty or April nineteen forty-one – the Albanian records we have are contradictory on that point. Either way, he was a slow learner compared to Gröber. Alexander wasn't recruited by the Sigurimi until he was twenty-one or twenty-two. Karl, on the other hand, first volunteered for the Stasi when he was fifteen.'

'The Sig-ur-imi?' Coleman repeats, carefully mimicking Flint's pronunciation. 'Again, for the record if you will.'

'Directorate of State Security, or the secret police. Albania's version of the East German Stasi and more or less a carbon copy; same galloping paranoia, same urge to know everything about everybody, the same brutal methods of repression – total isolation of so-called dissidents, arbitrary arrests, torture, sometimes murder. It's difficult to say which was worse but the Sigurimi may just have had the edge, if only because for much of the time Albania was virtually cut off from the outside world. No outside scrutiny, you see, whereas the East Germans at least made some pretence of running a democracy.' Flint pulls a sour face. 'Not that you would have known it, not if you were on the Stasi's list.'

'The Stasi and the Sigurimi, they were never allies?' Coleman asks.

'Far from it, not after nineteen sixty-one when the Soviets and the rest of the Eastern bloc broke off relations with Albania. In fact, for much of his Sigurimi career – after nineteen seventy-eight, when the Albanians also fell out with the Chinese, who were the last friends they had left – Çarçani was the deputy head of the foreign intelligence section, and one of his targets was East Germany. In that sense, the Sigurimi and the Stasi were in direct opposition.'

'So, can we assume that Çarçani and Gröber did not begin their alliance until after the collapse of the communist bloc?'

'Correct, Senator, although both of them knew it was coming, and both of them had been planning for the future. In Gröber's case, in nineteen eighty-four, while he was attached to Department Twenty-One, the Stasi's Central Group of Analysis and Information in Berlin, he established a sub-group to study the Western banking system, on the pretext of establishing the best way of disguising the source of operational funds that the Stasi sent to its agents and collaborators abroad. The sub-group worked for three years without ever producing a report – and by then Gröber knew every trick in the book. As for Çarçani, by nineteen eighty-nine he was up to his neck in the so-called Greater Albanian Movement that wanted to liberate Kosovo from the then Yugoslavia, and much of the funding for that came from Albanian gangs operating here in the US, primarily in New York and New Jersey. It was fairly standard criminal activity – drug trafficking, prostitution, coordinated robberies from automatic teller machines – but what law enforcement began to suspect was that the perps – excuse me, the perpetrators – were employing sophisticated surveillance and counter-surveillance techniques. The FBI got involved and what it established, to its own satisfaction, was that the gangs had been reorganised into small, self-sustaining cells and intensively trained by Sigurimi agents.'

'Sent to this country by Mr Çarçani?'

'Yes, sir.'

In the ensuing silence Flint glances at her watch and realizes she has been testifying for nearly two hours, and she hasn't even scratched the surface. She feels a tug of panic because she is running out of time.

'Let me see if I have this right, Agent Flint. It is your testimony to this committee that Alexander Çarçani, a high official of a foreign intelligence service, sent espionage agents to the United States to further an organised criminal enterprise?'

'Exactly that.'

'According to the FBI?'

'According to the bureau, Senator, and everything we've learned subsequently fully supports that view.' Somehow she stops herself from adding, *for once*.

Then it is Senator Coleman's turn to check the time, and he ducks his head for a whispered conference with the ranking minority member of the committee. Flint senses Cutter stir like a snake waking from slumber, hungry for its next meal.

'Director Cutter.'

'Senator?'

'It's become obvious to us that in eliciting testimony from your strike force we have seriously underestimated the time necessary to adequately cover the ground.' An understanding nod from Cutter and Coleman continues, 'I'm going to have to bring this hearing to a close, because we have business on the floor of the Senate, but it is our intention to schedule a continued hearing, or hearings, as soon as possible, and ask you and Agent Flint to return.'

'It's Deputy Director Flint,' Cutter says, though without a hint of reproof. 'DD for short.'

'Excuse me, *Deputy Director* Flint – and that goes to my point. For while it is vital that this committee obtains the fullest understanding of the threats to this country posed by Gröber and Çarçani and their organisations, it is implicit, and we are very aware, that our need for information diverts you from your task of finding them and bringing them to justice. Simply put, Director, can you and your deputy afford the time?'

'I can't think of anything more important than informing the legislature of the threats we face,' Cutter says. 'I don't see how we can *not* afford the time.'

Snake oil, Flint thinks. *What's your game, Mr Cutter?*

Senator Coleman is conferring with his chief clerk who is flicking through the pages of her diary, shaking her head.

'Director Cutter, we're going to have to do some rescheduling and get back to you on dates. Provisionally, I'd ask you to see if you and DD Flint can both clear your itineraries for Wednesday and Thursday of next week. Does that seem feasible to you?'

'Whenever it's convenient for the committee, Senator, we'll be here.'

'Good, and I thank you for your cooperation. Speaking of which,' Coleman continues, making a show of searching through his papers, 'I have no doubt that it would greatly assist the committee if, in the meantime, your office could provide a written briefing that is more substantial than . . . this.'

Coleman holds up the terriers' file, Operation Payback – except, as Flint immediately recognises, it is wafer thin, no more than a few sheets of paper, decidedly not the nearly two hundred pages of narrative that her copy of the terriers' file contains.

Cutter doesn't blush, doesn't even blink.

'Reducing the product of our investigation into a useful summary – and, Senator, we're talking here about enough paper to fill this room – and getting that much information summarised is going to be one hell of a task. But, yes, sir, we'll do our best for you in the time available.'

Flint doesn't know where to look. She just knows that if she even glances at the file in front of her the mask of her face will crack.

'Well, don't overburden your people,' says Coleman. 'Perhaps you can just provide a chronology of events and a cast of the major characters?'

'Like *War and Peace*,' Flint says, quietly enough for only Cutter to hear – and once again she feels the press of his thigh.

'You bet, Senator,' says Cutter brightly. 'We'll do whatever we can.'

In the soaring atrium of the Hart Building, where Flint and Cutter wait for the car that will take them to the airport, Cutter stalls. He can see that Flint is seething, wonders how long it will be before she boils over.

'You know about Hart?'

'Excuse me?'

'The senator this building's named for?'

'No, sir.'

'He was quite a guy,' says Cutter as though he's speaking of a personal friend. 'Someplace here,' he continues vaguely, turning slowly on his heels, searching the wall with his faded blue eyes, 'there's an inscription . . . talks about his courage and integrity . . . and, if I remember right, there's something about, what is it now . . . yeah, I remember: his inner grace and outer gentleness, quote unquote. Not a bad epitaph, right?'

'Wonderful,' says Flint, picking up her briefcase, putting it down again.

'Something bugging you, Flint?'

'Not really, Mr Cutter. Why would there be? Only, I just sat next to you while you flat out lied to a senate committee under oath.'

Cutter flinches. 'I didn't lie, Grace, I delayed.'

'Oh, really? And after you'd *delayed*, what if Coleman had asked me what I had in my copy of the file?'

'You'd have thought of something.'

In sheer frustration Flint aims a kick at her briefcase and marches away from him. She is attracting attention from the Capitol police guards and Cutter is giving them what he intends as a reassuring glance.

'Why didn't you give them the full report, Mr Cutter?' Flint demands, coming back. '*Why?*'

Now Cutter is smiling broadly, not to placate Flint but because he's seen Bob Tyrer, the subcommittee's chief investigator, emerging from the elevator, scanning the atrium, spotting Cutter and Flint, heading their way like a man on a mission.

'Because it's too damn good, too seductive. Anybody reads that, they think they know the whole story, and we'd have been lucky to get a couple of hours in there. Now we've got two whole days.'

Flint looks at him as though he's mad. 'You want to spend two days in front of a committee?'

'Two days? Hell, I'll take two weeks if we can get it. Listen, Grace, you're a great cop, and a lousy politician, which is why you don't begin to understand how important this is to the strike force, and right now I don't have time to explain because we have a visitor.'

Turning Flint by the shoulder, raising one hand in a greeting, Cutter indicates the imminent arrival of chief investigator Tyrer.

'Try me,' says Flint through gritted teeth, not yet willing to surrender.

'As one of you Brits once said, time spent in testifying is seldom wasted.'

'He said reconnaissance, Mr Cutter. Time spent on *reconnaissance*.'

'Same thing,' Cutter replies. 'Or, anyways, same result.'

Tyrer is angular, bony, with a way of stooping his shoulders as if to minimise his height. His long, pale face has lines that shouldn't be there, not at his age, but his eyes are clear, a startling blue, regarding Flint with frank enjoyment.

'Sorry about that,' he says.

'About what?'

'Dragging you back here next week. You must feel it's a complete waste of your time.'

'Not according to my boss,' Flint says primly. She is beginning to find Tyrer's gaze unnerving and she looks away, pretending to search the atrium for any sign of Cutter, who had made an excuse about going to check on the car.

'The thing is,' Tyrer says, talking to the side of her head, 'I wondered if we could have dinner.'

'What?'

'I mean next week, when you come back. I know this French restaurant, nothing pretentious, but they do serve—'

Flint, startled, spins her head round to look at him. 'Are you hitting on me, Mr Tyrer?'

'God, no. I wouldn't have the nerve.'

But his bright eyes never leave her face and his smile doesn't lack for confidence.

'The thing is—'

'You keep saying that.'

'I know I do, and that's because you're making me nervous. The thing is, we need to talk.'

'About?'

'If I tell you, will you promise not to go ballistic?'

'No,' says Flint. 'You'll have to take your chances.'

She folds her arms, and so does he, and she can't help but notice the delicate beauty of his fingers.

'The thing is, I was at Columbia, class of ninety-eight, with some of your – what do you call them? Your terriers? Well, we keep in touch, some of us, and sometimes we talk about things of mutual interest, and there's stuff about the relationship between Gröber and Çarçani that I don't understand, and—'

He breaks off because, though neither her expression nor her posture has changed, he can sense the menace in her stillness.

'You know, this would be so much easier if we could just talk over some decent food and a glass of Côtes du Rhône.'

'No it wouldn't. Are you going to tell me their names?'

'My friendly terriers? Never,' he says defiantly, smiling all the while.

'Then goodbye, Mr Tyrer,' says Flint, and she picks up her briefcase, turns her back on him, walks towards the exit intent on finding Cutter or, failing that, a cab on Constitution Avenue, and it is only by shouting, 'IS IT TRUE THAT GRÖBER TRIED TO KILL ÇARÇANI?' his voice booming around the atrium, that he stops her, brings her hurrying back.

'Are you out of your mind?'

'I think it's important.'

'What is? And keep your voice down.'

'Tirana, the summer of nineteen seventy-nine, Scanderbeg

Square, some kind of celebration of the Glorious Revolution, Chairman Hoxha, eternal First Secretary of the Party, on the podium. Someone takes a shot, sniper's rifle, range of about one hundred metres, but it's not Hoxha who's the target, it's Alexander Çarçani. The shooter misses, only creases Çarçani's skull, but the thing is,' – Tyrer nods to acknowledge his verbal tic – 'I'm told that, in all probability, Karl Gröber was the shooter.'

'And your point is?'

'Is it true?'

'Who knows?' and Flint shrugs.

'But what if Çarçani knew? I mean, what if Çarçani believed that it was Gröber who tried to kill him? Wouldn't that, couldn't that, disrupt their relationship?'

'He already knows,' says Flint.

'He does? How?' But Flint is once more heading for the exit, and this time she does not turn around.

Because that's what I told him, is what she doesn't say.

England

Five

As Flint's pregnancy approached the stage when airline regulations would no longer permit her to fly, she had suspended her relentless hunt for Karl Gröber and returned to England and to her father's home in Oxfordshire to wait out the last few weeks before her son was born. To take her mind off the physical discomforts – the indigestion, the breathlessness, the backache, the swollen legs – she had absorbed herself in the intelligence reports on Çarçani. Since those reports came from MI6 – the British Secret Intelligence Service, which Flint had every reason to deeply distrust – she was unwilling to take anything she read at face value. Even so, she had become intrigued by MI6's assertion – no more than speculation, really – that it was Karl Gröber of the Stasi who had attempted to assassinate Sasha Çarçani of the Sigurimi in Scanderbeg Square in the summer of 1979. It had occurred to her that it didn't really matter if the allegation was true. What if Çarçani could be persuaded to believe it? And how might the thought be planted in his mind? During the long uncomfortable nights when the repeated need to urinate had kept her awake – getting in and out of bed with no husband (grumpy or otherwise) to help her – she had gradually formulated a plan that she hoped might seed a civil war between Gröber and Çarçani.

Reaching Çarçani presented no problem since, unlike Gröber, he was not officially wanted for anything; not a fugitive and not in hiding. He lived openly, indeed prominently, in Milan where he was well known as a successful financier and, according to MI6's intelligence, a generous contributor to many of the city's good causes, including the frequent financial appeals of the basilica of San Ambrogio where, on most Sundays and most saint's days, he could usually be found. But Flint knew that she could not simply present herself to Çarçani and make the accusation against Gröber, however convincing the legend she might invent for herself. She would need 'proof' to show Çarçani: something tangible – documents, perhaps, conjured up from the voluminous files of the Stasi. They would have to be forgeries, of course. The question was, forged by who? A question she had raised with Cutter when she called him at the Marscheider Building in New York and told him of her embryonic plan.

'Talk to Ridout,' he said, meaning Nigel Ridout, head of the East European Controllerate of MI6, and Flint's nemesis.

She laughed as though he'd made a joke.

'I'm not kidding, Grace. Like it or not, Ridout's a player in this game and you're gonna have to work with him. You need to get over it, swallow your pride.'

Pride! Her *pride*! At the time she was prone to sudden bouts of weepiness – her body besieged by all those hormones, no doubt – and she'd almost burst into tears.

'This is not about *pride*, Mr Cutter. This is about the fact that Nigel Ridout is a lying, devious, double-crossing shit.'

'Right. Sounds to me like just the kind of guy you'd want on your team. Listen, Grace, I don't know if the scam you've got in mind is gonna fly. What I do know is that if you intend to try and start a war between Gröber and Çarçani then whatever you show Çarçani better be pretty goddamned convincing, otherwise save me some money and just buy yourself a one-way ticket to Milan because if you go in there half-assed you won't be coming home. Bottom line: if you want to pull this off – and I think it's worth a shot – then you need Ridout, lying, devious shit that he is.'

She couldn't believe what she was hearing. Caustically she said, 'You left out double-crossing, Mr Cutter. Have you forgotten what he did?'

'No, and neither have you – and that's the point. Sure, he'll have his own agenda, and sooner or later he'll pull some stunt, try and stiff you, like he did before. But this time you'll be watching out for it – leastways I hope you will. Use him, Grace, like he used you. And watch your back.'

Cutter wouldn't listen to any more of her arguments and after he ended the call – with a brusque 'I've gotta go' – she had dissolved into tears; sobbed so loudly she'd brought her father to her room to inquire what was wrong. 'Ridout,' she said, and her father instantly understood.

'Oh, dear Lord. Not again, Gracie, not again.'

This is what Nigel Ridout did to her; what she can never prove but knows in her bones and will never forgive. Three years ago in a crowded bar in downtown Miami a young man had asked to share her table and they'd got to talking. His name was Ben Gates and he was an ornithologist with an all-consuming passion for nature and she'd liked that about him; liked quite a lot about him, actually. They'd met again and started dating and become lovers and quickly fallen in love, and within eight months they were married – and it was perfect; all too perfect to be true, as it turned out.

None of it was true. His name was not Ben Gates and he was not an ornithologist and he did not love Grace Flint. He penetrated her in order to penetrate the Financial Strike Force; in order to learn from his wife in any way he could the most closely held secrets of her undercover operations – specifically her operation to bring down Karl Gröber – and he did that under orders and at the direction of Nigel Ridout who had his own interest in Gröber, and his own agenda. Flint's husband was Ridout's spy, his mole, and Ridout was his pimp.

Flint's husband was dead but, in a manner of speaking, he lived on – as the father of her unborn child.

'Aldus, Mr Cutter, he can't expect this of you, Grace,' John Flint said, the deep lines of his concern showing on his face. 'It's simply too much to ask.'

And she vehemently agreed with her father, and vowed she would see Ridout dead before she would ask for his help or trust him with the knowledge of any part of her plan.

A week later, when the birth of her child was imminent, she called him at home.

'Grace, what a delightful surprise! You're in rude health, I trust. Ready for the big event?'

'Never better.'

'Splendid. And what can I do for you?'

'I don't have a secure line so I've written it down. You need to send someone here to collect it.'

There was only the slightest hesitation. 'Of course, my dear. Post haste. When you say *here*, you're staying at your father's place, I expect?'

As if he didn't know.

Her son was thirteen weeks old when Flint received a message from Nigel Ridout saying he had 'something' for her.

She had travelled to London but declined to set foot in the headquarters of the Secret Intelligence Service, Ridout's lair. Instead, she had insisted that they meet for lunch in a subterranean restaurant, Orso in Covent Garden where, from the table in the back corner she had specifically requested, she could watch the stairs; see who came in, who left.

'So, you have a bonny boy, I understand.' Ridout beamed at her. 'And how is Jack?'

'Thriving, thank you.'

'Not too young to leave, you don't think?' Ridout asked, as though he cared.

Flint shook her head. *Go on, Nigel, why don't you ask if he's the spitting image of his father?* But Ridout had never acknowledged that Ben Gates was his malevolent creation.

He gave her a file, and while she read it he sprinkled salt on the tablecloth and drew an elaborate pattern of concentric circles with his fingertips. Then, 'It's rather good. Don't you think?'

'Not bad,' she conceded.

'It's remarkably authentic,' Ridout continued. 'If friend Çarçani has the file forensically examined – and, of course, he will have it forensically examined, suspicious bugger that he is – he will learn only that the paper, the ink, the official stamps – particularly the stamps, I'm told – are entirely pukka. Courtesy of Otto, of course, who, by the way, sends you his warmest regards.'

Dr Otto Schnell is senior director of the Bundesnachrichtendienst, the German intelligence service and, second only to Nigel Ridout, the man Flint least trusts in the world. It is her firm conviction that Schnell and Ridout are co-conspirators in the plot to obstruct and frustrate her pursuit of Karl Gröber; that two years ago, when Schnell presented evidence that Gröber and her fugitive husband had died together in a helicopter crash, Ridout knew the evidence was false.

Nevertheless she smiled, as though she was pleased.

Misunderstanding, Ridout said, 'You know, Grace, you really should give Otto some latitude, a little leeway for his . . . what shall I call them? His necessary deceptions?'

'If you like,' she said.

'For that's what they were, you know: necessary deceptions – in the circumstances, your circumstances at the time.'

'I see.'

'Do you? Do you really, Grace?' Ridout leaned towards her across the table, a sudden bitter urgency to his tone. 'Because I sometimes wonder if you do understand, if you have the faintest fucking notion what the game is actually about.'

'What game, Nigel?' she asked evenly, nothing more than a polite inquiry.

'The quest, the grail, Grace – the holy fucking grail that all of us seek, together but separately, in our separate ways and by our different means and, if I might say, with varying degrees of success. You think you own Gröber, Gröber and Çarçani, that they are only yours, to have and to hold. What you forget, what you choose to forget, is that we – Otto and I – had comrade Gröber in our parallel sights many moons before you knew he even existed. And before you remind me that it wasn't one of my agents that Gröber killed, or one of Otto's, allow me to remind you that we had no hand in your wretched operation; that you chose to fly solo, if you'll allow the metaphor; which is, perhaps, why you crashed.'

An unfortunate metaphor, Nigel, Flint might have replied, for Special Agent Ruth Apple – Flint's Special Agent Ruth Apple, her responsibility, her call, her fault – did indeed fly solo, having been thrown from Gröber's helicopter at a height of some six hundred feet.

'Your point being, Nigel?' she replied instead.

'My point being, dear girl, that if our file enables you to get close to Çarçani, which I'm sure it will, and if it enables you to get out of Milan alive, which I hope it might, you should not, for once, forget your friends – meaning me, meaning Otto. We are legitimate shareholders in this enterprise, Grace Flint; we are your partners, we stand united – and, as our great leader is fond of reminding us, when we stand united we are greater than the sum of our parts.' Ridout showed his fine white teeth. 'Or something like that.'

'Our great leader? For Christ's sake, Nigel!'

'How are you getting there?' he asked abruptly, withdrawing his smile, using his fingers to flick away imaginary breadcrumbs from the cover of the file. 'To Milan, I mean, keeping in mind that your Frau Fischer is an impoverished widow, is she not? No money to waste on ruinous air fares. Not if you don't want to alert the rude suspicions of friend Çarçani.' His tone, now brisk, businesslike, implied that he was merely seeking basic facts.

Flint shook her head. 'Partners or not, Nigel, I don't want to be tripping over your outriders, your minders, your shadows, or whatever you call them.'

'Of course not,' said Ridout, as though the idea had not even occurred to him.

'I'm going there alone. It's what I prefer.'

'Was it ever any other way?'

'So you don't need to know.'

Ridout leaned towards her, closer than he'd ever been. 'If I might suggest, take the bus,' he confided. 'Frankfurt to Milan by way of dreary Switzerland; Eurolines, I think you'll find the operator's called. Bit of a long haul, I'm afraid, but amazing value that even an impoverished widow might credibly afford.'

'Really?' said Flint. *You bastard*, she thought, for a Eurolines ticket – Frankfurt to Milan – was already in her bag.

Milan, Italy

Six

San Ambrogio is Milan's oldest church and, in its austere way, the most beautiful. Within the basilica, where nine kings of Italy were crowned, is the Golden Altar that contains the remains of the patron saint of Milan, making it a place of pilgrimage for the most devout Milanese, and the most fashionable, especially on a sparkling Sunday morning in April when many of their children, or their children's children, waited to receive their first Communion. On this particular Sunday there were more pilgrims than the basilica could accommodate and the overflow spilled into the courtyard, to where the audio of the service was being relayed by concealed loudspeakers.

Easing her way through the crush of spectators and ranks of baby carriages, Flint observed how Çarçani's bodyguards, lounged against Roman columns, had placed themselves strategically to reduce the risk of wounding each other with crossfire in the event of trouble breaking out.

Scusi, scusi, per favore – polite but insistent, Flint pushed her way into the church. From her headscarf to her stockings and sensible shoes she was dressed entirely in black; a young widow seeking solace, perhaps, which was exactly the impression she wished to create. Not that it earned her any respect from the bantam guard blocking the stairway that led to the high gallery overlooking the nave. Before he would let her pass he ran his eyes and then his hands over her body, brushing her breasts and her buttocks and the insides of her thighs.

Alexander Çarçani waited alone on the gallery, statue-still, gazing down on where his youngest grandchild would shortly be anointed with oil and received into the Church – a boy with deep-set eyes that, in the muted light of the chancel, appeared to be black.

'What do you want?' Çarçani asked, scarcely bothering to look at her.

'Justice,' Flint said, and Çarçani nodded, as though that was something he might be inclined to dispense. He had lost some weight and he seemed a little taller than MI6's surveillance photographs suggested but the head, seen in profile, was unmistakable: that long, imperious chin; the fleshy lower lip; the Roman nose; the same deep-set eyes that his grandson had inherited; the broad slant of his forehead. 'Looks a bit of a mongrel, doesn't he?' Nigel Ridout had remarked to Flint in that disdainful tone of his, but there was no doubting that, in the flesh, Çarçani was imposing. The waves of thick silver hair swept back behind his ears set off the deep tan of his face which was only marred by a paler horizontal stripe, running like a groove from just above the corner of his left eye to behind the top of his ear.

'I know who did that to you,' Flint said softly, pointing at his disfigurement.

Çarçani seemed not to have heard her. His gaze remained fixed on the chancel while he mouthed the words of the Gloria that the congregation was now reciting.

Gloria immensa, Signore Dio, Re del cielo, Dio Padre onnipotente. Signore, Figlio unigenito, Gesù Cristo, Signore Dio, Agnello di Dio, Figlio del Padre . . .

'That's why I asked you for an appointment,' she said. 'That's what I came here to tell you.'

'My husband is . . . excuse me, my husband *was* Peter Fischer,' Flint said in passable Italian, though she hoped it was tinged with strong German inflections. 'For two years he worked for the Firm, in *die Zentrale* in Berlin, for Department Twenty-One, the Central Group of Analysis and Information. Karl Gröber was his boss.'

There was not a flicker of reaction from Çarçani. He seemed lost in the scene below the gallery where children dressed in creamy-coloured cassocks now stood in neat ranks before the Golden Altar.

'After *die Wende*,' she pressed on anyway, 'after the Wall came down, Herr Gröber instructed Peter to remove certain files from the centre; many of the files of Department Twenty-One. There was no time to be selective because every day the mob outside Normannenstrasse grew stronger and we did not know, Peter did not know, how long it would be before they seized the building. So Peter just removed what he could, working at night, bringing the files back to our apartment in the trunk of his car until it was impossible to continue, because there was no more room to store them. Our apartment was full of those files. Believe me, Signore Çarçani, there was scarcely room to move!'

Tu sei pie-tran-go – la – re, Signo-re – a lone treble's angelic voice, tentative on the first note but growing stronger, drifted up from the chancel.

'When Peter reported the problem, Herr Gröber immediately proposed a solution. Somehow he knew that my parents . . .' She broke off and laughed softly, as though she was embarrassed by her own foolishness. 'Not somehow, of course he knew, Herr Gröber knew *everything*. But, excuse me,' she continued quickly. 'Herr Gröber knew that my parents lived near Potsdam and that on their land there were outbuildings that might accommodate many, many files. You know Potsdam, Signore Çarçani?'

Nothing from Çarçani.

'No matter. It is not far from Berlin: a forty-minute drive – less when the traffic is light; two hours for a round trip, including unloading time. So, four trips a day – that was Herr Gröber's solution. If I made four trips a day, I could transfer the files from our apartment in East Berlin to Potsdam in less than a week, that's what he said. Of course, meanwhile Peter would be bringing home more files and more files and there would be more trips next week, and the week after, and so it would continue until Herr Gröber was satisfied – or until I was caught.'

Believe it, Flint, had been the mantra of the instructors at the academy. *Whatever lie it is you're telling, believe it. Because if you don't, if you don't feel the fear or the pain or the joy, or whatever else it is you're selling the target, if you don't believe it really happened, neither will they.*

It was not the chill of the church that caused Flint to shudder but the scene vividly created by her imagination: her Trabant pulled over at a *Polizei kontrol* on the road to Potsdam; excited search dogs and the heavily armed righteous guardians of a new German order in the East about to discover the trunk full of pilfered Stasi files, tokens of a regime that, almost overnight, had morphed from all-powerful to most-vilified. *And you have stolen these files for what purpose, exactly?*

'Anyway, I moved the files to Potsdam,' Flint said, 'including this file. Your file, Signore Çarçani.'

There was now a full choir singing in the chancel, their voices glorious, pulsating, overwhelming even the insistent ringing of someone's mobile phone.

Alexander Çarçani held the file – *his* file, pilfered from the archives of the rapidly disintegrating Stasi, if he believed the softly spoken words of Frau Fischer, beguiling in her widow's weeds.

'I apologise for not providing a written translation, Signore Çarçani,' Flint said. 'My Italian is simply not sufficient. I will do my best to tell you what it says, but I'm sure you have the means to obtain an accurate conversion of—'

Çarçani dismissed her excuses with an impatient flick of his hand.

'Very well. The first two pages are the original – the *original*, Signore Çarçani – of a memorandum from Oberst Martin Braun, Colonel Braun, director of Department Ten, within Main Department Two, of the Ministry for State Security. As you can see,' she said – though Çarçani was not looking at the file, only, intently, at her ghostly pale face – 'the memorandum is dated twelve January nineteen seventy-nine and it is addressed to the minister himself, General Mielke. I should explain, perhaps, that Main Department Two was responsible for counterintelligence and, within that remit, Colonel Braun's Department Ten was specifically responsible for liaison with the other intelligence services of the Warsaw Pact. The subject heading of Colonel Braun's memorandum is: "The counter-revolutionary and terroristic activities of the Sigurimi". The opening paragraph states that, at the request of the minister, Department Ten has fully consulted with its fraternal allies and established the following: one, that the Sigurimi has and continues to conduct hostile operations against member countries throughout the Pact; two, that these hostile operations include espionage, subversion and intimidation of Albanian defectors and attempted sabotage; three, that the chief architect and orchestrator of this "campaign of anti-Socialistic activities" – those are Colonel Braun's words – is the deputy director of the foreign intelligence section of the Sigurimi. In a word, Signore Çarçani, you.'

Widow Fischer was not reading from a copy of the file; she spoke like a newsreader who had learned her script by heart.

'In paragraphs two through six, Colonel Braun summarises incidents of Sigurimi activities ... perhaps I should say alleged activities' – she glanced away to escape Çarçani's gaze for a moment – 'in the GDR, Czechoslovakia, Poland, Hungary and the Soviet Republics. The incident reported – excuse me, alleged – in paragraph six, concerning the death of the defector Meksi, Adil Meksi, is elaborated in paragraphs seven through nine. In summary, Signore Çarçani, Colonel Braun informs General Mielke that you personally authorised the elimination of the defector Meksi, and his common-law wife, Nikki, and their child, Ramiz. This, says Colonel Braun, is the irrefutable conclusion of the Moscow police, as reported to him by the Soviet Ministry of State Security, otherwise known as the KGB. Paragraph ten states that, on your orders, before their throats were cut, Ramiz Meksi, aged twelve, and his mother were repeatedly raped.'

Ramiz Meksi, when he was repeatedly raped, before his throat was cut, was approximately the same age as the black-eyed grandson of Alexander Çarçani, the boy in the nave with the golden voice, and part of Flint wanted to take Çarçani by the neck: two steps forward, parry his defensive thrust, use his momentum to swing him round, her forearm pressing inexorably on his thyroid cartilage, her knee in the small of his back – and even if the bodyguard at the bottom of the stairs heard the commotion he wouldn't have a chance of getting there before she was done.

But Frau Fischer was entirely circumspect. 'Colonel Braun provides no substantiation for this allegation,' she said as though she was inclined to dismiss it. 'He simply states it as fact.'

Alexander Çarçani, she noted, had the gift of stillness. Confronted with ghosts from his past, he remained motionless, unmoved.

'In paragraph ten, Colonel Braun refers to discussions he has held with Boris Letkin of the KGB liaison directorate in Berlin regarding the degree of the threat posed by the Sigurimi's activities, and he reports Comrade Letkin's unequivocal opinion that retaliatory action against the Sigurimi – and against you, specifically, Signore Çarçani – is required. In the next and final paragraph, Colonel Braun respectfully proposes to the minister that the matter should be referred to the Kollegium to consider what that action should be. The Kollegium was the minister's advisory body but it is well known that General Mielke was not . . .' Widow Fischer hesitated while she searched for the appropriate word.

'Sympathetic, I think – General Mielke was not *sympathetic* to advice; he was, after all and as he frequently remarked, the Minister. At the bottom of Colonel Braun's submission, you will see what the Minister has written in his own hand: "Refer to Gröber." Not the Kollegium, Signore Çarçani, but to Oberleutnant Karl Gröber of Department Twenty-One, the Central Group of Analysis and Information. Why?'

No answer from Çarçani.

'The reason, I suggest to you, is to be found within the next three pages of the file. First we see a travel authorisation, signed by General Mielke over his personal seal, an authorisation that permits Oberleutnant Gröber to visit Moscow. The sections of the authorisation requiring the date, the duration and the purpose of the visit are left blank. Oberleutnant Gröber has carte blanche to travel to Moscow when and for how long he chooses, because the Minister says so. This, I assure you, Signore Çarçani, is most irregular. In Potsdam, at my parents' house, I have examined thousands of the Firm's files and never have I seen such an authorisation so lacking in detail. It was General Mielke's doctrine, indeed his rigid directive, that everything should be written down – and yet here he leaves us with mysteries. Who was Gröber going to see in Moscow, and why?'

Preghiamo, said the priest below them, his entreaty for the ritual *pausa di silenzio* that precedes the final act of the celebration of Communion, and Alexander Çarçani raised a warning finger to his lips. But Widow Fischer would not be silenced, for Flint knew she was running out of time.

'The next page,' she whispered, moving closer to Çarçani – so close that their clothes touched – 'provides the answers. It is a letter from Minister Mielke to Arkady Sobolev of the First Chief Directorate of the KGB in which he affirms that in the forthcoming discussions about you, Signore Çarçani, Oberleutnant Gröber is acting with his personal authority.'

Çarçani placed his hands on her shoulders and pushed her away.

'The next page,' she said, becoming slightly breathless in her haste, 'is a memorandum from Oberleutnant Gröber to Minister Mielke, marked "Eyes Only", which reports on his meeting in Moscow with officials of the First Chief Directorate. The subject is "The recommended elimination of the Albanian terrorist Çarçani". The text of the memorandum describes exactly when and how, with Moscow's full approval, Gröber proposed to kill you.'

Çarçani had his back to her, heading for the stairs.

'Like my husband was killed by the pig, Gröber, shot in the back of the head. Shall I tell you what happened?'

E Spirito santo, chanted the priest.

Amen, the congregation responded.

Before she could say any more, Çarçani was gone and the bantam guard was standing at the head of the stairs, his face moulded into a grin, the index finger of his right hand beckoning.

Come to me, he seemed to be saying. *Because you have no choice.*

New York

Seven

Contained in Grace Flint's personnel file at the Marscheider Building is a red flag notation from Human Resources that her continuing appointment as Deputy Director (Operations) of the Financial Strike Force is 'subject to quarterly review'. That is because, in the opinion of Human Resources, recent events in Flint's life – in particular the treachery of her husband and the birth of his child – have left her in a fragile mental state. The people in Human Resources claim that Flint exhibits many of the symptoms associated with borderline depression: arbitrary interference (into any aspect of the continuing Karl Gröber investigation); magnification (of Gröber's place in the scheme of things); minimisation (of just about everything else); that she also suffers from anxiety (particularly about flying, but not, it seems, the welfare of her child). And, they say, she drinks too much – and since Flint drinks mainly alone, away from prying eyes, late at night in the solitude of her apartment, they don't know the half of it.

Now, if further proof were needed, has come what the media has dubbed the Kissimmee Massacre, an event which further reflects badly on her judgement, in the view of Human Resources. Flint should be history, or, at the very least, on indefinite compassionate leave and it's only Cutter's legendary stubbornness, his dogged insistence that her talents are unique and invaluable to the strike force, that has saved her. The price she pays is the compromise deal that Cutter struck: Flint keeps her job so long as she agrees to undergo weekly counselling with a psychotherapist selected by Human Resources – a former Russian doctor whose last name Flint cannot easily pronounce and whose English syntax is sometimes as wild as the mass of silver hair that seems to double the size of her head.

'When I was last here,' Flint is saying, seated uncomfortably in an overstuffed chair with broken springs that serves as Dr Przewalskii's consulting couch.

'When you were last *not* here,' says Dr Przewalskii.

'I called to cancel, Dr P, I left a message on your machine. And I sent you a cheque.'

'Money! You think I care about your money?'

Obviously not, for the general shabbiness of Dr Przewalskii's office is evidence that most of her patients are recent arrivals to the United States from parts of the former Soviet Union, damaged refugees who often cannot afford to pay even her discounted fees. Flint pays the full fee of $300 per double session but Dr Przewalskii does not always remember to cash the cheques.

'So?' she demands, jutting out her chin, fixing Flint with eyes that sparkle with unspoken accusations. She's trying to provoke her, trying to get Flint to develop the same feelings for her therapist that she holds for her dead husband and maybe her father, the forbidden feelings that are hidden in the unconscious part of her mind. In the jargon of psychoanalytic psychotherapy, it's called 'transference' and it often works, but only if the patient is willing to play the game.

'I was out of town on an operation and I couldn't get back in time.' Flint shrugs as if she can hardly be bothered to explain. 'I thought I would be back but I got delayed.' Another slight lift of the shoulders. 'It happens.'

No mention from Flint of a phosphorous bomb or the screams of dying men, no mention of a body folded in a box. Nor does she mention her own injuries or her hospitalisation (the reason she was 'delayed') and there is no explanation for the blue headscarf that is tied tightly around her head like a bandanna, concealing the fact that her skull is bald.

But of course Dr Przewalskii knows all this because Human Resources will have informed her. *You can talk to her as though she were your priest*, they'd told Flint, implying that Dr Przewalskii was 'secure', meaning thoroughly vetted and cleared to receive even the most sensitive operational information.

That was only their opinion – and, anyway, Flint never, ever talks to priests.

Dr Przewalskii wastes a few dollars of Flint's money on silence, leaning forward in her chair, staring intently at the headscarf. Flint knows, because the therapist has proudly told her, that Przewalskii is also the name of the only surviving breed of truly wild horse and sometimes – like now – she affects to toss her head with equine impatience.

'Shall we get on?' asks Flint, not waiting for consent, opening her briefcase, taking out a small leather-bound notebook, turning the pages to find the one she wants. 'Here we are, what we were talking about at the end of last session.'

Dr Przewalskii lifts her head and snorts exactly like a horse. 'Why do we need to refer to that? We're not having a meeting, are we? I want to know why it is that you take notes each time you are here. Is it about being an agent? Am I under *investigation*?'

Flint resists the urge to smile. Calmly she says, 'I write things down. It's what coppers do.'

'But you don't write things down when you go to a café with a friend and talk about your life, do you? You don't take *notes*?'

'No, Dr P, but then I'm not paying my friend three hundred dollars a time, am I? It's not the same thing, is it? If I could get to the place I want to be by talking to a friend, I wouldn't be coming to see you, would I?'

Another snort and Dr Przewalskii shakes her head as if to say, *Nice try, but I'm not buying.* 'Some psychotherapists would want to interpret this but I'm not going to, I'll let you off the hook just this once. But by writing everything down, do you know what you're doing? You're blocking – blocking what unconscious thoughts you may be having because you're afraid of them. I had a patient once who wrote down every word I said to her, literally every word, to the point that I would have to wait for her to catch up.'

'Sounds good to me,' says Flint.

This is the game, this is how it's played, this is what has happened half a dozen times before: Dr Przewalskii making her forays, trying to get inside Flint's head, trying to probe the secrets in her superego; Flint resisting the intrusions, finding ways to avoid facing the truth and getting better at it, more lateral in her thinking, more cunning. She senses, perhaps for the first time in the presence of Dr Przewalskii, that she might be the one in control.

'Is this what this is about, you and your notes? You write to block, yes? To block your thoughts?'

'No, Dr P. What this is about is respect. Respect for you, because what you say is worthwhile and relevant and useful. Respect for me, that I care enough about this process to make sure I retain it.'

Dr Przewalskii looks bemused; for once she doesn't have a thing to say.

Collapse of one stout psychotherapist, thinks Flint.

But the contest isn't over until the session ends and, as Flint knows from reading a lengthy profile of her in the *New York Times*, Marina Przewalskii has played mind games against the very best. When she was still in Russia, when she was denounced to the KGB as a subversive, when she was held in the Lubyanka and interrogated for eighteen straight days, when she was threatened with the Gulag, when they took away her job and her apartment, when they frightened away her friends; when, for more than a year, she lived in Moscow as a non-person, someone who didn't officially exist, she didn't crack, didn't confess, didn't sign the confession they fabricated for her – she *argued* with them. In the end they grew tired of her, kicked her out of the Soviet Union, let her go to America but without her dependent mother, her two-year-old son or her cat. It was nine years before the boy was allowed to leave Moscow and join Dr Przewalskii in New York. By then, her mother and the cat were long dead.

Before Human Resources gave Flint a copy of the *Times* profile of Marina Przewalskii, someone had thoughtfully highlighted with a yellow marker the kicker paragraph, the one that revealed that the informant who had denounced her to the KGB was her husband, the father of her child. Perhaps Human Resources thought this would encourage some empathy between Grace and Marina, two women similarly betrayed.

Fat chance.

'The last time you were here,' says Dr Przewalskii, commandeering Flint's opening line, 'I asked if you killed your husband because of the baby or in spite of the baby.'

'It was a foetus, Dr P, a tiny, tiny foetus. I wasn't even sure I was pregnant. And' – Flint shifts in the chair – 'I did *not* kill him; I was just there when he died.'

'But is that what you feared, do you think?'

'Feared what?'

'That you were pregnant, that you were going to have Ben's

baby. After every fantastically terrible thing he'd done to you, now his seed was inside you, *growing*.'

'His name wasn't Ben, Dr P. That was just another of his lies. His real name, if you want to know, was Errol – Errol Flynn, in fact, and I'm not kidding.'

'Why you don't answer the question?'

'I thought I just did.'

'I don't think so.'

'*Christ, Marina!*' Flint is out of the chair, on her feet, heading for the window that is coated with grime. 'It's so bloody hot in here. How do I get this open?'

'It won't open, it's sealed. And you're still blocking.'

Flint spins round from the window, a flush on her face. 'No I'm not, I'm dissimulating. I'm doing what any perp does when they're cornered, because that's what it feels like, Dr P – like I'm a perpetrator you're interrogating. You're trying to get me to say something that isn't true and when I won't you accuse me of *blocking*, whatever that means, and I can't win, can I? Because the more I deny the feelings of guilt you want me to have, the more you're convinced I'm suppressing hidden emotions. It's called catch-22, isn't it?' She folds her arms and leans her back against the window. 'I'm interested, Dr P, did you learn your technique from the KGB?'

Dr Przewalskii smiles but there is a blaze of anger in her pencil-grey eyes. 'No,' she says quietly. 'From the KGB I learnt other techniques that are illegal in this country, fortunately for you.'

'I'm sorry. That was gratuitous.'

The doctor nods a curt acknowledgement, then nods again towards the overstuffed chair. Reluctantly, Flint resumes the patient's position.

'The point is, you keep insisting that I killed him and—'

'You told me you shot him many times.'

'Shot at him. I shot *at* him, Dr P, nine times, because he was trying to kill me – or at least I thought he was . . . at the time.'

Dr Przewalskii waits.

'Listen, this is not something I really want to talk about. What's the bloody point?'

And still she waits.

'He was a plant, a mole, sent to deceive me from day one. He married me under false pretences, not because he loved me or to sleep with me – though he did that whenever he wanted – but to get access to the files I was sometimes stupid enough to bring home from work. He made copies of those files and gave them to his masters. He betrayed me and, much more important, he betrayed the most sensitive operation the strike force has ever run and, as a direct result, one of my agents got thrown out of a fucking helicopter. Now *he's* dead, and now I have his child . . . That's it, end of story. What more is there to say?'

'How could I possibly know?' Dr P's eyes are wide with innocence.

Jesus!

Now it is Flint's turn to resort to silence. She concentrates her attention on a spider that is climbing up the wall behind Dr Przewalskii's head.

After a while, 'What did you and your husband have in common, do you think?'

'Once you strip away all of his lies, absolutely nothing.'

'Except the lies, of course.'

'Sorry? You've lost me.'

'The pretences. You both liked to pretend to be somebody else, no?'

Flint comes out of the patient's chair. 'Not me, Dr P. Not at home . . . not in the marital bed.'

'But when you are working, many times you are . . . what do you call it? On cover?'

'Undercover.'

'And isn't that what your husband was doing – working undercover, even in the marital bed?'

'Oh, *come on!* There's *no* comparison. When I adopt a false identity it's to investigate criminals, to get inside their heads and their schemes; to uphold the law – and I don't deceive my family or my friends, ever. He deceived his wife, me, in order to further a criminal conspiracy that led directly to murder.' She's trying to keep her voice down, trying not to shout. 'You don't think there's a difference?'

Dr Przewalskii is resting her chin in her hands. 'No,' she says. 'No comparison at all.'

Eventually Flint surrenders, but only on her terms. She paces up and down the threadbare carpet, refusing to sit in the patient's chair.

'All right. After he blew my operation and after my agent was murdered – even if he didn't know that would be the consequence – he bolted. He ran from me, of course, but also from the spooks, the spies he was working for: MI6 in London, the German intelligence service. He thought he might have outlived his usefulness to them, that he was expendable. They, the spooks, didn't want me looking for him, they wanted to find him for themselves, so they rigged some evidence to convince me he'd died in a helicopter crash in Croatia – him and Gröber – and I was stupid enough to believe it, for a while. Anyway—'

'Why don't you call him by his name?'

'I've *told* you: Ben wasn't his name, just another of his endless lies.'

'Errol, you said.'

Flint thinks about this, rejects the implicit suggestion. 'His M16 code name was Mandrake.'

'Very well then, Mandrake.'

'Anyway, by that point he, Mandrake, was also on the run from Gröber and his hoods because he'd blackmailed Gröber by threatening to tell me that, firstly, Gröber wasn't dead and, secondly, where I could find him.'

Dr Przewalskii looks startled. 'I don't understand. You were supposed to believe that Mandrake was also dead, yes? That he and Gröber were killed in the same accident? How could he reveal that this Gröber was still alive without—'

'Exactly. But he'd calculated that he could get hush money out of Gröber – which he did – and still betray Gröber to me – which he also tried to do, by sending me a letter. He thought if he gave me Gröber I might forgive him. Or, at the very least, that Gröber would be my first target and while I was concentrating on Gröber, he could slip away. Vanish.'

'Mandrake?'

'Yes.'

'And was his calculation correct?'

'No.'

'Because you hated Mandrake even more than you hated Gröber? This is possible?'

Flint is still pacing the carpet, reliving moments and feelings she would rather keep suppressed, hugging herself with her arms.

'It wasn't about hate, Dr P – though, God knows, I despised them both. But if you're asking me who was the more evil, the more culpable, then I would say Gröber, without a doubt. Despite what he'd done to me, I always knew that Mandrake was a pawn, more the monkey than the organ grinder, and there's no question that if I'd known where Gröber was he would always have been my primary target, my first choice ... Would have been, if Mandrake hadn't seriously miscalculated. He waited too long to write me the letter, you see. On the day he sealed the envelope, took it to the post office, I already knew where he was.'

In La Rochelle in western France, living on an ocean-going yacht that he'd bought with money extorted from Gröber; a handsome sloop which he'd intended to sail into oblivion. But Gröber's hoods had followed the money trail, and Flint had followed the hoods, and before they could kill Mandrake – which was certainly their intent – an elite intervention unit of the French national police had, well, intervened.

'With violence?' asks Dr Przewalskii, who is clearly not immune to the pleasure of learning vicarious detail.

'With extreme violence,' Flint says deadpan, which is as far as she will go. 'Mandrake escaped, sailed his boat off into the Bay of Biscay, heading for Spain – and who knows where beyond – unaware he had a stowaway on board. Me.'

The boat was an hour out into the bay when she'd emerged from her hiding place in the forward cabin with a nine-shot Beretta in her hand.

'Hello, Mandrake,' she said.

The light has faded to murk and all that illuminates Dr Przewalskii's office is the jaundiced glow of the street lamps and the headlights of the traffic on Upper Broadway, filtered through the grime that coats the sealed window. The doctor sits in the cast of a shadow, almost invisible to Flint, except for the pinpricks of light reflected in her eyes.

Back now in the patient's chair, Flint says, 'He told me his story, beginning with his real name, date and place of birth, where he was raised; that kind of thing.'

Dr Przewalskii smiles. 'So simple. You found Mandrake and he told you the truth.'

'More or less.'

'Why? Do you think he was afraid of what you might do to him?'

Flint shrugs. 'I guess,' she says, as if she doesn't know.

Listen to me. You think you know me but you don't, not really, not any more. And you have no idea what I'm capable of doing to you, what I will do if you make me. I'll ask you again and for the last time . . .

'And what would you have done, do you think?'

No answer from Flint.

'Would you have killed him?'

'Yes.'

The next question is how but Flint shakes her head, unwilling to go there. Instead she hurries through the crux of Mandrake's story.

'He was a drug dealer, a supplier of cocaine and heroin to a bunch of wealthy Arab kids living in a flat in London – a couple of Saudi princes, an Egyptian banker's son, and so forth. One night there was a party at the flat and a girl died with a syringe in her arm; an overdose they thought, or her heart gave out. Anyway, Mandrake volunteered to dispose of the body, dump it into the River Thames – only he was interrupted by the police, just after he'd dragged her out of the back of his car. While he was in custody awaiting charge, a man he'd never seen before – a spook, as it turned out – let himself into the interrogation room and told Mandrake that the heroin the girl had injected was contaminated with a lethal toxin; showed him surveillance pictures of Mandrake buying the stuff. Told him that he was looking at a charge of murder. Oh, and by the way, I forgot to say that the dead girl was the daughter of a minister in the British government, so this was a charge that was likely to stick. Mandrake was given a choice. The spook said, in effect, work for me, do whatever I tell you to do, or they'll put you in jail and throw away the key. Being the pathetic creep that he was, Mandrake couldn't wait to sign on the dotted line. He became a deniable, deep-cover penetration agent for MI6. Once he'd learned the ropes, his mission, his target, was . . . well, me.'

'And you believed Mandrake's story?'

'Most of it. Most of it fitted with what I knew about the way Nigel Ridout works.'

'Ridout?'

'MI6. The man in the interrogation room – Mandrake's recruiter; his controller, his pimp.'

'Ah, yes, the *spook*,' says Dr Przewalskii, relishing the word. 'You hate this Ridout, I think.'

'Yes' – no hesitation from Flint.

'But you say you don't hate Gröber, you only despise. Do you think the distinction is—'

'I loathe Gröber for what he is and what he does but there is no pretence that he is anything other than the enemy. Ridout is supposedly an ally; we are supposed to be on the same bloody side!' Flint's temperature is rising again. 'And I know what you're thinking, Dr P, and you're out of line. When I pretend to be something – someone – I'm not, when I deceive, I do it for specific purposes of law enforcement and I'm accountable to both the strike force and the courts. Ridout cheats and lies in the shadows for reasons that have nothing to do with law enforcement – which sometimes *obstruct* law enforcement – and he is *never* accountable.'

'So, you shot Mandrake because you hate Ridout?'

'*No!* I shot *at* Mandrake because we made a deal and he broke it. He agreed to help me bring in Gröber, dead or alive, and if that meant using Mandrake as live bait, so be it. He also agreed to help me bring Ridout to account, whatever that took. I told him to take us back to La Rochelle, and then he pulled a stunt: made the boat suddenly swing so that I was hit on the head by the boom. I fell into the cabin, and that's when I saw him coming for me. I fired at him until the clip was empty but I was stunned, firing blind. Then I grabbed the signalling pistol and I was going to put a hole in his chest – except he was no longer there. I didn't think I'd hit him because there was no blood on the deck so I figured he'd either fallen or jumped into the sea. I had to get the boat under control – get the sails down, get the engine started – and I had no idea what I was doing, so it took a while. Finally, I was able to look around and I saw him in the water, about two hundred feet away, and I went to get him; or tried to.'

She can see him bobbing in a trough between the waves like a cork, one arm raised, waving to her.

'So, he tried to kill you and you tried to kill him, and now you wanted to save him so he could try again. Is that what you're telling me?'

'He wasn't any threat to me in the water. I was going to throw him a life jacket and a rope, but he wasn't coming back on board, not until the gendarmes arrived.'

'But you didn't.'

'Didn't what?'

'Throw him a life jacket.'

'Because he disappeared. One minute he was there, very close to the boat, and I went to the locker to get a life jacket, a whole armful of jackets in fact. And when I turned around he was gone; no longer on the surface.'

'And all of this time – when you were questioning him, when he was trying to kill you, when you were trying to kill him, when you were trying to save him – you never thought of what was growing inside you?'

Dr Przewalskii's question comes from the blindside and it takes a moment for Flint to comprehend.

'You mean the baby? No, not then.'

'When? When did you think?'

'Later. After he'd drowned. After I fired the emergency flares. While I was waiting for the gendarmes' launch.'

'What did you think?'

'That I was pregnant. I mean, I suddenly knew what I suppose I'd been denying to myself ever since I'd missed my period. I *knew*.' Flint pauses while she searches for a fuller explanation that can't be found. 'I just knew,' she adds lamely.

'And what did you feel?'

'I'm not sure. Panic, maybe. Anger, certainly.'

'Did you think, *I've got to get rid of this monster's child*?'

'No. Oh, later on I thought about an abortion but at the time my instant reaction was, okay, that sets the deadline: seven months. I mean, my first thought was that I only had seven months more, seven months at most, to find Karl Gröber.'

'And then what?'

'Find him and make him pay for what he'd done.'

'But you didn't find him.'

'Not yet. I ran out of time.'

'If you'd had the abortion that wouldn't have been a problem, yes?'

'I couldn't do it.'

'But you thought about it.'

'For a few days, maybe a week. I wanted to but . . .' Again, Flint runs out of words.

'You didn't want the child, not his child?'

'No and yes. I didn't want *his* child so I had to try to separate them in my mind, make him my child, not his; nothing to do with him.'

'And can you separate them in your mind?'

'Mostly.'

'Mostly? What is mostly?'

'Sometimes I think I see physical characteristics in Jack that come from Mandrake, characteristics or mannerisms. It's purely my imagination, I know, because the last time I saw Jack he looked like . . . well, a baby, but—'

'When did you last see Jack?'

'Five months ago, five and a half, but my father sends me pictures, videos—'

'Five months?'

'I haven't been able to get back to the UK. Because of Gröber.'

'That is what? Half his life? You haven't seen your son—'

'And you didn't see your son for, what? Nine years, wasn't it, Dr P?'

'I had no choice.'

'Neither do I.'

'Rubbish! That is absolutely the most fantastic rubbish! You could give up this crazy job of yours tomorrow and—'

'No, I can't.'

'Why?'

'Because of Gröber.'

'You think you are the only person in the world who can catch this Gröber? You really think you are that special?'

'It's more like destiny. I know I'll find him, just as surely as I knew I was pregnant.'

'So, when will you become a mother to your son?'

'After Gröber.'

'And then you'll go home to your son? Do you believe that, really?'

'Of course,' Flint lies.

Flint is still in dissimulation mode: now she is dissembling about why she won't be coming for any more therapy sessions for the indefinite future.

The real reason, the unspoken reason, is that once more she's going undercover, deep cover, shedding her real identity like a snake sheds its skin. For as long as it takes she will not meet or communicate with anyone she knows: nobody at the strike force, not even Aldus Cutter – except when there is real progress, or grave danger, to report; not her father nor Jack's full-time nanny; certainly there will be no communication with Dr Przewalskii. For as long as it takes, Grace Flint will vanish, effectively cease to exist.

'I'm going to be away for a while,' she is saying, breaking the news. 'A few weeks, maybe a couple of months.'

'Going? Where are you going?'

'I can't tell you that.'

Dr Przewalskii snorts.

'I can't tell you because I don't know. I'm following a lead and I'll go wherever it takes me.'

'A lead? This is more of your obsession with Gröber, of course?'

'I'm following a lead to Gröber, yes.'

'And your employers, they approve of this?'

'If you mean your friends in Human Resources, I wouldn't say they *approve* exactly. But Director Cutter has cleared my operation, which is all that counts. It's official, Dr P, I even have it in writing: I'm officially excused your weekly ministrations until and when I get back to New York.'

'Show me,' Dr Przewalskii demands, leaning out of the shadow, holding out a hand.

Reaching down into her briefcase Flint knows exactly where to find the clearance that Aldus Cutter has signed. She hands it to the doctor who makes a great pretence of studying the text.

'Do you want me to turn on a light?' Flint asks.

'I want you, before you go, to answer one more question.'

'Go ahead,' Flint says nonchalantly. 'Fire away.'

'Was Mandrake's body found?'

'No.'

'So, if there is no body there is no proof that he really drowned?'

'No proof I didn't kill him – shoot him, or whatever? Is that what you mean?'

'No, no. I mean, there is no proof he is dead. Maybe he fooled you, maybe he survived, waited until you had gone. Maybe he swam to the shore, maybe he got picked up by another boat. It's possible, yes? Have you ever thought he might still be alive?'

'The chances of that have got to be a billion to one against – but, yes, it has occurred to me. In dreams, usually. Nightmares, I suppose.'

'And in your dreams, does he ever come to claim his child?'

Even in this impoverished light it is impossible for Dr Przewalskii not to notice that Flint's face has turned very pale.

'Sometimes.'

'And what do you do?'

'I kill him.' Flint leans forward in the chair and points a straight arm at the mid-point between Dr Przewalskii's shining eyes, fashioning her hand as though she's holding a gun. 'I shoot him in the head.' Her hand jumps to mimic the recoil.

'Always? Always in your dreams you shoot him?'

'No, not in my dreams. When I imagine shooting him, killing him, when I see his head go back and his neck snap, I'm always awake, Dr P. Believe me, I'm *wide* awake.'

Eight

In the bedroom of her small apartment on West 11th Street, Grace Flint is shedding her identity. She has done this many times before but never more meticulously: now, unpicking the threads to remove labels from her clothes that might contradict the legend Aldus Cutter has created for her; now, sorting through her toiletries to discard any that are not widely available in the United States; now, emptying her wallet, her briefcase of every piece of her real identity. The woman who will leave here in the morning – slipping away in the small hours, when the risk of meeting a neighbour is remote – will be newborn, entirely imagined, as much of a lie as a counterfeit dollar bill.

To keep her company the television is on – Ted Koppel and *Nightline*, something about Iraq – but the sound is muted. She's listening instead to the latest Annie Lennox CD; Annie, as always, finding the words, hitting the spot.

Flint sings along, sotto-voiced, wandering the room, trying to remember where she's put down her glass of wine. Annie has a line about erasing someone from her memory; all erased. But you can't erase a memory that grows inside you to term, that emerges from you like a miracle spluttering for breath, that still lives and still grows – seems to grow more like *him* with every passing week, marked by the clockwork arrival in the mail of fat envelopes from England.

All of her father's envelopes are on the bed, in the discard pile – the pile of her possessions that the Cleaners from the strike force will remove tomorrow morning after she's gone, along with every other trace that Grace Flint ever existed in this apartment. The last five envelopes are unopened because she can no longer bear to see the images they contain.

And can you separate them in your mind? Dr Przewalskii

had asked, meaning her child and the father of her child.

Mostly, Flint had lied, mainly to herself.

Christ, it's hot in here – even hotter than in Dr P's office, but at least the windows aren't sealed. Flint goes to crack one open and finds her glass on a ledge by the window, finds that the wine has lost its chill, and she heads for the refrigerator in the kitchen to replenish it. There is a picture of Annie Lennox on the fridge door held in place by a couple of magnets, a publicity still for the *Bare* CD that shows her apparently naked behind a large guitar, wearing a startling wig of untamed black hair that makes her look a bit like a younger Dr Przewalskii. Flint also has a black wig, a less extreme version of Annie's, that will be part of her new persona. In the privacy of the apartment she does not wear the headscarf. She's checked in the bathroom mirror to confirm that all the burn blisters from Kissimmee are now forming healing scars.

Flint refills her wine glass and returns to the bedroom where she stands by the open window feeling the bite of the draught, listening to the hum of the traffic on Fifth Avenue. She has her back to the bed but in the windowpane she can see the reflection of the discard pile, see her father's unopened envelopes. They tug at her like a guilty conscience until finally she has to do something. It's on her mind to return to the kitchen and get a rubbish bag, to fill it with the envelopes, to march right out of her apartment and down the corridor to the garbage chute, to rid herself of – to erase – the things she can't bear to see.

And then Annie intervenes – or rather Flint becomes aware that the CD player has randomly selected the eighth track, the one Annie calls 'The Saddest Song I've Got', and she's not kidding.

Annie's voice, wrenching, as pure as pain, cutting like a knife, asking if it hurts a lot, and Flint is moving towards the discard pile, being pulled towards the discard pile as though she has no will of her own. Now she's picking up the envelopes one by one, tearing them open, spilling their contents onto the bed; notes from her father that she doesn't even glance at, five video cassettes each labelled with a date. Annie's remembering something she forgot – and Flint can scarcely breathe, scarcely see what she's doing because of the moisture in her eyes.

At random she selects one of the cassettes without registering the date on the label; she's pushing it into the video machine, feeling resistance because she's trying to insert it the wrong way round. She reverses the cassette and tries again and the machine accepts it with a mechanical sigh. Annie is still singing in her angel's voice as Flint punches the play button on the video player.

On the television screen there is momentary fuzz and then Ted Koppel's reassuring face is replaced by a face that is distorted, even grotesque, because it's far too close to the camera. Then the camera pulls back and the face snaps into focus and it's her father, who looks equally reassuring in his own way.

'And now,' he says theatrically, hamming it up, 'we present . . . we very proudly present . . . the show we've all been waiting for . . . The . . . JACK . . . FLINT . . . SHOW.'

His grinning face ducks out of frame and now Flint can see the kitchen terrace at Glebe Farm, apparently empty. Then the camera pans slowly, teasingly, to the right until it reveals her son and for a moment she is totally thrown, for this is not the baby she remembers. Jack Flint wears bright yellow dungarees and a matching floppy hat and he's standing on his own, holding on to a chair with one hand for support, holding in his other hand a red rubber ball.

'Give that to me, give that to me,' says a woman's voice – Sally, the nanny, Flint assumes – and with a shriek Jack throws the ball to where she might be standing and, off camera, John Flint roars his delight.

The boy beams. 'Ma-ma,' he says, looking directly into the lens.

In the morning when the Cleaners arrive, letting themselves into the apartment with a copy of Flint's key, they will find – and they will report to Director Cutter – that everything is in order, everything as it should be. Flint has made an inventory of every item that would or might identify her, and every item she has listed will be found neatly arranged in discard piles on her bed.

They will report with particular approval that she has left behind even those items that some undercovers find difficult to discard: her personal diary that records her most intimate thoughts, her private address book, her photographs, her correspondence.

'All of it?' Cutter will ask.

'As far as we know, sir.'

'Letters from her father?'

'Yes, sir, letters and some that are more like notes. Seventeen in total.'

'Photographs of her kid?'

'A hundred or more.'

'Videos?'

'Sorry?'

'Videotapes of her kid. She told the shrink that her father sent her videos, it's in the transcripts.'

There will be a pause on the line, then, 'She left no videotapes, Mr Cutter.'

Friendship Heights
Maryland

Nine

If we are to believe Aldus Cutter, Grace Flint has more cunning than any fox. When she's undercover she knows instinctively how to cover her tracks; how to double back or go to ground; when to potter or jog or run for her life and vanish completely. On the other hand, Cutter says, when she is the hunter Flint can pick up the faintest scent, and she has a foxhound's stamina to follow it. There is a legendary occasion – legendary within the Financial Strike Force – when she single-handedly maintained pursuit of a major target for 104 consecutive hours. A chase that began in the Bronx on a bleak Monday night led her zigzagging across America and halfway back again, until she engineered the arrest at a cheap motel near Coin, Iowa, at four o'clock on Friday morning, and in the interim she never slept in a bed or ate a proper meal or changed her clothes. 'And, get this,' Cutter says, spreading her legend to all new recruits, 'she got the perp to waive extradition, brought him back to New York, did the interrogation, did the paperwork, got herself a bunch of arrest warrants – and Friday afternoon she was back in the Bronx running a follow-up op on Arthur Avenue that netted a further eight violators. It was Sunday morning before she would quit – before I *made* her quit, sent her home. And what did she do? She spent the rest of the day and half the goddamn night writing up an after-action report.'

But just four weeks into her new fictitious life Grace Flint's fabled endurance seems completely spent. When her alarm goes off at 5 a.m. – as it does every morning, Monday through Saturday – she can barely find the strength to crawl from her bed and stumble to the dresser to silence the clock's escalating din. Neither the hot shower she takes nor the three cups of coffee she drinks do much to revive her. She feels bone-tired, as though her whole frame is leaching calcium.

Even so, a few minutes before 6 a.m. she leaves her apartment on the ninth floor of 4550 Park Avenue North and takes the elevator to the second level of the underground garage where her Ford Mustang is parked in its assigned space. A ritual glance in the driving mirror to check the make-up she is not accustomed to wearing, a second glance to ensure that her wig is properly in place, and then she guns the engine of the little red car and seems to absorb some of its energy.

'Good morning, Kathy McCarry,' she says cheerily to herself, 'and how are you this fine morning?'

Still bloody, is the truthful answer, but now there is some weave to the day. She's slipping into her role and her adrenal glands are secreting and pretty soon she'll be where she needs to be, where she belongs; right there on the edge.

Gup Securities occupies a drab three-storey building on Rockville Pike in North Bethesda that was built in the days before architects favoured the expansive use of glass. The monotonous rows of small windows, all of an identical shape and size, and the solid wooden entrance door which requires a swipe card to open give it a fortress-like appearance, as though within its concrete walls there are secrets to be guarded. According to the Financial Strike Force analysts, Cutter's terriers, this is an entirely accurate impression, for after examining tens of thousands of financial transactions that have been deemed 'suspicious' by banks and other institutions and dutifully reported to the authorities, they have concluded that among the clients of Gup Securities is one Alexander Çarçani; that through Gup Securities Çarçani has invested millions of dollars of his illicit revenues in entirely legitimate enterprises. Çarçani does not deal openly with Gup Securities of course; not in his own name. The funds that he invests are filtered through complex webs of banks and front companies and law firms located in offshore havens, mostly in the Caribbean. Nevertheless the terriers' computer programmes, which are also highly complex, have detected distinctive patterns and telltale 'signatures' and trails that lead back to Çarçani and specifically to the handiwork of his money launderer in chief, Karl Gröber.

Which is why, under deep cover, Grace Flint now works for Gup

Securities as an expert on taxation – or, rather, on how the clients of Gup Securities might best avoid it.

'This could be our last shot at Gröber and Çarçani,' Cutter had said when he'd approved Flint's operation – given it his blessing and all of the considerable resources it would require. 'Three strikes and I reckon we're out.'

Strike One was Flint's failure to provoke a civil war between Gröber and Çarçani for reasons she still doesn't understand. Why didn't Çarçani take the bait? 'Perhaps he's biding his time?' Flint had suggested, holding on to hope, not really believing it. Strike Two was the murder of Vincent Regal at Kissimmee. Was that also her failure? When it came to apportioning blame in the Gröber case, Cutter had always been careful to ascribe it generally: to *we* and *us*, never to *you*. But it wasn't *we* who hauled Regal in and threatened to walk away from him – to hang him out to dry – if he didn't deliver Gröber's rotten hide. It wasn't *us* who sent Regal in search of a psychopath. Sometimes in her sleep the spectre of Regal's body, of how it looked unfolded from the TV carton, comes back to haunt her; to remind her of what she did.

But she cannot allow the shadow of those failures to distract her, to get in the way of what she has to do. Burying the memories in her deep subconscious, she enters the Gup Building, steps up to the plate.

'This is good,' says Joseph Gup, the senior partner of Gup Securities. 'No, this is better than good, this is inspired.'

'If it flies,' says Nathan Gup, his younger brother.

'Oh, it'll fly, Nat, no doubt about that. The question is, for how long? Well, Kathy, what do you think?'

Kathy McCarry takes her time to answer. The Gup brothers have not agreed to pay her $280,000 a year, plus generous benefits, plus a bonus of two per cent of the firm's declared profits, for glib advice. If you believe her curriculum vitae, and the impeccable references Aldus Cutter arranged, she was previously a highly regarded divisional counsel with the Criminal Investigation division of the Internal Revenue Service – until, that is, she changed sides.

'IRS is not a problem, not in the short term,' she begins carefully. 'I can see problems down the line, see them challenging some of my interpretations of the tax code, for example, or the tax shelter provisions, and we could end up arguing about it in court. But that's a while away, after the complex is generating significant revenues, and by then, as I understand, the client will be out of it.'

'Long gone,' confirms Joseph Gup.

'Okay, so what we're concerned about, what we need to be concerned about, is not so much what we're doing but who we're doing it for. I'm not worried about the client, because you've made him invisible. I am worried about the other partners and the visible principals because we don't know enough about them and, post nine eleven, that poses a substantial risk.'

'Why?'

'Because of terrorism, because of possible links.'

'Oh, come on, Kathy!' To date in their working relationship, Joseph Gup has treated Kathy McCarry with great civility, as though he's determined not to offend his prize recruit, but now he's clearly offended. 'We don't work with terrorists. The visible principals, they're lawyers, accountants, bankers – all eminently respectable folks.'

'No they're not,' McCarry comes back matter-of-factly. 'Either through gross negligence or actual complicity, they're involved in a scheme to launder money, to legitimise funds that have no provenance – as are we, gentlemen' – and each of the Gup brothers receives in turn her baleful stare – 'and let's not kid ourselves,' she continues, 'that we and they don't know exactly what we're doing.'

Nat Gup is the younger of the pair by five years and, in all the dealings that Flint has witnessed, he defers to his brother – but he's the one who worries her. Twice in the past four weeks she has looked up from her desk to catch him lurking in the doorway to her office. The first time, she'd given him a flustered smile, and he'd walked away. The second time, when she was working late, when she thought she was the only one left in the building, she'd challenged him – 'Is there something you want?' – and, once again, he had walked away. And then there was the night when she'd left her apartment at around 9 p.m. too tired to sleep and too tired to cook, thinking she might drift over to Clyde's for a drink and a bite to eat. With her copper's instinctive suspicion, she'd been alerted by a car parked illegally alongside a fire hydrant on Park Avenue North, and the shadow of someone inside, and when she'd stopped to take a second look the car had pulled away. She'd noted the make and colour of the vehicle, and the first three digits of the licence plate, and scribbled them down on the palm of her hand. The next morning, when she arrived for work at the Gup Building on Rockville Pike, she had searched the parking lot until she'd found a metallic-grey Cadillac Seville with the same first three digits on the licence plate parked in the space assigned to 'N. Gup'. She'd started work as usual, waited an hour or so and then strolled along the corridor to Nat's office and said, as though she was merely passing the time of day, 'Mr Gup, were you watching me last night? Outside my place, parked in your car?'

He'd pretended not to hear her, keeping his nose buried in whatever file he was reading, until she'd insisted, 'Mr Gup?'

And then he'd leaned back in his chair, fastened his hands behind his head, looked at her, looked her up and down, and finally responded, 'Why would I do that?'

'My point exactly.'

'And what is your point, exactly?' Nat Gup says now.

The three of them are sitting around an oval-shaped conference table in the anteroom of Joseph Gup's office, a room that has no windows or exterior walls and one that is swept for all manner of electronic bugs on a random but frequent basis. The lighting is subdued except for spots recessed into the ceiling that cast pools of light on what Kathy McCarry has brought to the meeting: three identical copies of a hefty report that is the product of a month's intensive work, entitled 'San Ambrogio Project: Proposal & Analysis'. McCarry sits between the Gup brothers and she must choose which one to face, and though it was Nat who asked the question it is towards Joseph that she turns.

'It is likely to the point of near certainty that the visible principals have acted, are acting, for other parties in similar ventures. In other words, they are or they have in the recent past fronted for shell corporations that were designed to hide or wash or move money, because that is what they do. The question is, are any, or were any of those entities connected in any way to individuals or groups or countries suspected of any kind of link to any form of terrorism? Because if they were, my point is' – and now she turns her head to look hard at Nat – 'their names are very likely to be on one or more federal watchlists and, if that is the case, and if any agency for any reason runs the names of our visible principals through the system, then Project San Ambrogio will not merely not fly, it'll implode. And,' she adds, turning back to look at Joseph, 'in that event, you'll very likely see a SWAT team coming through your door.'

In the silence that ensues while the Gup brothers absorb this alarming scenario Flint can hear a faint hum coming from the air-conditioning ducts above the false ceiling, and her mind imagines where she could place her hidden cameras and her microphones if that became expedient, for there are bugs she has access to that will never be detected, no matter how often the room is swept.

'You're talking about IRS, or the FBI?' Joseph Gup asks.

'The watchlists? Neither really. I'm much more concerned about the Financial Strike Force, and the Bureau of Intelligence at State. It's not widely advertised that the state department has the most comprehensive database on suspected terrorists. It was designed in the late nineteen eighties to stop them getting visas to enter the US but, since nine eleven, it has finally been recognised that you can't run terrorist operations, or maintain terrorist cells, without money, and money has to be moved, and the movement of money can be just as good an indicator that something's in the pipeline as the movement of people. So, after nine eleven, State and the FSF combined their resources and their databases to create a system called TIPOFF – acquiring tip-offs about possible terrorist plots being the point of the exercise. TIPOFF contains the names and all and any aliases of not just suspected terrorists but also their known or suspected or even potential facilitators: diplomats, lawyers, accountants, bankers, brokers, couriers and so forth. As well as State's overseas posts, any intelligence or law enforcement agency, domestic or foreign, can submit names for inclusion, and the database is huge, effective and growing exponentially.'

Nat Gup is in denial. 'I don't get it,' he says petulantly. 'Even if some of the principals, or some of the partners, are on your fancy watchlist, why would anybody run their names?'

'If they need and apply for visas to travel to the US, it's automatic.'

'Say they don't.'

'If, when we start filing documentation, someone at IRS or the SEC, maybe the local planning commissioner, maybe someone who doesn't want a resort complex built in their backyard and they call their congressman, maybe a reporter with time on their hands – if anyone thinks to ask just who is behind these offshore corporations, and if they ask that question in the wrong place, then sooner or later IRS or the SEC or the FSF or DEA, FBI, CIA, INS, ICE – choose your own acronym – somebody is going to come and ask you for the names. And, if they do, the odds are very short: the names will be run.'

'Kathy, let me ask you a question,' Joseph Gup says, and then he waits until she turns her head towards him, and finds him closer to her than she had expected. 'When you were at IRS did you run names through the system?'

'No, it wasn't part of my job description. But special agents I worked with did, requested State to run the names, and, towards the end, they did so increasingly.'

By 'the end' she means Kathy McCarry's bitter resignation from the Internal Revenue Service a year after the shocking diagnosis that she was suffering from breast cancer, and months of sick leave; after she had realized that, whatever federal employment guidelines might say, her promising career had been derailed, irreparably wrecked, by the chance detection of a small, malignant tumour.

Or that is what her legend says, what the brothers Gup have been carefully led to believe.

'And who else can run names through TIPOFF?'

'Any state department post that handles visa applications, and any intelligence or law enforcement agency that's in the loop. Essentially, any provider of information to the system is, ipso facto, a potential recipient; if they ask, they will get.'

'But we can't ask? We can't approach the Department of State as Gup Securities and say, we have these potential clients and before we take them on we'd like to make sure they're not members of al Qaeda, and would you run the names? We can't do that?'

'No.'

'But you could.' This is Nat Gup, talking to the back of her head. 'You could run the names, or get someone to do it.'

For a moment, Kathy McCarry freezes. Then slowly, and for the first time in the presence of the Gup brothers, she removes her glasses that have full-moon lenses that seem to cover half of her face, and when she places them on the table the frames rattle on the polished oak because her hands are trembling.

'Mr Gup,' she says, addressing Joseph, for now she will not turn to look at Nat, 'before I joined this firm—'

'I know,' he says, trying to placate her.

'Before I joined this firm,' she stubbornly repeats, 'I made it absolutely clear to you what I would and what I would not do.'

Again he tries to interrupt but she holds up a hand to stop him.

'I said I would provide you with my knowledge of the tax code, of the loopholes that I know to exist, and, to some extent, of the procedures of IRS to enable your clients to avoid any . . . pitfalls, any errors of judgement that could land them in jail.'

From behind, she hears the harsh scraping of chair legs on the hardwood floor and then Nat's explosive voice. 'This is pure bullshit! You said it yourself. We all know exactly what we're doing.'

Joseph says, 'Shut up, Nathan' – the first time Flint can remember him using his brother's full name.

'It's complete bullshit,' Nat insists.

'Nathan, shut up and sit down!' – and now it's Joseph's chair that's scraping on the hardwood, his voice that's explosive. He's a good three inches taller than Nat, and thirty pounds heavier, and for many tense moments he stands looking as though he's prepared to fight, glowering at his brother over Flint's head, his hands curled into huge fists. But Nat does not take up the challenge.

'Nat, sit down, please,' Joseph says at last, moderating his volume, and Flint hears the sounds of Nat settling back into his chair.

'I'm sorry, Kathy,' Joseph adds as he, too, resumes his place at the table.

'What I also told you, Mr Gup,' Kathy said, picking up the thread of her declaration as though nothing has happened, 'is that I would not use my inside knowledge, or any contacts within the service I may still have, to break US law. I told you, I will help your clients to avoid but not evade.'

'That's precisely what you said,' Joseph agrees, 'and we wouldn't want it any other way.'

'So, no, Mr Gup. Even if I could, which I can't, I will not ask anyone at IRS to run the names of your visible principals – even if I knew their names, which I don't – through the TIPOFF system. Is that clear?'

'Perfectly clear.'

'So?' says Kathy McCarry, picking up her glasses with steadier hands, indicating that her indignation is running out of gas.

'So, how do we ensure that our principals are not engaged in terrorism?'

'You can't, so dump them.'

'Dump them?'

'At the very least, the lawyers. Bring the project management onshore and appoint the most prestigious law firm in South Carolina you can find to represent it. Bring in a high-profile figure-head as CEO – maybe a former state governor or a congressman, someone with very public credentials who's never been tainted. Appoint an executive board and pack it with the great and the good of Charleston. Get at least one local bank involved in part-financing, even if the loans have to be secured out of New York or Chicago. In short, Mr Gup, do everything you can to keep the focus onshore, where it belongs. That way, I believe, there's far less chance that anybody will become overly curious about the folks on the islands, or start running names through TIPOFF.'

Joseph Gup looks very glum and Kathy McCarry adds, 'You pay me for my advice, Mr Gup. You don't have to take it.'

'No, no, we value your advice very highly. I'm just thinking about the repercussions.'

'If you mean financial repercussions, there are certainly negative tax implications.'

'How negative?'

'I don't know yet. I'll work on it.'

Nat Gup has been silent for a while but now he says assuredly, 'The client is not going to like this.'

'I'm afraid you're right,' Joseph agrees.

'Then the client needs to understand,' McCarry snaps, sounding as though she's losing patience. 'If San Ambrogio attracts the wrong kind of attention, if they run the names, if – God forbid – they score any hits, then the client stands to lose not just a few million dollars, but all of it, every cent.'

'Oh, come, you're surely not suggesting that the client is breaking American law?' This is Nat, his tone as sarcastic as he can make it.

McCarry spins round in her chair and says, 'Listen to me' – and though she doesn't add *you jerk*, the epithet is implied. 'It doesn't matter if the client is not a US citizen or resident. It doesn't matter that you tell me the funds did not originate in the United States. It doesn't matter that he's offshore and so are the funds. None of it matters because, if the terrorism flag is raised, the United States will go after his assets wherever they are, in any jurisdiction where it has agreements or influence, which is most of them, and his assets will be seized or, at best, frozen, and he will not get them back unless and until he can disprove any connection to terrorism and prove that the assets have legitimate provenance. I don't care where he hides his money – the Cayman Islands, Switzerland, Jersey, Antigua, Liechtenstein – because we're living in a different world and when even the hint of terrorism is raised, remember all those secret doors we could never unlock? Well, now, post nine eleven, post Bali, Istanbul, Casablanca, Madrid – they just fly open. Unless the client plans to do his banking in Myanmar or North Korea, what he's going to need is a hole in the ground because that's the only place his assets might be safe. Do you understand? Are we clear on that, Nat?'

The look on Nat's face causes Flint to worry, causes her to think that Kathy McCarry may have overdone it; may have scared the Gup brothers into abandoning their San Ambrogio scheme. But then she sees the slyness enter his eyes. She relaxes and gives silent thanks to whatever gods there are for the immutable law on which all good coppers rely: the law which states that a perpetrator's caution is almost always outweighed by their greed.

'You'll need to explain this to the client,' says Joe Gup – and somehow she manages to keep her face a mask.

Ten

It is the next morning, a Friday morning, when Joseph Gup comes to her office, not lurking in the doorway like his brother but rapping on the frame and inquiring politely, 'Can I have a word?' He closes the door and indicates a chair – 'Mind if I sit?' – and unbuttons the sporty plaid jacket that complies with the policy at Gup Securities, International Financial Consultants, that Friday is a day for 'dressing down'. He sits and smiles at Kathy McCarry, cradling in his lap his copy of the San Ambrogio report.

'You do fine, fine work, Kathy.'

'Thank you, Mr Gup.'

'But not too much work, I hope.'

'I'm sorry?'

'This,' he says, showing her the San Ambrogio cover, 'is a superb proposal, exquisitely researched and argued, the most thorough of its kind I've seen. In fact, I find it difficult to believe you produced this on your own in – what? Just under a month?'

Flint's mind is racing for she did not produce one word of it. The credit for the San Ambrogio report belongs entirely to Aldus Cutter's diligent terriers and the joke around the Marscheider Building is that now they know so much about how to develop a tourist complex, they're thinking of going into business for themselves.

Kathy McCarry narrows her eyes and peers at Mr Gup. 'What are you saying?'

'I'm saying that I'm worried about you. I can't imagine how many hours, how many all-nights, how many weekends you must have invested in your report, but I can certainly see how tired you are. Kathy, I'm worried about your health.'

'If you mean my illness, I'm fine.'

'Really?'

He doesn't look convinced and since Flint is never a better deceiver than when she lies extemporaneously, she hurries to reassure him.

'I'm finished with the chemo and my last two scans have been absolutely clear. The tumour didn't metastasize, apparently, because they caught it in time. That's not to say it won't come back, but . . .' She shrugs and smiles. 'The only thing that's bugging me is this' – and she puts her hands to her head and jiggles the wig.

'Your hair's not growing back?'

'Yes it is, like stubble, and it itches like mad.'

'Well, if that's the worst of it.'

'Exactly,' says McCarry, and now they smile together. 'Honestly, Mr Gup, I like to work, and I like to do it well, and I know how to pace myself.'

'Joseph,' he says, 'or, better still, Joe.'

'Excuse me?'

'I thought that in private we might drop the formality.'

'Okay.'

'Okay, Joe,' he admonishes, and now Flint's mind is racing again, trying to anticipate where this is going.

Slowly, biding his time, his eyes sweep her office, taking in the desktop that is almost clear, the computer stand that is uncluttered by any personal knick-knacks or photographs, the shelves that are crammed with tax manuals and law books she has never read, the walls that are bare except for a counterfeit Certificate of Appreciation from the IRS.

She waits for him to make his move.

'Got any family, Kathy? Back in England, I mean.'

'My father.'

No mention of the son she hasn't seen for more than half his life.

Gup nods. 'Do you get to visit with him much?'

'Not often.'

Gup nods again as though he was expecting her answer. 'That's a shame for him, I expect. Same with my daughter. She's out in California, at Berkeley, studying for her doctorate, and I rarely get to see her. Not since her mother died.'

'I'm sorry, I didn't know.'

He shrugs away her apology. 'You never married, did you, Kathy?'

Are you hitting on me, Mr Gup?

'I'm married to the job,' she says, and he laughs softly in appreciation.

'Do you miss it?'

'What?'

'England. Do you miss the old country?'

'Not really. I came here, to the States, when I was seventeen so this pretty much feels like home.'

'But you like to go back, from time to time?'

Perhaps, she allows.

'Maybe to see old friends?'

She knows she's losing the thread and she doesn't like the feeling, as if she's flying too close to the ground.

'Mr Gup – excuse me, Joe. Is there something you want to say to me?'

Gup leans forward in his chair to place the San Ambrogio report on her desk and he remains there, his elbows propped on the edge and says, 'Let me ask you a question. Yesterday, when Nat made his entirely improper suggestion about you running the names—'

He gets no further because she's standing up, pointing an accusatory finger at his head like she might point a gun. 'Mr Gup, we're not going there!'

'Just hear me out.'

'I said—'

'I know what you said and you were right, damn right.'

'Then drop it.'

'Okay, okay,' he says, leaning back in his chair, holding up his hands to express his surrender.

'Are we done? Because I've got work to do.'

He seems to consider her invitation to leave. 'Well, since we're on my dime, I'd like to visit with you for a little while longer. If you don't mind.'

If we are to believe Aldus Cutter, a good undercover needs, among many other talents, the skills of an expert angler. Entrapment of a target – tempting them to do what they would not have done of their own volition – is a constant risk in every undercover operation, and the rock on which too many cases have foundered. 'You might sell dope to the President,' Cutter tells the new recruits, 'but no jury's gonna believe you didn't twist his arm.' The skill lies, Cutter says, not only in knowing when and where to cast the line but, if the lure is taken, knowing when to let the fish run and when to reel it in.

Reel him in, Flint, she tells herself.

'Ok, Joseph, I give in. Tell me what you've come to say.'

'Not if you're going to jump down my throat.'

'I promise.'

'Promise what?'

'I won't jump. I won't say a word until you're done.'

Gup, who has occupied the last half-hour with pointless chatter, and seemed willing to continue indefinitely, grins at her as if to say I knew I'd wear you down. And then he begins his pitch with silken praise.

'The thing I'd hate most is to see all of your fine work wasted' – and when she tries to interrupt, he raises a finger to his lips to shush her, to remind her of her promise. 'I'm not saying we shouldn't bring some of the project onshore, I think there's some merit to that. But what I don't want to see destroyed is the essential architecture of your proposal because, I tell you, Kathy, the structure you've conceived is magnificent. Truly. To me it has all the magnificence of a cathedral.'

Blimey! Flint thinks, and she imagines the strike force's terriers with swollen heads basking in the compliment, and, uncomprehending, Gup likes the fact that Kathy McCarry is smiling broadly.

'Hey, did you know there is actually a cathedral called San Ambrogio? In Milan – Milan, Italy, that is, not Michigan.'

As a matter of fact I did, Mr Gup, because I was there – with your scumbag of a client, or your client's client, as a matter of bloody fact, Mr Gup – and her smile fades as her episodic memory fast-forwards through the seventy-two hours that she was held a virtual prisoner in two small rooms above a pasticceria while Alexander Çarçani had his supposed Stasi file forensically examined; subjected to the sexual taunts of the three leering guards who would never allow her to close the bathroom door.

'Anyway,' Gup presses on, 'what I want to do is preserve the integrity of your cathedral as much as we can, and if that requires making some changes to the façade, so be it. But we can't have the foundations undermined, or any rot in the woodwork, which means we've got to make damn sure that none of our principals has the slightest connection to terrorism, and that means we've got to run the names. Now, Kathy, how do we do that?' he asks rhetorically. 'How, I've been asking myself, do we check the names without compromising your integrity, which, let me tell you, is something I would never tolerate, never in a thousand years.' Gup pauses as though he is pondering this conundrum and then he adds, 'I think – I only think, Kathy – I may have found the answer.'

Here we go, thinks Flint.

Now Gup is on his feet, pacing the room, using his hands and arms like a conductor to lay emphasis on the finer points of his construction. Would it compromise Kathy McCarry's professional integrity if the request to run the names through the TIPOFF system came from an agency for which she had never worked? What if that agency was in the TIPOFF loop but foreign, based in the old country, the country that Kathy McCarry left when she was not much more than a schoolgirl, and – 'so you see, Kathy' – an agency with which she cannot have the remotest connection? Better still, what if there were intermediaries who were in a position to approach that agency on her behalf? Intermediaries who would neither know nor care who she was; who would have never heard of Kathy McCarry, or the San Ambrogio project – or, come to that, Gup Securities. And, if such distance were maintained, could it possibly be ethically wrong to go to these lengths if the only purpose – 'the *only* purpose, Kathy' – were to make damn sure that they were not getting into bed with the facilitators of terror, destruction and death?

'Because, Kathy, if we find out that's what's happening, if that's who the principals are, the first thing we do is we call the FBI.'

Gup contrives to make this ringing declaration leaning across the desk, towering over her, his hands planted on the desktop, and Flint sees that he has an actor's sense of the stage. He keeps the position for several moments, maintaining eye contact, letting her see the strength of his righteous sincerity. 'If that turns out to be the case, we don't dump the principals, Kathy. I say we *bury* them.'

Resuming his pacing of the room, Gup admits that he is not the sole architect of his construction. Last evening, after their meeting, he had explained the dilemma that Gup Securities faced to a close confidant, a trusted friend – 'and not on the telephone, Kathy, I can assure you of that' – and it was the friend who had told him of the intermediaries.

'They're private security consultants in London, a very discreet outfit with a profile so low they almost don't exist, but with major, major clients. My friend says they're first-rate, not least because of their contacts with official agencies; stellar contacts, Kathy, that go right to the top. Whether we're talking about law enforcement or the intelligence community, or both, I don't know – and I'm sure you don't want to know.'

Oh, you're dead wrong there, Mr Gup.

'What matters is, my friend knows from his own experience that these people can get the job done. Now, they're very fussy about who they do business with and they don't take on new clients without an introduction, but I've got that covered.' At this point in his perambulations Gup has his back to Flint but he times a pivot to perfection. 'My friend has agreed that he will introduce you, Kathy, personally.'

Me? Why me, Mr Gup? Because you don't like flying? Or you think you can keep your hands clean?

And this, finally revealed, is Joseph Gup's proposal.

Kathy McCarry will travel to England – 'first class, soup to nuts, every step of the way' – taking with her the full list of names of all the hidden partners and principals in the San Ambrogio project, a list of names that Gup will retrieve from the bank vault where it is held. She will present the list to the intermediaries, together with $25,000 in cash that is already available in London – 'Hell, I know it's expensive, Kathy, but when it comes to protecting your integrity, I don't care what it costs' – and in due course – 'a week, maybe ten days, I'm told' – she will learn if any of the names are dirty.

'And while you're waiting, I want you to rest and relax. We'll put you up at the Savoy or the Ritz, wherever you like so long as its top-rate. See some shows, do some shopping – on my dime, of course. What do you think, Kathy?'

I think you fly too close to the sun, Mr Gup.

'Perhaps you could take some time to visit with your dad,' is Gup's final suggestion.

Or my son, Flint imagines, but she pushes that scary thought away.

Eleven

When Kathy McCarry is on her way to London – when it is certain the flight is airborne, headed out over a calm Atlantic, and she's definitely on board – a red Mustang pulls into her assigned parking space in the underground garage of 4550 Park Avenue North. It is more or less identical to Kathy's car and it bears the same licence number, and the driver is a woman in her mid-thirties with tousled black hair that could be a wig who is wearing dark glasses with full-moon lenses that seem to cover half her face. For the benefit of anyone at the front desk watching the CCTV monitors, she unloads paper sacks of groceries from the trunk and then busies herself searching for something she can't find, apparently, killing time until she sees a likely mark heading towards the locked door that leads to the elevators. Now she slams the lid of the trunk and gathers up the paper sacks in both arms, her laptop computer and her bag hanging precariously from their shoulder straps, and hurries after her unsuspecting target. The echoing tattoo of her heels on the concrete announce her approach, and the mark pauses in the entryway and turns, and hears a flustered woman call, 'Could you hold the door for me, please?'

The mark holds open the door as though his life depends on it and is rewarded with a stunning smile. He summons the elevator, asks her for the number of her floor, presses the button for nine, ten for himself, and then, on second thoughts, offers – with overdone casualness – to help with her packages, carry them to her apartment, and she says, 'Only if you know how to conjure up a risotto in . . . Jesus! What's the time?'

She affects to look at her watch, and almost spills the groceries, and so he tells her the time and she says, 'Excuse my total panic but I've got my ex's parents coming to dinner in less than an hour!' Her reference to her 'ex' suggests that she is no longer attached, and possibly available, and whatever the mark is thinking does not include the possibility that he is assisting in the commission of a felony. The elevator is slowing, approaching the ninth floor, when he holds out his right hand and says, 'Frank Delaney' – and they both laugh at the futility of his gesture.

'Kathy McCarry,' she says, as the doors open.

'If you're sure you can manage?'

'I'll be fine.'

'See you again, I hope.'

'Only if you like risotto, because that's about the extent of my repertoire.'

'I adore risotto.'

'Then you know where to come.'

She exits the elevator, turns the curve in the hallway, presses her back against the wall, gets her breathing under control, waits until she hears the doors close.

Now comes the tricky part. He temporary employers were unable to provide a duplicate set of keys to Kathy McCarry's apartment so she must pick two locks that are a cut above basic domestic security. This will take a while and, meanwhile, because of the curve in the hallway, and because the floor is carpeted, she can neither see nor hear the approach of anyone coming from the elevators. She has her excuses ready – the contents of her handbag spilled on the carpet to indicate her thorough search for the right set of keys – but if anyone comes, and sticks around, she will have to admit that she must have left the keys at the office and hightail it out of there before they call the front desk: *Look, it's none of my business, but there's a woman trying to get into nine thirteen, and I'm not sure that it's her apartment . . .*

She's timing herself and it's two minutes and forty seconds before she hears the second lock turn.

Inside the apartment, the door closed, she remains in the entryway to take her bearings. To her right is a passageway leading to the kitchen. Straight ahead is a combined living/dining room and beyond that, through sliding glass doors, a covered terrace. To her left is a passageway that she knows from the floor plan she was shown – but not allowed to keep – leads to two bedrooms and two bathrooms, one of them en suite. There's a lot to search if you're going to be meticulous, but she takes her time because she has all the time she needs; hours, days if that's what it takes.

In the second bedroom, which evidently serves as Kathy McCarry's study, there's a glass-topped desk, a swivel chair, a two-drawer file cabinet on wheels, an inexpensive laser printer, a flat-screen monitor and a broadband connection. There is no sign of a computer to hack into, which suggests that McCarry uses a laptop she's taken with her, but the neatly arranged contents of the file cabinet reveal fragments of the subject's life.

She has rented the apartment for one year, and the furniture and the television from Aaron Rents. She has bought her kitchen stuff from Williams-Sonoma and Sur La Table, the towels and the bedding from Linens 'n' Things, her books and her CDs from Borders – all of those stores in Friendship Heights, all within a mile of where she lives.

To buy her computer peripherals, the mini hi-fi and the VCR, she went to the White Flint shopping mall, within a mile of where she works.

In other words, within this leased apartment there is little that Kathy McCarry owns, and what she does own – with the exception of her clothes, and we'll come to them because the clothes are interesting – was bought locally and within the last six weeks.

'She brought almost nothing with her,' Kathy McCarry's impostor types into her own laptop which she's set up on the glass-topped desk, attached to the scanner she is using to acquire images of the more significant documents she finds in McCarry's files. 'Why?'

In the file cabinet there is ample evidence that Kathy McCarry has a past: bank statements going back five years; correspondence from her stockbroker going back even further – and even the earliest letters begin 'Dear Kathy', suggesting a pre-history; tax returns dating back to 1992 and, in the same file, correspondence with the IRS about the financial terms of her severance; medical files detailing an enduring struggle with interstitial cystitis that seems to have plagued her since her late teens and, much more recent, her battle with breast cancer which might have been caught in time.

And then there is trivia from her past: letters from college friends and class reunion invitations; flirtatious postcards sent from Marrakech in the summer of 1988 by someone who signed himself 'Scooter'; more postcards from Scooter, these postmarked Bali, circa 1991, the tone of them now more neutral and distant; five birthday cards signed 'Dad' under messages that are affectionate but sometimes tinged with disappointment ('Hope to see you this year'); an envelope containing a silver chain with a broken clasp, and a single diamond earring; a folded, discoloured menu from a restaurant in San Francisco with snatches of a Tim Hardin song lyric – 'Knowing how you lied straight-faced while I cried' – written on the back in angry green capitals; a photograph of a gawky girl in a swimsuit; another photograph of the same girl, now filling out, with her arms round the waist of an older man – Scooter, or Dad? the impostor wonders.

'Contrived?' she types into her laptop, and then she deletes the question and poses another, more complete, one: 'Why are there so many gaps in the subject's history? Like a jigsaw puzzle with half the pieces missing.'

She has already decided she will spend at least one night in the apartment. She has brought her own supplies and she drifts out onto the terrace with a vacuum flask of hazelnut decaf and a pasta salad in a plastic container, to be eaten with a plastic fork. Although it's late and dark, the temperature is still in the high eighties and the air is heavy with swampy humidity, and the protective suit she brought with her – to protect against the shedding of any particles of her DNA – feels as clingy as a wetsuit. She removes the hood, unzips the suit, strips down to her underwear, lurks in the far left corner of the terrace where there is no backlight to expose her, and considers what her well-tuned intuition is insistently telling her: that Kathy McCarry is a twenty-four-carat fake.

A con artist? A fugitive? A fantasist? An undercover cop?

The terrace overlooks the communal garden and swimming pool where there is a sign which she can read from the terrace through her sniper's night scope warning that no lifeguard is on duty after 8 p.m.; that you swim at your own risk. She scans the surface of the pool until the cross hairs of the scope find the head of a solitary swimmer, male – the guy from the tenth floor who adores risotto, if she's not mistaken – who's performing laps with a lazy crawl.

Kathy McCarry doesn't use the pool, apparently, for there are no swimsuits among her meagre collection of clothes, from most of which the makers' labels have been carefully removed.

'To conceal what?' is another question already typed into the laptop. 'Where she's come from, or where she's been?'

Growing restless, the impostor closes the lid on the unfinished pasta salad, gets back into the protective suit and re-enters the apartment. Now begins the serious work of taking it apart room by room. She will empty every cupboard, every drawer, every shelf, move every piece of furniture and all of the appliances, lift the carpets if she has to, looking for the hiding place that she is certain must exist.

Why is she so certain?

Because her initial search of the apartment did not reveal the presence of a single videotape, and who would go to the trouble of buying a VCR at the White Flint mall when they have no tapes to watch? The impostor has considered the possibility that Kathy McCarry rents her tapes from the Friendship Heights branch of Blockbuster Video but there is no evidence of a Blockbuster account in her files, no payments to Blockbuster on her credit card statements, no payments to Blockbuster from her checking account.

So, the impostor has decided, there are two logical possibilities. Either McCarry has taken the tapes to London – and why would she do that? Or she has hidden them somewhere in this apartment.

Again, why?

Perhaps because they are pornographic videos that she wishes to conceal from the prying eyes of anyone who may enter the apartment during her absence; the maintenance man, for example, come to fix a leaking water pipe.

It's possible.

Perhaps because they are home movies that reveal something embarrassing or that is at odds with Kathy McCarry's account of her past.

Also possible.

Either way and in any event the impostor will search the apartment until she finds the missing videos or proves to herself they do not exist, for she is scrupulous in her work, thorough to the point of obsession. It is her marque, the reason she was hired.

First she makes her necessary preparations. Shelf by shelf,

drawer by drawer, cupboard by cupboard, room by room she captures the position of everything with a digital camera so that having dismantled the apartment she can put it back together with every item in its place.

However long it takes.

It is the following morning. The dawn light is a dull bluish-grey, the colour of gunmetal, and through the open terrace doors comes the persistent hum of the commuter traffic on Wisconsin Avenue. She has not slept, nor will she until her search is completed. Four-fifths of the apartment is in a shambles, the floors strewn with Kathy McCarry's possessions – though, on closer inspection, the piles are fairly orderly, the items arranged in the order in which they were removed. There are two areas left to search. She is leaving the kitchen until last.

For now her focus is the passageway leading to the kitchen which is lined on one side by storage cupboards set behind three pairs of louvered doors. Two of the cupboards are practically empty, containing only a wok, one cooking pot, one pan, two plates, two side bowls; not much entertaining goes on here, she thinks. There are, however, six wine glasses and six squat tumblers and, on the bottom shelf of the second cupboard, a dozen bottles of wine, a half-empty quart bottle of whisky and a full one in reserve.

A lush? she thinks and then she thinks about it some more and drifts into the office to pose more questions on the laptop: 'Is alcohol compatible with the cancer medication she's supposed to be taking? Does she really have cancer?'

The third cupboard presents more of a challenge. There are brooms, a vacuum cleaner, two umbrellas, two pails, a shelf crammed with cleaning materials, all of it wedged into a narrow gap alongside a washing machine with a clothes dryer stacked on top. She needs to look behind the appliances but the gap is too narrow for her to squeeze into, so she has to get them out of there. The question is, how?

Placing her hands under the front edge of the dryer she attempts to lift it, to judge its weight, and it doesn't budge at all, and now she sees why. The machines are not free-standing as she had assumed but embraced in a metal corset that is attached to a

spindle. There is a simple catch that she releases with one press of
a foot pedal and the whole contraption swings towards her in a
ninety-degree arc revealing an alcove where, nestled among the
water pipes, are five unlabelled video cassettes.

Watching the videos in their entirety takes less than one hour,
which is precious little time to learn so much. She returns to the
laptop to type what will become the opening words of her report.

'The subject's real name is not McCarry but Flint. And she has
a kid, named Jack.'

Lake Lugano
Switzerland

Twelve

Karl Martin Gröber lives for now on the southern shore of Lake Lugano in a part of Switzerland that is a masquerade. The car number plates are Swiss, as are the banks and the currency, the police, the telephone provider, the mail service – all efficient as clockwork, as you would expect – but that is merely for the sake of convenience. Inconveniently, the electricity supply comes from Lombardy, carried by cables that spill down the mountainside on spindly pylons, maintaining an umbilical link with Italy that has existed for almost a millennium and a half, ever since a landowner named Campione ceded his small parcel of Lugano lakefront to the church of San Ambrogio in Milan. This curious arrangement has never been disturbed and Campione d'Italia remains an Italian exclave within a foreign land, financially sustained by a municipal gambling casino that boasts half a million visitors a year. Karl Gröber appreciates irony and he likes the idea that his present refuge depends on chance and is anomalous, as irregular as his own identity.

For now he calls himself Klimt, Oskar von Klimt, and he holds an Austrian passport that states he was born in Salzburg, Mozart's birthplace, in July 1949, which makes him two years older than he really is. His application for residency in the tax haven of Campione (tax free because of the bountiful profits of the casino) described him as a financier of independent means, and since property values in Campione rival those of Tokyo (because of its tax haven status), and since he had the wherewithal to buy a waterside villa on the Via Matteo da Campione outright for cash, the Italian authorities – much less pernickety in these matters than the Swiss – took him at his word. When he's not travelling, which he does extensively, Herr Klimt lives quietly, listening to recordings of Mozart's music at a volume that will not disturb his neighbours, reading modern histories that dwell on the collapse of communism in Eastern Europe, eating lunch alone at the Rally Club pizzeria, sitting by the lake, sometimes venturing onto it in an open motor launch that he moors alongside a wooden jetty just beneath his house.

Tonight the lake is restless. There is a capricious breeze coming from the direction of Lugano, skidding across the surface, causing sudden squalls and a chop that rocks the launch from side to side as Gröber edges alongside a Ferretti motor yacht – fifty feet of sleek opulence that, in Gröber's view, represents an absurd extravagance on a lake that is landlocked. A handful of the many bodyguards who habitually attend Alexander Çarçani lounge against the guard rails, watching Gröber's progress with insolent indifference. Despite their slick hair and the expensive black linen suits that they wear like uniforms, they look to Gröber what they are: Tosks from southern Albania, come to Italy by way of the war in Kosovo, lifelong members of the Çarçani clan, indifferent to any law except the clan's brutal code; cunning, cruel, frequently lethal.

Çarçani himself stands on the flying bridge. At the last moment, as he watches Gröber reaching perilously for the mooring rope that hangs from the Ferretti's stern, he calls out in Russian, which is the language the two men share with equal fluency. Roughly translated, what Çarçani says is, 'Don't you fucking dare scratch my boat.' Gröber grins, raising his right arm in mock salute, using his middle finger to make the gesture obscene. 'Up your arse,' Çarçani replies, making a crude gesture of his own.

On the flying bridge of the Ferretti, Alexander Çarçani turns suddenly from the guard rail and throws a punch, one of those fake swings that misses Karl Gröber's head by a narrow margin, and then they fall into an embrace, wrestling bear hugs that almost lift them off their feet.

Çarçani is in an excellent mood tonight. Breathless, laughing, he breaks free of Gröber's grip. 'You've brought me something? You'd better have brought me something, you prick.'

'Don't I always bring you something, Sasha?' Gröber says, but he does not yet remove his jacket and his shirt to retrieve the waterproof pouch that is taped to the small of his back. 'I'm just another of your whores.'

'Sure you are, but you think I pay *them* five per cent?'

Oh, not five per cent, Sasha, not this time, Gröber thinks. *This time, we're looking at a lot more than five per cent. Because of the complications and the extra costs and, my ignorant friend, because you need me.*

He offers a wan smile.

'You're nothing but a parasite.'

'If you say so,' says Gröber, watching Çarçani's eyes.

There is a muted giggle that comes from the shadows that conceal the innermost reaches of the bridge. Çarçani flicks his fingers and, instantly, the shadows are erased by the beam of a searchlight. Two girls are on a banquette, pinned by the beam like moths, lying on their sides head to head, their lips scarlet, their bare limbs bleached white in the light. It is difficult to guess their ages but Karl Gröber would give serious odds that they are considerably younger than either of Çarçani's granddaughters.

'Fresh meat,' says Çarçani. 'You want them?'

'I want to drink.'

'You want to *drink* them?'

'Whisky,' says Gröber. 'I want to drink whisky and, Sasha, if it's all the same to you, I want to get out of this fucking wind.'

Çarçani chuckles. He signals with his hand to kill the searchlight and then he grips Gröber's shoulder, steering him towards the companionway.

'This wind,' he says, 'this is a *breeze*. You know what, Karl? You may think you have the balls to steal my money, but I think you're growing soft.'

Thirteen

In the salon of the Ferretti, Alexander Çarçani stands over a chart table on which he has laid an artist's impression of a marina complex that Gröber, in his role as financial facilitator, insists should be Çarçani's next substantial investment in real estate. There is an Anglepoise lamp clipped to the table that illuminates the drawings, made with a draughtsman's care, showing in some detail the façades of a low-rise luxury hotel, two adjacent blocks of condominiums, a half-moon-shaped boulevard of boutiques and cafés fronting a natural harbour where expensive-looking motor yachts are moored alongside jetties, parallel-parked like cars. The complex is to be built in South Carolina, a couple of hours' drive north of Charleston, and the legend on the drawings proposes the name of 'San Ambrogio' – which, given the generosity of his contributions to the basilica strikes Çarçani as a nice touch.

'So what does this cost me?' he says, searching impatiently through the other documents that Karl Gröber has produced from his waterproof pouch. These documents are written in largely obscure English, littered with legal jargon, and Çarçani cannot understand them, which is one of the reasons for his impatience.

'Your share is seventy million dollars,' says Gröber, 'give or take. With the fees, say seventy-two, maybe seventy-three.'

'My *share*! I give you seventy-three million dollars to own a *share*?'

'You'll own nothing, Sasha. You are making a loan – no, not even that. You're *guaranteeing* a loan. What you'll own is a note.'

'A piece of paper?'

'Exactly that, but not directly, through intermediaries. There will be nothing that can be traced back to you.'

Çarçani removes his glasses and rubs the knuckles of one hand along the groove in his head.

* * *

A Milanese lawyer named Umberto Belli who is fluent in the arcane language of international commerce – of Heads of Agreement and Deeds of Confirmation, of Bearer Bonds and Certificates of Deposit – now stands at the chart table examining the documents that Karl Gröber has provided from his waterproof pouch. Gröber is slumped on one of the sofas in the salon of the Ferretti, nursing a glass of whisky. Alexander Çarçani has retired to his cabin where, Gröber is sure, he feeds on fresh meat. The bodyguards are passing shadows, glimpsed occasionally through the portholes as they prowl about the deck.

Umberto Belli is a study in contrasts. He wears scuffed trainers with his Armani suit; a diamond ring and yet a cheap watch with a plastic strap. He is unshaven, two days' growth of stubble on his cheek and chin, but his jet-black hair is immaculately groomed and held in place with gel. He flicks through the documents impatiently, as though he can hardly spare the time, but he's here to find fault and his dark eyes miss nothing.

'This,' he says, fingering one of Gröber's documents, 'this is a joke?'

It seems unlikely, for Karl Gröber is not noted for his sense of humour.

'This guy Lindling . . .' Belli taps the page that offends him. 'This Garfield Lindling, who is he?'

'He is a lawyer.'

'I can see that, but who *is* he? What's so special about him that he gets to hold seventy millions dollars of Sasha's money?'

'In an escrow account.'

'Terrific! *Fantastico!* You think he can't steal from an escrow account?'

Gröber prefers to answer the original question. 'He runs the most prominent law firm on the island. His brother-in-law is the prime minister and his sister, his older sister, is the attorney general. His younger sister runs the bank.'

'Who runs the army – his mother?' Belli asks with wasted sarcasm.

'There is no army, only the police,' Gröber says, and then he adds straight-faced, 'the chief of police is, I believe, his first cousin.'

Belli groans. 'So, he has the perfect set-up. He is untouchable, protected on every front, no?'

'He will not steal, Umberto.'

Another groan from Belli, this one even more theatrical. 'Trust me, Karl – and I should know: all lawyers steal.'

'Not from us.'

'Why? Why are you so sure?'

'Because Garfield Lindling has a wife, a very pretty new wife he does not want to lose. And, during the three weeks that the money is in the escrow account, she will be with me, under my ... protection.'

A raucous laugh announces the arrival of Alexander Çarçani. He stands naked in the doorway of his cabin, towelling his hair still damp from the shower.

'Karl, Karl' – Çarçani shakes his head – 'you *piccóne*. You ever know a woman who was worth seventy million dollars?'

'No,' says Gröber, slowly getting up from the sofa, 'but I am not sentimental, Sasha. Lindling, his woman is pregnant. It is a boy, he has been told, and he does not want to also lose his son.'

Now Çarçani nods his head as though he thinks the answer reasonable. He ties the towel round his waist and pads bear-like to the bar to fix himself a drink. He has his back to Gröber but he's watching his face in the mirror when he quietly asks, 'And do you have the balls to kill someone, Karl, to put a bullet in their head? I mean close-up, not from a distance, not with a sniper's rifle – because that's what fucking cowards do, right?'

'The problem with shooting from a distance, Sasha,' Gröber evenly replies, 'is that sometimes you miss.'

On deck, the prowling bodyguards once again hear their master's chilling laughter.

England

Fourteen

Grace Flint is in the shower, scrubbing off the dirt. The London grime that has left an inky ring on the inside of her collar dissolves easily enough. What she can't seem to wash away is the intangible stain of her meeting with William Goodheart, or the smell of his cologne.

'No offence,' he'd said, 'but I need you to unbutton your shirt.'

Flint was sitting in the front passenger seat of his BMW in an underground car park off the Tottenham Court Road. He had parked strategically, reversing into the space, giving himself the widest possible view of their surroundings.

'Do me a favour,' he'd said in response to her stony stare. 'When I said no offence, I meant nothing personal. Meaning, you're not my type. The only reason I want to see your skinny tits is to make sure you're not wearing a wire. You've got two choices. Either undo your shirt or bugger off. *Comprendé, amiga?*'

She had unbuttoned her shirt.

'Now the skirt,' he'd said. 'Hitch it up, show me your thighs.'

Again, she'd done as she was told, endured in submissive silence the smirk on his pink, fleshy face. He was an ex-copper if ever she'd seen one, probably a DI with the Met who'd been allowed to take early retirement to avoid embarrassment, just before the boys from the anti-corruption group came calling. His clothes, his shoes, his watch, the signet ring on his pinkie finger, the cologne he wore – everything was too obviously expensive, statements of his conceit. She would have bet her pension that he had a converted riverside loft in somewhere like Canary Wharf, an ex-wife in the suburbs who had to pester him for maintenance, kids he never saw, a girlfriend half his age. *Remember, it's never personal* was Cutter's mantra but right then it was; right then what invaded her senses, along with the cologne, was the stench of corruption so powerful it almost made her gag.

'Give me your bag,' he'd said and he'd rummaged through its contents, taking particular interest in her mobile phone, making sure it wasn't also a voice recorder.

'Right,' he'd said, finally satisfied. 'Let's get on with it.'

'No, not right.' And then she had pointed at his chest and added, 'Your turn.'

His face contorted as though he had been slapped and it was very much on Flint's mind that when she was a British copper – an undercover detective working for Major Crimes – it was in a London car park similar to this one that she had been attacked by a Los Angeles lawyer named Clayton Buller and beaten to a pulp with the butt of a nine millimetre Browning and then the heel of his handmade Italian boot; that she had endured months of surgery to reconstruct her face. William Goodheart wasn't in Clayton Buller's league, and she doubted he was carrying a gun, but his body language said he was close to violence. She'd moved quickly to assert control.

'Listen, you need to understand that the people I work for care about the confidentiality of our arrangement as much as you do. Indeed, they *insist* on it and, frankly, they're the kind of people you wouldn't want to disappoint. So, if you'll just show me that you're not wearing a wire, then we can get on with our business and those bloody things' – now she was pointing through the windscreen to a concrete pillar where a clutch of CCTV cameras monitored the garage – 'won't be capturing images of me tumbling out of this car with my clothes in disarray and yelling "rape" at the top of my voice.' He was still absorbing her threats when she'd added quietly: 'Come on, Billy – it is Billy, right? That's what your friends call you? I'm just trying to do my job, get the job done, so, help me out, won't you, Billy?'

Now he didn't know whether to be angry or amused.

'You think you're a clever bitch, don't you?'

'Just a working girl,' she'd said.

And then he'd decided to play along, and taken off his tie and begun unbuttoning his shirt, and the smirk had returned to his mouth as he'd asked, 'You'll also want to see inside my trousers, I expect?'

She'd seemed to consider his proposition for a moment.

'No, I don't think that'll be necessary. No room to hide anything inside *your* pants. Right, Billy?'

The list she had given him contained twenty-three names of principals, partners and nominee directors of the San Ambrogio project, together with their nationalities, countries of residence and dates of birth. For the directors she also supplied certified photocopies of their passports and Goodheart had studied these with some care before declaring dismissively, 'Lawyers, straw men.'

She'd shrugged and said, 'Of course, but that doesn't mean they're clean. We need to be sure.'

'Fair point.'

The bulky envelope she'd given him had contained $25,000 in used, non-sequential one-hundred dollar bills, money she had collected earlier that morning from the Gup brothers' solicitors in London – another encounter that had left her feeling grubby. She had arrived at their offices in a Marylebone mews precisely on time to be left sitting unattended in a poky waiting room for forty minutes, until she had sought out the pinched-faced receptionist and asked, 'Tell me something, do all the clients get treated this way, or are you being especially rude to me?' There was no apology from the receptionist but she'd picked up the phone to mutter something incomprehensible and a few minutes later Flint was ushered into a pristine office where Mr Atherton, the most junior of the partners, waited behind his desk.

'Sorry about that,' he'd said cheerfully, not offering to shake her hand, 'I'd forgotten you were coming.'

'You do this all the time, I suppose?' she'd replied, nodding at the stacks of bills lined up on the desk, each stack held by a paper wrapper.

Ignoring her taunt he'd opened a drawer, produced a single sheet of paper with two lines of type. 'When you've counted it, I need you to sign this receipt.'

'You don't think I should trust you, Mr Atherton?'

'No, Miss McCarry. And, speaking of trust, I need to make a photocopy of your passport, for purposes of identification.'

'In case I'm not who you think I am?'

'In case you're not who you say you are. Exactly. Your passport, please,' he'd added, holding out his hand, 'and then, count.'

Billy Goodheart had not counted the money. He'd merely glanced inside the envelope with the assurance of a man who always got paid what he was due.

'How long before we get the results?' she'd asked.

'Depends. If they're all clean, no hits on the system, we should get the all-clear in seventy-two hours, maybe less. If there are hits . . . well, it depends on where the alarm bells start ringing – which agency, how responsive they are, if you know what I mean. In that event, maybe a week, maybe ten days. So' – he was affable now, the buttons of his shirt still undone, perfectly comfortable with showing her his chest, – 'where are you staying? We might have a bite to eat.'

She'd taken a pen from her bag, and taken his hand, and scribbled some digits on the palm.

'My UK mobile number,' she'd said. 'Call me when you know.'

'Give you a lift somewhere?'

'No, thanks, I've got a car.'

'Kathy,' he'd said when she was halfway out of the passenger door, 'what I said about you not being my type, that could change.'

'Billy,' she'd said, 'if only there was time.'

Fifteen

Grace Flint, marooned in London, could have easily killed the time. There were former colleagues from the Metropolitan Police she would have seen – not many, it's true, but certainly Tom Glenning, her former commander, who would have taken her to Simpson's-in-the-Strand and spoiled her with rare roast beef, a bottle of good claret and his avuncular concern. But as Kathy McCarry she had no old friends to look up, nobody to talk to. And though she was confident in her disguise – confident that even Tom Glenning wouldn't recognise her if he bumped into her in the street – she didn't want to run the risk of a chance encounter that every undercover operator dreads: *Grace? Grace Flint, is that you?*

So, for the most part, she stayed in her room at the Connaught – actually a corner suite, since Joe Gup had insisted that no expense would be spared – watching television, switching between CNN and Sky until she knew the news by heart. Growing tired of room service, she'd slipped into the hotel's Grill Room for a meal, and twice into the American Bar for a drink and a snack, and the second time she'd done that she'd found herself registering a familiar face. She'd looked away while she hastily ran the image through her memory bank, and made the connection, and realised she was sitting two feet away from Bob Tyrer, the chief investigator for the Senate Permanent Subcommittee on Investigations.

You know, this would be so much easier if we could just talk over some decent food and a glass of Côtes du Rhône.

Well, you almost got your wish, Mr Tyrer, she'd thought as she signalled for her bill and made a hurried exit.

For all its sumptuous comfort the suite had taken on an oppressive feel and she paced its rooms as though they were prison cells. It was now four days since her encounter with Billy Goodheart, and he had not called, so now he must know that some of the names on her list had scored a hit on the TIPOFF database. Somewhere across the Atlantic, in the headquarters of some agency or other, alarm bells were ringing, but it would be a while before Billy knew where. 'Depends,' Goodheart had said. 'Maybe a week, maybe ten days' – and, either way, it seemed to Flint like an unbearable eternity.

At eight o'clock on Saturday morning she'd called down to the concierge and asked him to arrange a hire car for two or three days.

'Certainly, madam. Chauffeured or self-drive?'

'Self-drive. Something with a bit of zip, maybe a convertible.'

'And when would you like the car?'

'As soon as you can get it here.'

An hour later he'd called her back to say there was a Mercedes coupé waiting for her at the door and a man from Hertz waiting for her to sign the papers. Whenever she was ready.

She had no real idea where she was going and she didn't care. She headed south capriciously on a zigzag course towards the sea, taking the back roads, feeling the heady rush of her liberation and a warm breeze on her fuzzy skull. The signposts she passed pointed to villages with deliciously quirky English names: Thakeham and Partridge Green, Coldwaltham and Amberley, Madehurst and Lavant. At every junction she chose her direction at whim and it was therefore entirely by chance that in the early afternoon she found herself in Chichester and decided, this will do. She scouted for accommodation and settled on the Ship Hotel where she secured a room with a four-poster bed. She put on shorts and a pair of sandals, leaving her legs bare and, defiantly, the wig and the headscarf in her overnight bag, and set off to explore the town like any other tourist.

The cathedral and the cloisters; tea and scones in the rectory; the permanent collection at the Pallant House Gallery – she did all of the obvious things and then took a taxi to Chichester harbour, south of the town, and found a peaceful spot from where she could watch the boats navigating the deep-water channels, and sharp-billed waders probing the mudflats for their supper. The juxtaposition of the two inevitably brought to mind Mandrake – and it was only because of her late husband's infectious passion for birds (the only genuine thing about him, she now believed) that she thought she could identify curlew and whimbrel and bartailed godwits. Thoughts of Mandrake brought thoughts of Jack and, suddenly, an impression of emptiness so profound that she felt as though her insides had shrivelled.

For a long time, an hour or more, she wandered the flats barefoot, feeling the sticky mud between her toes, struggling to resolve the conflicts among a ragbag of emotions until, barely conscious of what she was doing, she found her mobile phone in her hand and dialled a number in New York and, after two rings, heard a recorded message.

'You have reached the office of Dr Przewalskii. This is the weekend and I'm not available. Only if this is an emergency should you leave a message on this answer-call machine, after you hear the tone. Speak slowly and clearly, and let's see what happens. Goodbye.'

Hi, Dr P, it's Grace Flint, your most reluctant patient, the one who takes notes. I don't think I'm crazy and what I'm feeling at the moment is just about unbearable. You see, I'm in the UK, chasing up a lead on Gröber – I shouldn't be telling you that, but what the hell – and, as of right now, I'm about a hundred and fifty miles away from my son, and I could be there in three hours, and I've got nothing else to do, nothing in the way to stop me, and the thing I most want to do is go and see Jack and hold him in my arms – and I can't bloody do it. I'm scared, Dr P; scared of what I'll feel, or maybe what I won't feel. Do you understand? It's like I'm paralysed. Marina, I need your help and I'm sorry it's the weekend, and this is not about any lack of respect for you. In fact the opposite is true, which is why I'm reaching out to you. So, if you could call me back, please . . .

That's what Flint might have said, what she wanted to say. Instead, she said nothing and cut the line.

In her dream Flint is dressed entirely in black: black leather shoes; a shapeless black skirt that reaches her ankles; a black satin jacket that is buttoned to the neck; black gloves and a black, stiff-brimmed Puritan's hat with a veil that covers her face. She's at the doors of a cathedral trying to press her way through the throng – *Scusi, scusi, per favore* – but she can't seem to make herself understood and she feels a growing sense of dread that she will arrive too late. Too late for what? She doesn't know; she only knows she must reach the altar or something terrible will happen, and she presses harder, and Alexander Çarçani turns round and places his hands on her breasts and shoves her with such force that she loses her balance and sprawls backwards onto the steps, losing her hat, exposing her bare skull.

'Show some respect,' says Çarçani, speaking in English as though he was born to it. 'Do you have no respect for the dead?'

Nobody is dead! is what she screams but in the dream what she hears herself say is, *Nessuno è morto.*

She tries again.

Nessuno è morto. Questo è il punto, esso è tutto un terribile errore. Queste è ciò che devo dire a loro, prima che sia troppo tardi. Dovete lasciarli passare.

'Bloody foreigners,' a woman in the crowd says.

Flint is trying to tell them it's all a terrible mistake; nobody is dead and that's why they have to let her through before it's too late but the words will only come in Italian.

'Speak English, can't you?' the woman says.

And there is another disconnection. Lying on her back, staring up at the cathedral, she can see that it is the façade of Chichester, not San Ambrogio – so why is there a gaggle of uniformed carabinieri watching her as she struggles hopelessly to remove Alexander Çarçani's hand-made Italian boot from the middle of her chest?

'Help me, please help me!' is what she calls (*Aiuto, vi prego aiuto!* is what she hears) but the carabinieri only laugh, and Çarçani presses harder with his boot, and now he has a gun in his hand, pointing at her head.

'Why did you do it?' he says. 'Why did you kill your child?'

Nessuno è morto, nessuno è morto! she screams, but he pulls the trigger anyway, and the resonance of the shot rings and rings and rings . . .

She wakes up tangled in the sheet, her body drenched with sweat. The ringing persists and she thinks it's in her head and she squeezes her temples to try to make it stop.

No go. The ringing is getting louder and she finally works out that it's coming from her mobile phone.

'Wake you?' asks Cutter, his voice so distinct he might be in the room.

'Not really,' she says, trying to untangle herself from the sheet.

'Only I just got some news I thought you'd want to hear.'

'Just a moment, I'm a little tied up.' She drops the phone and tears the sheet, the only way to free her arms. 'That's better,' she tells Cutter. 'What?'

'Jerry Crawford, he's out of danger – in fact, he's out of intensive care.'

Flint can't help herself: she whoops with joy until Cutter says, 'Grace, I hope you're in a soundproofed room.'

'Oh, God, Aldus, that's just fantastic. When? How? What more do you know? *Tell me.*'

'Not a lot. I got a call from Christie saying he's fully conscious, breathing on his own and bitching like hell about the feeding tubes. He says he wants *proper* food.'

'He's got it: all the caviar he can eat, on my tab.'

'Jerry and caviar? I don't see it.'

'Okay, lobster, prime rib, whatever he wants.'

'I'll tell him.'

'You're going to Orlando?'

'As soon as I can get a flight.'

'Aldus . . . Mr Cutter, will you do something for me? If there's any part of Jerry that's not too sore, will you give him a kiss from me?'

'No,' says Cutter. 'But I'll tell him you asked. Now, are you ready for some bad news?'

Flint flinches, goes into a mental crouch.

'I also just heard from State, about who submitted your list to TIPOFF. Take a guess.'

But she doesn't need to guess. Suddenly, in that instant, she knows – just as certainly as she suddenly knew she was pregnant with Mandrake's child.

'Fucking Ridout,' she whispers into the phone.

'Close,' says Cutter. 'The request was transmitted by MI6 under the signature of a guy called Sullivan, James Sullivan, but it came from Ridout's department, no doubt about it.'

Flint shivers with cold, pulls the torn sheet around her bare shoulders.

'What do you want me to do?'

'First thing Monday, I think you should talk to Tom Glenning, and not on the phone. Go see him if you can, put him in the picture, ask him if he's got a discreet way to join the dots. We need hard data. We need to know how your Goodheart guy, and maybe the Gup brothers, are connected to Ridout's mob at MI6.'

'Mob is exactly right,' says Flint.

'Excuse me?'

'No, correction: he's worse than any mobster.'

'Don't make it personal, Grace.'

'Right!' There are moments of tense silence until she continues, in a more conciliatory tone, 'Commander Glenning might need to talk to you, Mr Cutter, just to clear the formalities.'

'Sure. Get him to call the office on a secure line as soon as he's ready. Wherever I am they'll patch him through.'

'Will do.'

'So, seen your dad yet? What about your boy?'

'I'm going to see them today,' she replies without a thought – and in that instant she knows that's exactly what she'll do.

There is no evidence of a night porter when Flint slips out of the hotel at 4 a.m. leaving behind a brief note of explanation, the cash to pay for her room and an extra twenty pounds for the torn sheet.

Cocooned in the Mercedes she heads almost due north, driving fast on near-deserted roads, watching bugs in the headlights, Annie Lennox on the CD player keeping her company.

New York

Sixteen

Heading home to see Jack it is not thoughts of Glebe Farm that occupy Flint's mind but memories of another of her sessions with Dr P; one that was easily the most searing.

'So, how exactly did you feel during the final stages of your pregnancy?' Dr Przewalskii asked, a Biro in her fingers poised close to her lips like an unlit cigarette.

'Feel? I don't know – the usual, I suppose.'

'And what is *usual*? This was your first child, I think, your only child, so how can anything you felt be *usual*?'

'I meant, I felt what most women feel, I suppose. Tired because of being so huge. Indigestion, breathlessness, having to get up a hundred times a night to pee. Backache with this really strange dragging feeling that makes you want to sit down; swollen legs, which means you *must* sit down. Anxiety about the waters suddenly breaking when you're nowhere near a hospital. So, a little scared of the unknown; tired, certainly; fat, undoubtedly. Oh, and ugly. That's for sure, I definitely felt ugly.'

Dr Przewalskii had put the tip of the Biro between her teeth and sucked as though her life depended on it, and then exhaled a long plume of non-existent smoke. This was only their fourth session, or maybe their fifth, and Flint hadn't yet learned to spot the traps.

'Doctor, if you want a cigarette, go ahead. It doesn't bother me.'

'Smoke? I never smoke, not any more. What I'm showing you now' – and she had sucked mightily on the Biro again, exhaled again – 'is what you are doing: blowing smoke. You understand? Do you think you can remember what you *felt*?'

Flint shrugged her shoulders.

'Joy?'

'No.'

'Excitement?'

'No.'

'Anticipation?'

'Not exactly.'

'What, then? Perhaps anger? *Resentment?*'

Flint was silent and Dr Przewalskii turned the screw. 'Guilt,' she said firmly, not phrasing it as a question.

'I felt guilty about what?'

'Not then, now. Now you suffer guilt, yes? Now you feel guilty because, all the time he was inside you, you resented your unborn child. Is that possible, do you think?'

'No!'

'What is no? No, you were not resentful? Or no, you feel no guilt?'

'Neither,' said Flint. 'Both,' she added, feeling her eyes grow wet.

Calmer now, Flint had said: 'Frustration is what I felt most of all, Dr P; sheer bloody frustration. You see, I kept on working well into the third trimester, because I'd traced Gröber to Brazil, to São Paulo, where he'd bought himself a whole new identity. He'd also bought himself protection – from some fairly senior cops, rogue elements of the intelligence service, a few politicians – but it wasn't bullet-proof. That kind of protection never is because corrupt officials, they'll always sell you out to a higher bidder, and I let it be known that I was very much in the market for Gröber's head.'

'You bribed *policemen?*'

'We pay for information, Dr P, when we have to; when there isn't any other way. Does that shock you?'

'Nothing shocks me. Go on.'

'Anyway, I was going backwards and forwards to Brazil, chipping away at Gröber's defences. I got the American Consul in São Paulo on side and he was putting pressure on the Brazilian authorities to begin a real search operation for Gröber, rather than the bullshit one the police had going. I knew I was getting closer to Gröber all the time, closer to cracking his new identity and, more to the point, I knew *he* knew. I made damn sure of that. I was giving media interviews, going on TV, holding press conferences at the airport, whatever it took. And the bigger I got, so did the story: "Clock ticks for pregnant cop in relentless hunt for killer" – that sort of thing; I was all over the front pages.'

'Why do you think you wanted so much attention?'

'I was trying to provoke Gröber. I reckoned, or hoped, that he would either make a run for it, in which case I was betting he'd get picked up at the airport or the border – I'd made sure that the immigration department was very much on side – or . . .' Flint had shifted in the overstuffed chair, as though the springs were making her uncomfortable.

'Or?'

'Or that he would take out a contract . . . To have me killed.'

Dr Przewalskii had a fixed expression on her face. It seemed to Flint that she was smiling.

'Now I have shocked you, haven't I?'

'To have you *both* killed,' said Dr P.

'What?'

'You wanted to provoke this Gröber, this *animal* as you call him, so that he would kill you *and* your unborn child. Is this what you are telling me?'

'No, I—'

'Or did you hope that you might somehow survive the attack – a knife, a bullet in the stomach, perhaps, penetrating the womb – and only your child would die?'

'*Jesus*, Marina! *No!* I didn't plan on actually being attacked! I just wanted him to take out a contract on me because, if he did, the chances were we'd get to know about it, and even in Brazil – even in São Paulo – that would have put him totally beyond the pale. You don't plan to kill a foreign cop, particularly a pregnant cop with a media profile as big as her belly, without causing an uproar. If he'd done that, and we'd found out about it, it would have been the lead story in every paper in São Paulo, trust me, and I don't think he would have lasted more than twenty-four hours.'

'Lasted?'

Flint, feeling suddenly, desperately tired, only half suppressed a yawn.

'Honest cops would have found him, arrested him; the pressure on them would have been intense. Or, more likely, before that could happen, the rotten cops or the spooks, the ones who'd been protecting him, taking his money, they would have killed him – for their own protection. Either way, within twenty-four hours, he'd have been off the streets.'

'And did you care which way?'

'Not really. Oh, sure, I would have enjoyed bringing him back to New York – and I would definitely have been on that plane – but getting him extradited before he could bribe the judge, competing jurisdictions, plea-bargaining, it could have got messy. And even if I had got him back to New York, there would have been the trial with all of its uncertainties: jurors can be bought or intimidated or bamboozled, or sometimes they come to verdicts that are just plain dumb. Then there's the whole appeal process' – Flint was counting off her reservations on the fingers of her left hand – 'and if he'd drawn a death sentence the appeals could have dragged on for twenty years. So, on balance ... I honestly don't know what I would have preferred, Dr P, but if they'd killed him – and if they said they had, I would have wanted custody of the body, and personally supervised the matching of his DNA – then at least I could have been certain about one thing: there would have been no more wiggle room for Herr Gröber, would there?'

'Would you have killed him?'

'If he'd given me cause, directly endangered my life or anybody else's? Yes. That still applies.'

'If you find him.'

'When I find him, Dr P.'

'But you didn't find him in Brazil, did you? Despite your very best efforts, you did not manage to provoke him. Do you know why?'

'Airline regulations,' Flint said glumly.

'Explain, please.'

'What we heard, what I was told, was that Gröber had eventually got fed up with me, that he'd discussed taking out a contract on me with one of his chums from intelligence, but that he'd been talked out of it on the grounds that airline regs would do the job for him – get rid of me, I mean – and it wouldn't cost Gröber a cent, or cause the slightest ripple. You must know that when you're pregnant most airlines won't fly you after twenty-six weeks without a note from your doctor saying you're in perfect health, and after thirty-four weeks they won't fly you even if you've got a note from the Surgeon General. By the time Gröber decided to make his move, his intelligence buddy knew that I was coming up to thirty-two weeks, so I only had another week or so before I had to leave São Paulo; either that or stay in Brazil and have the baby there – and I was never going to do that. So—'

'If this Gröber was so important to you, why would you not stay in Brazil to have your baby?'

'Because I'd promised my father I'd go home – his home, I mean, in England, where I grew up. I'd promised my dad I'd go home to have the baby there.'

'Ah, yes,' said Dr Przewalskii brightly, and it seemed to Flint that in her mind she was turning an imaginary notebook to a fresh page, writing a heading with her Biro that she smoked like a cigarette. 'Let us talk, please, about your father.'

Seventeen

When Mandrake went on the run – from Karl Gröber whom he had blackmailed; from MI6, for which he had operated as an irregular, clandestine agent that they now wished to permanently deny; not least from his wife, who was too blind to see that he had penetrated her, both literally and metaphorically, only because that was his job – he had turned up unannounced at Glebe Farm, Flint's father's home, determined to retrieve his escape kit: a cache of fake identity documents and $130,000 in cash that he had hidden under a floorboard in Flint's childhood bedroom; a deception he'd achieved when he and Grace had spent a night at Glebe Farm as part of their honeymoon – and, if you think about it, an indication that he always knew the day would come when he would need to escape. Unsuspecting, unaware that his son-in-law was the subject of multiple international manhunts and a psychopathic liar who had betrayed everyone, and especially John Flint's daughter – unaware, because John Flint's daughter hadn't yet found the strength to tell him that his son-in-law was an utter fake – John Flint had welcomed Mandrake into his home with open arms, given him whisky, insisted that he stay the night, spend one more night in Grace's bed.

And how had Mandrake returned this kindness? By sneaking up on John Flint in the middle of the night, when John Flint was attempting to call his daughter to say how pleased he was that 'Ben' had come for a surprise visit; by beating him over the head with a heavy table lamp with a base made of cast iron; by stuffing him unconscious, gagged and bound, into a dog cage—

'A dog cage?' Dr Przewalskii had asked, interrupting Flint's reverie, clearly startled by the last assertion.

'My father's a vet. His surgery is in the barn at Glebe Farm and there are cages – more like pens – where he keeps his post-op patients if they need to stay overnight. The pens are comfortable enough for dogs, even large dogs. Not so comfortable for an unconscious man with a fractured skull who's six foot three in his socks. Bloody Mandrake had to practically bend him double to get him inside. And then he left him there to die.'

Hearing herself talk, Flint was struck by how remarkably calm her voice sounded.

'But your father, he did not die?'

'Obviously not. He was found in time – barely, and in a coma, but . . . There was some permanent damage to the neurons in the basal forebrain; so, some memory loss, some attention deficit. But, yes, he lives, and works; he still has his practice; he manages.'

'And what did your father say when you told him you were carrying the baby of this man who had tried to kill him?'

'Nothing.'

'*Nothing?*'

'He held me very tightly for a long time and waited for me to cry – which I did, eventually, in buckets.'

Flint thought that her voice no longer sounded quite so composed.

'Later on that night, I told him I wasn't going to have an abortion – not that the thought had even occurred to him. I told him that as soon as the child was born, I'd put him up for adoption – I already knew it was a boy; I just *knew* that bloody Mandrake's child would be in his image. When I said that, it was Dad's turn to cry. When, finally, he could speak, he said he couldn't bear the thought of me giving up my child.'

Dr Przewalskii knows when to remain silent.

'We rowed. I mean, for once we really rowed. He said, how could I possibly think of doing that? I said, it was only half my child, and I didn't want the other half – and, anyway, I had a full-time job to do, finding Gröber, et cetera, et cetera, and adoption was the best solution. Fine, he said, I'll adopt the child, and I said he was being ridiculous, he couldn't raise a child, and he got on his high horse and said, let me remind you, young lady – which is what he calls me when he's cross – let me remind you, young lady, that I raised you on my own – with some success, I might say. Yes, I said, but let me remind you that I was six when Mummy disappeared, and what we're talking about here is a newborn baby. And, I said, when I was six, you were not much more than thirty and now you're . . . What are you doing?'

Flint could tell that, in her mind, Dr Przewalskii had turned to another new page in her imaginary notebook and was scribbling furiously.

'You say your mother disappeared when you were six?'

'Died.'

'I thought you said she disappeared.'

'Same thing, in her case.'

'You have a body?'

'I have a what?'

'Was her body ever found?'

'No, Dr P, I don't have a body – and, if it's all right with you, can we just turn back that page in your head?'

'You don't think this is *relevant*?'

'To you, maybe. I just don't want to talk about it, not now.'

'But how can we—'

'*Drop it!* Drop the subject of my mother right now, Dr P, otherwise I'm walking out of here, and I don't give a stuff what Human Resources says.'

Flint was on her feet, white-faced, furious. For a moment Dr Przewalskii looked as though she might take up the challenge but then, with elaborate motions, she indicated with her hands that she was turning back a page in her imaginary notebook, flattening the spine with her palm.

'And your father was how old when he proposed to adopt your child?' she said as though nothing had happened.

'Sixty-two,' said Flint, not placated, still on her feet and ready to leave.

'Too old, you thought?'

'Not necessarily. Not,' she continued icily, matter-of-fact, 'if my *fucking* husband hadn't beaten him half to death with a table lamp. Not if he hadn't robbed him of his faculties, or some of them. Not if my *fucking* husband hadn't turned him into a prematurely old man. Do you understand, Dr P? Are you getting the plot?'

'My child, please, sit down.'

'I'm not your child.'

'Then, excuse me. *Deputy Director* Flint, please . . . Please, that you sit down.'

Flint remained standing.

'You drink?'

'You know I do – too much, apparently.'

'But do you drink vodka? Genuine Russian vodka, not the rubbish they sell you in America.'

'Rarely.'

Then, without a further word, Dr Przewalskii had hurried to her desk, opened a drawer, pulled from it a flask and two shot glasses into which she poured colourless liquid. She came to where Flint was standing – the top of her bushy head barely reaching Flint's shoulder – and pressed one of the glasses into her hand.

'We drink to your father, that he survived, that he gave you his love, that he gave you back your son.'

Flint sniffed the glass suspiciously. 'Dr P, is this appropriate?'

'Absolutely not! To give alcohol to a patient is entirely inappropriate, *fantastically* inappropriate. If Human Resources find out they will have me shot, I think – and I don't give a stuffed.'

'Stuff,' said Flint. 'You don't give a stuff.'

'That's right,' said Dr Przewalskii. '*Stoi!*' and she drained her glass.

Afterwards Flint thought it must have been the alcohol, one hundred proof, that had seeped through her defences, dissolved her resolve.

'About my mother,' she'd blurted out, the words forming in her mouth rather than her head. 'When I was a teenager, about sixteen, I think—'

'Sixteen? You said you were six when you lost your mother, when she disappeared.'

'I was. I'm talking about something else.'

'Please,' said Dr Przewalskii in apology for interrupting.

'When I was about sixteen I started having a recurring dream in which I saw my father beating my mother to death . . . With a hammer . . . In his surgery, by the operating table. Night after night I would see the same thing: hammer holes in her head; him standing there with the hammer in his hand, blood all over his gown.'

Sometimes, even now, twenty years on, those images return.

'The school – I went to boarding school when I was twelve – knew something was wrong because, more often than not, I woke up with a migraine or a panic attack. It got worse and worse until

I really thought I was going mad. Eventually, after about a month of this, I had a complete breakdown and I was admitted to a psychiatric clinic on an emergency basis. They really put me through the mill – transactional analysis, hypnosis, regression therapy – trying to find out what was wrong. They got nowhere, until they switched to what they called drug-mediated interviews.'

'Sodium amytal?'

'Right.'

'And you were sixteen years old?'

'Yup. You can probably guess the rest, Dr P.'

'Oh, my poor child,' Dr Przewalskii said – and this time Flint did not object to her solicitousness. 'They gave you sodium amytal to free what was hidden in your deepest subconscious and concluded that your dream was a repressed memory coming to the surface. Yes?'

'Exactly.'

'And you believed them? They made you believe you really had seen your father kill your mother?'

'Yes.'

'Did they tell this to the police?'

'Yes.'

'And you were interviewed by the police?'

'Yes – and, yes, I made a statement accusing him of murder.'

'And he was arrested?'

'Yes, and they dug up the floor of his surgery with a JCB looking for her body.'

Nothing shocks me, Dr Przewalskii had claimed earlier but that was belied by what Flint now saw in her eyes.

'It was all utter bollocks, of course. My father didn't kill my mother; he couldn't have done. I was with him when she took Hector, our Labrador, out for a walk and never came back. I was still with him when he went searching for her and we found Hector in the lane at the bottom of our meadow, half beaten to death. She was abducted, taken away and presumably murdered – and not by him . . .' The pain of recollection was becoming unbearable and Flint sought refuge in a question. 'Did you ever use sodium amytal, Dr P, to get to the so-called truth? I mean, when you were still in Russia?'

'No. But I've seen it used many, many times. I know what it does.'

'So?' Flint said brightly, as if to say, are we done?

Far from it.

'How long did it take for you to realise that your so-called repressed memory was – what did you call it? Bullocks?'

'Bollocks – which is what bullocks don't have once they're castrated.' A faint smile from Flint to suggest that she can still see the funny side of things. 'Oh, I don't know, Dr P. Months . . . My father arranged for me to go to a psychiatric clinic in Paris where there was this incredible guy, Dr Holt, who slowly repaired the damage; allowed me to work out for myself what was true, what was false. I was there for about fifteen months, I guess. I do know that I went home, back to Glebe Farm, on my eighteenth birthday.'

'And your father forgave you?'

'Oh, no! He never *not* forgave me, if you know what I mean. What I did to him, when I accused him of murder, it was never my fault, not in his eyes. He blamed the quacks – excuse me, no offence. He blamed the doctors, the drugs, the police; anyone and anything but me. The one absolute certainty I have is that he's never, ever stopped loving me, Dr P.'

'Then you are very fortunate, do you think?'

'Yes.'

'So, I wonder if you know why you are so angry. Where does your anger come from, do you think?'

'*What?*'

'Are you angry with your mother for leaving you, perhaps?'

Flint out of the chair, back on her feet, leaning over Dr Przewalskii's cheap desk. 'She didn't *leave* me! She was *abducted*! You're talking rubbish, Marina; complete and utter bullshit.'

'Probably. You are probably absolutely right – I am speaking bullocks. So, let me ask you something else. Did you become a police officer to avenge your mother's murder?'

Flint lifted her hands from the desk and held them in the air to express her exasperation. 'Hardly. How could I?'

'This Gröber, other people like him, when you hunt them, when you go on cover, when you risk your life so recklessly and with all of your rage, do you think it is possible that, in your mind, they are surrogates, proxies, for your mother's killer?'

Always is the answer Flint doesn't provide.

'Because you know you will never find him?'

'Says who?' said Flint.

* * *

They returned to calmer waters.

'Your father, you think maybe he swamps you with his love?'

'I wouldn't say he swamps me. He loves me a lot and he knows that I know it, but it's not demanding love, if that's the right expression.'

'So, unconditional love, perhaps?'

'I think so.'

'And what about your love for him?'

'I'm not as generous as he is, Dr P, or as nice. But of course I love him, and I try to make sure he knows it. He certainly knows he's the most important person in my life.'

There was a longish pause until Dr Przewalskii said, 'So, when did you decide your father could adopt your child?'

'Not adopt, take care of, at least for a while. After the amniocentesis test results came back negative. Until then, because they'd warned me there was an increased risk of genetic defects – particularly of Down's syndrome and spina bifida, because of my age – I suppose it had been in the back of my mind that I might be offered a termination; that if the test results showed a serious defect they would recommend a termination, and . . . I don't know . . . I'm pretty sure that if they had I would have taken it.'

'The easy way out?'

'Easier, or it would have been. But, no, every test I had said the baby was absolutely fine, and I was in perfect health, and that was in England – the amniocentesis, I mean. I'd taken two months' leave – Gröber had disappeared, I didn't know yet that he was in Brazil – and I was living at Glebe Farm, and when the results came back my father was just so damn thrilled. Overnight he seemed to shed ten years; he was back to the way he was before Mandrake nearly killed him. It was just extraordinary. Shortly after that I had to go to London for a few days, to brief my former boss about Gröber – I wanted the Brits to monitor some bank accounts I thought he might be using – and when I got back, the house was like a building site and there was my father, stripped to the waist, shovelling sand into a cement mixer, singing something from Gilbert and Sullivan at the top of his lungs. He said he'd decided *on a whim*, quote unquote, to knock through the wall between two spare rooms and create what could be – just *could* be, mind – a nursery suite with a separate bedroom and bathroom for a nanny. Oh, and by the way, he said, he'd been in touch with an agency in London and they were sending him details of several highly qualified candidates. *Just in case*, he said. Just in case.'

'Did that make you angry?'

'No. Exasperated – for about five seconds. And then I had this feeling of unbelievable relief, as though some huge, crushing weight had been lifted from my chest. I just threw myself at him, grabbed him around the neck and blubbered. And he was trying to push me away: *Gracie, Gracie, you're getting wet cement all over your nice suit.* As if that mattered; as if I cared a damn about my suit.'

'So, he made a nursery?'

'He did. I got him to see sense and hire three local lads to help with the heavy work; I think he'd found two days of lugging cement more than enough. But, yes, he made a brilliant nursery, and a lovely room for Sally, the nanny he eventually chose, and—'

'Your father chose the nanny?'

'Well, we chose her together but he's the one who's got to live with her so, obviously, it was very important that they hit it off. Dad's not always the easiest person to be around. He can be distant – no, not distant, more like preoccupied, as though he doesn't even know you're there. Anyway, we both agreed that Sally – Sally Beaumont is her name – was head and shoulders above the other girls we saw. Not that she's a girl, really; just a couple of years younger than me. She trained as a nurse before deciding she would rather be with kids. She loves living in the country, loves to ride. She's bright, good fun, entirely self-sufficient, knows how to change a fuse. Oh, and she loves to cook, which is just as well because my father can barely boil an egg.'

'She is perfect.'

'Not quite,' said Flint pulling a face. 'She's Australian, from Melbourne, and so was Mandrake – although I only discovered that on the day he died – and every time I hear that Melbourne accent, when I haven't heard it for a while, it gives me the creeps. It's really crazy, I know; Mandrake's accent was Canadian, which is what he pretended to be, but I can't forget his association with Melbourne. Anyway, the clincher was Mrs Gilbert. She's Dad's housekeeper cum cleaning lady, has been for aeons, comes in five mornings a week, and she's the one who rules the roost. Nothing much happens at Glebe Farm without her approval. *Why don't we run it by Mrs G* – I can hear my father saying it now. So Sally got *run by* Mrs G and, fortunately, Mrs G decided Sally was wonderful. Actually she said that Sally was sent by destiny, as likely as not. Mrs G's very big on destiny.'

'Do you think you resent the other women in your father's life?'

Flint had instantly flared. '*What?*'

'You seem hostile to this Mrs G.'

'On the contrary. As far as I'm concerned the G stands for gold, and she's worth her weight in it. I don't know what my father would have done without her, especially after Mandrake tried to beat his brains out with a table lamp.'

'So, everything *was* perfect.' Dr Przewalskii smiled.

'I don't know about that but I do know that in the last couple of months, when I was still going back and forth to Brazil, my father was in pig-heaven. Boy, did he shop! I don't just mean the usual baby things. Every time I went back to England, about the first thing he'd say was, Gracie, come and look at this. Don't you think it's wonderful? And there would be a new cradle or a Moses basket – he must have bought six of them – or a rocking chair or a rocking horse, or a playpen, or a safety gate, or a walker. I said to him, Dad, the baby's not even born and you've bought him a *walker*? And, of course, he got on his high horse: Nothing wrong with being prepared, young lady. He bought a baby monitor, and I don't just mean one. There was a monitor in every room, every place you can imagine, including all the loos and his surgery and the stable. It was as if the whole farm had been wired for surveillance. Oh, I almost forgot – and baby books! He must have bought every book on pregnancy and baby-raising that was ever published; there were scores of them. Sally told me that whenever he was expecting me home, he'd hide the latest ones he'd bought, like an alcoholic hides the empty bottles, in case I thought he was overdoing it.'

'Sally was already living at the farm?'

'Yes. She needed a job straightaway and we didn't want to lose her, so my father hired her a couple of months in advance. Gave her a chance to settle in, get to know the area, make some friends. It was also good for me to have her around for company when I finally went back to await the birth – or J-day, as Dad insisted on calling it; J for Jack.'

'And how was it?'

'The wait? It seemed to go on forever. I read in one of those many, many books my father had accumulated that long walks, curries and sex are generally supposed to trigger the birth. Well, it was December, just after Christmas and really icy, so walking outside was not a great idea, and I hate the smell of curries, and sex wasn't an option. So, I just waited.'

'Until?'

'January the sixth. I went into hospital early on Sunday morning and Jack was born at nine o'clock that night.'

Dr Przewalskii toyed with her empty glass, twirling it between the palms of her hands, watching Flint's face intently before saying, 'Do you want to speak about it?'

'No, but I will, on two conditions. First, you give me one more shot of your vodka. Second, you give me the most disapproving look in your repertoire so we can get it over with in advance.'

'You think I disapprove of you?'

'Dr P, let's face it: I don't fit the motherhood mould and, for me, childbirth was not the ultimate miracle it's supposed to be; anything but. In my time I've been shot, stabbed, almost raped and beaten to a pulp – but nothing had prepared me for giving birth.'

Dr Przewalskii poured them each another shot of vodka and gave a mock glare of disapproval that was belied by the sparkle in her eyes. 'Was your father present?'

'No, he was outside the delivery room. He wanted to be with me but I wouldn't have it. I was determined to be a martyr. *I have no partner so I'll do this alone, and no epidural for me and none of your painkillers, thank you very much – because I can take it.* I was very clear about that. Ha! They put me on gas and air and I became very quickly very high, out of control, and I think I had a panic attack. I announced I was going home and tried to get off the table, and the midwife slapped me on the leg, really hard, and told me to stop it. By the time I was begging for painkillers it was too late and when Jack finally arrived I felt totally numb and confused, maybe in shock. Then they gave me an injection of something called syntometrine, to speed up the delivery of the afterbirth, and that made me feel sick to my stomach. God, what a ghastly feeling! So, when they tried to get me to hold Jack, or to lay him on my stomach, I'm ashamed to say I didn't feel any of the things you're supposed to feel. I looked at this wrinkled, blood-streaked thing they were holding out to me and told them, in no uncertain terms, to bugger off. There, now you know,' Flint added, and took the vodka in one swallow.

'You think you are the only woman who has felt like this? You think it is always like in the magazines and the movies?'

'No, but when it comes to childbirth, motherhood, we're not supposed to own up to our true feelings, are we? We're supposed to *bond*. And it wasn't just that I didn't instantly bond with Jack, or that my feelings were ambivalent. My feelings were very, very . . . negative.'

'You hated the sight of him?'

'Yes.'

'Because he reminded you of Mandrake?'

'He didn't remind me of anyone. I was just incredulous that this baby could have anything to do with me.'

'And how long did this feeling last?'

'Days. All the time I was in hospital and even when I took him home. I just dumped him on Sally and fled to my bedroom. I wouldn't come out even for meals. My father, who was totally devastated by my behaviour, had to leave a tray outside my door.'

'So, you did not breast feed, I think?'

'No.'

'Had you intended to?'

'Yes.'

'But, even so, you were eventually able to bond with your baby, I think. Your feelings changed, yes?'

'I think what happened is that I adapted; adapted to the idea that this baby was mine, that I was his mother – and, yes, my feelings changed, grew, into what I recognised as love. Unbidden love, maybe, but real enough.'

'And then after, what – three months, a little more? – you left this baby you loved. At the first opportunity you ran away. Is that what happened?'

'I didn't run, Dr P. I took a taxi to Birmingham airport and I *flew*.'

Mid Compton

Eighteen

If a record exists for the fastest road journey between Chichester and Mid Compton, Flint reckons she must have broken it. The first red flush of the sun is barely above the horizon when she takes the sharp curve into the driveway of Glebe Farm, feeling the rear end of the Mercedes losing traction on the gravel, flicking the steering wheel to regain control. She allows the car's speed to drop to less than walking pace as she edges up the hill to where her father's house and the barn that is his surgery stand like citadels etched against the backdrop of altocumulus clouds tinged with blood. Having broken the record to get here (and, frequently, the speed limits), she's no longer so certain that she wants to arrive.

Cresting the brow of the hill she drives onto the grass verge and cuts the engine, coasting to a stop some fifty metres short of the house. She's not concerned about disturbing Jack or Sally because the nursery and the nanny's room are at the back of the house, but her father's bedroom overlooks the driveway and she half expects to see his light come on; half expects the window to open, to see his head emerge, his tousled hair; to hear him asking, 'Hello? Who's there?'

And suddenly it's very important to her that he doesn't wake up – not yet – because, if he does, she knows exactly what will happen. She can hear him now – *Gracie, is that you? You've come to see Jack! Marvellous, bloody marvellous* – and he'll go rushing off to fetch the boy – *Jack, Jack, guess who's here!* – and the truth is she's not ready to see the child she has abandoned for more than half of his life – not yet. She feels she's like a diver coming up from the deep and thinking about the bends; she knows she's got to do this slowly, give herself time to adjust to changes in pressure.

And so she waits until she's sure her father has not been disturbed, then, easing out of the car, pressing closed the driver's door with a barely audible click, she heads swiftly for the house,

keeping to the grass, avoiding the gravel. The front door key is in
the niche where it's always been hidden for as long as she can
remember. It turns the lock and she slips inside, silent as a thief.

Now she's in the darkened hallway, navigating a careful passage
towards the kitchen where she intends to make herself coffee when
she is stopped, arrested, by an abrupt awareness of something;
something wrong, something out of place. She shallows her breathing and concentrates her senses, willing herself to see or hear or
taste or smell what she cannot yet identify. It is the auditory nerves
that respond, telling her brain that the membranes in her outer ears
are detecting the faintest sound waves of human laughter. Slowly
she turns her head from side to side until she is certain the sound
waves are coming from upstairs.

One by one she climbs the stairs, pausing on each step while
she searches her episodic memory for data from her childhood
on the parts of the treads she must avoid because they creak.
Now the auditory nerves report that the laughter is interspersed
with the muffled sounds of conversation.

Reaching the top of the stairs she advances along the L-shaped
corridor that leads eventually to her father's bedroom: past the
nursery/nanny suite, the door to which is closed; past her own
bedroom, where Mandrake royally screwed her in more ways than
one; round the corner – and now she can see in the growing light
that her father's door is ajar, and she can make out every word that
she hears.

'. . . now that he sleeps all the way through,' her father is saying.

'*Almost* all the way through,' says Sally in that Melbourne
accent that still gives Flint the creeps.

'Did he wake up, darling? I didn't hear.'

Darling? Flint registers the word but not yet its implication.

'As if.'

'I'm sorry, you should have woken me.'

'Old men need their sleep if they're going to perform.'

'Old men, indeed!' Her father gives his mock roar – and now he
must be doing something to Sally because she's squealing like a
piglet. 'And do we have specific complaints about the performance
of this particular *old man*?'

'None that I can think of,' Sally says eventually, sounding out
of breath.

'Are you sure?'

'Absolutely certain.'

'So, what do we do now?'

'Well, I fed and changed Jack an hour ago so he'll be fine until about nine. We could maybe . . .'

'Y-e-s?' says Flint's father, teasing out the question.

'We could . . . go back to sleep?'

'Um.' There is a pause and then he says, 'You know what, my girl? I don't think I want to sleep.'

'Really?' Sally sounding playful. 'And what is it that you think you'd like to do, old man?'

'I think I would like to kiss you. Stroke you, lick you, suck you, *fuck you*.'

'Again?'

'Oh, yes. Again and again and again, *and* again.'

'Enough!' Sally laughs. 'You're just bloody insatiable, aren't you?'

'I sincerely hope so.'

'And you won't take pity on a working girl?'

'You know, the problem with young people today is that they've got no stamina.'

'Is that a fact? Try me,' says Sally, sounding as if she means it.

Flint feels as though she can't move; as though the seagrass matting she's standing on is quick-drying cement that has encased her feet. But she has to move because there is vomit in her throat and she's going to choke unless she can get out of here, get some air. And perhaps it is the effort of freeing herself from the sense of paralysis that causes her to scream.

She's flying: back along the corridor, down the stairs, through the hallway, out of the front door, across the gravel, down the grass bank – tumbling, getting to her feet, tumbling again – making it to the meadow, running for the treeline; running, it seems to her, for her life.

'*Gracie, Gracie, Gracie . . . Please, stop. Gracie, please come back.*'

She hears, ignores, her father's frantic pleas.

Nineteen

Grace Flint with her back against the wall; a low, drystone wall that marks the western boundary of Glebe Farm. Overhanging the wall, the canopy of a stunted white ash provides her with some shelter from the persistent drizzle – not that she gives a damn about the rain. The tree marks the spot where, in all likelihood, her mother was abducted more than thirty years ago, where Madeline Flint vanished so comprehensively she might never have existed. And since the tree was planted as a memorial to her mother on Grace's twelfth birthday at Grace's request, and since it is where Grace has often come in search of solitude or solace, it is an obvious place to look for her.

Yet more than an hour has passed before John Flint makes his cautious approach to the spot, plodding warily down Glebe Rise, stopping well short of where his daughter waits as though he's afraid she might bolt.

'Gracie, you'll catch your death,' he says as she stares straight through him. 'Look at you, you're soaked.'

With his peaked cap, his trousers tucked into green gumboots, a knee-length oilskin jacket that glistens with moisture it has repelled, he's dressed for the weather. He holds out a similar jacket for her.

'Please, Gracie, please come home.'

Because she does not respond, because she seems as though she might be in a trance, he takes tentative steps towards her, taking himself under the shelter of the ash's canopy, still holding out the jacket like a peace offering.

He tries again. 'Gracie?'

Now he's very close to her, squatting on his haunches, getting on a level so he can look directly into her vacant eyes.

'Gracie, believe me, this is the last way I wanted you to find out. I was going to tell you, of course I was, but I didn't know you were coming. If I had known . . .' The thought is lame and he leaves it unfinished. 'I had hoped you might be pleased for me,' he substitutes with just a hint of peevishness in his tone.

Pleased for you?

'Please send her away,' says Grace flatly.

'What?'

'Please get that woman away from my child.'

John Flint stands up quickly, like a man with cramp in his calves. There is a look of bewilderment on his face, his eyebrows arched in surprise.

'I mean it, Dad,' Flint continues relentlessly. 'I want her out of here, gone. I don't want her anywhere near Jack ever again.' Now she's getting to her feet, a little stiffly, drops of rain on her cheeks that look like tears.

'Grace, *please*.'

'I can't stand it,' she says. 'You have to ask her to go.'

Her father holds out his hands in supplication. 'I can't possibly send Sally away. Don't you see? For God's sake, Grace, I'm in love with her.'

He registers a look of sheer confusion on his daughter's face, hurt in her eyes that are now the colour of violets. She turns away from him, leaves the shelter of the ash, begins her weary ascent of Glebe Rise.

'I know you're angry, Grace,' he calls after her. Then, more quietly to himself, he adds, 'I just wish I knew why.'

She has decided she will take Jack away from Glebe Farm and nothing will dissuade her; no amount of pleading from her father to see common sense. The rented Mercedes coupé does not have a child seat, nor can one be properly secured. There is nothing like enough room for Jack's buggy, his travel cot, the sheets and duvet, his high chair, the sterilising kit, his nappies, his potty, his clothes, his toys.

Jack's nanny – the woman he's surely entitled to regard as his mother – makes similar pained contributions until, slamming the car door, Flint says, 'Listen, Sally, you're fired, all right? What you and my father get up to is your business. I just don't want you around my son.' Sally whimpers and flees inside the house; runs upstairs to her room, locks and bolts the door.

'Grace, for heaven's sake!' her father says before following his lover into the house.

Jack observes all of this soundlessly through huge eyes, sucking on a rubber teat, fingering a corner of his precious blanket. It is not until the Mercedes is heading down the drive, skidding on the ruts, that he begins to realise the extent of his loss. Strapped into the back seat like a hostage, he begins to cry at a pitch that skewers his mother's brain.

In a lay-by on the A40, Flint steps out of the car so she can hear herself think and uses her mobile phone to call the duty officer at the headquarters of the Financial Strike Force. Even though it is a Sunday, and early morning New York time, she asks to be put through to Rocco Morales, sure that he will be at his desk, for Rocco has no other life. Sure enough, he answers the phone on the first ring and, after the courtesies, Flint says she needs him to hack into the database of Human Resources to find the home number of Dr Przewalskii. No can do, says Rocco, even though it is a well-known fact within the FSF that there is no computer system extant that Rocco cannot hack into.

'What's the problem?'

'It's a discrete system.'

'So?'

'I don't have the necessary permissions. Meaning, I'm not authorised.'

Flint knows she is coming to the end of her tether.

'I could ask?' Rocco suggests.

'Ask?'

'Ask Human Resources for the number. You never know, they just might—'

'Rocco, stop sucking about!'

'Sucking?'

The tether snaps. 'Rocco, *listen to me*! What I'm giving you is an order, and you can put it in the log, and if there's any comeback . . .' She breaks off and makes herself count silently to five. Then, much more calmly, she pleads, 'Just do it, Rocco. *Please*.'

'Hello? Who is speaking?' Dr Przewalskii's voice is laced with caution.

'Dr P, it's Flint, Grace Flint, your least favourite patient. Listen,'

Flint hurries on, 'I'm sorry to be calling you at home but I wanted you to know.'

'Know?'

'I wanted you to be the first to know that I've reclaimed Jack. For keeps, Dr P. He's with me now. I'm bringing him home.'

Dr Przewalskii, while recognising hysteria when she hears it, chooses not to respond.

'Okay, okay, I know I'm being impulsive but I've got no choice.'

Flint paces the lay-by, watching her imprisoned son through the Mercedes' side window.

'The thing is, I found out . . . I'm in the UK, chasing Gröber – and I shouldn't be telling you that but what the hell – and I had some time on my hands and I went home to see Jack . . . no, not home, definitely not home, not any more. So, correction, I went to my father's home and I found them in bed together, him and the nanny. Can you believe that, Dr P? My father's sleeping with a woman young enough to be his daughter . . . No she's bloody not! She's younger than I am, she's younger than his daughter! He won't give her up. He thinks he's in love. Love? Didn't sound much like love to me, not what I heard, not the way he was talking . . . Anyway, I had to get Jack out of there. You do see that, don't you? Get him out of there before he . . . I don't know . . . Before he suffocates on his own vomit while they're fucking each other stupid because she's not doing what she's paid to be doing, which is taking care of Jack, not screwing my father. What do you think, Dr P?'

'I think you are angry.'

'Yes.'

'Even disgusted, I think.'

'I'm numb.'

'Do you know why?'

Silence on the line. Flint has not yet begun to understand the emotions that have overwhelmed her.

'I think you are in shock, and so is your child. He is crying?'

'He won't stop.'

'That is because you have broken his routine, taken him away from everything he knows.'

'Because I had no choice,' Flint says while her son screams, his face a picture of misery behind the glass.

* * *

At Dr Przewalskii's suggestion Flint has changed Jack's nappy, fed him a bottle and at last he sleeps. She has adjusted the rear-view mirror so she can watch his face – and bugger the cars behind – and the relief she feels is close to euphoria.

The Sunday evening traffic heading into London is heavy, near to gridlock in places, and she finds herself navigating through the side streets, following the half-remembered rat runs that used to be part of her daily life. Just the act of driving, of making progress, is cathartic, allowing her to believe she's doing something useful. When even the rat runs become clogged she diverts herself by rehearsing what she will tell the hotel to explain Jack's unexpected arrival.

My best friend's child . . . No, my sister's boy . . . Sudden illness in the family . . . Or maybe a road accident. Both parents in hospital and no one else to take care of Jack. So, I'm going to need some things brought up to the suite: a crib, a high chair, maybe a playpen if you have one. And tomorrow morning I need to find practically full-time help, somebody who knows about taking care of babies because, frankly, I hardly know a thing.

In the back seat Jack whimpers in his sleep and his mother wonders, *What do babies dream?*

London

Twenty

Flint has spent an entirely sleepless night but now, flying high on four hundred milligrams of modafinil, she feels no fatigue at all as she strides along the Thames embankment on her way to meet her former boss, Tom Glenning. No one really knows how modafinil works, how it manipulates the brain, but work it does, at least for Flint, and those little white tablets – her 'go pills' as she calls them – are the well-kept secret of her legendary endurance. She had sworn off them, after reading in the *New York Times* that laboratory animals subjected to chronic sleep deprivation invariably die of overwhelming bacterial infection. But just the first few hours alone with Jack in the hotel suite had convinced her that sleep was not an option, not tonight. Not while he screamed constantly; not while he refused to eat and instead hurled his food about, making indescribable messes on the Connaught's lush carpet; not while, released from his high chair, he crawled about the room attempting to probe every electrical socket with his sticky fingers; not while he dismantled the TV remote control and attempted to push the batteries into his nostrils. So when Jack finally, fitfully slept she dug down deep into her bag to find the bottle of modafinil that she always carries just in case and took twice the normal dose. US Air Force pilots who have taken modafinil on an experimental basis reckon it allows them to remain alert and fully combat-ready for up to eighty-eight hours – which, Flint thinks, is about what she will need to get Jack home.

With all possible luck. With Tom's help.

Commander Glenning waits at their hastily agreed rendezvous, punctual as ever, his elbows resting on the guard rail, gazing across the river to the south bank of the Thames and the headquarters of MI6; Nigel Ridout's lair. Twice he has dipped his head and glanced to his right, monitoring Flint's approach, without any sign of recognition. Whether this is tradecraft, or simply his failure to identify her, Flint doesn't know.

She walks behind and just beyond him and then spins round to exclaim, 'Uncle Tom!' and ducks under the arm he throws up in surprise to embrace him, kiss him on the cheek.

'Jesus, Grace!'

'It's Kathy, Tom,' she says and laughs as though she is delighted to see him. 'And since I'm supposed to be your favourite niece, and in case anyone is watching, a bit of visible affection on your part might be a good idea.'

Obediently Commander Glenning gives her a clumsy hug and returns her kiss but, clearly, he's rattled.

'How do you do that?' he asks. 'The rest of you, I can see what you've done. But how do you change the way you walk?'

'It's the shoes.'

'The shoes?'

'Yeah. They're half a size too small, and one heel's higher than the other. Cocks the pelvis, changes the gait.'

Hands on her shoulders, he holds her at arm's length and studies her face as though he's seeing her for the first time.

'Are you doing yourself harm, Grace?'

'No, honestly, I've got a great osteopath. He eases my pelvis back into alignment whenever—'

'That's not what I meant,' Glenning interrupts.

'I know.'

'Well, then. Are you in trouble?'

'Some,' Flint says 'but not what you might think.' She takes his hands in hers. 'Can we walk, please? Walk and talk?'

Crossing the river via Vauxhall Bridge, turning left onto Albert Embankment, pausing to gaze at MI6 HQ – out of range of the obvious surveillance cameras, until, even so, Flint shivers and says, 'Let's get out of here' – they head briskly north to Lambeth Bridge, crossing back across the Thames, finding a pub on the Horseferry Road where there is no jukebox and only a small lunchtime crowd. Commander Glenning nurses a glass of Guinness that he barely touches and Flint drinks white wine. They are sitting at a table in the back where they can both watch the door – and all the while she talks, narrating the history of Operation Payback in exquistie detail. Commander Glenning listens with a priest's solemnity, saying almost nothing, showing barely any reaction on his broad freckled face, until she comes to the part where she is describing her penultimate meeting with Joseph Gup.

'So the next morning Gup comes into my office. *Can I have a word*,' Flint mimics in a fair impression of Joseph's deep, conciliatory tone, 'and then he puts on a dog and pony show that was enough to make my head spin. I do great work, he says, but maybe too much work and he's worried about my health; I'm recovering from cancer, by the way, that's part of Kathy's legend. I tell him I'm fine, in remission and all the tests are negative, and then he slips in a question: do I ever go back to the *old country*? Meaning here, to visit my father, which is also part of Kathy's legend.' Glenning raises an eyebrow and Flint explains, 'It's what you taught us at Hendon: when you're building a legend, always add some truth to the mix. Anyway, then he switches back to my analysis of the San Ambrogio project and gives me some more claptrap about the *magnificence* of my work, and what a shame it would be to waste it all, but of course he understands that I can't run the names of the principals through TIPOFF without compromising my integrity, blah, blah, blah – and then, finally, he comes to the point: he says he's got this friend who knows of *intermediaries* who can run the names; intermediaries in the *old country*; private security consultants, he calls them, *very discreet*. Says they've got contacts with official agencies, *stellar contacts*. Then he says,' and once again Flint adopts Gup's tone, '*Whether we're talking about law enforcement or the intelligence community, or both, I don't know – and you don't want to know.*'

Glenning fingers the tobacco in the bowl of his unlit pipe. 'Wrong about that, wasn't he, Grace?'

'He surely was.'

'Did he give you the names of these intermediaries?'

'Not then, not until I agreed to go. The bait on offer was a free trip to London, first class all the way, stay as long as I liked; get to see my father, if I wanted. All I had to do was collect some dirty dollars from a firm of scumbag lawyers' – and from the pocket of her raincoat Flint takes a folded slip of paper on which she has written the details of the Gup brothers' London solicitors, and pushes it across the table. Commander Glenning looks at it and nods.

'Know them?'

'They're in the frame,' Glenning replies cautiously, and Flint
gives him an old-fashioned look, and he responds with a rueful
smile. 'I can't tell you why, Grace; nothing to do with your case,
obviously. I'll just say that they came to our attention a while ago,
on various matters, and one of these days we're going to knock on
their door with a search warrant. A statement from you could
help.'

'Gladly, though not while I'm Kathy McCarry.'

'In your own time,' says Glenning and then he takes a sip of his
Guinness, waiting for her to continue.

'So, I kept brother Joe waiting for a day while I *thought it over*
– didn't want to appear too keen, obviously – and then I said I'd go
– come to London, I mean – and that's when he gave me a name
and a contact telephone number.'

Once more Flint reaches into the pocket of her raincoat, and
another slip of paper crosses the table. Commander Glenning
glances at it, fully aware that Flint is watching him for the slightest
reaction.

'I jumped to a conclusion,' she says when Glenning remains
stone-faced. 'About Billy Goodheart, I mean. Two minutes in his
company – in the bowels of an NCP car park off the Tottenham
Court Road – and I was pretty sure he was a former copper, ex-
Met, a high flyer; probably a DI on the fast track to promotion
until he came under a cloud. I suppose the brass knew he was a
dirty copper but they couldn't quite nail him, right? So they came
up with the ever-ready compromise: he got early retirement, on
health grounds or whatever, and they let him walk away because,
so far as the Met was concerned, better out than in.' Flint keeps her
voice low but her tone is taking on a hard, relentless edge. 'Now,
my guess would be that the brass hoped, even expected, that Billy
would take his ill-gotten gains and buy himself a pub somewhere in
deepest Essex, or a used-car dealership, and that would be the end
of it. Instead of which, Billy teamed up with a couple of his chums
– equally dodgy ex-coppers, I expect – and they set themselves up
as so-called security consultants.'

Flint pauses for breath and Glenning breaks his silence. 'Risk
control,' he says.

'What?'

'That's what they call themselves: risk control specialists. Which means that, for a few hundred pounds, they will access records they shouldn't have access to and sell you details of bank account trans-actions, monies in and out, of anyone you're interested in. Mobile phone records, calls made and received; vehicle registrations; a criminal records check and, if you pay a premium, anything that's logged on the national intelligence database; anything they can get their hands on by bribing former colleagues, serving officers.'

Flint's anger is infectious, apparently. From the matter-of-fact way he speaks, Glenning could be talking about the weather but there is a telling flush to his cheeks, almost as red as his hair.

'Your instincts about Goodheart were more or less right. He was Robbery Squad and well enough considered by his superiors, until the rumours saw him banished to Brixton. Even so, he was made an acting DI – until the rumours amounted to near-certainty and his position became untenable. Grace, I don't know if he could have been prosecuted, or even disciplined. I do know it *was* a case of better out than in – and, as a matter of fact, the pension he got was the very minimum. I'm not saying it's a perfect world but, trust me, Billy Goodheart did not escape entirely unscathed.'

'Except he's still out there, selling your secrets.'

'For now. His time will come.'

Flint is inclined to argue but Commander Glenning doesn't give her the chance. Standing up, on his way to the bar, he says, 'What I need is a proper drink. You too, I expect – and by the way, how's your father, and your boy?'

'I'm coming to that,' says Flint.

Glenning's driver – the driver of the black Jaguar that Flint spotted dogging them for the last two hours – puts his head round the pub door and points to his watch as if to say, 'Time to go, sir?' Commander Glenning sees him in the mirror behind the bar and waves a hand to send him away.

Now there are two glasses of malt whisky on the table between them, so far untouched, and Glenning's pipe is still unlit, and Flint says, 'Tom, I'm not talking about minor corruption. I didn't pay Billy Goodheart a few hundred pounds in order to run some names through the Yard's computers. I paid him twenty-five thousand dollars to have the names run through TIPOFF, because to get that done he needed somebody with clout; somebody expensive, I suppose – and that's exactly what happened. Four hours after I gave him the list, the names were submitted to TIPOFF by . . . well, maybe you can guess who.'

'Six, I expect,' says Glenning.

'Exactly. Bloody MI6.'

'Ridout?'

'Not directly. The formal request to TIPOFF from Six was submitted by one James Sullivan, but Cutter's pretty sure that he—'

'Works for Ridout?' Glenning suggests. 'Indeed he does.'

'You know him?'

Glenning's eyes search what has become the nearly empty bar before he gives Flint a brief, affirmative nod.

'Is he dirty?' she asks.

'Sullivan, bent?' Glenning rubs the knuckles of his thumbs along his eyebrows before he adds, 'Would he take a bribe from the likes of Billy Goodheart? I seriously doubt that, Grace.'

'Then when Sullivan submitted the names to TIPOFF it would have been official, on Ridout's say-so?'

'At least with Ridout's knowledge. I've known the lad a long time and from what I've seen, from what I know, Jamie Sullivan is about as straight as two parallel lines, meaning he goes strictly by the book. I can't see him tapping into TIPOFF without his superior's tacit approval.'

But Glenning's assertion seems half-hearted, spoken as though he's been distracted by some troubling second thought. His eyes wander again until they rest upon her glass. 'You're not drinking,' he says, raising his own glass in a silent toast of encouragement.

Flint is thinking that a mother with a young child to take care of shouldn't be drinking straight whisky in the middle of the afternoon. Even so she acknowledges Glenning's toast, takes a generous swallow, feels the warmth in her throat. 'So,' she asks, 'what's wrong, Tom?'

'It doesn't make sense. As I say, Sullivan's as straight as they come, and Ridout's a devious bastard, I'll grant you. But, trust me, Grace, Ridout doesn't need to take a bribe. It's not money that drives him.'

Flint knows she is on the cusp of learning something important so she pretends not to care. 'Maybe,' she says, 'but you know the saying: we're all whores, the only question is the price.'

'And you believe that?'

Flint shakes her head. 'Not really, not in your case. Nor Cutter. Nor me, I hope. But Ridout?'

Glenning rests his elbows on the table and leans towards her. 'It's a little-known fact – and not one to be repeated – but I see the vetting reports. Ten years ago, when Ridout's father died, he inherited more money than you and I will earn in our lifetimes, combined and multiplied many times over. And he hasn't spent it, not much of it. Oh, he's paid off his mortgage and he buys ludicrously expensive plants for that garden of his, but that's just him squandering a little petty cash. By most standards he is a very wealthy man.'

Absorbing this intelligence, staring glumly at her glass, Flint says, 'I'll tell you something else that makes no sense. This morning, just after I called you, I got a call from Billy demanding a meet; same RV, same grotty car park. Billy's all smiles, pleased with himself – and he wants me to be pleased too. *Nothing for you to worry your pretty head about*,' Flint adds, now perfectly mimicking Goodheart's south-London drawl. 'All the names had come back negative, he said; white as snow, clean as whistles.'

'That was it?'

'More or less,' replies Flint, deciding not to replay Billy's tiresome sexual banter.

'And?'

'What he said was total crap, Tom. Because we also ran the names through TIPOFF and got eleven double zeros: zero, zero – that's what the computer throws up when you score a hit. Turned out seven are on the immigration watch list, two more are red-flagged as Arrest and Detain and the other two are on the No Fly list; they wouldn't even make it onto the plane. So, the question is, why is Billy Goodheart lying to me – or, more likely, why are Ridout's people lying to Billy?'

'Are you certain that MI6 got the same results from TIPOFF?'

'Yes, Cutter made sure of it. Once we knew there were dirty names on the list, Aldus spoke to the Bureau of Intelligence at the state department and got a guarantee that any subsequent requestor would be given the unvarnished truth.' Flint provides a rueful smile. 'We were hoping to help Kathy cement her legend,' she explains. 'The plan was, I'd go back to Maryland to confirm that my worst fears about the names had proved fully justified and the Gup brothers would be all over me with gratitude for saving them – not to mention the client – from their greedy selves. Kathy's stock would rise exponentially and the client – who we're ninety-nine per cent sure is Gröber – would get to hear how this brilliant lawyer with her insider's knowhow had saved them from walking into a trap – thanks, of course, to the Gup brothers' foresight in hiring me in the first place. And in that case, we reckoned, the client would definitely want to meet Kathy McCarry, if only to find out what other inside knowledge she had that might one day save his ass. Now . . .' Flint shrugs. 'Now we're buggered.' She shrugs again and lapses into silence.

'You would have gone in alone?' Glenning asks, meaning without back-up, without the reassurance of any support.

'Yes. When I promised Cutter that I'd find a mousehole, a way into Gröber's organisation, I always knew I'd have to go in alone.' She can see what Glenning is thinking, see the unease in his eyes. 'Hey, sometimes it's better that way,' she adds with forced jollity. 'After all, Jerry Crawford crawled through his mousehole with what was virtually a SWAT team – and look what happened to them.'

Now Glenning's eyes are telling her that he's not buying her dubious logic.

'What's the matter?'

'For God's sake, Grace! Gröber killed one of your own agents in broad daylight. Threw her out of a helicopter while you watched.'

'He certainly did, and thanks for reminding me' – this she says with a touch of sarcasm – 'but that's exactly my point. When Gröber abducted Ruth, when he dragged her into that bloody chopper, there was so much back-up we were practically falling over one another. And yet all we could do was watch. Couldn't open fire because he was using her as a shield; couldn't reach them because we were taking fire from his goons; couldn't stop him from taking off except by shooting him *and* Ruth down.'

Flint is replaying the scene in her mind.

'In fact, if you want to know the truth, I believe the reason he did what he did was precisely because we *were* watching. He had no reason to kill Ruth. If there had been no back-up present, all he had to do was tell Ruth he knew who she was and walk away. She wasn't armed; nothing she could have done to stop him.'

'But you'll be armed?'

'What?'

'Carrying a firearm? If and when you get to meet Gröber?'

'I certainly plan to be.'

'And then?'

Flint doesn't answer. She is suddenly aware of the whine of a vacuum cleaner being pushed around the carpet by a young man with a silver stud piercing the corner of his left eyebrow, who returns her glare of annoyance with open insolence. Time to get out of here, she thinks.

'I need to get back to my hotel,' she says, 'but before I go I want to ask you—'

'I've got a car outside,' Glenning says, and Flint feigns surprise. 'I'll give you a lift, we can talk on the way.'

But he shows no sign of moving. While Flint gets up from her chair, gathers her things, checks her BlackBerry for messages – sees there are three, all from Cutter, and inwardly groans – he remains seated, his plump arms planted firmly on the table.

'Are we going?' she asks brightly.

'When you've answered the question. Grace, before I can help you, I have to know what you intend to do.'

Flint sighs, a long weary sigh as though she's past the point of caring. She slumps back down onto the chair, resting her bag on her lap, and says as evenly as she can, 'Tom, I'm a copper, by instinct and by choice, and I play by copper's rules, you know I do . . . If Gröber's alone when I get to him, and when the circumstances seem right, I'll show him my credentials and arrest him for the murder of Ruth. If he resists arrest, I'll show him my gun, and if he still resists, or offers violence, I'll use whatever force is necessary to defend myself and restrain him; the *least* force necessary. If I can't do that for any reason – if, for example, he turns up mob-handed, or there are civilians in the immediate vicinity who might get hurt – he won't see my credentials or my gun. I'll remain Kathy McCarry, tell him whatever he wants to hear, and wait for another meeting, another day; another hundred days if that's what it takes. For the record, I'll go entirely by the book. Is that what you needed to know?'

It's hard to tell. Without a reply or even an acknowledgement, Commander Glenning gets up from the table and leads the way towards the door.

Twenty-One

So, here's the thing, Tom Glenning; here's what I need you to do. You asked about my father? Well, physically he's fine, never better, or not for a long while, but in other ways he's *not* fine, he's not himself; in fact I would say he's totally out of order. I'll spare you the details and my own embarrassment, if you don't mind. Suffice it to say, I can't trust him to look after Jack any longer so I'm taking my boy back to the States. Problem is, Jack doesn't have a passport, and I don't have his birth certificate – and even if I did, I can hardly turn up at the passport office claiming to be his mother when the only ID I'm carrying is for Kathy McCarry. You see the problem, don't you? There's no way I can get Jack out of the UK unless you use your influence to get him a passport, no questions asked. Then, if you'd be so kind, I need you to have a quiet word with British Airways, the check-in people, to say it's perfectly okay that Kathy McCarry is travelling with a baby boy with whom she has no obvious relationship – different surnames, different nationalities – and, for reasons of national security, or whatever else you can dream up, would they just turn a blind eye, and then forget about it? All I need to do – what I need *you* to do – is get us both on the plane. Once we reach the States, I can handle it. I know it's asking a lot, Tom, but *please*?

That is, more or less, the speech Flint has rehearsed, the appeal she had intended to present. But sitting alongside Commander Glenning in the back of his official Jaguar, no glass partition separating them from the driver – and, although the driver pretends to listen to Classic FM on the radio, Flint is sure there is no way he would not hear every word – she finds herself with nothing to say.

It's not just the presence of the driver that is inhibiting; it's the gap between them that Glenning has imposed, sliding away from her along the leather seat until he's pressed against the door, as if he is distancing himself from Flint and her questionable intentions.

Or, that's the way Flint is reading the situation.

You don't believe me, do you? she might have said to Glenning if she wasn't so close to the driver she can count the broken capillaries on the back of his neck where he's been worrying a rash. *You think that, come what may, I'm dead set on killing Gröber*, she might have added if she didn't suspect that Glenning's answer would be a blunt, *yes*.

Instead she sits in resentful silence watching the wipers make intermittent passes across the windshield as the Jaguar edges towards Hyde Park Corner at a snail's pace, locked as they are in an interminable queue of vehicles. Stretching ahead of them as far as Flint can see is a river of brake lights that glow brilliant red in the gloom.

Until Glenning says softly, 'What is it you want me to do?' and, when she doesn't immediately reply, he adds, nodding at the driver, 'It's all right, he's practically deaf. Just keep your voice down.'

Still no word from Flint so Glenning says, 'What are you going to tell them when you get back?'

'The Gups? What can I tell them other than the names are clean? Or so Billy Goodheart swears. And then, I suppose, they'll go ahead with their original scheme and there will be no need for Kathy McCarry to meet with the client. After that,' Flint sighs, 'I suppose the dirty names will get busted if and when they enter the States and there will be a SWAT team at the Gups' door; we won't be able to stop it. By then, of course, Kathy McCarry will be long gone – as will Gröber when he smells the first whiff of trouble, crawling under a new rock somewhere that even the Gups don't know about. Then there's nothing they can say – assuming they say anything at all, which I doubt – that will lead us to Gröber . . . Jesus, Tom, what a waste of a good operation.'

Despite Glenning's caution, Flint has let her voice rise as she vents her frustration. She catches the driver's eyes watching her in the rear-view mirror.

'All I needed,' she continues more softly, 'was for Billy Goodheart to know the truth, to tell the truth, and I'd have had a decent shot at Gröber – metaphorically speaking, of course,' she adds quickly, and that gets her a glimmer of a smile from Glenning.

'Now, thanks to bloody Ridout, we're worse off than when we started.'

'What's his angle?' Glenning inquires.

'I've been asking myself that over and over and I still don't have a clue. The paranoid side of me says that he's somehow got wind of the Kathy McCarry operation and is out to sabotage it. He knows something about Operation Payback, the Çarçani part of it, because Six has a legitimate interest in Çarçani's sex trade, and we agreed to a standard reciprocal exchange – share info and coordinate ops – in order to avoid getting our wires crossed. So, for example, he provided the fake Stasi file I needed when I went to Milan to see Çarçani; knows I was posing as a German widow with a huge grudge against Gröber. But, Tom, Ridout *can't* know about the McCarry element because nobody does. Nobody inside the strike force, except for Cutter and a handful of others, and nobody outside of it – except, now, for you.'

And perhaps your practically deaf driver, thinks the paranoid side of Flint as she keeps her eyes planted on the rear-view mirror. And, by the way, what does 'practically deaf' mean, exactly?

As if he's reading her mind, Glenning leans forward to tap the driver on the shoulder, getting him to turn his head, and then says slowly, as if he was dictating a letter to a secretary whose shorthand isn't up to scratch, 'When you see a gap, use the lights; the siren if you have to.'

'Mainly, he lip reads,' Glenning explains as he settles back in the seat, now much closer to Flint so that their thighs are almost touching. 'A car horn he can hear, music and anything high-pitched, but words for him are mainly a distorted hum. Which is why I hired him – that, and the way he can drive. You'll see. You might want to buckle up.'

They edge apart and put on their seat belts and wait for a gap in the traffic to appear.

'But what's the longer game Ridout's playing?' Glenning asks. 'Does he want Gröber for himself, a feather in his cap, or do you think he could be protecting him? Perhaps Gröber's an asset who's feeding him intel. Have you thought of that?'

'But, Tom, what a risk to take. I mean, if it ever came out that Six was shielding a scumbag like Gröber – Jesus, can you imagine the consequences?'

'I didn't say Six, I said Ridout. Maybe Gröber's one of his assets that he keep off the books. Maybe the product he gets from Gröber is so bloody good that no one asks where it comes from.'

'You think so?'

'It's possible. Wouldn't be the first time.'

Glenning's theory seems to cast a shadow over Flint and for a while she sits in gloomy silence staring out of the window. Then, 'Well, whatever Ridout's angle, whatever game he's playing, I can't see a way around it. I've considered lying to the Gups, telling them that Billy says some of the names are dirty, but I can't risk it. For all I know, Billy's going to follow up with a written report and—'

'Say that, did he?'

'No, but then I didn't ask him. I went to the meet absolutely certain he was going to tell me the *bad news*' – Flint extends her index fingers to indicate her insertion of quotation marks – 'and when he didn't, when he told me the complete opposite of what I knew to be the truth, I was just so . . . unprepared.'

So, how about we celebrate? Billy had said, allowing his hand to touch her knee. *How about we go to your hotel and order up a bottle of champagne? Put a bit of sparkle into your life, eh?*

'Anyway, I just wanted to get out of there, get away from him.'

'I can imagine,' says Glenning, as if he knows how Billy might behave. 'So, as you said, you're buggered.'

'Yes.'

'Unless Billy is . . .' Glenning begins but does not continue.

'Yes? Unless Billy is what?'

'Discredited. As a source. What if . . .' And Glenning breaks off again, as if the idea is still forming on the edge of his consciousness, and it's all Flint can do to stop herself from wriggling with impatience. Eventually Glenning continues, 'What if, sometime between now and when you're due to go back to the States, Billy gets banged up – very publicly banged up? Let's say the Met carries out simultaneous forced entries into his home and business premises, lots of noise to wake up the neighbours. They might bring in his associates, too. Ex-Scotland Yard detectives arrested in dawn raids across the capital,' adds Glenning, adopting a newsreader's sonorous tone. 'That should make the front page of the *Evening Standard*. Might even get on Sky News, if they happen to acquire some decent footage of the raids. Either way, you're going to hear about it and, I suspect, the first thing you're going to do is call the Gups and tell them you don't know what's going on but your source has just been busted, he's all over the news, and you're on the first plane out of here before the cops come calling on you. That should get the Gups nice and jittery. Then, when you get back, you tell them Billy said the names are clean, but how can we trust him? And even if what he said was true, how do we know he's not now spilling his guts to the authorities, telling them about the names he ran – if, that is, they don't already know. In other words, Grace, you cast a lot of doubt. You say, even if the names were clean, they are now thoroughly compromised. We have to walk away from them, gentlemen, find another way. Do you think the Gups will listen to you?'

Flint is staring at Glenning open-mouthed. 'You'd do this for me?'

'I don't see why I can't put in a word. Billy had it coming to him sooner or later, and it may as well be sooner. We already have enough intel on him to enable the Anti-Corruption lads to obtain the search warrants, enough for them to charge him and his associates. Before Billy comes to trial they're going to need a witness statement from you, back-dated to today, but that's months away. Yes, I don't see any reason why they should delay. I can talk to Putney in the morning.'

'Putney?'

'Where the ACG lads are based, some of them.'

'Are they still called the ghost squad?'

'Not to their faces, no.'

'Is it all right if I kiss you?' asks Flint.

Glenning looks alarmed and moves hurriedly away from her towards the door. 'Behave yourself,' he says gruffly. 'I said he's deaf, not blind.'

Finally, just as they edge into the sprawling roundabout at Hyde Park Corner, a gap in the traffic materialises and the driver presses a button on the dashboard and blue strobes concealed in the Jaguar's grille alongside the headlights begin to flash. Flint feels a surge of power that presses her back into the seat, sees the gap closing, hears the whoop-whoop-whoop of a siren and a squeal of brakes, leans into the slide as the rear wheels fight for traction, braces herself and closes her eyes, waiting for a crunch of metal that doesn't come. She dares to look again and somehow they are through the gap, now barging, bullying their way across multiple lines of traffic towards the Park Lane exit, the reflection of the strobes bouncing off the wet road like shell bursts that illuminate staring, often angry faces with ghostly light. Glenning stares back impassively, as if he were the Queen.

Now they are into Park Lane, changing lanes, heading north, threading in and out of the new gaps that open up in response to the keening siren. By Flint's estimate they're doing up to 60mph, pushing their luck – and Flint wonders if she should push hers. Glenning gives her the perfect opening.

'So, how is your dad – and your boy, of course?'

Well, since you ask, here's the thing, Tom Glenning; here's another thing I need you to do.

But she doesn't say that. Instantly, without giving herself time to change her mind, she replies, 'Absolutely fine. No, better than fine. Great.'

'You've seen them?'

'At the weekend.'

'And your dad's coping?'

'Totally.'

'I mean, looking after a baby, it can't be easy at his age even if he does have help. What's he got? A housekeeper, a nanny?

'Both.'

Flint is worrying that her smile is a little too brilliant, a little too fixed.

'And you, Grace, how are you coping? How do you reconcile losing all this time with your son?'

'I try not to think about it. I've got a job to finish.'

'Yes, well . . .'

'What we do, it's not like working at the post office or in a shop, is it? I mean, if something comes up and you can't reach me because it's six o'clock and I've gone home to be with my son, and that's all I really care about, then I need to get myself another job. I like to think that going after the likes of Gröber and Çarçani, that's important, it matters. I like to think it isn't just a job.'

The Jaguar barely slows as it makes a sharp right turn, passes through a red light, darts recklessly across the southbound lanes.

'Yes, well, your dedication, that's never been in doubt. But I tell you frankly, Grace, I worry about you, about how much emotional strain all this Gröber business is putting on you. You need to take care of yourself – your head and your heart as well as your body.'

If Glenning doesn't stop this nonsense, if he utters one more understanding word, Flint knows that she will unbuckle the seat belt, lunge at him; before he can prevent her, he will get that forbidden kiss.

Twenty-Two

Jack Flint is indeed absolutely fine, apparently. Lying in a cot that is hand-decorated with Winnie the Pooh motifs, located and acquired by the Connaught's ever resourceful concierge and delivered to her room within one hour – he looks content, even serene. At the first glimpse of his mother, his face crumples into grief and he lets out a wail that rapidly rises to a shriek, but Marjorie Bennington, one of two nannies also found by the concierge to provide round-the-clock coverage – at a cost of £600 a day – immediately takes charge of the situation. Lifting Jack in her arms, she says to Flint, 'My dear, you look terribly tired. Why don't you go and have a nice hot bath, and leave this to me?' Guiltily, but with profound relief, Flint retreats. She is barely out of what is now Jack's room when she hears his distress transformed into delicious giggles.

Miss Bennington has many things in her favour, so far as Flint is concerned. She comes with impeccable child-minding credentials; she is ample in both body and spirit; she does not speak with a Melbourne accent; and, her résumé says, she is fifty-three years old.

So, not my father's type, Flint thinks bitterly. She knows she should get over it – move on to the next page, as Dr P would surely say – but snatches of the conversation she overheard at Glebe Farm keep replaying in her head like a bad tune she wants to forget but can't.

While the bathtub fills, she checks her BlackBerry once more and finds there are now seven messages from Cutter: four emails, two text messages and, the last one, a voicemail. Reluctantly, she listens to what he has to say.

'Flint, it's Cutter. I've spoken with your father. Let me ask you something. Are you out of your frigging mind?'

Good question, Mr Cutter.

She thinks about fixing herself a drink, decides not to.

You depend on alcohol? Dr Przewalskii had asserted at one of their early sessions, no doubt reliably informed by Human Resources.

I don't depend *on it, Dr P. I enjoy it, from time to time.*

Surveying the well-stocked bar of her Connaught suite, Flint reconsiders her decision, decides to change her frigging mind.

Cutter must be on the road or in the air; either way, somewhere that is not amenable to satellite communication. After the strike force Ops Room assures Flint, 'Patching you through,' what she hears is silence punctuated by short bursts of static. She's about to ring off, with a sense of relief, when Rocco Morales comes on the line.

'Hey, Grace, it's Rocco, there's a problem with the link.'

'That much I know.'

'But the Director's adamant he wants to talk with you. He'll be on the ground in . . . wait one . . . I reckon he'll be calling you in one hour forty-five, two hours max. You need to have your phone turned on.'

'My phone is turned on, Rocco. Otherwise we wouldn't be talking, would we?'

'Hey, give me a break, Grace. I'm just the messenger, right?'

'Fine, I've got the message. So, where's he headed?'

'I can't say, not on an open line.'

'What can you say, Rocco?'

There is a pause, more static on the line while Morales considers how frank he should be.

Then, 'The Director's really mad at you; I mean, he's really, *really* pissed. I don't know what's going on but, whatever you're doing, whatever you've done, he's pulling you out of London, pronto. You and your . . . your package, you're coming home, cattle class – and, Grace, don't blame me, I'm just the facilitator; it's the best I can do.'

'What package? What do you mean, cattle class?'

'I gotta go,' says Morales and, before Flint can say another word, he cuts the line.

Campione d'Italia

Twenty-Three

Karl Gröber insists that the Ferretti is too large to moor in the porto comunale and far too ostentatious. The yacht will attract attention to its owner and therefore to Karl Gröber, and since Gröber goes to considerable lengths to avoid attention in Campione, to stay well below the radar, this is unacceptable to him. Even Alexander Çarçani sees the sense of this, though he cannot resist tweaking Gröber's tail.

Gröber stands patiently in a Swisscom telephone kiosk on the quayside, holding the handset away from his ear, waiting for the flow of gratuitous insults about his manhood to subside; waiting for Çarçani to concede that he will cruise in a leisurely manner from Porlezza, cross the invisible maritime Italian-Swiss border, moor the Ferretti in Lugano's more spacious harbour and then take one of the ferries that regularly cross the lake bringing punters from Switzerland to try their luck at Campione's municipal casino.

'And come alone,' says Gröber, meaning without Çarçani's habitual retinue of linen-suited bodyguards who in Campione, he is sure, will stand out like soldiers guarding a mafia convention.

Çarçani grumbles his reluctant acquiescence. 'This better be important,' he warns.

Gröber's safe house on the Via Matteo is set under gable roofs in a small garden that separates it from its neighbours. At the western edge a long wooden jetty reaches out into the lake like a slender finger, which is where Çarçani's bodyguards amuse themselves skipping stones across the water's surface, competing like boisterous boys. For, of course, he didn't come alone – but there are only two of them and, dressed in jeans and open-necked shirts, they could almost pass for tourists, though, to Gröber's critical eye, they still look like the Tosks they are. His trained eye has also noticed the slight bulges in their jeans made by their ankle holsters.

'So, who is she?' asks Çarçani, talking to Gröber's back. He asks the question indifferently, as if he doesn't care.

Gröber remains at the open window watching the guards who, grown tired of their game, now stroll towards the end of the jetty, lighting cigarettes that leave wisps of smoke in their wake. 'Patience, Sasha,' is all that he says.

Patience will certainly be required, for the PowerPoint presentation that Çarçani watches on Gröber's laptop computer has been programmed to show each slide for thirty seconds, and Kathy McCarry is only at the beginning of her journey. The first shot Çarçani saw was a grainy black and white frame taken from a CCTV surveillance tape that captured McCarry coming out of customs at London Heathrow's Terminal Four seventeen days ago; at 08:06.35 precisely, according to the legend at the bottom of the still. The second and the third slides, vivid in comparison, were taken with a high-resolution digital camera and showed McCarry with her bags on the floor beside her, apparently searching the terminal with her eyes.

The fourth slide, the one that Çarçani now stares at with irritation, shows what might have been the subject of her search: a nondescript middle-aged man holding against his chest a piece of card on which the name 'Ms Kathy McCarry' has been scrawled in thick black letters. The name means nothing to Çarçani. 'Any way to speed this fucking thing up?' he asks.

'No.'

So Çarçani must wait until, in its predetermined good time, comes the fifth slide, a photograph taken outside the terminal that shows the woman in profile as she watched her bags being loaded into a car, and there is something familiar about her; something about the lines of her body, or the length of her neck, or the set of her head – *something* that triggers in Çarçani's episodic memory the vaguest sense of recognition. The sensation is both fleeting and elusive and, because of that, mildly disturbing. Çarçani needs a closer look.

His fingers randomly search the laptop's keys. 'How do I blow this up?'

'Wait,' says Gröber, still with his back to the room, counting off the seconds in his head.

Slide six, and this is what Çarçani wanted to see: a close-up of the woman's startling face, tilted at an angle of about thirty degrees. There is a trace of a smile on her wide, inviting mouth, as though she is silently acknowledging some small favour; perhaps the driver is holding open the door as she ducks into the back seat. Apart from spidery traces of fatigue lines at the corner of her eyes shaped like laurel leaves, her skin is flawless. This is the seductive face of a woman Çarçani would want to have and Çarçani is certain he's seen her before; seen, not met, because if Çarçani had met her he would have remembered – in all likelihood *would* have had her, taken her or bought her. So, he decides, he must have noticed her image and filed it away. Seen her face in some glossy magazine, perhaps; maybe the movies. He ventures a guess. 'She's an actress?'

Gröber is on the point of denying it when the irony strikes him and he turns his head away from the window to look at Çarçani with a pretence of appreciation for the Albanian's perceptiveness. 'Yes,' he says softly. 'In a way, Sasha, that is exactly what she is: an actress, a player of parts.'

'What the fuck does that mean?'

'Watch, Sasha.'

Çarçani sighs and Gröber turns back to the window to see the bodyguards now sitting on the end of the jetty. They have taken off their shoes, rolled up their jeans, unstrapped their ankle holsters. They bask in the morning sun, dangling their feet in the water. They appear harmless, which they are certainly not, but careless of their duty they certainly are. Gröber calculates that if things go badly he will have all the time he needs.

Ten more pictures, five more minutes, to go.

Kathy McCarry exits her limousine in front of the Connaught Hotel ... Kathy McCarry walks a London street ... Kathy McCarry enters an anonymous office building ... exits the same building – and Çarçani audibly yawns.

Now more grainy stills from CCTV footage. Kathy McCarry gets into a car, gets out of the same car; a BMW that is parked in what appears to be an underground garage. In the next slide the car is closer to the camera. No sign of the woman but through the windshield Çarçani can make out the features of the driver's face and, right on cue, Gröber says, 'Code name, Starwood. Real name, Goodheart, William Goodheart. We paid him twenty-five thousand dollars . . . forgive me, Sasha, *you* paid him twenty-five thousand dollars. To tell us a bunch of lies.'

No response from Çarçani. Seated at Gröber's writing desk, looking intently at the laptop's screen, he is motionless, without expression. The only hint of his likely agitation is the throbbing vein in his left temple that bisects the deep groove in his skin.

Three more slides to go and Gröber makes his mental preparations.

The next slide and Çarçani sees a burly man leaning on a rail, gazing into the middle distance. There is a body of water in the foreground, a lake or a river, and the shot seems to have been taken from the opposite bank through a long lens or even a telescope for the image is over-magnified, not fully defined. Still, Çarçani can clearly see that this man is not Starwood, not the asshole in the car who is stupid enough to think he can take Alexander Çarçani for $25,000. Çarçani waits for Gröber to reveal this new character's identity but Gröber keeps his silence for now.

Çarçani is content to play the game. The rhythm of the slideshow has become familiar, the predictability of the intervals making them seem shorter – and, anyway, Çarçani is not always an impatient man. In his Sigurimi days, when the terrorisation of Albania was his sworn duty, Chairman Hoxha once said that Alexander Çarçani had the patience to outlast Stalin; meant it as a compliment. 'Seven years!' Hoxha had said admiringly, after calculating how long it had taken Çarçani to track down the traitor Meksi to his hiding place in Moscow; Meksi and that whore of his, and their bastard child. 'How long did they take to die?'

'Two days,' Çarçani replied, and Hoxha had frowned as if to say *too quick* until Çarçani added, 'The boy, three days. The woman, five.'

Hoxha, it is said, waited more than thirty years to kill a cousin who had refused his hand in marriage; forbade any doctor and every hospital and clinic in all of Albania to treat her when she was diagnosed with cancer.

Now comes the McCarry woman who has her arms round the neck of the burly man. From this shot with its longer focus it is apparent that the camera was positioned at some considerable height; on the roof of a tall building, perhaps?

The bodyguards have found a new distraction: two young women in a pedalo who drift teasingly close to the jetty, feigning their disinterest in the banter of the boys. Gröber turns away from the window, faces Çarçani, waits.

Finally, the last slide – or, rather, what Çarçani will assume is the last slide, for PowerPoint has been programmed to pause indefinitely on this shot until Gröber presses the key that will command it to continue. It is a formal portrait of the burly man that shows him in a sober suit, seated, his forearms resting on a desktop, his hands lightly clasped alongside a plaque on which there is lettering too small to easily read. Çarçani leans forward to peer more closely at the screen.

'You see the sword, Sasha, the sword of justice pointing at your balls?'

Çarçani can just distinguish a horizontal line, running through the last three letters on the plaque.

'I think it is meant to be symbolic, a representation of their intent.'

Coming closer, until only the writing table separates him from Çarçani, Gröber continues, 'The letters you cannot read are N, C, I, S. You are looking at the logo of the British National Criminal Intelligence Service whose business is to conduct a covert war against what they call organised crime: drug trafficking, people trafficking, trafficking in human organs, guns – in other words, *your* crimes, Sasha. And, since concealing the profits of your activities is another of its concerns, also mine. The fat guy in the picture is Commander Tom Glenning, head of operations for NCIS. He means to destroy us, if he can.'

Çarçani's quick brain is sorting through the implications, not liking what it finds. In a disbelieving tone, as though the question is absurd, he poses the first of his suspicions. 'What are you telling me, Karl? That the bitch you sent to London to give away my money, her boyfriend is a *British spy*?'

'Not her boyfriend, I think, and certainly not a spy.' Gröber's tone is flat, entirely matter-of-fact. 'Glenning', he continues, 'is a police officer, a very senior police officer – and she is an agent, also very senior, for the American strike force. You understand?'

The look on Çarçani's face says he can scarcely believe, let alone understand, what he's hearing. 'This is *Flint*?' he asks, and now he is truly incredulous. 'You have allowed *Flint* to penetrate my organisation?'

Before Gröber can reply, Çarçani slams both fists on the tabletop, his gold watchband hitting the protective glass with a crack that sounds to Gröber like a rifle shot. Then Çarçani is on his feet, leaning across the table, the vein in his forehead throbbing as though it's fit to burst, bellowing at Gröber, 'YOU CRETIN! YOU PRICK! HOW COULD YOU BE *SO FUCKING STUPID?*' bellowing so loud his voice is bound to carry far beyond the open window, bound to bring the bodyguards running. Gröber moves quickly, leaning over the laptop's screen to press the Escape key. 'The show's not over, Sasha,' he says in what is still the voice of reason. 'Please, my friend, sit down, watch.'

Çarçani stays on his feet but he does look at the screen and what he sees in the first slide of this new presentation is the beginning of a video clip that comes complete with ambient sound. The opening sequence is confused and confusing: erratic, shaky glimpses of legs and buttocks shot from a low angle, as though the camera is close to ground level, hurrying through a crowd of half-people. The soundtrack broadcasts brief snatches of myriad polyglot conversations, amplified music in the background, the persistent toll of bells.

From the ground floor of Gröber's house comes the crashing echo of a door opened under extreme force.

Then the image steadies, snaps into focus. It is evident the camera has been raised from its lowly position to shoulder height in order to pan, in both vertical and horizontal planes, the marble façade of a towering cathedral, a façade that is decorated with hundreds, even thousands of statues. Inexorably, the camera lens seeks the spire and reaches the crowning gilded copper figure of what is unmistakably the Madonna. Çarçani knows exactly what he's looking at: the third largest church in Christendom, the Duomo in Milan; *his* Milan as he has come to regard it with an intruder's insolence – rather like Napoleon, another invader of Milan, who had himself crowned king of Italy in this very cathedral.

The sound of hurried footsteps on the stairs. Gröber moves round the table into position, standing next to Çarçani, and says calmly, 'Sasha, if your goons come through that door . . .'

'Go fuck your mother,' Çarçani says even as he gets to his feet, goes to the door, wrenches it open, disappears from Gröber's view. Gröber hears quarrelling voices speaking in Albanian, Çarçani's growing louder, more insistent. Whatever it is he finally says – two booming words that must surely echo throughout the house – brings the argument to an abrupt end. There is a moment of silence, then the sound of footsteps retreating along the hallway, down the stairs.

Gröber had paused the video. Now, on Çarçani's return, he commands it to resume and the camera begins a slow pan of the Piazza del Duomo on what was evidently a shining Sunday morning shortly before Mass. At the entrance to the cathedral the devout and the sightseers wait in lines for their bags and knapsacks to be cursorily searched by bored polizia while in the piazza itself mounted carabinieri, resplendent in black uniforms and wide white shoulder belts, stand by their motorcycles in scattered groups, keeping a weather eye for pickpockets and bag-snatchers lurking among the multitude of tourists. The camera lingers on a north African street vendor with watches strapped the length of both arms who is pestering a young woman, refusing to take no for an answer – until two carabinieri blow their whistles and head purposefully in his direction.

'Ah, *La Benemerita*,' says Çarçani as though he is proud of them, as though the carabinieri are also his.

Now the camera focuses on an egg-yolk yellow tram that is disgorging passengers on the northern edge of the piazza. Çarçani sees a dozen or so people getting off the tram, and nothing to interest him – until one more passenger comes into view, hesitating on the step as though she is unsure this is her stop and, for the second time today, Çarçani experiences a flicker of recognition; a feeling that, once again, he's looking at a snapshot of some encounter or some memory from his past.

No beauty, this one. As she falters in the doorway of the tram the camera zooms in on her face, filling the screen with her skinny neck, her pinched features, her dull eyes, her lank hair. She's not that old, not in terms of years, but she looks parched, sucked dry by a history of disappointment and wilful neglect. Not, then, the face of a woman Çarçani would have wanted or cared to remember. And yet Çarçani *knows* he has seen her before, and not in any magazine or the movies. He closes his eyes and he can hear her voice; not what she is saying but her shrill, relentless tone.

'Do you recognize her?' Gröber is also watching the screen, leaning over Çarçani's shoulder.

'Not yet, not for sure.'

'In a few moments, perhaps.'

Now she is walking away from the piazza, the camera following at a discreet distance, entering a narrow street of tall houses. She is dressed entirely in black, in clothes that make her seem without shape. Though she appears to be hurrying, her gait is short. She has an old woman's walk, almost a shuffle – and that is what finally triggers Çarçani's recollection. Just before she turns a corner and the street broadens, just before the twin towers of the basilica of San Ambrogio come into shot, Çarçani knows precisely who she is.

'Her name is Ingrid Fischer,' he says. 'Her husband worked for you, until you killed him.'

'Yes.'

Widow Fischer is in the courtyard of San Ambrogio, pressing through the crowd, the camera now much closer to her, the soundtrack playing back above the sound of choral music her plaintive, insistent pleading: *Scusi, scusi, per favore.*

'Yes – and no,' Gröber elaborates.

'Spare me your riddles, Karl.'

'Very well, Sasha. Yes, Peter worked for me and, no, I didn't kill him – or not deliberately. It was an accident, I didn't mean to shoot him. And, no, Sasha, she was never his wife or even in his bed.'

Widow Fischer is mounting the stairs to the gallery where Alexander Çarçani waits alone, statue-still.

'What the fuck are you saying?'

'I'm asking you the same question you asked me, about the penetration of your precious organisation.' Gröber has his mouth very close to Çarçani's ear. He whispers, each word spoken as a sentence, 'How . . . Could . . . *You* . . . Be . . . So . . . Fucking . . . Stupid.'

'No! It's not possible.'

Nevertheless, Gröber sees the truth dawning in Çarçani's eyes. 'Oh, yes, Sasha, I am afraid it's true.'

'You are telling me that hag is *Flint*?'

'Yes.'

'I don't believe it. Even my men wouldn't touch that shrivelled shrew. Even they didn't want her.'

'Even so.'

The cameraman had found a place in the chancery from where the zoomed lens had captured images of Flint and Çarçani on the gallery, their faces so close together they might have been lovers about to kiss. But at that distance, and in that setting, the camera's built-in microphone could not pick up the words that Flint spoke. On the screen of Gröber's laptop, Çarçani sees Flint's lips urgently moving while what he hears coming from the soundtrack is the congregation's recitation of the *Gloria*.

It doesn't matter. He remembers her every word.

I know who did that to you, the woman had said softly, pointing at his disfigurement.

'Perhaps you should not blame yourself too much, Sasha. As you suggested, she is an actress – a very good actress, don't you think?'

'I'll tell you what she is, what she will be when I'm through with her,' says Çarçani, not raising his voice; as calm as you like in the circumstances. Deadpan he adds, 'She's finished. Fucked. Fucking dead.'

'Wait.'

Çarçani shakes his head, begins to get out of his chair.

'Please, Sasha. Killing Flint is not the only option. Maybe not the best option. Watch.'

PowerPoint presents the last slide, another video clip; this one a second generation copy of a home movie, but clear enough.

A man's face, initially distorted, then in focus. 'And *now*,' he says, 'we present . . . we very *proudly* present . . . the show we've all been waiting for: The . . . JACK . . . FLINT . . . SHOW.'

Çarçani sees a young child, not much more than a baby, wearing bright yellow dungarees and a matching floppy hat, holding on to a chair with one hand for support, holding in his other hand a red rubber ball. 'Give that to me, give that to me,' says a woman's voice off camera. The boy does as he is told and, also off camera, a male voice roars encouragement. 'Ma-ma,' says the child, smiling into the lens.

'Flint's kid?' asks Çarçani.

Gröber doesn't answer, not immediately. Instead, he leans over Çarçani's shoulder and presses a series of keys to close and then erase the PowerPoint presentation from his computer's hard drive.

'Yes,' he says. 'Lunch?'

It is a ten-minute stroll from Gröber's house to the Rally Club pizzeria where the proprietor keeps a table by the window for one of his most constant customers.

'You have guests today, Herr Klimt?'

'Just one,' says Gröber holding up a finger. Çarçani gets the message and gives the bodyguards a signal that tells them to get lost.

'Then a bottle of my best wine. With my compliments, Herr Klimt.'

'You're very generous.'

'Please, sit, sit.'

They speak English, which Çarçani poorly understands, but he gets the drift of their exchange and he is amused by it. The revelation that Flint has a child, a potent vulnerability, seems to have lifted his spirits considerably.

'What else does he speak?'

'French, some German, Italian of course. But not Russian, Sasha, not a single word.'

'Then tell me, in Russian, Karl, since you think you are so well informed, what brought Flint to Milan? What did she want me to know?'

'That I was the one who tried to kill you.'

Çarçani sniggers as if he was expecting Gröber's answer. 'And you thought I wouldn't mind?'

'I was sure you wouldn't believe her.'

'Oh, really? And why wouldn't I believe that those KGB shits would choose Oberleutnant Gröber as their lackey to do their dirty work? That is right, isn't it, Karl? You were only ever a first lieutenant, never promoted? Why is that?' Çarçani's fingers are toying with a packet of bread sticks that he is crushing into crumbs. 'Because your bullet missed?'

'Because I didn't need rank. Because I had General Mielke's personal authority. He preferred it that way.'

'So, did General Mielke give you his *personal authority* to be my assassin, to hide in the shadows like a stinking coward?'

'No, Sasha, and you know it isn't true. Because if it were, my friend, you know you would be dead.'

There is a moment's silence before Çarçani responds with a roar of laughter that seems to erupt from his belly. '*Prego, prego*,' he calls for the wine – Chianti Classico, the exceptional Reserva of 1997, the proprietor says, which comes directly from his first cousin's vineyard in Collelungo. Çarçani demands of Gröber that they drink a toast. Raising his glass he says, 'We will drink to all those Kremlin turds; to your great, late leader, General Mielke, the arrogant shit; to the traitor Meksi and his bastard child – and, Karl, it isn't true the boy was raped; the woman, yes, but not the boy. To the bitch Flint and to *her* bastard son, and may she always regret the day he was born. To every imperialist American agent wherever they pollute the earth; to all British faggot spies—'

'And to Hoxha, too?' Gröber suggests. 'We should also drink to your great mentor, I think.'

Another roar of laughter from Çarçani. 'And to Hoxha, too, the greatest asshole there ever was.' Çarçani drains his glass in one swallow. 'May they putrefy in hell.'

'You believe in hell, Sasha?'

'Yes, I've been there. It is called Albania.'

Gröber's turn to laugh.

'What shall we speak of now, Sasha? The dossier?'

Caught unawares, Çarçani parries. 'What dossier?'

'The file that Flint gave you. The file she said her husband had removed from the archives at Normannenstrasse. Your file, Sasha, the one you had forensically examined and, I think, authenticated.'

Çarçani is still smiling but there is wariness in his eyes.

'It was authenticated, wasn't it? I do hope so, after all the trouble they took. The paper, the ink, the official seals, they were all correct. Even the language – the syntax, the jargon, the euphemisms – was entirely authentic; so authentic I might have written it myself. But no, Sasha, your file was not removed from the archives of Department Twenty-One by a man who was never that bitch's husband, because no such file ever existed. It is counterfeit, prepared in Pullach in the weeks before Flint came to see you by the forgers of the Bundesnachrichtendienst, competently aided by a woman who was for many years a functionary in the Ministry of State Security. You might say that she knew our little ways.

Actually, to tell you the truth, she worked for me – until she crossed the Wall, until she sold herself to the West, an embarrassment which did not please General Mielke. Her name was Krüger, Elsa Krüger. I say *was*, Sasha because, two days before Flint came to see you in Milan, poor Elsa was killed in Regensburg, not far from Pullach; run down in the street by a car that did not stop.'

A raised eyebrow from Çarçani.

'No, no, Sasha, it was nothing to do with me. Oh, certainly, when I was told that Elsa was the author of your file—'

'Told?'

'By MI6, by those same British spies we have just toasted, may their hides rot in – well, you said it, Albania.'

Çarçani's smile has been eclipsed. 'You talk to *British spies*?'

'If I am to be precise, I talk to one British spy. I tell him things about our competitors; things I hear, things I know. I give him small victories and, in return, he tells me what our opposition is up to; specifically, what Flint is up to. He has no love for Flint. You will understand he prefers that our relationship is entirely confidential, for obvious reasons. But he is a senior spy, Sasha; very highly placed in the British intelligence service, I promise you.'

'Suck my cock.'

Sensing there's a problem, the proprietor hurries to their table to inquire if there is something wrong with the wine.

'No, no, it's excellent,' Gröber assures him. 'In fact, it's magnificent. I should ask your cousin to send me a case.' And then, when they are alone again, Gröber says to Çarçani, all joviality gone from his tone, 'They tried to fuck us, Sasha. The Germans, they constructed an elaborate deception and they gave it to the British to give to Flint to feed to you, like fresh bait to a hungry fish. They hoped she would provoke you to move against me. But the British, they don't really trust the Germans – well, why would they? – so my British spy, he calls me to tell me what they've done. Karl, he says, you're totally screwed. Remember Elsa? She wrote the file, so now you know how good it is. He hoped to convince me that the file would be declared genuine, that you were certain to believe Flint's lies, and the only chance to save myself was to eliminate you before you could move against me. Elsa's dead, he said. She can't help you. They wanted a civil war between us. I don't think they cared who won.'

Çarçani is cautious, still weighing the evidence.

'This Elsa, who killed her?'

'Who knows? Elsa was a whore. She had sold herself once and might do so again, like any whore. So she was not to be trusted and, having done her work, she was entirely expendable. Christopher implied that it was the Germans who killed her, but I'm not so sure. Christopher lies to me most of the time.' Gröber shrugs. 'Frankly, Sasha, the Germans or the British – what's the difference, who cares?'

'Who the fuck is Christopher?'

'His work name, the name I am required to call him. I know it's not his real name, of course. I know his real name, his blood group, his date of birth. I know where he lives and the alarm code to his house; I even have floor plans. I know where he buys his groceries, and plants for his garden and the different routes he takes to work. I know the car he drives and who he fucks – and, Sasha, this will surprise you: here is one British spy who is *not* a faggot. I know everything I need to know about him. The fact that he thinks he controls me, well, it amuses me.'

'What did you say to him?'

'I said, Christopher, you're full of shit. I said, there's no way that Grace Flint could ever have got within a million miles of Alexander Çarçani to show him your crappy file. I said, I'm never going to believe another fucking word you say unless you show me proof; pictures, close-ups. A day later he called back and said, "check your email".'

'The pictures I saw?'

'Most of them. The video of Flint's kid, that I acquired. As you know, the Gup brothers were very proud about their hotshot defector from the IRS. Me, I wasn't so sure. I had her checked out.'

'Karl, Karl . . .' Çarçani shakes his head but his pacific mood seems to have been fully restored.

Gröber says, 'As a matter of interest, why didn't you move against me?'

'You think I don't trust you?'

'Do you trust anyone, Sasha?'

'On Sundays, I trust God.'

'Seriously, I would like to know. The file, Widow Fischer, they were persuasive, I think. If it had been me, I might have been persuaded.'

Çarçani smoothes the spotless tablecloth with his hands. 'I was going to have you brought to me, so I could cut off your balls and shove them down your throat. Then I thought, no, wait, he is more useful to me alive – for now. What do you think, Karl, do you think you will always be more useful to me alive?'

'I think we should eat.'

They eat fresh sole cooked in butter and sauté potatoes and green salad with a balsamic vinegar dressing, and the proprietor presses on them a crisp Orvieto Classico that, he claims, comes directly from a vineyard owned by his *second* cousin.

As they enjoy the pleasant meal, Çarçani asks, 'Karl, in our day, were we ever so devious?'

'Oh Sasha, we were much more devious,' says Gröber, and they both laugh.

Friendship Heights

Twenty-Four

When Jack Flint is finally asleep his mother slips out of the bedroom they now share, pausing in the hallway to count silently to sixty, and he doesn't stir. For the eleventh night in succession there were no tantrums before bedtime. Standing in the orange glow of night lights that are plugged into every other electrical socket throughout the apartment, Flint allows herself to wonder if, after all, she might have some instinctive talent for motherhood. Unlikely, she admits, but a warm, dry, tearless Jack who smells of talcum powder and baby oil – a gurgling Jack who, held in her arms, endlessly explores her face and neck with tiny soft fingers – triggers in her psyche feelings of maternalism that are amazingly, confusingly real. Of course, she only plays at being a mother: for most of his days, Jack is the recipient of professional, expensive childcare. But at six thirty each weekday evening – 'Seven o'clock at the very latest, and that's an instruction, Kathy' – Flint leaves her office at the Gup Building, Joe Gup beaming in the doorway, reminding her, 'It's time to go, Kathy, time to go.' She collects her son from the minders, takes him home to the apartment; feeds him, changes him, diverts and amuses him; reads him stories, plays with his toys. Then, bed – and, if you can believe this – Grace Flint serenades her son with lullabies; lyrics she makes up as she goes along and sings to the tunes of Annie Lennox.

Jack watches her with wise, inquiring eyes. He may not yet regard her as his natural mother but he seems to have reached a state of equilibrium, as though he recognises he is safe with her and therefore reasonably content.

Another minute passes while Flint remains in the hallway listening to Jack's gentle breathing relayed to her through the speaker of the baby monitor that is clipped to her belt. It sounds to her like waves lapping on a shore. She has no idea what she's doing

– and, when she dwells on the responsibility she's taken on, it scares her half to death – but Jack's presence in her life is becoming a pleasure that is as overwhelming as it is unexpected.

So, hey, what do you make of that, Dr P?

Which reminds her. She needs to call.

Flint and Dr Przewalskii have a deal, thanks to the intervention of Director Cutter. Vouched for by Human Resources, Cutter had turned up at Dr P's rent-controlled apartment on West 98th Street late in the evening and stood in her living room, towering over her, and said, 'This is Rocco, he works for me. He's here to fix your phone.'

'Something is wrong with my phone?'

'It leaks – potentially. Rocco's going to make it secure.'

'The phone *leaks*? What does it leak?'

'Words, Dr Przewalskii, things that shouldn't be said on an open line. Listen, I want you to understand that Grace is in real trouble and she badly needs your help but she can't get to New York to spend some time with you, not right now. So she's going to be talking to you on the phone, from wherever she is, until she has completed her current assignment – or, more likely, until it blows up in her face – and I can't have other people listening in on your conversations because that could get her killed. It could also . . .' Cutter broke off and smiled, as if he wanted to soften the blow. 'It could also get you killed, but that's only in our worst case scenario.'

Looking up at Cutter from the level of his chest, Dr Przewalskii did not seem in the least bit fazed.

'So, I have to make sure that nobody can tap into your phone line – or, if they do, all they'll get to hear is white noise. That way Grace can be as open with you as she needs to be, which is *wide* open, if I'm reading this right. She had a pretty rough time in the UK. I know she called you about the business with her father but it didn't help that the operation she was working on didn't pan out the way we'd expected. Plus, I had to bring her home on an air force freighter, and this freighter didn't have seats in the back, and the bottom line is she spent near enough nine hours swinging in a hammock with her boy who let her know that he didn't want to be there, every mile of the way. Right now she's trying to put her operation back together *and* cope with childcare, which is not one of her natural talents. All in all, there are some pretty complicated issues she needs to resolve – most especially, her relationship with her boy. And I want you to know something else: this is absolutely her call. The only reason I'm here is because she asked me to fix it; so she can talk to you, one on one. That's because she's in desperate need, close to meltdown, and she knows it, and I can't help her, not the way you can, and that's a breakthrough, right? I mean, the fact she's asking for your help, that's something pretty important. What do you think?'

'If she were a nuclear reactor,' said Dr Przewalskii, 'you would shut her down?'

'No doubt about it, as a precaution. But right now I don't have that option. I need Grace to stay where she is, to maintain her cover for as long as she can, and I need you to be available for her whenever she wants to talk. She's counting on you, doctor.' Cutter placed his hands on her shoulders as though he was applying a blessing. 'And I'm counting on you too, as I guess you can tell.'

'When do we talk?'

'Late in the evenings.'

'At what time?'

'Can't tell you that. After her boy's asleep, I expect.'

Dr Przewalskii shook her head of untamed silver hair. 'No, no. She has to make appointments, as if she was coming to my office. Every evening she has to say to herself, I have to call Dr P in one hour, two hours – at nine o'clock, ten o'clock, midnight, it doesn't matter to me what time she specifies to call. But she has to make a commitment to our sessions, do you see? She has to set a time and stick to it, so she is mentally prepared.'

'You're saying she should call you *every* evening?'

'You said meltdown.'

'I said she's *close* to meltdown.'

'Then we will need only . . . yes, let me see, let me consider.' She looked up at Cutter with mocking eyes. 'If she is only *close* to meltdown then perhaps we need no more than five sessions a week. On Saturdays, Sundays, maybe we can have the evenings off. Yes? Only close to meltdown, why panic?'

And then she'd said, 'Come, please,' and led Rocco Morales to her study so that he could fix the phone – and afterwards Cutter would swear he'd heard her say to Rocco, 'You want a bucket for your leaks?'

The secure phone rings, and Dr Przewalskii answers, and Flint says softly, 'Hi, Dr P, it's me. Am I calling you too late?'

'Why too late?'

'I meant, I'm worried that I might have woken you. Were you asleep?'

'At my age, I prefer to read. But, yes, you are late; twenty minutes late in fact, which means there are only thirty minutes left of our session.'

'I see,' says Flint in a tone that says she doesn't see at all. They've not even begun the session and she's already pacing her kitchen, feeling prickles of tension on her skin. 'I didn't realise it was quite so important to call you at precisely . . . Well, whatever.' She pauses and then she adds, 'Marina, I didn't call you at ten o'clock – not precisely, not on the dot – because I wanted to wait until I was sure Jack was settled, so he wouldn't disturb us. And, if I inconvenienced you, then I'm sorry, okay? I apologise, all right?'

'It's not for me to tell you this,' Rocco Morales had said while lying on his back on the floor of Dr P's tiny study, under her cluttered desk, working on her phone socket, fixing the potential leak. 'But Grace, you know, she can take your breath away, moving from zero to one hundred mph faster than a stripped-down Porsche. Then, before you know it, when she's got you all riled up, she's down to forty, cruising in the slow lane asking you, hey, what's your hurry? It's the way she is, especially now, since the business with Mandrake, since she had her kid. It's one of her defence mechanisms, I guess. If you're going to help her figure out her stuff, well . . . Hey, it's none of my business but I thought you ought to know.'

Following her instincts, Dr Przewalskii is also cruising in the slow lane. 'So, you say Jack is settled. That is fantastic. Yes, really, I'm entirely happy for you. You must be very pleased.'

Flint allows herself to relax her guard just a little. 'You could say that. If you want to know the truth, Dr P, what I am is truly amazed. About us, I mean, Jack and me. Now that we're finally together, how quickly we've started to . . . I'm not sure how to put it . . . relate?'

'Now that he's no longer Mandrake?'

'Excuse me? What did you say?' – Flint instantly back on her guard, nought to one hundred faster than a Porsche.

'I might be wrong but I wonder if all the time he was inside you, you thought of him not as your child but as Mandrake, the *monster* you had every reason to hate. Even when he was born, and you called him Jack, perhaps you still saw him only as an extension of Mandrake, not a person in his own right. It is only now that your Jack is emerging from the chrysalis of Mandrake that, very much against your will, perhaps, you see him for what he really is.'

Silence on the line until Dr Przewalskii adds, 'Yes, well, I may be absolutely wrong.'

'Is this another of your bombs, Marina? Another of your booby traps that you plant and walk away from?'

'It is just an idea, a possibility. Something for you to think about, perhaps.'

'Right.'

'So, tell me, what are you thinking now about your father?'

'Not a lot. Listen, that's not why I'm calling you. I don't want to talk about him.'

'Do you know why?'

'Of course I know why! You once said I was blocking. Well, that's exactly what I'm trying to do now, block my father totally out of my thoughts as much as I can because otherwise I get so . . . Even now, just telling you I'm *not* thinking about him I can feel my blood pressure soaring. It's like when I was a teenager and I went to France to stay with a girlfriend and one Sunday we made a fish stew for lunch using salt cod, only we didn't know you're supposed to soak it in water first, get rid of the salt. I ate two mouthfuls of what was practically pure brine and half an hour later I felt as if my skin was on fire and my heart was trying to jackhammer its way out of my chest. Same thing now . . . So, please, let's just drop the subject of my father, shall we? I don't want to think or talk about him, certainly not now. Jack is what I care about.'

'Of course. If I was you I probably would not want to talk about him either. I just wonder if you know why you are so angry.'

'Isn't it obvious?'

A pause and then Dr Przewalskii says, 'Yes, I think so, but is it obvious to you?' and nothing else, and Flint doesn't respond and they wait each other out in silence.

Here we go, Flint is thinking. She knows that Dr P is determined to make her talk about her father – as determined as she is not to. That's because, for all her attempts at blocking, she hasn't been able to put the scene at Glebe Farm out of her mind. It lurks in her subconscious like the memory of a migraine and there is a nagging question that goes with it: why were you so upset? And worse still is the answer that she pushes away and pushes away and still it comes back to haunt her: because you were jealous. And she *hates* the answer, and denies it – I've never been jealous in my bloody life! – and her subconscious replies, *not until then*, and then twists the knife by reminding her of two short lines from William Blake: 'Cruelty has a Human Heart/And Jealousy a Human Face'. And she knows that it's true, and that the face she sees is her father's face, and that truth disgusts her.

Oh no, Dr P, we're not going there.

But Dr Przewalskii continues the game, this contest of wills to see who will break first. There is only static on the line and Flint must resist the urge to ask, you still there, Dr P? She reminds herself that it is not only therapists who know how to use silence as a weapon. To break a stubborn perpetrator or witness, Jerry Crawford reads a book, a paperback edition of Kurt Vonnegut's *Hocus Pocus* that he carries in his jacket pocket to all interrogations, and when he gets to the bits he likes he whistles a tuneless rendering of 'Danny Boy'. As everyone who has worked with Crawford can testify, his whistle is particularly hard to bear and Jerry claims that no perp has lasted beyond page twenty-three.

Flint sometimes prefers a more elaborate method. Faced with an especially recalcitrant suspect she has been known to wordlessly leave the interview room and return, ten or fifteen minutes later, with a tray on which is set out a light meal that she places on the table opposite the perp and proceeds to eat. The menu doesn't matter. What seems to get to them is the cloth on the tray, the pristine white cotton napkin, the little silver condiment shakers, the fact the Flint eats off real plates with real cutlery; the basket of crusty bread rolls, the real glass from which she sips what could be white wine. She seems to be saying, I don't care how long we wait because I'm up here in first class enjoying my meal while you're down there in the cargo hold where you don't get so much as a glass of water, and the affront is so gratuitous and so huge that, almost invariably, the perp breaks. Either they'll ask for something for themselves, or they say something like 'I hope you fucking choke' or, as on one occasion, make a lunge across the table and a grab for the knife, and end up with a broken arm. It doesn't matter what they do: any response and they lose the game.

With this is mind Flint says, as if she's talking to herself, 'While I'm waiting, I'm going to put this call on the speakerphone and fix myself a drink, maybe something to eat.'

'Yes,' replies Dr Przewalskii, 'you should definitely eat.'

And now the only sounds travelling along the secure line between Friendship Heights and New York are those of Flint's supper preparations: the opening and closing of a fridge door and the popping of a wine cork; the clatter of dishes, the sound of chopping on a board, the sizzle of oil heating in a pan on the stove. While she works she softly hums some Mozart and Dr Przewalskii may recognise the overture from *The Marriage of Figaro*.

Now Flint lays her place at the table, pours a little of the wine to taste it, the glass positioned right next to where she has set the phone. *Mmm* – a murmur of appreciation.

I should check on Jack, she thinks and she is about to do so when she hears Dr Przewalskii say, 'Yes, well, that was a very interesting session, I think, and we should continue tomorrow and let's see what happens,' and the line is cut.

'Mama,' says Jack on the baby monitor, calling out to her in his sleep.

Twenty-Five

In the anteroom of Joseph Gup's office, Kathy McCarry has set out her stall: four neat stacks of colour-coded files laid out on the polished surface of the conference table like so many decks of cards. Today she has contrived to sit opposite the brothers so she can watch their reactions as she presents her proposed solution to what Joe Gup calls 'the San Ambrogio problem'; her 'Plan B' as it is described on the title page – a small joke at Director Cutter's expense perpetrated by the youthful terriers at the Marscheider Building who have adopted Cutter's endlessly repeated forewarning to his troops: *You've always gotta have a Plan B, pilgrims.* For this Plan B is entirely the work of the terriers, although the Gup brothers are fully entitled to believe it is Kathy McCarry who has worked untiringly – 'sweated blood,' Joseph Gup says – pulling it together, and he has not let a working day go by without expressing his admiration for her 'fortitude'.

Not so Nathan Gup. His reception of the news she'd brought back from London was muted, even frosty, and his mood has not changed. He seems to imply that it is somehow Kathy's fault that the names are, in her words, 'completely unusable'; that, clean or not, they have been 'totally compromised' by Billy Goodheart's dramatic arrest (news of which did indeed make it onto Sky News as well as the front page of the *Evening Standard*). In the past three weeks, Nat has made a point of repeatedly describing the consequences as 'your shit' and Kathy has held her tongue – until the last time he said it, when she'd simply picked up her things and walked out of the meeting, and Joe Gup had followed her into the corridor.

'Kathy, you need to understand that Nat is, how can I say this? Nat is distressed because the client is very, *very* upset.'

'When what the client should be is very, *very* grateful.'

'I understand.'

'Because I saved his ass.'

'I know. I hear what you say.'

'Then perhaps you should explain that to your brother?'

But there is something else that is bugging Nathan Gup: the fact that Kathy McCarry has returned from London a single parent, at least for the time being; her sister's child, she'd explained, in sudden need of her care.

'How come you never mentioned you had a sister?' Nathan had said accusingly, as if she had failed to meet some unwritten requirement.

'You never asked, Mr Gup, and, for the record, she's my *half*-sister, the product of my father's second marriage. And, she and I, we've never had much time for each other, and precious little contact over the years, and I was only vaguely aware she had a child, and I only called her because I was in the UK with time to kill, and Joe – excuse me, your brother – had encouraged me to use the down time on my trip to be in contact with my family. And I thought, why not give Sally a call? Which was when I discovered that she was in a psychiatric hospital, and her worthless partner was long gone, and Jack, her boy, was in the so-called care of Social Services, on the fast track to a foster home and there was no one else to look after him, and I thought, for once in your life, Kathy, you can do something that doesn't advance your career. And so I brought him home with me because, until my sister gets well, I'm the only functioning family he's got – and frankly, Nathan, I don't see how this is any of your goddamn business.'

'Kathy, Kathy,' said Joseph Gup, trying to appease her. 'It's just that Nathan and I are . . . Well, we were a little taken by surprise.'

'You know it's not affected my work.'

'Of course not,' said Joe.

'It had better not,' said Nat, 'because it's totally down to you to clear up your goddamned shit.'

Which was when Kathy walked out on him, eyes on fire, her body language saying she was *this close* to slugging him. When she reached the sanctuary of her office, Joseph had followed her inside and closed the door and said, 'Kathy, please sit down' and, 'Kathy, I want to apologise to you for Nathan's behaviour. I also want you to know that as a single mother, de facto' – and Joe had contrived to make it sound like a blessing – 'you are fully entitled to take off whatever time you need to deal with any emergencies; if young Jack gets sick, for example. And if it suits you to work at home, say two or three days a week, that's also fine by us. It's company policy and we're proud of it. Applies to all of our single carers, and you are not the only one at Gup Securities who's in that position, far from it. So, whatever you need, just tell us.'

Kathy had thanked him, remembered to call him Joe, thanked him again when he'd made her promise she would not stay late in the evenings or come into the office on weekends. 'You're a decent man,' she'd said, the Kathy part of her half meaning it, even though the Flint part knew that no amount of decency could save him. Watching his still-handsome face respond to Kathy's gratitude, Flint could easily imagine how it would sag and crumple when the time came for her pretence to end: *Mr Gup, Joseph Gup, I'm a federal agent and you, sir, are under arrest.*

Would he call her names – 'bitch', 'cow', maybe worse – as so many other perps had done when she'd reached the orgasmic moment when she could reveal her true identity? Flint doubted it, for, say what you like about him, Joseph Gup presented himself with dignity. More likely, she imagined, watching him banter with Kathy McCarry, he would stare at her in disbelief, trying to gauge the depth of his shattered illusions, and say something along the lines of, *But, Kathy, I thought I was like a father to you.*

Well, yes, Mr Gup, but when it comes to fathers, I have a problem.

'Excuse me?'

He was in the doorway of her office – half in, half out – and he'd asked Kathy a question that Flint hadn't caught.

'It doesn't matter.'

'No, please.'

'Back there in the meeting, when Nathan got out of line, I was just wondering how close you came to slugging him.'

'Out of respect for you, Joe, not close at all.'

'Pity' – giving her his winning smile.

'Plan B,' says Kathy McCarry, selecting two red files from the first stack, passing one each to the Brothers Gup. 'True Right Developments is a Nevada corporation in good standing, if that's not an oxymoron. They're property developers, primarily of strip malls and small apartment blocks, been established for twenty-nine years, listed on the NASDAQ, no adverse findings at the SEC, nothing to worry about at IRS. Mind you,' and Kathy wrinkles her nose to demonstrate her allegiance to her former employers, 'since Nevada doesn't share information with the IRS, that's not saying a hell of a lot. Still, True Right is clean, or as clean as it gets, which is why I'm proposing they take over the San Ambrogio project.'

'Take it over?' says Joseph Gup flicking through the file, not really questioning Kathy's proposal, more like trying it out for size. Nathan Gup leaves his copy of the file untouched and watches Kathy's face with sour eyes.

'The directors and principal stockholders of record – not that Nevada requires stockholders of record – are Dorothy and Sherman Childs, who don't live in Nevada but in Palm Beach, Florida, when they're not at their condo in Bermuda. Dorothy is sixty-nine and she told me on the phone that she likes younger men, which may explain why Sherman is only sixty-five. Until nineteen ninety-nine, the driving force behind True Right was their only child, Dale, and, that year, declared revenues were a little under thirty million dollars. Then, in December of ninety-nine, Dale flew his Cessna into a mountainside near Boulder, Colorado – fog and a faulty altimeter was the best explanation the accident investigators could come up with – and, since then, True Right has been moribund. Annual revenues are running at under half a million, which comes from residual interests in some of the apartment blocks True Right has developed, and the stock is trading on the NASDAQ at forty cents – not that anybody's buying.'

'And you're proposing this *moribund* company takes over San Ambrogio?' asks Joseph Gup, and this time he is posing a question.

'This is pure bullshit,' says Nathan.

Pressing on, ignoring Nat as though she hasn't heard, Kathy continues, 'So my proposal is, True Right will raise a loan to acquire the land for the asking price, which is two point seven million dollars. That's not going to be any problem. Dorothy Childs – or Dot, as she likes me to call her – has already spoken to a couple of Miami banks and the money is hers whenever she wants it. Next, to finance the construction, True Right makes a new stock offering through a market maker – one hundred and seventy-five million shares at forty cents a share, which the client buys in the names of various corporations that we will establish or acquire in Nevada. If you'll turn to page eighteen' – and Joseph Gup does as he's asked while Nathan continues to stare at Kathy, his copy of the file still untouched – 'I've itemised the corporations and how I'm proposing the stock be divided between them; twenty-three corporations in all. The client will control the corporations, of course – and therefore True Right – but only and always through nominees. He will be entirely invisible. Now, gentlemen . . .'

Kathy removes her glasses, placing them on the table in front of her alongside the spare pen she doesn't need to use. 'Now, it could be said that the structure I'm proposing is over-elaborate and even unnecessary. The fact is, we don't need twenty-three corporations to veil the client's identity, or even one. Under Nevada law, the stockholders of any corporation are not a matter of public record and, except in cases of proven fraud, the Nevada courts have *never* allowed the veil of corporate secrecy to be pierced. Better still, Nevada allows bearer stock certificates on which the owners can write their names – or Mickey Mouse and Donald Duck, or just The Bearer, or nothing at all if that's what they choose. Whoever holds the certificate owns the stock, and therefore the corporation, completely anonymously.'

'So, what's wrong with that?' – the first words Nathan has spoken.

'Nothing, nothing at all if you want to take the risk that the certificate doesn't get lost or stolen or destroyed in a fire.'

'You think the client is likely to be careless with a bit of paper that's worth – what? – seventy million dollars?' Nathan has loaded his voice with sarcasm.

'It's happened, Mr Gup. Or the client gets unlucky. He stashes his *bit of paper* in a nice secure bank vault, and the vault gets robbed – because there is no such thing as a vault that can't be robbed – and, because that *bit of paper* has no practical value to the thieves, they burn it. And then, when the time comes for the client to sell his stake, the only way he can prove ownership is to go to court and demonstrate that he was the source of the development funds – and I don't think the client will want to do that. Trust me, Mr Gup, it's happened more times than you would care to believe.'

Joseph Gup nods as though he knows this to be true.

'There's another issue. In Nevada True Right can operate behind a veil but it's going to be doing business in South Carolina and there the veil will get lifted, at least partially. We can't know if anybody is going to concern themselves as to who the investors in True Right are, but they might and, if they do, I'd sooner not have a six-hundred-pound, no-name gorilla attracting their attention. Twenty-three named corporations with officers of record – albeit nothing more than shells – are less likely to get anyone excited. At least that's my view, Mr Gup.'

'What's the cost, in terms of time and money?' asks Joseph.

'Time to form the corporations is twenty-four hours and I can do it online. The cost is eighty-five dollars per corporation. Taxes are zilch: no corporation tax, no capital stock tax, no corporate share tax, no stock transfer fee. We're going to need directors but Nevada allows one-person corporations so that means twenty-three nominees—'

'Why twenty-three corporations? Why not ten or, for that matter, thirty?'

Kathy smiles. 'Twenty-three is my lucky number, Mr Gup. Twenty-three, after I got my degree, was when I thought I really had it made.'

'And these nominee directors, they have to be residents of Nevada?'

'Residents of anywhere you like. Anywhere in the world.'

'So, bottom line, Kathy: what's the cost of getting that six-hundred-pound gorilla off our backs?'

'Bottom line, Joseph: you give me ten thousand dollars to spend and I'll bring you back some change.'

Joseph Gup looks very pleased.

But this is merely foreplay. For the next four hours the brothers Gup will dissect and analyse Kathy McCarry's Plan B – Nathan coming out of his sulk, even warming to the task. Concealed in the stems of Kathy's glasses are two microphones the size of pinheads, and two transmitters the thickness of a human hair, and in the casing of her spare pen is a digital receiver and a microchip that can record up to ten hours of conversation, and tonight, when he listens to highlights of the playback over Flint's secure line, Director Cutter will say of Nathan Gup, 'Pernickety sonofabitch, isn't he?'

'What you're proposing is basically a reverse takeover, right?'

'In all but name, Mr Gup. But Dot and Sherman Childs will remain the directors of record of True Right, insomuch as there is a record, not least because they bring experience to the project, and therefore credibility. After all, they're property developers with a long track record of bringing projects home on time and, as often as not, under budget. Nothing on this scale, I grant you, but when San Ambrogio is announced they can stand up at the press conference, or the launch party, or whatever it is, and plausibly say, this is the project we've been working towards for almost thirty years. And when they do that, with their history, they're not going to set off any alarms.'

'They're our camouflage?' Joseph Gup helpfully suggests.

'Exactly.'

Nathan, on a more practical note, asks, 'And what does this camouflage cost? What's their take?'

'With their existing shares in True Right, they'll own fifteen per cent of the project.'

A long, low whistle from Nat. 'Wow! You don't think, do you, that ten point five million dollars for laundry service might be just a little on the pricey side?'

'If I looked on this as simply a washing operation then, yes, I might think that.' Kathy rolls her eyes to suggest this would be a foolish decision. 'If, on the other hand, I recognised the deal for what it is – a double opportunity for the client to legitimise his funds with minimal risk *and* make a rock-solid investment – then, no, Mr Gup, I wouldn't think it's pricey. Look . . .' she begins, breaking off to search among the files for the one she wants, 'each completed phase of the project adds value to San Ambrogio: when planning permission is secured; when the land is cleared and the roads and the utilities go in; when the harbour is built; when the condos go up; when they break ground for the hotel – each step of the way adds value exponentially. If the client sticks with the project until it's finished, my analysis suggests that he could walk away with somewhere between one hundred and one hundred and fifty million dollars; clean dollars, Mr Gup, dollars the client can wire to the bank. But, better than that is what could – what very well might – happen to True Right's stock price. If, little by little as the project develops, the client releases some of his shares onto the true market – a million here, a million there – the chances are the price is going to rise. By how much I can't tell you but I think that anytime the development reaches a major landmark – say, for instance, Ritz-Carlton or another prestige chain picks up the hotel – we could expect to be looking at a significant increase in the value of the stock.'

'How significant?'

There is a hint of a smile on Kathy's lips as she shakes her head. 'Sorry, Mr Gup, I can't help you. Because, let's face it, if I could predict the stock market I wouldn't be sitting here talking with you guys' – and this earns her a broad grin from Joseph. 'But, for what it's worth, I have done some analysis of historical NASDAQ data to see what might happen and my guesstimate – and, gentlemen, please be very clear, this is only a guess – my guesstimate of the likely price of True Right stock two years into the project ranges from a dollar ten to . . .' Kathy breaks off to search for another of her files which she briefly consults. 'From a dollar and ten cents at the low end to five dollars and fifty cents.'

'That's one hell of a range,' says Nathan.

'Sure it is, so let me put it another way. Two years into the project, the client's investment of the seventy million dollars that he can't bank and can't account for today could be worth one hundred and ninety-two million entirely legitimate dollars, and that's the low end – and if you know of a better investment than that, Mr Gup, I'd like to sign up for a piece of it. At five dollars and fifty cents a share, the client's going to be walking away with . . . Well, you can work it out.'

Joseph Gup is scribbling on a pad, doing the sums. 'That's just a little shy of one *billion* dollars,' he says slowly, wonder in his voice.

'Less fifteen per cent for the laundry fee,' Nathan tartly reminds him – and, listening to the replay, Cutter will say, 'What's wrong with this guy?'

'The brothers Gup, they stand to make only five per cent,' Flint will explain.

'That's still fifty million dollars, right?'

'A couple of million shy of that, but the amount doesn't matter. I think what Nathan was objecting to was the principle; what he saw as their rightful place in the feeding chain.'

'You're kidding me.'

Bone-tired, her face the colour of ash, Flint will wander over to the window of her apartment and say into the phone in a voice so hollow it might have come from her grave, 'Even Nathan has his principles.'

Three hours after the meeting is over – Plan B provisionally approved, subject, of course, to the client's instructions – Joseph Gup re-enters Kathy McCarry's office without knocking and closes the door. For what seems like an age, he stands before her with no discernible expression on his face, not saying a word, his arms crossed protectively over his chest as though he is trying to reach a difficult decision. Then before she can move or do anything to stop him he leans across the desk and takes her face in his hands and kisses her lightly on the forehead.

'Kathy, I've said it before and I'll say it again – and this time I *really* mean it: you do fine, fine, *fine* work. If I wasn't old enough to be your father, I'd ask you to marry me. Hell, I might ask you anyway! What do you say, Kathy? Make an old man happy – and let me make you very rich?'

Joseph, beaming, has disturbed Kathy's wig and she is clumsily attempting to re-settle it.

'You're proposing to a de facto single mother?' – all she can think of to say.

'No, well, there you have a point,' and Joseph laughs delightedly. 'The marriage proposal, I was just kidding. The part about making you rich . . .' Now Joseph perches one buttock on the edge of her desk and his face is a mask of absolute sincerity. 'That part, what I said, was very, very real.'

There is silence until Kathy asks, 'If?'

'If the deal goes through. If the numbers are anywhere near what you've suggested. Kathy, with this client Gup Securities gets paid by results and, as you can surely see, the results for the firm could be spectacular. In which case, you're in line for – no, you're *entitled* to – a substantial bonus; a *very* substantial bonus. I'm talking seven figures and the first digit isn't a one, Kathy.' He pauses for a moment. 'Not a one, Kathy, it's a five, maybe even a six.'

'If?' Kathy asks again, removing her wig and putting it on the desk as if to say she has nothing to hide.

Joseph doesn't answer immediately. He slips from his perch on the desk and begins pacing the room, hands in his pockets, like a prudent man preparing his thoughts. Eventually, 'It's your cathedral, Kathy, your fine, inspired architecture, and you're the one who should sell it. No, not sell; that's the wrong word. *Present* it is what I mean; you're the one who should *present* Plan B to the client because you know exactly how it's constructed. When he asks a thousand questions – and he *will* ask a thousand questions, count on it – we need you there to answer them.'

There?

It is not Flint's face that could give her away, she knows, but the pounding of her heart.

'The question is, can you travel? We go to him, Mohammed to the mountain, and that means a four- or five-day trip, perhaps as early as next week. Is there any way you can manage that?'

'Of course,' she says without thinking – without thinking about Jack – and as soon as the words are out of her mouth she understands what he's getting at and she feels a stab of shame.

'What about your boy?'

'I'll fix it.'

'You've got someone who can take care of him?'

'It's not a problem, Joe.'

'You're sure?'

Kathy McCarry stands up and fixes Joseph Gup with a look that is meant to imply, *we are two of a kind*; that, for a seven-digit sum beginning with a five, or maybe a six, her young charge can go to the orphanage, if that's what it takes. They are breathing in unison when she says, 'Joe, believe it, I am absolutely certain.'

Joseph studies her face before he smiles and says, 'I was sure I could count on you, Kathy.'

Gotcha, thinks Flint.

Twenty-Six

Tonight Jack Flint is fretful. He won't eat his food or play with his toys and each time she puts him down in his cot he whimpers and whines, and outright screams if she leaves the room, and she has to go and get him because she can't stand the noise. And she hasn't eaten, either – not that she cares – and she's already fifteen minutes late in calling Dr Przewalskii, *again*. The only good news is the breeze that is coming through the open sliding glass doors diluting the lung-sucking humidity.

Jack in her arms, his chin resting on her left shoulder, his compliant body pressed against her breasts, she wanders out onto the terrace and replays in her mind her telephone conversation with Aldus Cutter.

'We're taking a private charter out of Dulles, so I won't know where we're going until we get there. He told me to pack a sweater, because it might get cool in the evenings, but that could mean just about anywhere. As to when, Joseph says we leave tomorrow night, or maybe Wednesday. He said he's waiting for word from the client.'

'Out of Dulles, you're sure?'

'It's what he said.'

'If that changes—'

'Aldus, you'll be the first to know.'

'Okay, we'll run a check on all the private birds scheduled out of Dulles in the next seventy-two hours, see if we can't narrow down the possibilities. But, Grace, depending on where you're going and given the time frame, I don't know how much support I can provide.'

'I know.'

'You could be flying solo, at least for a while.'

'I know.'

'And that worries me.'

'I know.'

Silence on the secure line until Cutter said, 'You're not licensed to hunt, Grace, not this time.'

'No.'

'This is a sales trip, nothing more.'

'Right.'

'If it is Gröber you're meeting, your job is to sell him the idea that San Ambrogio can make them more money than all of Çarçani's toxic rackets put together. And you have to sell yourself.'

'Absolutely.'

'You've got to persuade him you're central to their future prosperity because – and let me be very clear about this, Grace – I don't just want Gröber and Çarçani in jail. I want their assets seized, *all* of their assets, and I don't want to spend the next twenty years looking for them. So, to begin with, I want Çarçani to invest seventy million dollars in the San Ambrogio deal for the very good reason that, when the time comes, I'll know exactly where to send the Brinks Mat truck.'

'More than one truck, I think.'

'Whatever. Listen, Grace, you've done better than you know. We didn't have a case against Gröber – leastways, not one we could prosecute, not after Regal got flattened and put in a box – and now we do, thanks to you, because what we're looking at is a RICO conspiracy if ever there was one, and that's not just my opinion. I spoke with Rufus Hardy at the US Attorney's office an hour ago, filled him in on what you've got, and he was practically salivating about the number of indictments he sees coming down the road. But you've only got Gröber on a hook, him and Çarçani. They're not yet landed on the bank and if you're going to land them you have to reel them in *slowly*. However tempting it may be for you to grab these assholes at the first opportunity, what you have to do is build a case that's going to stick. And I don't want just them. I want to demolish their whole rotten edifice and that's going to take a while, maybe a long while. I don't have a single doubt you've got the skills and the stamina. What I worry about, Grace, is have you got the patience?'

'As long it takes.'

'Don't blow this, Grace. Don't let your anger get in the way.'

'No, sir.'

That is what she'd said; what she'd even half believed, at the time.

Twenty-Seven

There is no sound, no distant crack or warning whistle of a small projectile approaching them at supersonic speed. Afterwards Flint will say that a nanosecond before it hit she had an impression of immediate danger, but she cannot describe what physical properties alerted her senses.

Nor does the impact make any great impression. Jack's body does not lurch or stagger in her arms and she is not knocked backwards in her chair. Rather, she feels his body shudder and slump. He does not cry out. All she hears is a whimper and a whisper that sounds to her like the sudden escape of air.

She looks down and on his lower back, two or three inches above his right buttock, she sees a spot that in the subdued lighting of the terrace is inky black. It's no larger than an eraser on the end of a pencil and she brushes at it with one hand as though it might be a fly, but it doesn't move. Gently she probes the spot through the terrycloth of Jack's sleepsuit until she finds a hole in his soft flesh, a tunnel with the bore of her little finger, and her right prefrontal cortex is immediately registering urgent alarms about an *entry wound*. Instinctively she ducks her head and upper body into a defensive crouch, using the momentum to take her out of the chair in a forward roll, flipping herself over in a somersault so that she lands on her back, Jack clamped tightly to her chest by the uncommon strength of her arms.

Still on her back, she uses the power of her legs to propel herself across the terrace, scuttling like a crab, craning her neck as a backstroke swimmer might to see where she's going, heading for the open glass doors. She slightly misjudges her approach and the back of her head hits the raised sill at the entryway, jarring her neck. For a moment she feels stunned but her legs continue working, driving like pistons, pushing her through the gap between the doors and into the living room. Her upper body, the part of her on which Jack lies inert as a corpse, is across the sill when the floor-to-ceiling glass panel of the right-hand door disintegrates.

Ignore! Ignore the pain! Keep moving! MOVE!

Her face feels as though it has been thrashed with stinging nettles and there is what might be blood leaking into her left eye. She resists the compelling urge to remove her hands from their protective positions, guarding Jack's back and the back of his head, and sheer willpower keeps her legs pumping, driving her and Jack fully across the sill.

Then the glass panel of the left-hand door shatters – and afterwards she will say that this time she was certain she heard a bullet passing only millimetres over her head.

Safe for now, Flint lies on her back in a corner of the living room, feeling the faint flutter of Jack's breath on her neck, and reviews their situation. It is not good for they are trapped. The nearest telephone is in the kitchen which she cannot reach without crossing what is now the killing zone in front of the shattered windows. Neither can she reach the wall switch to turn off the two table lamps that light the room, or pull the night lights from their sockets, not without exposing herself to the sniper. Her only option, she decides, is to crawl along the wall to the cupboard where, under a pile of never-used dinner napkins, she has concealed a semi-automatic pistol she has no authority to possess.

But to do that she will have to remove Jack from her chest and the prospect terrifies her, for she is convinced there must be an exit wound in his abdomen the size of a grapefruit and that only by using her body as a compress can she prevent him from bleeding to death.

Do it, or he'll die anyway says the reasoning part of her brain and she knows this to be true.

Unwillingly, preparing herself for the dreadfulness of what she might see, she loosens the grip of her arms and turns on her side to lay Jack on his back on the floor. And then she dares to look and stares in disbelief for there is no exit wound, only spots of *her* blood dripping from her face, discolouring the snowy whiteness of his sleepsuit. Her sense of relief is visceral, rising from her gut – until, in an instant, reality hits her like a punch and what emerges from her throat is a sob. The lack of an exit wound, she is sure, can only mean the sniper is using bullets that are designed not to leave the body, but explode inside it like a small grenade.

Despair overcomes her. She cannot move, or think; she can barely breathe. There are messages coming from her brain that are screaming to be heard but their meaning is lost in the cacophony. All she comprehends is that Jack's face is whiter than his sleepsuit; that his eyes are huge and filled with fear.

Perhaps it is her son's look of dread – the look that says he somehow knows he is close to something unimaginable – that gives Flint the strength to move. She does not remember getting to her feet but here she is, her back pressed against the wall, taking rapid sidesteps. From the angle of the last shot she's guessing that the sniper is positioned on one of the upper balconies, or maybe the roof, of the adjacent condominium and, if she's right, when she reaches the cupboard she knows she will be in the line of fire. Two steps short of her objective, she pauses. Surprise is her only weapon. She counts to three and then – *Do it* – and she is spinning away from the wall, pulling at the cupboard door, grabbing at the napkins and the gun, falling to the floor – registering the fact that, as she falls, her best wine glasses on the second shelf of the cupboard explode – rolling across the carpet, getting herself out of the killing zone; lying on her stomach, lifting the pistol, firing at the first table lamp, missing by a mile.

Bloody do it right!

Now she's on her knees, getting her breathing under control, taking her time to adopt the correct firing position. Her gun hand outstretched, the other hand bracing the wrist, she closes her left eye and sights along the barrel and fires twice, and both lamps are instantly extinguished. The two night lights are much smaller targets and take four shots to kill. In this confined environment, the noise of each shot she fires seems deafening.

Two silent answering shots from the sniper, but they slap harmlessly into the living-room wall at well above head height and Flint is sure he's now firing blind.

Bolstered by her small victory, she's at Jack's side, lifting him gently in her arms, whispering to him with a mother's might.

'Don't be afraid, I'm here . . . Nothing bad is going to happen to you, I promise . . . I know it hurts, darling, but I'll make it better . . . Oh God, Jack, I love you so, so much . . .'

On that evening the Incident Log of the Maryland State Police records six emergency calls from residents of 4550 Park Avenue North, in the township of Friendship Heights. The first four, all received within two minutes, reported sounds of gunfire coming from the ninth floor of the condominium. The fifth call, received at 22.27, was from a Miss Martha Skelhorn, a visitor to the building, who said she had been waiting for the elevator on the ninth floor when she was confronted by the sight of a 'deranged woman' running along the corridor towards her. The woman was practically bald, her face was splattered with blood, she held within her shirt – also bloodstained – the body of a small child. She was barefoot and, stuffed into the waistband of her jeans, was a gun. 'Call nine one one,' was all she'd said as she'd brushed by Miss Skelhorn, practically knocking her over. The deranged woman had not waited for the elevator but taken the stairs as though the building was on fire.

The sixth emergency call, received some three minutes later, recorded the theft of a car from the driveway of 4550 Park Avenue North. Actually, the caller said, his SUV had been hijacked, virtually at gunpoint.

'Drive, Daniel. Just get in and drive.' Flint was not pointing the gun so much as waving it.

Daniel is the night manager of the condominium and he and Flint – or Miss McCarry, as he knows her – have an affinity because Daniel comes from the Caribbean island of Martinique, and he and she sometimes speak French together, which lessens the homesickness he often feels.

Taking his life in his hands, responding to increasingly frantic calls from alarmed residents, Daniel was about to take the elevator to the ninth floor when Flint burst into the lobby yelling for his help, demanding to know the whereabouts of the nearest Accident and Emergency hospital. He'd said there was a late-night ER clinic not too far away, told her where it was, tried to give her directions; changed his mind, said he would take them in his car and set off at a loping run to get it. And then she'd seen the empty Chevy Blazer parked in the driveway, and the keys in the ignition, and she'd called Daniel back and said, 'We're taking this.'

As Flint was opening the passenger door, a middle-aged man dressed in running shorts and a jaunty red top had come striding from the building, calling to her with outrage in his voice, 'Hey, what the hell do you think you're doing?'

'Is this your vehicle, sir?'

'Damn right it is.'

'Do you know how to get to the nearest emergency room?'

'What?'

'Do you?'

'Get the fuck away from my car.'

'Sir, this is a medical emergency and I'm requisitioning your vehicle. If you've got a problem with that, call nine one one. And, sir, if you don't step back, so help me . . .' Which is when she'd pulled the gun, waved it around.

Drive, Daniel. Just get in and drive.

Speeding along Wisconsin Avenue, threading his way through the traffic with surprising proficiency, Daniel has apparently put aside any concerns about the consequences. In the rear-view mirror he can see in the far distance the flashing blue lights of police vehicles in apparent pursuit but he can lose them, he firmly believes. The next time there is a curve in the road, when the chase lights are no longer in the mirror, he'll leave Wisconsin Avenue, take a hard right and vanish into the side roads.

'Not long now,' he says. '*Ne vous en faites pas, ne vous en faites pas.*'

Flint doesn't hear him. She has no awareness of time or where she is. What occupies her is a mantra from her police training days when the instructors had drummed into her the ABC of major trauma care: *airway, breathing, circulation.* She knows that the first hour after the infliction of devastating injury – what emergency medics call 'the golden hour' – is when survival or not is frequently decided. *Keep the airways clear. Keep the patient breathing. Do not let the blood pressure plunge, or the heart jackhammer.*

She has used her fingers to remove the sputum from Jack's mouth, noting with a shudder that it is laced with clots of blood. Now she breathes into his puckered mouth, trying to force additional oxygen into his lungs.

In between each breath, she pleads for Jack's life. Flint does not have time for religion or faith in any god – not after all the lowlifes she has encountered, not after all the shittiness she's seen – but what Daniel hears her repeating, over and over, sounds to him very much like prayer.

Twenty-Eight

At the North Bethesda Family Health Center, Dr Robert Dolnick is winding down from another long day of dealing with mainly minor ailments and injuries. He is sitting at a desk in the reception room catching up on the paperwork when he hears the entrance doors to the clinic burst open and looks up to see a bloodied woman coming wordlessly towards him, a child in her arms that she holds out like an offering. His first thought is *car wreck*, for her face looks as though it has been driven through a windscreen. He is getting to his feet when she disabuses him.

'My son has a gunshot wound,' she says in a voice of unnatural calm. 'Entry wound in his right lower back, no exit wound. I think the bullet was a soft nose, fired from a high-velocity rifle.'

Gently she lays the child on the desk, her right hand cradling the back of his head. 'His name is Jack, doctor, and I don't want him to die. Please help him.'

Dr Dolnick has worked in emergency medicine for twenty-five years and seen all manner of catastrophes, but nothing like this. The child lying before him, his sleepsuit speckled with his mother's blood, wears an expression on his ghostly-white face – entirely white except for the crimson stain coming from his nose – that conveys a mixture of terror and helplessness and unbearable pain; an expression that Dolnick has only ever seen before on the faces of soldiers brought in from the combat zone. The pathos of it freezes him into immobility. All he can think of to say is, 'Mother of God, who *did* this?'

Flint feels as though she is drifting through a dream, which may account for her preternatural poise. It is the sight of this doctor just standing there doing nothing that snaps her composure like a thread. Before she can stop herself she's yelling at him – *For pity's sake! DO SOMETHING!* – grabbing at his green smock with her hands, trying to drag him down towards Jack.

But his body is rigid and, leaning over the desk, she can't get the leverage, and he remains frozen, just staring down at the boy. So now she's started calling out for alternative aid – *Help me! Somebody, please, help!* – twisting her head to direct her voice down the dimly lit corridor leading from the reception room, hollering as loud as she can.

Until finally she hears the hurried approach of footsteps and a woman's voice responding – *What on earth?* – and maybe that's what makes the difference.

'Loretta,' Dolnick says, snapping out of his trance and placing his hands tenderly on Jack's abdomen, 'fetch the battle gurney, please. As fast as you can.'

A woman in a nurse's uniform with a handsome ebony face comes into Flint's view, pausing just long enough to take in the scene, then turning on her heels and retreating down the corridor with a deceiving gait, like an airline stewardess who needs to get to the flight deck fast without wishing to panic the passengers.

'When did this happen?' asks Dolnick as he cautiously turns Jack towards his left side to examine the wound on his back.

Flint doesn't know because she's lost all track of time.

'When was he shot?' – this time urgency to the question.

'Twenty minutes ago, maybe half an hour?' Flint guesses. *Please let it be less than the golden hour*, she silently implores.

Done examining the wound, the doctor eases the child onto his back and, avoiding eye contact with the mother, leans over the desk to press the call button of an intercom.

'Charlie?'

'Hey, Bob, what's up?'

'Charlie, I've got an infant here with a serious gunshot wound. Possible organ failure and, from what I can hear through the scope, blood in the lungs – and I need all the help I can get.'

There is a slight reflective pause and then Charlie says, 'On our way.'

Organ failure, blood in the lungs? Flint is trying to work out the implications when, to her left, she hears what sounds like a gurney being rammed through double doors and, almost simultaneously, to her right, the slamming of other doors – and suddenly it seems to her she is in the midst of an invasion. Here, from the corridor, comes Loretta pushing a trolley to which is clamped precariously swaying saline drips and IV lines and oxygen bottles and monitors and other equipment Flint can't identify. And here, through a doorway on the opposite side of the room, comes a small army, a line of men and women – one, two, three, four, five, *six* of them – dressed from head to toe in surgical gear, masks swinging from their necks like lanyards, their rubber shoes squealing on the linoleum floor. They do not surround Jack so much as engulf him and Flint has the sense to scramble out of their way. On the edge of the crowd, she hears someone say, 'Let's get him sedated and into the trauma room.'

She cannot really see what they are doing, understands little of what they say. The next thing she knows, Jack is on the gurney and five people are pushing – one at the back, two on either side – heading for the corridor at breakneck speed. Flint is in pursuit, until Nurse Loretta blocks her way.

'Honey, what's your name?'

'Kathy McCarry,' Flint says automatically, before spooling through the complications that this deception is likely to cause when the police arrive.

'Okay, Kathy—'

'Actually, my real name is Grace.'

'Okay, Grace,' Loretta says evenly, as though people switching names on a dime is an everyday event at the centre, 'let me explain to you what's happenin'.'

'I know what's happening,' says Flint.

'You do?'

'Law enforcement experience,' she offers vaguely.

'Well, good. 'Cause then you'll know what I'm sayin' when I tell you, the folks you just saw taking your boy to the trauma room, they're the best emergency team you're gonna find in Montgomery County. What you've got on your side is two surgeons, one anaesthesiologist, three highly experienced triage nurses, and Dr Dolnick, who's an army doctor, in the reserves, and he's seen more battlefield injuries than he cares to tell. So, what I'm saying to you is, your child's in fine hands. And, Grace, if you know about these things, then you know that while they're trying to save your boy,

what they don't need, the last thing they need, is his momma gettin'
in the way. You understand what I'm saying?'

No, not really – but, by her body language, Flint seems to
acquiesce.

'Besides, you and me, we've got paperwork to do. Now, Grace,
this might not seem like the best time to be filling out some damn-
fool forms but there's basic information I need about your baby
and, right now, that's the only way you can help him.'

Loretta reaches out to take Flint's arm, feels the steely tug of her
resistance, sees the fear in her eyes.

'Honey, I *know* how hard this is for you.'

'Do you?'

'Believe it. Some other time, I'll tell you how I know, if you
want. For now, what you've gotta do is trust me.'

And for reasons she doesn't really understand, Flint does decide
to trust Loretta – or perhaps she has simply exhausted her will to
resist. Placidly, she allows herself to be led to a small consulting
room off the reception area and settled in a chair, where – for how
long, Flint can't grasp – she is made acutely aware of how little she
knows about her son.

Previous ailments? She doesn't know.

Any allergies? She doesn't know.

Well, is he allergic to any medications? She doesn't know.

His blood type? She doesn't have a clue.

Loretta keeps her wide, chocolate-brown eyes on the forms,
ticking the appropriate boxes, without the slightest sign of surprise
or criticism, as if to say this is par for the course – hey, mommas
comin' in here knowing nothing about their babies, happens all the
time. Flint, on the other hand, feels acute discomfort and the need
to justify her dire lack of knowledge about her son. She is rapidly
fashioning some kind of explanation in her head, an elaborate lie
that she hopes will not blow her cover, when she hears a man's
voice calling, 'Loretta? Nurse?'

The door to the consulting room opens and here comes Dolnick.
He enters slowly, even reluctantly, and as he positions himself
alongside her chair, Flint catches the sombre glance he exchanges
with Loretta. He looks shattered and as though he's aged ten years
in as many minutes, and there are traces of fresh blood on the front
of his smock. Flint would say something but she knows if she opens

her mouth all that will come out is something incoherent or, more likely, a scream.

'I'm sorry,' Dolnick says wearily, 'I don't know your name.'

'Grace,' says Loretta. 'And, my guess, doctor, is that you can spare her any bullshit.'

'Yes, well, Grace . . .'

He's about to tell her that Jack is dead, that he has succumbed in the trauma room to internal injuries that a miniature human frame cannot possibly absorb; that, in a baby's body, the vital organs and lungs are simply located too close together to escape the scattered shrapnel of a soft nose projectile entering the lower back at something close to twice the speed of sound.

'The bullet disintegrated like confetti,' Dolnick is saying. 'Whether it was designed to do so, or whether it struck a rib and shattered – and two of his ribs *were* broken – I can't say. In any event, the X-rays show that the fragments lacerated both of Jack's lungs, his liver, his spleen and his stomach. There was, I'm afraid, a great deal of internal bleeding.'

Unconsciously, Flint has slipped into defensive copper's mode. For the sake of her sanity, she is absorbing these bleak specifics as though she is back with the Met; a young detective inspector in some white-walled, brightly lit autopsy room, trying not to gag on the stench of formaldehyde, learning with professional detachment the cause of yet one more violent death. Her detachment is entirely spurious and will not last, of course, not in this case. But for now, defining Jack as just another victim is the only way she believes she can cope.

'Now, fortunately,' Dolnick is saying, 'the capacity of young lungs to regenerate is extraordinary, and the same is true of the . . .'

Fortunately? Flint's mind is churning, a little too far behind the curve. She's trying to grasp the meaning of what he's saying but her capacity to process and evaluate input in a timely manner has somehow deserted her.

What did he mean? – her cortex urgently demanding clarification. There is none available from Flint.

Dolnick is still speaking. 'And, so far as we can see – and, mind you, this is very much a provisional diagnosis – there appears to be no damage to the heart. This can only be confirmed when Jack reaches hospital. Here and now, we simply don't have the facilities . . .'

Flint has lost the thread but found the weave. It has finally got through to her that Jack is alive, or not yet dead – and that's a whole lot better than the prognosis she thought she had just received. Out of her memory bank bursts an intoxicating line from Hunter S. Thompson, what he said about the triumph of hope: about plunging to your death down an elevator shaft and then you land in a lake of mermaids.

Falling out of the darkness into the light. Flint reborn, *electrified* in the company of mermaids, comes out of her chair.

'Now, *please*, you *must* understand, your son is gravely, gravely ill.' Dolnick, flustered by Flint's abrupt display of euphoria, is trying to drag her back to earth – back to the elevator shaft into which she has fallen, where any hope of survival is very likely a desperate illusion.

'I know, I do understand.'

'He's on a ventilator, and we're doing what we can to control the bleeding, but he has six or even seven life-threatening injuries that require immediate surgery – surgery this clinic simply isn't equipped or qualified to carry out. As soon as we can, as soon as he is sufficiently stable, we need to move Jack and, I must warn you, that entails immense risk. Ideally, I wouldn't move him at all, but . . .' Dolnick holds up his hands in surrender to the inevitable. 'We have to get him to Children's as quickly as possible.'

'Children's?' Flint asks.

'Children's Hospital in DC.'

Flint, disbelieving, says, 'Washington DC? It's *miles* away.'

'Grace, your son needs the best there is and, given his injuries, Children's Hospital is it; there is simply no question about that. And the hospital is not much more than five minutes away by air, and the state police have a medivac helicopter standing by at Andrews Air Force base, only waiting for word from us that Jack is ready to go. The members of the trauma team at Children's – that's *eighteen* people, by the way – have been alerted; they're assembling as we speak. And once Jack is on the helicopter, they will be able to constantly monitor his vital signs in real time and throughout the journey, so that by the time he arrives at Children's they will be as prepared as it is possible to be, in the circumstances.'

'DC? That's what I said,' says Loretta, 'after my youngest was shot. Like it was the other end of the world.'

Flint had lost sight and track of Loretta, wasn't even sure she was still in the room. Now she turns her head to find the nurse perched on the edge of an examination table, watching her with those extraordinary soulful eyes.

'I'm sorry, I had no idea . . .'

'No way you could.'

'What happened?'

'To my child? She's alive – in a wheelchair, but *alive*. And, honey, there isn't a day goes by that I don't give thanks that when Dr Dolnick here said we're takin' Lorraine to Children's, I had the God-given sense to know that he was right.'

Flint's euphoria is rapidly evaporating. Already she can taste the all too familiar nausea that signals a migraine attack is on its way. She rubs her forehead in pre-emptive self-defence, winces at the pain she causes.

'Can I ask you what happened to your face?' While she wasn't looking, Dolnick has advanced a couple of paces.

'Flying glass. The first bullet hit Jack while we were on the terrace of my apartment. The next two broke the glass doors while I was getting him inside.'

'How many shots in all?' asks Dolnick, hoping to distract her while he takes her face in both hands and turns her towards the light.

'Six, I think – ouch, that *hurts*!'

'Yes, well, the cuts are superficial but some of the shards are still embedded. I'm going to give you something to dull the pain and then I need to take them out.'

Flint protests that he should be attending to Jack but Dolnick shakes his head; the boy, he insists, is getting all the help he needs. She says she doesn't want anything for the pain, but Loretta is already flicking off the neck of an ampoule, filling a syringe with ten milligrams of a colourless liquid.

'Believe me,' says Dolnick, 'with all the epinephrine that's in your bloodstream, and without sedation, getting the glass out of your face is really going to hurt.'

So, reluctantly, Flint allows herself to be led to the examination table where she lies down and feels the prick of a needle entering her arm. Dolnick says that while the sedative takes effect he's just going to check her out for any other injuries – injuries she might not know she even has, not in her hyper-protective state. 'You've probably got no idea how your body can fool you,' Dolnick is saying as he gently probes her abdomen. 'We once had a patient in here . . .' but she's not really listening. She's staring at the ceiling where her imagination has projected an image of Jack's face. Not the pinched white face that is rigid with fear, but the untroubled angelic one he wore when he was last asleep in her arms and the possibility of his imminent death from any one of six or even seven life-threatening injuries was inconceivable.

And it's entirely your fucking fault – the black truth lunges at her from out of nowhere.

No!

Because you took him away from where he was safe.

Don't!

Because you put your baby in the line of fire.

'Did that hurt?' Dr Dolnick's concerned face dodges into view. 'Because when I touched you here, your whole body shuddered.'

'Rabbits,' says Flint. 'Just rabbits running over my grave.'

'Um,' says Dolnick in a tone that implies he's not convinced. He tells Flint to loosen her jeans and remove her shirt and turn over onto her stomach, and he begins probing the regions of her kidneys, and calls to Loretta for an ultrasound examination – and Flint wonders if an ultrasound machine can see the turmoil inside her head.

If you hadn't been such a selfish, stupid cow he'd be at home now, his proper home where he belongs, safe and warm and fast asleep, not thousands of miles away lying on some battle gurney in a trauma room with tubes coming out of him, trying to suck the blood out of his lungs. This is your war, not Jack's, but he's the first casualty because you put your baby in harm's way. And for what? To get back at your father because he'd taken another woman; given himself to a woman who wasn't you. And Dr P's right, isn't she: you were jealous—

No!

Yes, you were. You were jealous because another woman had come along and broken up your happy little family: John and Grace Flint, the perfect couple, practically married in all but name, except for no sex. Fine for you because you had whatever other relationships you wanted. Not so great for him though, was it? Did it ever occur to you that his life was entirely sterile, lacking any human intimacy? I don't think so. Now, finally – after how many years? – he takes a woman into his bed – and why do you care how old she is? – and it's like she's taken away something that belongs to you and you couldn't bloody stand it, could you? So you lashed out like a drunk with a broken bottle in your hand, wanting to hurt him; wanting to punish him by taking Jack away. Except it isn't your father you've punished, is it? It isn't your father they'll be putting on a helicopter, with six or seven life-threatening injuries, on his way to bloody Washington DC . . .

Dolnick says her kidneys seem to be okay but he's not yet ruling out the possibility of internal injuries. She turns onto her back and complains that she's cold and Loretta lays a blanket over her chest while the doctor goes to work on her face with tweezers and a probe and swabs of antiseptic. 'These scars on your scalp, they look like blister injuries.'

'Right.'

'You were in a fire?'

'Something like that.'

'My, you do get yourself in some wars.'

'Not on purpose, doctor. Can we talk about something else?'

'Not right now we can't because I need you to keep your face absolutely still.'

The sedative is working, apparently, because she feels no pain; no physical pain, that is. Even the tumult in her head is subsiding, perhaps because there are other thoughts distracting her.

Dolnick's caution notwithstanding, she has to speak. 'The sirens you can hear . . .' She has been listening to their approach for the last few minutes and deciding on her strategy. She knows full well what is likely to happen when their keening stops.

'Just a minute.'

'It's the police,' says Flint regardless, 'on their way here, I expect. It's very likely they think I've got a gun, which I don't, because I left it in the car – the car I stole at gunpoint in order to get here. The point is, they'll be coming through your door like—'

'Yes, I think I get your point. Now, *please*, be quiet.'

'Because you don't want scars, not on your pretty face,' – this from Loretta, sounding like a mother who knows what's best.

Flint forces herself to keep still and silent until Dolnick says, 'Okay.'

'Doctor, you know I don't have a weapon.'

'Yes.'

'But they don't know that, and somebody needs to tell them. Otherwise, they're liable to be edgy and that's when accidents can happen. And, doctor, before they arrest me, I need someone to make a phone call.'

'Yes, well, just one more,' says Dolnick evenly, his face very near to hers. 'This one is embedded in your right eyelid so, please, whatever you do, don't blink.'

The sound of sirens is no longer approaching. It's here, right outside.

'All right, nurse, if you'll finish up for me, I'll go and have a word.'

Dolnick leaves the consulting room and Flint hears the door close and, very soon afterwards, a babble of raised voices.

'The gun,' says Loretta quietly while applying a soothing cream to Flint's face. 'You get to use it?'

'I'm sorry?'

'Did you shoot the sonofabitch who did this to you?'

Not yet, thinks Flint but she merely shakes her head. 'Loretta, about that phone call,' she says.

Loretta has given her a nurse's smock to wear, to replace her bloodied shirt, and a cap to cover her head, and green rubber boots for her feet – and perhaps that's why they barely glance at Flint and don't immediately pull their guns. There are six of them, two state troopers and four uniformed police officers, filling up the reception area, bristling with weaponry and radios, and Dolnick is there with one of the surgeons who is cataloguing the extent of Jack's injuries.

'There's severe damage to the spleen,' he is saying. 'It's haemorrhaging badly and even if we knew his blood type, which we don't, we don't have a blood bank, just a couple of units of O negative, which is universal and better than nothing, but not enough. Which is why speed is essential.'

A radio crackles and one of the troopers presses with his fingers on an earpiece to better hear the transmission. 'Wait one,' he says and then, 'Chopper Trooper Two is on its way. ETA is four minutes.'

'I'll get the boy,' says Dolnick and hurries towards the trauma room, and Flint stays where she is, as inconspicuous as she can be, her back pressed against the wall, preparing herself to bear the unbearable.

The second trooper – the one who seems to her to be absurdly young – is watching her intently through tinted glasses, working out that she's not a nurse, beginning to wonder who she might be. She's watching him back, watching his right hand move slowly towards the butt of his gun, willing him to wait for a few more minutes before he embarks on his predictable routine: *Freeze! Keep your hands where I can see them* . . . And so forth.

Just wait!

The surgeon is saying, '. . . impossible to repair, like trying to sew a wodge of wet Kleenex with a . . .'

Flint is keeping her hands nowhere near her pockets, or anywhere else she might have concealed a weapon, and the young trooper's gun is still in its holster. Both are biding their time, waiting for the moment when she must reveal herself.

'. . . he can live without it, of course; it's while it's haemorrhaging that we've got a problem. If he loses much more blood, there's a severe risk of organ failure, brain damage . . .'

The rest of what he says is lost to Flint in the racket of Trooper Two approaching, the relentless chop of the rotor blades.

'. . . also damage to the tail of the pancreas, and that's a real bitch. Emergency surgeons have a saying: always eat when you can, always sleep when you can – and *never* mess with a pancreas . . .'

Flint maintains her position at the junction of the corridor, with her back pressed against the wall. Towards her comes the gurney bearing the child she never wanted but now wants more than life, Dolnick striding in the lead, his hand resting on the head rail, acting as a brake. When he reaches her he stops, and steps aside, and she can't bear to look and can't bear not to, and when she does she feels as if her heart has stopped.

Jack is lying on his back, encased in a body brace, his eyes closed. There are tubes everywhere: coming from both his nostrils and one corner of his mouth; from both sides of his chest; three more tubes from his abdomen and one from his left groin, and it seems to Flint there is barely a part of him that has not been punctured and invaded. He looks so much more tiny than when she last saw him, as though his whole body has shrunk.

She leans over the gurney and threads one hand carefully through the forest of tubes and monitoring wires and gently strokes the side of his neck with her fingers, feeling the clammy coldness of his skin, and whispers, 'It's all right, darling, Mummy's here.'

'I'm sorry, we have to go,' says Dolnick.

'I'm coming with . . .' she starts to say, but Dolnick shakes his head.

'There are weight restrictions on the helicopter, and besides . . .'

He has no need to say more. Flint senses rather than sees the approach of armed men.

She says to her son, 'Bye-bye, Jack, I'll see you very soon,' and then she stands upright and turns to face them, now using the same fingers to wipe the wetness from her eyes.

Twenty-Nine

The unlisted telephone number Flint asked Loretta to call is strictly reserved by the Financial Strike Force for agents only, and then only for use when they are on undercover missions and the wheels come off, when their cover is blown and they've gone to ground, or are otherwise in clear and immediate danger. The number rings a dedicated phone on the command desk in the Ops Room at the Marscheider Building, which is manned 24/7, and it is equivalent to a panic button in that it sets in train a series of procedures detailed on a checklist, among the first of which is *Notify Director Cutter*.

Cutter was at home in his Manhattan apartment, stripped down to his undershorts, sitting at the kitchen counter talking on the phone to Jerry Crawford who was being surprisingly upbeat about the rate of his recovery from the burn injuries. He was still in Orlando but out of hospital, living in a rented apartment with Christie while he completed his outpatient treatment and, Crawford said, he was progressing so well he thought he might be back in the office, ready to resume light duties, in just a few more weeks.

No chance, Cutter thought even as he said, 'That's terrific, Jerry!' Then his cell phone rang and he'd put Crawford on hold to answer the call and heard the voice of the night-watch supervisor identifying himself.

'Just had a call on the panic line, sir. It seems that DD Flint is down.'

'Define down?'

'The caller – female, wouldn't give her name – she said that Flint's son was shot, and Flint herself has been arrested by the police for armed robbery. She used a gun to hijack a vehicle, apparently.'

'What friggin' gun?'

'Sir, I don't have the faintest idea. The caller didn't say. She just said that Grace – that's what she called the DD, by the way – she said that Grace had wanted us to know her child has been shot by a sniper, and is on his way to Children's Hospital in Washington DC in critical condition, and Grace is in police custody for hijacking a vehicle with a gun. Then the informant rang off.'

'Did you trace the call?'

'Yes, sir. Came from Maryland, somewhere in the Bethesda region. We should have the subscriber ID verified in the next few minutes.'

'Okay, call the cops, state and local; find out who's got Flint. She's got no credentials to show she's an agent so go as high up the command chain as you can get and make damn sure they understand who and what she is, and what's happened to her boy, and that they treat her with all due consideration.'

'Understood.'

'Meantime, get somebody to call the hospital, see if they can get a heads-up on Jack. And call Rocco, tell him to get a go team together, ready to roll. I'm coming in.'

Hurrying to the bedroom to dress, Cutter remembered that Crawford was still holding on the line.

'Jerry, I'm sorry, something's come up I've gotta deal with.'

'Sure, boss. Well, say hello to the guys for me, especially Grace. How's she doing? Still chasing Hustler? Up to her neck in trouble, I'll bet.'

Flint is in the back seat of a state trooper's car, behind the grille but no longer in handcuffs. The corporal who is driving her has little idea what's going on. The first he knew of her, she was a weird-looking felon in a nurse's smock being brought into the Rockville barracks in shackles. Next thing he knew, she was in the sergeant's office wearing a borrowed trooper's shirt that looked two sizes too big for her and he was being told to get her to DC in double-quick time. And, the sergeant said, since the order came from 'on high' he should definitely 'move ass'. Well, that he can do. With four motorcycle escorts – two in front, two behind, their flashing blue strobes lighting up the night, – he's leaving rubber all along the fast lane of the interstate, eating up the miles.

She hasn't said a word, not to him. She's sitting in the back like

she was it would say she was Kathy McCarry, and without her
agent's credentials to shove in front of their faces she knows she's
as impotent as any civilian up against the power of an unyielding
bureaucracy, and her temper's broiling in a dangerous way –
dangerous for them, that is, because she's quickly calculating how
she can disarm all three of them, leave two incapacitated and force
the third to take her to Jack – when, at the left periphery of her
vision, she sees elevator doors opening and a man emerging, and it
takes only a second for her to recognise the blessed appearance of
Director Cutter.

'Excuse me,' she says, dodging under the guard's raised arm,
jabbing him in the ribs with her elbow as she passes to send him off
balance, moving fast towards the elevator and ignoring the shouted
command for her to stop – and who knows what might have
happened had Cutter not urgently replied, 'It's okay, fellers! She's
one of mine.'

'Jack was admitted to the hospital as a VOV – meaning victim of
violence – and, since he was shot by a sniper who could still be
hunting him, he was assigned an alias for his own protection.
Standard procedure.'

Cutter and Flint are riding the elevator to the floor where Jack
is still in theatre, and Cutter is attempting to explain why Flint was
very nearly arrested for the second time tonight, or even shot.

'So far as the staff is concerned, and the hospital's computer
system, Jack's name is Wendell Young, and if you don't know that
alias, if you come here asking questions about Jack Flint, you
trigger alarms, as you found out. It's not just the hospital security
guards who are on high alert. Far as I can tell, half the uniforms
out of Metropolitan PD are here. This place is under virtual
lockdown.'

'Thanks for warning me,' says Flint po-faced, as if she's angry at
him, though the truth is, she's never been more grateful for his
presence. 'But then you couldn't warn me, could you, because you
never called me back.'

'Right.'

'Because?'

Cutter thinks about his answer and then, 'Grace, there's stuff
you need to hear and it shouldn't come from me because I wouldn't

know what I was talking about. It needs to come directly from the doctors.'

'Is Jack . . .' She can't bring herself to finish the sentence.

'No, he's not dead,' says Cutter quickly. 'But there are some . . . complications.'

She doesn't know how much more of this she can take. Sensing her hopelessness, Cutter puts a broad arm around her shoulders.

'Look, Grace, there's no point in anyone pretending that your boy is not in a bad way, but you already knew that. The fact is, he *should* be dead, should have died at the scene – most likely would have died at the scene if it wasn't for the fact that you've got more guts than any guy I know; or any other gal, for that matter.'

The briefest of smiles from Flint.

'You are also the craziest person I know, which is how you were able get him out of your place and to the clinic in time, and that's the *only* reason Jack is still alive, and this is not bullshit I'm feeding you. I spoke on the phone to the doctor at the clinic – Dr Dolnick, right? – and he said he was pretty certain that if you'd called nine one one and waited for an ambulance, the chances are that Jack would have bled to death. You saved your son from that, Grace. You gave him a chance to live, and that's the very best you or anyone could have done.'

Wrong, Flint knows, *because I should never have put him in danger in the first place* – but she takes a crumb of comfort from Cutter's sop.

They've arrived at their destination and the elevator doors open and Cutter chooses this moment to add, 'About that gun.'

'Yes?'

'You were jeopardising your cover. You shouldn't have had a weapon in your apartment or anywhere else.'

'I know.'

'Bet you're glad you did, though,' and he gives her a squeeze and a glimpse of his gap-toothed grin.

The hospital administrator looks to Flint like an investment banker facing a client with serious doubts about the reliability of his advice. He is perfectly polite to her, even solicitous, but he keeps himself at an emotional safe distance, as though he expects her to turn on him and start casting blame for her loss. Given the hour, she has no idea why he's here. Cutter's doing, she supposes.

They are in the administrator's office – *You'll be more comfortable in here* – waiting for the surgeon to arrive and tell Jack's mother about the complications he's found after slicing open her son from his sternum to his navel. 'It was the only way to assess the full extent of the damage, I'm afraid,' the administrator hurried to explain, reacting to the look of astonishment on Flint's face. 'X-rays only provide a one-dimensional view and there simply wasn't time to perform a CAT scan. Or that was Marty's expert opinion,' he added with just a note of caution. Marty is Martin Berger, the head of paediatric surgery and 'the very best there is', according to the administrator. *He needs to be*, was Flint's unspoken thought.

Running out of conversation, they wait in awkward silence because there is nothing else to do. And when Cutter says, 'Why don't you stretch out on the sofa and close your eyes?' she doesn't baulk. Fearing nightmares, she is determined to stay awake – but how could any dream be worse than the reality? In self-defence she allows herself to drift into a netherworld, a kinder place somewhere beneath awareness where the sharp edges are blunter; where Jack's life is not hanging from a frayed thread but merely suspended, to save him from unneeded pain.

'Grace' – Cutter's voice bringing her back to consciousness.

There is early dawn light coming through the office windows so she knows she must have slept. She is covered with a blanket and someone has removed the rubber boots. She knows exactly where she is but, for a moment, she can't remember why – and then the knowledge comes flooding back and with it the dread, and she sits bolt upright and blurts out, '*Aldus?*' Which is not so much a question as an expression of her fears.

'Grace, this is Mr Berger.'

Marty Berger doesn't look like a surgeon who has spent too many hours toiling in an overheated operating theatre (overheated to facilitate the clotting of blood). He looks freshly showered and he's had the sensitivity to remove his gown – stained with Jack's gore, no doubt – and replace it with a tweed jacket. With his mane of thick silver hair neatly brushed back over his scalp, emphasising the height of his forehead, and intense blue eyes that are candidly examining her over the rims of a pair of pince-nez spectacles, he looks to Flint like a particularly clever professor about to lecture the class on a matter of grave concern. He coughs to clear his throat and Flint feels hers constrict.

'Do you mind if I sit down?' – a purely rhetorical question since he is now settling himself next to her on the sofa. 'Miss Flint – Grace, if I may – your son came through the operation and is in intensive care. For now, his condition is stable.'

For now?

'Can I see him?' Flint hears her question emerging in a whisper.

'Yes, of course. But before you do, there are some things you need to understand. I've been told you would wish me to be entirely frank with you. Is that right, Grace?'

She says, 'Yes,' but she's not sure he can hear her so she also nods her head.

'Physiologically, infants are very different from grown-ups – they're not adults in miniature even if that's the way they seem to us. For example, their hearts are, generally speaking, strong and resilient and can withstand the strain caused by major trauma, whereas for us . . . well, put it this way, if you had been my patient, what would have concerned me most while you were on the table would have been the risk of cardiac arrest. On the other hand,' he continues, and Flint is thinking, *here it comes*, 'an infant's lungs are both smaller and weaker and the most common danger attending major trauma is respiratory failure – and I'm sorry to tell you, that's what happened to Jack.'

Cutter has moved a discreet distance away from the sofa but he's placed himself directly in Flint's sightline and he's watching her face, waiting for the moment when she breaks down.

'The second lobe of the left lung was severely lacerated by fragments of the bullet. I have to tell you that in thirty years of paediatric surgery I've rarely seen such extensive damage – blasting damage is the only way I can describe it – and never in a child so young. Nevertheless, because a healthy lung will heal itself, I decided against removing the lobe. It was while I was repairing it that Jack went into respiratory failure.'

Her face is a mask but there must be something in her eyes, for Cutter is edging towards the sofa.

'We were able to revive him, and machines are now breathing for him, but there was a period, perhaps ninety seconds, when

Jack's brain tissue was deprived of oxygen, and I can't yet tell you what the consequences of that might be. It is possible there was no damage to the brain whatsoever. On the other hand . . .'

There is a sudden, excruciating pain in Flint's chest and her vision blurs, and by the time Cutter reaches her she is no longer conscious.

Thirty

Even in the middle of the night, on this particular night, there are more people in the Bethesda branch of Kinko's than the sniper had expected, far more than she is comfortable with. Still, patience being one of the fundamentals of her trade, she connects her laptop to Kinko's WiFi hotspot and whiles away the time surfing innocuous websites, waiting until most of the other customers have left. Then, when there is nobody within ten feet of her, she fires up her Trojan Horse hacking software, loads the page on which she has recorded the Internet Protocol addresses of every hospital with an A&E department within a twenty-five-mile radius of Bethesda and begins her systematic campaign to access their patients' records.

She knows she hit the target, knows he should be dead, but doubts have emerged and she needs to make sure.

When she could no longer see what she was aiming at she had chosen to abandon the mission with the outcome still uncertain. *Don't kill the woman, just the kid*, the client had said – and he was *very* insistent on that. So, after the lights went out she'd fired two token fuck-you rounds into the target's apartment at well above head height and then disassembled her rifle, removed her latex gloves and the rest of her protective clothing, packed everything away in her knapsack, withdrawn from her position on the roof, taken the emergency stairs to the ground floor, slipped out of the service entrance, strolled around the block and joined the onlookers gathering on the sidewalk opposite the entrance to Flint's condominium; not an obvious sociopath, just another rubberneck exercising her fundamental right to be curious.

'What's happening?' she'd asked of nobody in particular.

'Some crazy woman with a gun stole that guy's SUV; that guy talking to the cops, the one who's fit to be tied.'

'Jesus!' she'd said. 'Everywhere you look, there are crazies.'

'Yeah,' another voice from the crowd, 'well, you might get crazy if someone had just shot your kid.'

'He shot her kid?'

'Not him. Some other asshole.'

'Why'd she steal the car?'

'To take her kid to the hospital.'

'She couldn't call nine one one?'

'Right. And the last time you called nine one one, how long did they make you wait?'

'But the kid's alive?'

'Why would you take a dead kid to the hospital?'

'Beats me,' she'd said, and edged her way to the back of the crowd and slipped away into the night – and, in the investigation to come, what will both surprise and dismay the investigators is the lack of impression she made. Between them, the FBI and the Montgomery County police will quickly identify, trace and interview nine people who were part of the crowd of onlookers and, as a result, will conclude, unhelpfully, that the suspected sniper was a white female aged somewhere between twenty-five and fifty; she was tall, or not so tall; she was skinny, or of average weight, or a little thick around the thighs; her eyes were dark blue, or black, or maybe an olive green; her hair was short and brown, or fair, or mousy; she was wearing jeans and a loose top that was either lemon or pink; she was carrying a knapsack or a canvas holdall, or nothing at all.

'She's goddamn Everywoman!' Cutter will say to Rocco Morales after he's read the investigators' report. 'What do you think the chances are that any of these deep-fried gumbos could pick her out of a line-up?'

'About zero,' Morales will reply.

She doesn't really know the area and the pecking order of the emergency rooms; doesn't know the local protocols as to who gets taken where when they're hurt. So she wastes some time hacking into the computer systems of hospitals in Montgomery County, and coming up with nothing, before turning her attention to the District of Columbia and targeting Children's. While her software searches for an open, unprotected port on the network, she considers what the client's reaction might be if she has somehow failed to kill Flint's child. That she won't be paid the balance of her fee is probably the least of her problems, she guesses. Then the appearance of a hash mark on the laptop's screen grabs her attention, telling her the software has found a way in. She is now free to roam the records of Children's Hospital as if she were there.

At the root of the system where she can conduct a global search she types in the child's name and hits the Enter key, and is not discouraged when the system responds *No match found*. She has good reason to know that victims of violence are sometimes admitted to hospital under a pseudonym. The only time until now she wasn't sure she'd made a clean kill – three years ago, in Tucson, Arizona – she'd followed the ambulance that had taken her target to hospital, and gone back two days later with fake press credentials to discover that the victim, an Albanian named Rexhep Kastrioti, was listed in the hospital's records as plain Ted Bryson.

Now she wants a list of that day's surgical admissions to Children's. It takes her Trojan software countless attempts to pose the question in the correct syntax but since this happens at lightning speed she is quickly rewarded with a list of seven names. Six of the seven patients were evidently admitted for day surgery because the records say they have also been discharged. That leaves only one candidate, a Wendell Young whose given date of birth does not match that of Jack Flint – but then, neither did Ted Bryson's DoB match that of Rexhep Kastrioti in the Tucson database. She asks to see Wendell's record, and is told that it is protected by a password which she must provide, and Trojan goes to work to crack the code on her behalf, and in less than one minute Wendell's record is on her screen.

It is succinct, even bare.

Wendell Young lives with his parents, Betsy and Bill, on 36th Street in the Georgetown area of DC, apparently, but no house number is given. The Youngs do not have a telephone, apparently – or no number is provided. Also not provided is any medical history, nor the name of the referring physician, nor details of the Young family's health insurance. Wendell was admitted to Children's tonight with 'acute breathing difficulties' – but what the diagnosis is, what treatment he's receiving, where in the hospital he is presently located, the record doesn't say.

Fake? A bit of camouflage hastily cobbled together without much subtlety or imagination?

She thinks so. Logging out of the system, cutting the connection to Children's, she already knows how she will swiftly, definitively establish that the Young family of 36th Street do not exist; that, in reality, Wendell Young is Jack Flint, and that she now knows where she will find him. But first she has a message to send, a message that is overdue.

On the laptop she logs on to her Instant Messenger service and clicks on the only name in her 'buddy list' and types, *You there?*

Yes.

I hear there's been a terrible accident: a child's been shot.

Tragic. Dead?

Not necessarily.

!!!

Not yet. In hospital, I think.

You'll be visiting, I expect?

As soon as conditions allow.

Good. And the mother?

Traumatised, I imagine.

Nothing worse?

No.

Then all will be well after your visit?

I'll take a gift.

Do that. And one more from me.

I think only one gift will be necessary.

Even so. Just to be sure.

OK.

:-)

Mid Compton

Thirty-One

John Flint is sitting on a stool at the kitchen counter when Sally comes downstairs. He looks wrecked: his face gaunt, his hair dishevelled, the stubble on his face the same tinge of grey as his skin, which has the curious effect of making it seem like a disfigurement. Protruding from his pyjama bottoms he sees an old man's feet, the toes twisted and knobbled. His fingers, also bony, are curled around a mug of black tea that is hours old, stone-cold. He is unaware of Sally's presence until she speaks to him in that inquiring, slightly shrill tone of hers that is beginning to get on his nerves: 'John?'

'Hello, old thing,' he says, switching on his tired smile.

'What are you doing?'

Her question baffles him. It is surely perfectly obvious what he's doing.

'How long have you been down here?' she presses.

'Oh, not long, I think.'

'*John?*'

'I couldn't sleep,' he admits.

'Again, for the umpteenth time,' she says. 'John, this *can't* go on.'

Unlike him she is radiant: buffed and crisp, fresh from the shower. She is wearing one of his twill shirts over a pair of tight blue jeans that emphasise the shape and length of her legs; no make-up and no jewellery, except for a simple gold pendant around her creamy neck. She looks virginal and so damn young and so out of his reach that he wonders, not for the first time, what on earth she's doing in his kitchen, her arms folded under her breasts, scolding him like a wife.

'You need to see somebody, John.'

'Yes, well . . . I'll drop in on Dr Potter, ask him for some sleeping pills, or something.'

'No! That's not what I mean. You need to talk to someone about what's going on inside your head, what's eating at you like a cancer. Pills won't fix this, John. It's like you're in mourning but you won't – you can't – grieve. You need professional help. You need to talk to somebody about . . . about Grace.'

There, she's said it now – the name he had forbidden them to mention. He glares at her, feeling a swell of anger that should be sufficient to send him flouncing out of the kitchen, out onto the terrace and down the steep bank to the barn, locking the door behind him, locking her out. If he could just summon up the energy to get off the stool; if only he wasn't so damn tired.

'Talk to me,' she says, and her pretty face is unexpectedly such a picture of misery that he can't bear to look at her.

'Please, Sally,' he says.

'*Please, John,*' she replies. 'John, if you love me, then please, please talk to me.'

'It's not about Gracie,' he hears himself saying, the truth revealing itself to him as much as to her. 'Not really. Of course I miss her, of course I do, but the fact is, Gracie left me a long time ago. It's the loss of little Jack I can't stand. I don't know why, I can't explain, but I feel as though Grace has stolen part of my soul and I hate her for that, and hating my daughter, that's what's tearing me apart and . . .'

And then the phone rings and, after a moment's hesitation, Sally answers it – and John Flint is momentarily distracted by the sound of car engines coming up the drive – and the next thing he knows, she is saying, 'Who's speaking, please?' and 'What's it about?' and 'Just a minute, please,' and then she's covering the mouthpiece with her hand, and there's a look of such intense unease in her eyes that he comes off the stool, starting towards her, and then she tells him what he doesn't want to hear: 'It's a Commander Glenning, the police. He says something's happened to Grace . . . to Grace and Jack.'

Armed policemen in the kitchen; four of them, wearing body armour and carrying stubby automatic machine pistols, herding Sally and John away from the windows.

John Flint resisting, roaring on the phone, 'Tom, what the bloody hell is going on?'

Tom Glenning trying to calm him down: 'John, please, just do as they say.'

'What's happened to Jack?' Jack, mind you; Gracie not his first thought.

'In a minute. Just *move*.'

Now they're in the hallway, not a window in sight. Even so they're told to keep their heads down, to sit on the floor, stay where they are.

'Tom, for God's sake, man. Tell me what's happened.'

'I'll tell you what I know, which isn't very much. An hour ago I had a call from Aldus Cutter. Jack's been shot—'

'Jack? *Shot?*'

'He's in hospital, in critical but stable condition, as is Grace – in hospital, I mean, in stable but *not* critical condition. She passed out with chest pains and they thought she'd had a heart attack. Seems that was a false alarm but, just to be sure, they're running some tests and keeping her under observation. Cutter says she should be out in a day or so, all being well.'

John Flint is trying very hard to comprehend but he feels like a dyslexic with a phonological deficit because he can't make sense of the words. Sally reaches out to touch his face with her hand and whispers, 'John, what's happened?' and all he can do is stare at her; stare at her and shake his head as if to say he doesn't know.

'Are you there, John?' – Glenning on the phone.

'I don't . . . I don't understand,' says Dr Flint, though shocking images are slowly forming inside his head. From the sounds he hears he is also becoming aware that the police are searching his house.

'Listen, I know this is hard for—'

'Where was Jack shot?'

'Where? In the back, I believe.'

'No! *Where?*'

'Oh, I understand. In Maryland, just over the line from Washington DC, in or just outside Grace's apartment in—'

Dr Flint interrupts again. 'Grace doesn't live in Maryland,' he insists, grasping at the wild idea that this is all some terrible mistake. 'She lives in New York.'

'Not any more she doesn't, or not at present. Even before she took Jack to the States, she was living in Maryland as part of an undercover operation. That's as much as I can tell you, at least on the phone.'

Grace living undercover with Jack? Was Jack a part of her cover? Is that why she took him away?

Sounds of hurried footsteps coming down the stairs, one of the policeman coming into the hallway. He's half Dr Flint's age, if that, but he speaks to him in a tone of absolute authority. 'All right, sir, the house and grounds are clear. Now, what I need you and Ms Beaumont to do is go upstairs and pack some things, whatever you'll need for four or five days away, maybe a week – but keep it to one suitcase each if you can, please.'

'What?' For all the sense he's making to Flint, the man could be speaking in Dutch.

'And I need you to hurry. I want us out of here in five minutes.'

'Leave? I can't leave here,' says Flint as though in the midst of all this madness it's the most preposterous thing he's heard. But the policeman is already striding away from him, heading towards the front door.

Into the phone Flint says, 'Tom, what in heaven's name are the police doing here? They say we've got to—'

'I was coming to that,' says Glenning. 'John, you need to understand that Jack was shot by a sniper with a high velocity rifle from medium to long range. This was no accident and Cutter says it has all the hallmarks of a professional hit, an attempted assassination, and that makes it likely, very likely, that Jack *was* the target. In other words, somebody was trying to get at Grace by killing her son and since they've failed – please God they've failed – they may try again by going after another member of her family, which could mean you. Cutter's very strong advice to me was to place you under protection, to move you somewhere safe until he's got some idea who's behind this, and I agree with that advice. I also agree that Sally, Miss Beaumont, should go with you because, in your absence, her life may also be in danger.'

'This is all so . . . so . . . bloody incredible!'

'No it's not, John, it's absolutely real, I'm afraid. Please, do as I tell you and go with the officers. They're going to take you to a safe place where I'll join you as soon as I can, once I know more about Jack's condition.'

Dr Flint has lost all will to resist.

'John?'

'Very well,' he says, defeat in his voice, as though he is accepting something as inevitable as death.

'Good. I'll see you later.'

'Tom? Please tell me something. How could Grace be so bloody wilful? How could she do this to Jack?'

New York

Thirty-Two

It is now eight days since her son was shot – a lifetime for Flint, Cutter is sure. Since discharging herself from Georgetown University Hospital – *There's absolutely nothing wrong with me*, she'd insisted when he'd asked if that was wise – she has spent every moment at Children's watching over Jack, who is being kept alive in a sterile bubble, watched over in turn by a police guard that has been doubled, following the detection of a successful attempt to hack into the hospital's computer system. There are also two minders from the strike force, Duncan and Fran, a taciturn pair sent by Cutter to keep a sharp eye on security and run errands for Flint, fetching clothes and toiletries and whatever else she needs from her apartment, bringing her food that she usually neglects to eat.

For fear of introducing infection, she cannot touch Jack or even get close to him. She watches him from eight feet away through a glass wall, perpetually scanning the monitors that will detect any sign of impending organ failure. The nurses could tell her that there is no point to her vigilance, since the monitors are wired to alarms that will sound instantly at the nurses' station, but they do not say that because they seem to understand her visceral need just to be there; perhaps to make some small amends for the harm she's caused. They have placed a camp bed on her side of the glass wall so she can sleep, though she rarely does, and never for long. She passes most of the time sitting upright in a hard wooden chair, her knees pressed against the glass, staring at her son.

But not today, for Cutter has called a council of war at the Marscheider Building – a 'must attend' meeting of all department heads and lead agents to urgently review Operation Payback – and Flint has asked to be present. Consulted by Cutter, Jack's surgeon, Martin Berger, had urged him to agree. 'Because the state of limbo her child is in, it could last for weeks, or even months, and she needs to get out of here, get some air,' he said. So Flint is on the Amtrak Metroliner, on her way to New York, dressed in a smart charcoal-grey trouser suit that Fran has selected from her wardrobe. She is escorted by four armed strike force agents who have orders to protect her against any perceived threat. 'At any cost,' Cutter had said to Rocco Morales. 'Meaning, whatever happens, they're to get her here alive.'

Among the strike force agents and support staff there is an air of edgy anticipation pending Flint's arrival. The detail of what happened in Maryland may be sketchy but everybody who works in the Marscheider Building knows that the Deputy Director (Operations) has compromised a major operation – and, at impromptu meetings around the water coolers, there is a general consensus that Flint may have finally pushed her luck too far. On the other hand, it is universally known that her child is on life support, and Cutter's not the kind of guy to kick one of his pilgrims when they're down, least of all Flint. The consensus is, she will draw indefinite compassionate leave, with the emphasis on indefinite. Question is, how will Flint respond?

Precisely on time the Metroliner arrives at Penn Station, where Cutter has provided an armoured SUV and a back-up car to bring her the couple of miles across town and, at just after 3 p.m., the escorts sneak her into headquarters through the unmarked basement entrance and take her by elevator directly to the fifth-floor conference room where eleven people are gathered; waiting for her, apparently.

All conversation dies as she enters the room and everybody's staring at her with frozen faces, as though somebody has stopped the tape, and she knows she looks like hell – but what the hell do they expect? And she's about to ask them exactly that when Cutter says, 'Welcome home, Grace,' and immediately the ice melts and she's aware of burgeoning smiles and a babble of murmured greetings and Kate Barrymore, the chief terrier, comes hurrying towards her with arms wide open to offer a hug.

'Great,' says Kate. 'It's really cool to have you back' – and Flint allows herself to think that perhaps she can get through this after all.

*   *   *

'Rocco, you're first up,' says Cutter. 'You wanna bring us up to speed?'

It's a rhetorical question, for Rocco Morales is already poised alongside the large screen onto which he will project his presentation. He is armed with a laser pointer and a remote control which he uses first to dim the room lights. Then the press of a second button and on the screen in blood-red letters a foot high appear the words THE CRIME SCENE, a title that dissolves to reveal a photograph of the apartment terrace. It has been taken from the sniper's perspective – perhaps even the sniper's position – and it shows an upturned café table, a chair lying on its side, two sliding doors with gaping holes and the litter of glass.

'And the interior,' says Rocco, and Flint sees her living room looking as if it's been hit by a bomb – glass everywhere, the interior of the armoire shattered, bullet holes in the wall, table lamps lying dead on the floor. She must have made some sound for Cutter touches her arm and inquires, 'You okay?'

'Uh-huh,' she says – only a half-truth.

'Seven rounds fired,' Morales is saying, 'not including the pistol rounds expended by DD Flint to extinguish the lights. The bullet that struck the victim shattered on impact, as it was designed to do, so that although the entry point was . . . here' – Flint snaps her eyes shut but not quite quickly enough to avoid a glimpse of Jack's naked back with the red dot of the laser pointer zeroing in on the wound – 'and the trajectory was downwards, most of the fragments travelled vertically, toward the chest cavity and the lungs. As you can see, the bullet fragments recovered from the victim are extremely small' – Flint opens her eyes and sees on the screen a close-up of shards of metal that look like pieces of gravel – 'and about all the forensics folks can tell us is that it was twenty-two calibre and soft-nose or hollow-point. Oh,' adds Morales, 'and one more thing . . .' and then he pauses, glancing around the room as though to make sure he has everyone's attention. 'It was like no other bullet I've seen since the Gulf, and then only once.'

'Rocco,' snaps Cutter, 'you can spare us your theatrics.'

'Yes, sir, but this is important. There was no way to put these pieces back together, no way to tell which fragments were part of the core and which were on the surface. So, forensics put each and every last piece under an electron microscope, and looked at them

from each and every angle, and what they *didn't* find were any
scoring marks. If you believe in miracles, then this bullet travelled
down a rifled barrel at five thousand feet per second and exited the
muzzle as smooth as a baby's bott— oh, shit! I'm sorry, Grace.'

'It's okay, Rocco' – and Flint summons up a small smile to tell
him that she means it. 'You think the shooter was using sabots?'

'That's exactly what I think. Look' – and Morales brings another
image onto the screen – 'these are the other six bullets the shooter
fired, and they didn't disintegrate. Okay, one through four are
pretty badly chewed up but look at these two, which were
recovered from the wall.' Morales shows them a huge blow-up of
two virtually pristine bullets side by side that look to Flint like the
menacing nose cones of ballistic missiles emerging from a silo. 'In
my opinion, there's no question about it,' Morales continues. 'Each
round the shooter fired was encased in a plastic jacket, or sabot, so
the bullet wasn't scored by the rifling as it spun in the barrel. The
jackets would have disintegrated on exit from the muzzle and the
bullets went on their way without a single mark to identify the
weapon that fired them.'

'Specialist bullets?' Flint asks.

'Believe it.'

'How special?'

'Handmade. You won't find sabot bullets in your local Wal-
Mart.'

Cutter says, 'And the six bullets that were fired into the
apartment, why didn't they disintegrate?'

'Because they weren't soft-nose or hollow-point.'

'Which tells you what?'

'That only the first shot was intended to kill. The next six
rounds that went into the magazine, they were regular rounds the
shooter loaded for insurance; for a just-in-case.'

'In case of what?'

Morales hesitates and glances at Flint and then looks to Cutter
as if to say, *She really doesn't need to know*, but Cutter shows no
sign of receiving the message.

Another look at Cutter that says, *Okay, don't blame me*, and
then Morales takes a deep breath and answers the question. 'In case
the first shot wasn't instantly lethal,' he says. 'The shooter was a
pro and pros know that hitting the sweet spot on a target at a range

of a little over one thousand feet – and I'll come to how we know the range – hitting the spot at that kind of range is never a guarantee, no matter how good you are. The trajectory of a bullet at that distance isn't flat; it's an arc, and the precise curve of the arc is dictated by several factors, some of which you can measure and some of which you can't. For example, both the ambient air temperature and the degree of humidity will influence the trajectory, and those you can measure, more or less. But the strength and direction of the wind is the greatest influence, and when both the shooter and the target are in and surrounded by high-rise buildings, the shooter has a problem because the wind speed and direction is going to vary significantly. At one hundred feet it might be ten mph from the east, and at three hundred feet, twelve mph from the south-east, and at six-hundred feet, no damn wind at all. The point is, you can't *know*. The best you can do is look for telltales – the breeze in the trees, if there are any; dust swirling in the air; curtains moving in open windows – and make a guesstimate of the likely arc, and adjust your overshoot accordingly. You always overshoot, by the way: cross hairs fixed on a point right between the target's eyes – that's just movie bullshit. But I'm talking now about millimetres, up or down. You aim at the head, and you guess the arc wrong, and you're just as likely to shoot off the target's toes. So, that's what I mean about insurance. The shooter would have aimed for the head, because that's instantaneous death, but also allowed for a hit lower down on the target. Now, anywhere you hit, you're going to cause a problem because a twenty-two calibre soft-nose will drop a moose in its tracks. But, depending on where you hit, it may take a while before you achieve the desired effect. What I'm saying is this: in the circumstances, the shooter couldn't be certain of a clean kill and, just in case, the other six rounds were in the magazine to keep DD Flint's head down; to keep her occupied and prevent her from getting help . . . until the target bled to death.'

Flint is feeling nauseous. She needs to get to the bathroom fast.

'Okay, pilgrims,' says Cutter glimpsing her pallor. 'Let's take a break.'

Flint is back from the bathroom, looking even paler. What Morales now has on the screen is a three-dimensional computer simulation of her apartment, and of her and Jack. She is on the terrace, represented by what looks like one of those mannequins in a shop window waiting to be dressed; naked, with an appropriately hairless head and impossibly pert breasts. (*I wish*, she thinks to herself.) Jack is represented by what looks like a large doll, also naked, cradled in his mother's arms with his back towards the shooter.

'Because DD Flint was seated,' Morales is saying, 'and because we don't know the precise position in which she was holding the victim' – and on the screen the head of the doll-like figure moves from her breasts to above her left shoulder and back again – 'the angle of the entry wound tells us nothing about the trajectory of the bullet, and therefore nothing about the shooter's position. Same is true of the next four shots, the regular rounds the shooter fired, because they ricocheted all over the room. But the last two rounds – five and six, or six and seven, depending on how you're counting – that's a different story. They penetrated here,' Morales says as the computer simulation zooms in on the far wall of Flint's living room, 'four inches apart. This wall is made of two sheets of high-grade gypsum plasterboard and the bullets left a trace that is almost perfect. So, we know that the last two rounds travelled at a downward angle of twenty-one point three degrees, which allows us to calculate the trajectory with a lot of confidence, and which puts the shooter . . .' the simulation on the screen swivels and Flint is looking out of her living room, across and over the terrace, following the converging tracks of two thin blue lines. 'Right here,' says Morales, the red dot of his laser pointer settling unwaveringly on the roof of a distant building. 'This is a condo on Willard Avenue.'

'And you say that's one thousand feet?' asks Cutter.

Morales presses a button on the remote control and a third line races across the screen, from a spot on the rooftop to the back of the doll-like figure, while a counter measures the distance in bold red digits: 1076.39ft is the final calculation.

'You found the sniper's exact position.'

'Yes, sir. As I've indicated, the shooter was a pro, and professionals clean up after themselves, but that's not so easy to do when it's dark and you can't use any form of illumination, and you're in a hurry to get out of there. Here,' he says – and the screen now shows a close-up aerial view of a part of the rooftop where there is an air-conditioning unit – 'we found traces of gunshot residue in cone-shaped patterns, which tells us where the muzzle was. And, just behind the cones, we found burlap fibres and a few grains of quartz, which tells us that the shooter used a sand sock to line up the shot, which is classic sniper technique, and—'

'A sock? You've lost me,' says Cutter.

'Well, it's called a sock but it's actually a homemade bag that you fill with sand to provide support for the barrel. Then, when you're lining up the shot and you want to fine-tune it, you just squeeze the bag to raise or lower the muzzle by a millimetre or so. It's not rocket science but it sure is effective.'

'Where'd the sand come from?' Cutter asks.

'Don't know, sir, not yet. The quartz particles we found are small and well rounded, which suggests water attrition, and they contain fairly high concentrations of salt, which suggests sea water and therefore a beach. Which beach, we don't know. The forensics guys are still working on that.'

'Okay, make sure you keep on top of it. Kate, you wanna come in here?'

'Yes, sir,' she says brightly – and of course she does, for Kate Barrymore loves a stage more than anyone Flint knows. With a quick smile for Cutter, the head of Research and Analysis claims the podium from Rocco, clutching a batch of folders that she and her fellow terriers have compiled and that Flint knows she will have no need to consult. Like all born performers, Kate will have mastered her lines perfectly.

Another brief smile, this one for the room, and then Kate begins. 'This is Joanna Fox' – and she presses a button on the remote control and on the screen appears a photograph of a woman's face; a middle-aged woman with short brown hair that leaves her ears exposed, a broad forehead, large green eyes that are looking into the middle distance, an aquiline nose and generous red lips that are pursed in a half-smile.

'The shooter,' says Kate with rhetorical flourish.

Now Kate is literally into her stride. Unlike Rocco, who stands resolutely at the podium throughout his presentations, she is a pacer, never still. She moves this way and that, left and right, sometimes facing her audience, sometimes turning away, twisting on her heels, punctuating her monologue with expressive hand gestures and sudden flicks of her head. She is tall and slim with graceful limbs, and the men in the room cannot take their eyes off her.

'Outside of the Marine Corps,' she is saying, 'most police SWAT teams and, we have good reason to believe, the CIA, professional snipers are a rare breed. In civilian life, hit men are a fact of life, especially in the drugs trade. And, all too often, some disgruntled citizen armed with a rifle will go on the rampage. But long-distance shooters who kill for a living – the kind of professional killer the victim never sees – they're uncommon, except in novels and Hollywood plot lines. In fact, in the last forty years there have been only eighteen documented cases of professional snipers operating in the entire United States.'

Is that excluding Rocco? Flint finds herself thinking, wondering about his time with Delta Force.

'And *female* snipers are practically unheard of,' Kate continues. 'Okay, in times of war, the Soviets, the Turks, the French Resistance, the Viet Cong, the Serbs and, most recently, the Islamists in Chechnya are all said to have recruited and trained women to act as snipers, but these are mostly unsubstantiated claims. Outside of war and within the US – and until now – no long-range assassination, or assassination attempt, has *ever* been reliably attributed to a female shooter.' Kate works the remote control and, with perfect timing, pirouettes to face the screen. 'With one possible exception.'

On the screen appears a grainy image of an overweight man wearing a short-sleeved lemon-coloured shirt over baggy shorts, ducking his head as he stoops to enter the back seat of a shiny white stretch limousine.

'Three years ago in Tucson, Arizona,' says Kate. 'This is Peter Slater, aka Peter Slavitch. On May twenty-third, a grand jury in Tucson returned a true bill charging him with running a Continuing Criminal Enterprise: namely, the largest prostitution ring in the south-west United States that relied, almost exclusively, on the services of illegal aliens. On the morning of May twenty-fourth, Slater was arrested at his home by the Tucson vice squad. That same day, he appeared in state court and was remanded in custody in lieu of bond of one million dollars. During the next three weeks, Slater's lawyers negotiated a plea bargain with the States Attorney's office whereby, in return for a recommended maximum sentence of ten years, he agreed to provide sworn testimony to the grand jury against the main supplier of the women he exploited. The day after Slater finished testifying to the grand jury his bail was reduced to fifty thousand dollars, which was part of the deal. He was released, he went home. An hour or so later he went outside to check on his pool – and took a twenty-two calibre bullet through the throat.'

Someone at the back of the room says, 'Ouch!' and someone else says, 'You can't say ouch with a hole in your throat,' and there is a murmur of laughter. Kate looks momentarily flustered, and even Flint manages a smile, but Cutter is not in the mood.

'Cut it out,' he says, without turning his head to identify the culprits. 'Kate, go ahead.'

On the screen there now appears a succession of photographs showing the exterior of a large pink stucco mansion set in a hollow of desert scrub and tall saguaro cacti surrounded by rocky foothills. The swimming pool at the rear of the house is diamond-shaped and the area around it, paved with pale marble tiles, is protected by endless yards of 'Do Not Enter' crime-scene tape. The crude outline of a body, drawn in lurid orange chalk, shows the approximate position where Slater fell.

'The police never established precisely where the shot came from, though they narrowed it down to somewhere in these rocks,' Kate says, using the laser pointer to indicate the sniper's possible positions. 'Which makes the range somewhere around one thousand feet, which may be nothing more than a coincidence – or maybe not. Maybe that's this shooter's preferred range.'

'And maybe it isn't,' says Cutter, discouraging speculation in what is supposed to be a factual briefing. 'Did Slater die at the scene?' he wants to know, bringing Kate back to the basics.

'No, sir. He made it alive to the critical care unit at El Dorado Hospital and survived for two days, albeit in a coma. And this is where our shooter – possible shooter – enters the story. Two days after Slater was hit, a woman who said she was a reporter for the *Tucson Citizen* turned up at the hospital asking questions about him. She was carrying press credentials in the name of Joanna Fox which, fortunately, some bright secretary at the hospital had the sense to scan into her computer. Now, the staff at El Dorado had instructions to deny any knowledge of a Peter Slater – who'd been admitted under a pseudonym – which is what they did, and the woman apparently left the building. However, an hour or so later, an alarm was triggered, indicating an unauthorised attempt to enter Slater's room. Eight minutes after that, his blood pressure dropped through the floor and he went into cardiac arrest. There was no way to save him.'

What little colour there is left in Flint's complexion seeps away. 'You mean she got to him?' she asks in a tone of what is either disbelief or dread.

'The hospital says not, and so do the police, and there was no evidence that Slater's life-support equipment was tampered with. And, since the bullet had nicked his trachea, and both of his lungs had collapsed, he was always a prime candidate for heart failure. But . . .' Kate allows her caveat to hang in the air.

'Grace,' says Cutter, breaking the heavy silence that follows, 'nobody's gonna get to Jack.'

How can you be so bloody sure? she wants to know, but since the question is futile she keeps it to herself.

'In any event,' says Kate, ready to move on, 'immediately after Slater's death, the police learned about the visit of the supposed reporter, checked with the *Citizen*, and discovered that she didn't exist. And then, credit where it's due, they moved amazingly quickly. They copied this picture' – the image of Joanna Fox returns to the screen – 'from the credentials the secretary had scanned and circulated it with an all-points alert. Within thirty minutes they had checkpoints on the interstate and all other major roads leading out of Tucson, and at the airport. They kept them in place until they had shown her photograph at every hotel and motel and car rental agency, and just about every gas station in the area, and had it broadcast by every TV station, and published in the paper – and they came up with precisely nothing. Except for five people at the hospital, nobody remembered seeing her. She came out of nowhere, did whatever it was she did, and vanished.'

Kate pauses and looks about the room, waiting for the mood of anticlimax to build, and then she adds, 'Until six days ago, in Friendship Heights' – and now she brings onto the screen a new photograph that shows what appears at first sight to be a shadow in a stairwell. And, unbidden, Rocco Morales takes his cue and joins Kate at the podium for what Flint supposes is now going to be a two-handed dog and pony show.

Rocco goes first. 'This is the emergency staircase of the Willard Avenue condo,' he says, 'which goes from street level to the roof, from where the shots were fired. The picture was taken by a fixed security camera, located immediately above and inside the street exit doors at eighteen ten, according to the time stamp, approximately four hours before Jack Flint was shot.'

Now Kate. 'The surveillance cameras at the Willard building are pretty antiquated. They're still cameras, not movie, and they're not triggered by motion sensors; they're simply programmed to take a picture every thirty seconds – and, as you can see, the image quality is, well, lousy.'

'But this is the same image digitally enhanced . . .' Rocco pauses while Kate works the remote control, and the picture on the screen sharpens and enlarges, and the shadow in the stairwell transforms into the back view of a distinct human form climbing the stairs, dressed in what looks like an urban camouflage suit, '. . . and what we can see now is an intruder, possibly the shooter.'

Male or female, it's impossible to tell.

Then another picture flashes onto the screen and Rocco continues, 'Okay, this shot is from the same camera in the Willard stairwell, taken more than four hours later, at twenty-two twenty-three, according to the time stamp. Which, as best as we can tell, was approximately five minutes after the last round was fired into DD Flint's apartment.' The picture is of a woman descending the stairs towards the camera. She is wearing jeans and a T-shirt rather than a camouflage suit, but it's what she's carrying in her right hand that grabs Flint's attention. 'Now, how can we be pretty sure this is the same party who entered the building?'

'The bag,' Flint says flatly, and Rocco raises his arms in apparent surrender, and Kate grins, and Cutter says, 'What's the joke?'

'No joke, sir. Kate and I, we had a bet on whether anyone would spot it, and I just lost. You see, the bag the subject is carrying' – and on the screen the woman's right hand and the bag it is holding are hugely enlarged – 'is made of the same camouflage material as the suit, and when the subject entered the building she was wearing the bag on her back, which is why in this picture' – the back view of the intruder comes onto the screen – 'it's pretty difficult to spot. Or so I thought,' he adds.

'Dumb bet,' says Cutter, and Rocco acknowledges that truth with a rueful smile directed at Flint, but she's not paying attention.

She's on her feet, slowly approaching the screen, saying to Kate, 'Put up the front view again,' and then, 'Now pull up the face,' and then, 'Now, put up the Tucson suspect and pull up the face.'

Side by side, two giant faces stare indifferently into the room – or is it one face, photographed from different angles, in differing conditions of light and three years apart? Flint can see some resemblance but just as many differences.

'Have you run these through FRT?' she asks.

Kate pouts as though she's disappointed. 'I was coming to that,' she says.

'Well, you've arrived. What was the similarity score?'

'Low' – said with just a hint of petulance.

'How low?'

'Two point three,' which, in terms of the face recognition technology the strike force uses, means beyond question *these subjects do not match*.

'Come on, Kate!' Flint snaps. She's getting annoyed because she'd bet her pension that Kate's dog and pony show isn't going to end on any such dismal conclusion, and she wants to know the bottom line *now*. 'Just tell us what you know.'

Kate glances at Cutter to see whose side he's on, and gets no response, and so she admits, 'That was the result the first time we ran them through the software.'

'And?'

'Then we programmed some algorithms to compensate for the differences in image quality, image size, lighting conditions and the angles of attack, and then we ran the pictures again and got . . .' Kate can't resist a teasing pause. 'And then we got a nine point four.'

'*Jesus!*' somebody exclaims, and Kate smiles as though she's won a prize. In the software programme the terriers have designed, a similarity score of 9.4 is about as close as it gets to a perfect match.

'What are the chances you could be wrong?'

'About one in one billion,' says Kate. 'So, beyond statistical

doubt, Joanna Fox and the Willard intruder are one and the same
– and so is she,' and Kate brings onto the screen moving pictures
that are startling in their clarity: the back and top of a man's head
in the foreground; beyond him, a woman standing at a counter, full
face to the camera, her lips mouthing monosyllables as she hands
over cash and receives change. 'This is security tape from the
Bethesda branch of Kinko's, the all-night copy shop, which is where
the hacker was traced to. She used a laptop and a wireless card to
connect to Kinko's WiFi Hotspot and get on the internet, and then
used some Trojan software to find a back door into the system at
Children's Hospital.'

Standing motionless before the screen, Flint watches the woman
turn away from the counter as though she has completed her
business, then change her mind; turn again towards the camera to
ask the counter assistant for something else. 'Freeze it, will you,
and pull up the face,' Flint says – and now she is staring into the
magnified eyes of Jack's would-be assassin. There is amusement in
those large eyes and her mouth is open, revealing upper teeth that
are slightly irregular, just the wrong side of perfect. The smile
makes her face pretty in an unspectacular way. She looks so
bloody *normal*; just another late-night customer at Kinko's, using
her charm to cajole some small favour out of the assistant.

Kate is saying, 'Now, paradoxically, the similarity score between
the Willard and the Kinko's images was only eight point two
because . . .' but Flint's not really listening. She is using all her
powers of concentration to burn the unique features of that face
into her long-term memory: the width of the forehead, the distance
between the eyes, the depth of the philtrum; characteristics that no
amount of disguise or cosmetic surgery can alter. Glimpsed on the
street, in a plane, on the TV news, in a file – tomorrow or in twenty
years' time – Flint is determined this is a face she will instantly
recognise.

Cutter knows what she's doing, and waits until she's satisfied.
Then, 'Questions?'

'I've got three,' says Flint.

'Shoot.'

'One, what's her real name?'

'We don't know,' says Kate. 'Not yet, though we're—'

'Two, where is she now?'

Kate shakes her head to admit a second failure. 'Obviously, we're circulating her picture to—'

'Three, who hired her?'

No answer from Kate.

Until, that is, on the very edge of her vision, Flint sees Cutter give a subtle nod of acquiescence, and Kate then says, 'We can't yet give you a case you can take to court but there's something else you need to know about the Tucson hit. The victim's real name wasn't Peter Salter or even Peter Slavitch. His real name was Rexhep Kastrioti, an Albanian national. And the perp he named to the grand jury as the supplier of his women was . . .' she hesitates for a moment and then, 'Alexander Çarçani.'

Flint is incredulous, gaping at Kate as though she can't believe what she's heard. '*Now* you know? *Now* you know that Çarçani has been under indictment in the US for three years? *Now* you know that a witness willing to testify against Çarçani was taken out by a professional shooter? Jesus, Kate! It's your *job* to know. Why the hell didn't you know before?'

Kate's cheeks are burning but she's standing her ground. 'Because the indictment of Çarçani was sealed by the judge – is still sealed, as a matter of fact – and our trawls don't detect sealed indictments. And, okay, we know that's a weakness in our procedures, and we're working on it. But, Grace, even if we had known, even if we'd known in real time, it wouldn't have made any difference.'

'Bollocks,' says Flint, and the tension in the room is palpable.

Until a voice at the back says, 'Right. With a name like Kastrioti, you'd think they would have shot his balls off.'

Thirty-Three

Cutter is in the kitchen separating egg yolks for a hollandaise sauce while, at his insistence, Flint takes a long hot shower. Part of her is still simmering at his refusal to allow her to return to Washington and the glass wall at Children's Hospital, on the unlikely grounds that he cannot provide an adequate security escort, not tonight. The larger part of her is relieved, even grateful, that for the first time in a week she will lie in a proper bed – Cutter's bed – while he takes the sofa. Her sense of relief is stained with guilt, of course – but guilt, like fear, is an emotion she can't sustain without fresh impetus and, on the telephone, Marty Berger has categorically said that her absence from the hospital has made no difference to Jack's condition: that he remains entirely stable, still in a coma but resolutely alive.

She reaches out with both arms to lean against the wall and arches her back to expose her shoulder muscles to the pulsating massage of the shower. What she's thinking about, what she cannot forget, is an excerpt from Marty Berger's post-operative notes that he allowed her to read: *At this point in the procedure, the patient's body temperature dropped to 28C and he went into DIC. An IV to administer AF-7 was immediately inserted . . .*

'I'm not sure I want you to tell me what this means,' Flint said to Berger, and he'd looked at her as if to say, *Right, you really don't want to know.* But, perversely, his reluctance to explain had only heightened her curiosity and she'd pressed, and pressed again, and eventually he'd told her that twenty-eight degrees Celsius was a catastrophically low body temperature, and that DIC stood for Disseminated Intravascular Coagulation, meaning the clotting of the entire blood circulatory system, and that Jack was not so much near-death as in a state of *pre*-death. Only the immediate intravenous injection of an anti-coagulant agent had brought him back from the abyss.

'How are you doing in there?' – Cutter calling to her through the bathroom door.

Flint turns off the shower and wraps herself in a freshly laundered towelling robe that bears the motif of the Buccaneer Hotel in Miami's Coconut Grove.

'Better,' she says, opening the door a crack so Cutter can see for himself. 'Much better, almost human.'

'Suits you, Mrs Breslin,' says Cutter nodding at the robe and they both grin, sharing the memory of an undercover operation that had reached its violent conclusion at the hotel where they were posing as husband and wife.

'Well, thank you kindly, Mr Breslin,' says Flint, putting on the brilliant, playful smile and the southern drawl that had been part of her undercover disguise – and, for a moment, the shadows of strain and fatigue are erased from her face and the sudden return of her singular beauty jolts Cutter because it stirs in him urges that he has forbidden but also struggles to suppress. Throughout acrimonious divorce proceedings, Cutter's former wife had bitterly maintained that the Buccaneer operation was designed by her husband to facilitate the start of an affair; that while posing as a married couple at the hotel, her husband had seduced Flint, or vice versa, and that Flint had subsequently obtained her much-elevated position as deputy director of the strike force by repeatedly lying on her back. And while the former Mrs Cutter was wrong on all counts, it was not for lack of secret wanting on Cutter's part.

'Here,' he says more abruptly than he intends, proffering a glass of white wine. 'I figured you'd need a drink.'

Flint opens the bathroom door wider to accept the glass and, still in the persona of Mrs Breslin, says, 'Why, honey, you read my mind,' and Cutter grunts. As he turns on his heels and trudges down the hallway and she calls after him, 'I just *love* your apron.'

Back in the kitchen Cutter decides he also needs a drink. Into a fat tumbler he pours two generous fingers of Maker's Mark bourbon and swallows them like a punishment.

They're eating shirred eggs laid on a bed of white asparagus and smothered with hollandaise, and Flint is astonished. It had never occurred to her that Cutter could cook, certainly not like this, and after a week of unaccustomed abstinence from alcohol the wine has gone to her head, lifting her dark mood to one of near euphoria, at least for now, and she feels a wave of gratitude towards him – and then he has to go and spoil it. 'There are some things you need to know,' he says. 'Things that Rocco and Kate didn't talk about this afternoon.'

No! If she has to hear one more word about the shooter today she knows her mood will crash, so she grabs the first thought that occurs to her and insists, a little too stridently, 'Aldus, the *only* thing I want to know is what's in this amazing sauce.'

He looks baffled by her question. 'Egg yolks, of course. Six yolks, and more clarified butter than is good for you.'

'Even I know that!' She laughs and reaches clumsily for her wine glass, brushing a burning candle with her hand, and Cutter has to stretch out a hand to steady it. 'I meant,' she says, 'what gives it the kick?'

'Tabasco sauce and cayenne pepper, and I use Key Lime juice instead of lemon.'

'Then I want the recipe. In case I ever learn to cook.' She laughs again and hears herself sounding just this side of hysteria.

'Grace, we need to talk.'

'I know.'

'That's why you're here.'

'I know, but Aldus, *please* not now. Please don't spoil this.'

Now she's stretching out across the dining table to touch his arm, pleading with him, and he studies her eyes in the candlelight and he can't bring himself to force the issue. 'When you're ready, then,' he concedes. 'After supper, right?'

'Right.' It sounds far more like a promise than she means to imply and, hurrying to change the subject, she asks him what he's made for dessert, and he tells her *oeufs à la neige* because, he says, he didn't want to waste the egg whites left over from the hollandaise sauce. She puts her elbows on the table and cups her chin in both hands. 'Aldus, seriously, I need to know: do you think I'm too skinny, or are you fattening me up for the slaughter?'

'Both,' he says deadpan, and although he smiles with his mouth she catches a brief glance of something alarming in his eyes.

* * *

'Grace, you blew it. You've gotta to face up to that fact because you've got no choice, and neither do I.'

Supper over, Flint is pacing back and forth along the same few feet of the living room like a caged animal, leaving tracks in the carpet while Cutter watches from the sofa. *This is so bloody unfair!* she wants to say but she doesn't yet trust herself to speak coherently.

'Somehow, somewhere, you made a mistake that allowed them to drive a truck through your cover. I don't know what you did, or didn't do, but this wasn't dumb luck on their part. They *made* you, Grace, saw through Kathy's disguise, and then they fucked with you – and that's the part that really worries me.'

'Meaning?' is the most she manages to say.

'Think about it. When they learnt you were Kathy, they must have figured out that the San Ambrogio project was a setup, a scam designed to entrap them. So why didn't they just walk away, cut off all contact with the Gup brothers? Why didn't they slither back under their rocks and leave Kathy McCarry to wonder how she'd messed up?'

'I don't—'

'Or,' Cutter interrupts, 'why not just have you killed, put you in a box like friggin' Vincent Regal?'

Flint has no answer.

'I'll tell you why. Çarçani and Gröber, they wanted you out of the equation because you're too much of a threat to them but, they decided, simply taking you out was too easy, too painless for you. My guess is they wanted you compromised, removed from the investigation but, twisted bastards that they are, they also wanted you to suffer, *really* suffer in the process. So, what better way than to hit your boy? The fact he wasn't killed is incidental because, God knows, you *are* suffering, and you *are* irredeemably compromised. Given your personal stake, given that it would look like a personal vendetta, there is simply no way you can continue to run Operation Payback, and no way you can continue as deputy director. Until and when we get Çarçani and Gröber – until and when they're located, arrested, extradited, tried and convicted – you can't be any part of what we do. Which means . . .' Cutter hesitates but only for a moment, 'I have no choice. I have to let you go.'

Now she has to say something, however badly it comes out. She halts her relentless pacing and stands over Cutter, coiled like a spring, her arms folded protectively across her chest, and struggles to find the words. 'You have to . . . you're . . . *Jesus*, Aldus, what are you saying? I don't believe . . . you're telling me . . . you're firing me? You're firing me *because my son was shot*?'

'No,' says Cutter. 'You're being placed on compassionate leave until we take them down; indefinite leave for the foreseeable future. But, Grace, let's not kid ourselves. Without you, it'll be a whole lot harder to find these assholes, and we have to start over from scratch. I don't have another infiltration agent of your calibre and, even if I did, Çarçani and Gröber will learn from this; they're not gonna fall for another San Ambrogio pitch. So it'll be a while before we get to them, maybe a long while, and sooner or later the bean-counters will come to me and say that keeping you on the payroll is not the best use of our resources, and they'll want to buy out your contract, and I don't have a whole host of arguments to use against them. Oh, for sure, I'll fight your corner; count on it. But in the end, Grace, the most I can do for you is get the best financial settlement that's available – and that's a promise you can take to the bank. Other than that . . .' Cutter holds up his hands to show that they're empty.

Flint can't believe what she's hearing. 'Aldus, do you really think I give a damn about the money?'

'No, I don't, but you should. Besides anything else, you've got a sick boy to take care of, and you could be looking at significant medical bills for years to come. I know your daddy's got money but—'

Now he's gone too far. At the mention of her father, Flint erupts. 'Don't go there.'

'What?'

'Leave my father out of it.'

'Why?'

'Because he's got nothing to do with this.'

'But he has, Grace.' Cutter comes off the sofa so suddenly that Flint backs away in alarm. 'Listen, Çarçani and Gröber threw a rock in your pool – and you think the ripples don't spread? You think your father's not involved? Bullshit. You want to know where he is right now? He's in a safe house guarded round the clock by armed officers who are wearing body armour; has been for the past

week. That's because Tom Glenning and I agree there is no other
way to guarantee his safety until the shooter is identified and
caught. And, even so, Çarçani and Gröber might have found
themselves a second shooter. I have to work on the assumption that
they're not going to quit until they've damaged anyone that matters
to you. Are you getting the picture?'

In an antique mirror hanging above the fireplace Cutter catches
Flint's frozen face and his own reflection, and moves beyond it.

'Unless,' he says vaguely, as though a thought has just occurred
to him.

Thirty-Four

Flint awakes to the sound of a telephone ringing, being answered; half hears in the distance the voice of Cutter saying hold on, he needs to close the door. The bedside clock tells her that it is almost 10 a.m., which means that she has slept for more than eleven hours. She lies between Cutter's sheets, allowing herself to relish the sense of rejuvenation she feels – until the memory of last night's events begins to seep into her consciousness.

I have to let you go, Cutter had said and then, throwing her a lifeline, *Unless* . . . And then he'd refused to tell her what he meant by that, and in her frustration she had practically screamed at him: '*Bloody hell*, Aldus, don't cock-tease me. Unless what?'

'Forget it. I didn't have my brain in gear.'

He'd clammed up and nothing she could say would budge him, and eventually she'd given up her lost cause and stomped off to bed without uttering another unnecessary word.

'We'll talk some more in the morning,' was the last thing he'd called after her.

Damn right we will, she thinks, suddenly stirring herself, throwing off the covers, hurrying to the bathroom to splash water on her face and pull on the Buccaneer robe. In bare feet, she sets off along the hallway towards the kitchen, sees that the door is closed. She slows her pace and approaches cautiously, trying to determine if Cutter is still on the phone. Apparently he is for she can make out the steady murmur of a voice and she is trying to decide whether to push open the door and interrupt, or wait for him to finish the call, when something – some sixth sense – sends a prickling sensation creeping down her spine.

The rhythm's wrong and so is the pitch. Whoever's talking on the phone in Cutter's kitchen it isn't Cutter – and, come to think of it, she knows there's never been a working day when Cutter isn't at the office by 7 a.m. – and now she's backing away from the door, from possible danger; backing down the entire length of the hallway until she reaches the bedroom, slips inside, soundlessly closes the door, eases home the lock. She leans with her back against the wall and commands herself to think.

Who is he, and how the hell did he get in? And, does Cutter keep a gun?

Of course he does and, urgently, she's pulling open the doors to Cutter's closet, searching through the orderly stacks of underwear and socks and handkerchiefs and sweaters and neatly folded shirts back from the laundry in cellophane wrappers. Nothing, and nothing either in the pockets of his suits or jackets or overcoats or inside the regimented rows of his highly polished shoes. She checks the drawers of the bedside tables and finds cufflinks and loose change and nail clippers and knick-knacks, and a small bottle of unidentified pills – and nothing remotely suitable to use as a weapon. She feels under the mattress, looks under the bed, checks behind the framed prints hanging on the walls. Zilch.

Come on, Aldus, where did you hide the gun?

She sits on the bed methodically examining all the possible hiding places in the room, trying to imagine herself inside Cutter's devious mind. *Not likely*, she thinks. *Not in a million years*.

Resigning herself to defeat, she hurries to dress. If she has to fight unarmed, she doesn't want to do it in a bathrobe; too much loose fabric for her opponent to grab and use for leverage. Instead she wears the trousers of her charcoal-grey suit, the bottoms rolled up until they are tight around her calves. From Cutter's closet she borrows a white T-shirt that is far too big for her, that she binds tightly at her waist with one of his belts. Glancing in the bathroom mirror, she sees the reflection of someone who looks vaguely like a samurai; a samurai without a sword.

Think, bloody think!

Behind the mirror is a cabinet which she searches and finds a pair of scissors with pointed three-inch blades and a bottle of aftershave that might be sufficiently astringent to cause disabling discomfort if thrown at the eyes. Better than nothing, she believes.

Now she finds her cell phone and, sitting on the lavatory, dials the number of Cutter's direct line at the Marscheider Building. It rings twice and then the tone changes to indicate that her call is being diverted.

'Duty officer.'

Keeping her voice down to not much more than a whisper she says, 'This is DD Flint. I need to speak with the Director.'

There is a pause and she imagines the duty officer checking his computer screen to establish the source of the call.

'The Director's in transit, DD.'

'To where?'

'Washington DC.'

Where Jack is, she thinks with a shudder of alarm. 'Why? What's happening in Washington?'

Another brief pause and then, 'I don't have that information, ma'am.'

'Is he airborne?'

'Yes.'

'Can you patch me through to him?'

'I can try.'

'Do that, please.'

Flint is put on hold and while she waits she goes into the bedroom and listens at the door.

'Ma'am?'

'Wait one,' she whispers and hurries back into the bathroom. 'Okay, go ahead.'

'I'm getting no response from the Director. Could be the plane's out of range of his cell.'

She hears the sound of the bedroom door handle being slowly turned.

'Ma'am? DD, are you okay?'

'Wait,' she says so quietly that she can't be sure he will have heard. Nothing she can do about that. She leaves the phone on the lavatory seat and returns to the bedroom, quickly moving into position against the wall, near to the door but also far enough away not to get hit by flying woodwork if it bursts open; the door lock, she is sure, will succumb to even a modest shoulder charge. She waits, watching the door handle make a second slow turn.

Who knows how long she stands there holding the scissors in her right hand, poised like a dagger. Then, after what seems like an eternity, she hears a single cough that seems to come from mid-hallway, suggesting the intruder is retreating towards the kitchen.

'Hello?' Back in the bathroom, back on the phone, she's working on her options. 'Listen, put me through to Rocca Morales.'

'Sorry, no can do. He's travelling with Director Cutter.'

'*Shit!*'

There is a pause and then the duty officer asks, 'DD, are you in trouble? Is there something I can do for you?'

Yes, she wants to say, *you can send in the cavalry* – but that means revealing that she's inside Cutter's apartment, that she's spent the night in Cutter's apartment, and she's fully aware that within the Marscheider Building there is already enough gossip about her relationship with Cutter; speculation that she doesn't want to feed.

'Do I know you?' she asks.

'It's Fletcher,' he says. 'We were introduced at the Director's New Year's party, though you probably won't recall.'

But Flint's ability to remember names and match them to their owners is almost uncanny, and now she's running Fletcher through her memory bank; recollecting a sweet-faced man with freckles on his cheekbones and a mop of curly ginger hair.

'It's James, right? James Fletcher. You joined us from DEA.'

'Yes, ma'am.'

'And your wife – Lucy, as I recall – is she still with the DA's office?'

Fletcher laughs quietly. 'That's pretty impressive, DD, seeing as how we talked with you for all of two minutes.'

'Yeah, well, as you can tell, James, you made a lasting impression. Now, I'm going to ask you to do something for me.'

'Shoot.'

'I'm at the Director's apartment, came by to drop off a package, and there are signs of an intruder, and I'm going to check it out, and what I want you to do is stay on the line, and if I start shouting my head off then—'

'You want to wait until I send back-up?' – sudden alarm in Fletcher's tone.

'There isn't time.'

'Ten minutes, fifteen at the most.'

'James, I'm going in. Just keep listening and if you don't like what you hear, send in the marines.'

'I really don't think . . .' Fletcher is saying, but Flint's no longer listening. The phone is clipped to Cutter's belt, the scissors are in one pocket of her trousers. She's taken the cap off the bottle of aftershave – her primary weapon, she's decided – and she's unlocking and opening the bedroom door. Taking two deep breaths, she steps into the hallway and immediately her senses are assaulted: by the smell of freshly brewing coffee; by the sound of whistling, an instantly familiar tuneless rendering of 'Danny Boy'.

She can't believe it. 'Crawdaddy?' she calls. 'What the hell . . .?'

In the kitchen doorway the grinning face of Jerry Crawford appears.

Crawford has lost weight, serious weight. Hugging him with both delight and deep relief, Flint can feel the sharp boniness of his shoulder blades.

'Should I be doing this?' she asks, thinking of the skin grafts on his back.

'No, because you're hurting the hell out of me, but don't stop.'

Flint remembers they are not alone. She lets go of Crawford, unclips the phone from her belt and says, 'James, false alarm.'

'I gathered.'

'So, if you sent in the dogs, which I'm sure you did, you can call them off.'

'Already done.'

'And, James.'

'Yes, ma'am?'

'The next time I tell you not to follow procedure, just ignore me again. And say hello to Lucy for me, and tell her that if she's half as bright as I think she is she's going to make DA. Now go away and leave us alone.'

'Roger all of that,' says Fletcher, and he cuts the line.

They drink coffee while Flint calls Children's Hospital, establishes that Jack's condition has not changed. Then she says she wants to walk, get some air into her lungs, and she and Crawford take a cab to Central Park, and it's not until they are strolling in Strawberry Fields that she demands to know what's going on.

'I've got something to tell you about the shooter,' Crawford begins, slowly, as though he's setting out on a long journey and might need to conserve his strength. 'Something nobody knows about except me and Cutter. Oh, and Blade; he knows most of it.' He sees the surprise register in her eyes.

'Singleton? What's Al got to do with it? I don't understand.'

'So listen,' says Crawford. 'And maybe you will.'

The night Jack was shot, Crawford was on the phone to Cutter, talking things over; Crawford was talking about coming back to work – which Christie said was just plain ludicrous since all the medication he was taking left him tired out. And Cutter was probably thinking the same, though he tried to be encouraging, and then Cutter had taken a call on his cell phone, and said he had to go, and it was another two days before Crawford learned what had happened – when Rocco Morales called him in Florida, brought him up to date.

'So, I called Cutter and told him I was coming back to New York, to help work the case. And he said, no, don't do that, because I may need your help and I want you to stay off the books. He told me to stay in Orlando, stay by the phone, wait for his call.'

Flint had promised to keep silent, to not ask questions, but she's losing the plot. 'Stay off the books?'

'Remain on sick leave, out of the loop. Deniable, if that's what it comes to.'

'Right,' she says, though she's still not sure what he means.

Then, the next night, actually way after midnight – but that didn't matter, Crawford said, because the weird thing about drug-induced fatigue is that however tired you feel, you still can't sleep, and he had been in the living room of his rented apartment watching *Mulholland Falls* on DVD, with the sound turned way down to avoid disturbing Christie – Cutter had called and asked him to take a trip to Miami to speak with a legendary former homicide detective named Al Singleton, also known as Blade.

'Cutter wanted a second opinion. He said to me, "Rocco thinks the perp we're looking for is a professional sniper and, having been one himself, he should know." But Cutter wanted the facts run by Blade – who was once a marine sniper with fifteen verified kills to his credit – so, Cutter said, there was a FedEx package on its way to me with details of the crime-scene evidence, pictures of the probable perp, and two thousand dollars in cash from the Director's slush fund to cover my expenses. He said to take Christie along if I wanted; find ourselves a decent place to stay.'

They had driven to Miami and, for old times' sake, checked into the Buccaneer in Coconut Grove and, early that evening, met up with Blade and his wife, June – 'You remember his foxy lady?' – at a place on South Beach called Lola's where Blade was treated more like an honoured guest than a customer. In fact, said Crawford, the folks at Lola's venerated Blade, practically lay down at his feet, on account of the fact that there had been a night a couple of years ago when he was still with Homicide, and he'd taken June to Lola's to celebrate her birthday, and there was this bunch of cowboys – big-shot dopers from Colombia, as it turned out – who'd gotten over-excited and one of them had pulled a gun, waved it around in a hostile manner, and there was panic in the place – until Blade intervened. Metro-Dade rules said that all detectives should always go armed, even off duty, and Blade had this peashooter that he always carried in an ankle holster, and he'd shown it to the Colombian and told him to behave, and the Colombian had looked at him as if to say, *You call that a fucking gun?* Maybe he said something else, maybe something about June. Whatever, the asshole continued to act in a threatening manner and so Blade got behind him, shot him in the elbow of his gun hand, and then dragged his sorry hide out of there. Turned out he was a mid-level importer for the Cali cartel with three outstanding warrants.

'Jerry,' says Flint, 'is there a point to this?'

'You bet,' says Crawford. 'Because what you don't know, what Rocco didn't tell you yesterday – because Cutter told him to keep it to himself – is that forensics tried matching the quartz from the shooter's sand sock to samples collected from salt-water areas all over the US. And though they didn't get a definitive match, they did get an eighty per cent. Do you want to guess from where?'

'Miami Beach,' says Flint, for she is now certainly getting the plot.

'Right,' says Crawford. 'South Beach, to be precise, because the fill they use is pretty distinctive. So, Cutter figured, if the sand did come from South Beach, why would a shooter go all the way to Miami to fill a sock that they're going to use in Maryland, unless they're a local? He said it was a long shot but, then, that's what we were after: a long shooter. Maybe, he said, we should ask around.'

'Which you did,' Flint says, trying to keep the tension out of her voice.

'No.' Crawford shakes his head. 'Blade had a better idea. He said, let's get Luis to ask around.'

'Luis?'

This was the way it went down. After the stone crabs and the prime rib and a couple of bottles of a decent Merlot, Blade had called over Luis, who was the maître d' at Lola's, and said, Luis, I need a favour, and Luis had said, Then you've got it. And Blade had shown Luis one of the photographs of the probable shooter and said, I need to find this woman but she can't know that I'm looking for her. She's local, or I think she is, and maybe there's some place on the beach where she hangs out? Well, Luis can't sleep at night, apparently, because just before seven the next morning Blade got a call from him. Luis said there was a waiter at the News Café called Jimmy who not only knew the woman for sure, he also knew where she lived.

Half an hour later, Crawford and Blade were sitting down with Jimmy at the News Café, buying him a healthy breakfast, listening to his story. Jimmy was a jogger in a serious way. Each morning, *every* morning, before starting his shift, he said, he would run at least eight miles back and forth along the beach. He never lacked for company but the dedicated runners, the ones you could count on to be there whatever the weather, were not that many. The woman – the woman in the photograph, the woman he would come to know as Courtney – was pretty much a regular but there were occasions when she wouldn't show up for two or three weeks at a time; travelling, Jimmy supposed.

She was older than Jimmy by a good ten years but she had the kind of taut tanned body that he liked and whenever he'd had the chance he'd let her know that he was interested: eye contact, a friendly greeting – *Hey, how are you this fine morning?* – that kind of thing. Nothing from her except total disinterest – until, that is, there came this particular morning when their paths crossed and Jimmy made his usual pitch and instead of ignoring him she'd stopped and asked him his name. *So, Jimmy*, she said, *do you want to come to my place and eat yoghurt for breakfast?* Hell, yes. So she took him to a two-storey villa off 3rd Street and fed him yoghurt and honey and then took him to bed and – 'Excuse my language, Grace,' says Crawford, 'but this is what he said' – fucked him senseless. They stayed in bed all day – fortunately it was Jimmy's day off from work, otherwise he would have lost his job – and then at about six in the evening she suddenly turned on him for no reason that he could discern. Told him to get up and get dressed and get the hell out of her house. And, the next morning when their paths crossed on the beach, she looked right through him, as though he didn't exist. Next two days he got the same treatment. But on the third she accosted him like nothing had happened and said, *Jimmy, do you want to go to my place and fuck?*

For about three months the pattern kept repeating itself. Courtney – the only name he knew her by – was either eating him alive in her bed or throwing him out of her house like he was vermin, and he never knew why. Finally, it got to him. There came this day when she suddenly turned once more into an avenging bitch, and told him to get lost, and Jimmy refused to budge from the bed. She screamed at him but he still wouldn't move. Then the bedroom door opened as though it had been kicked by a mule and in came a second woman; actually a young woman – sixteen, seventeen at the most. As Jimmy would shortly learn, she was Courtney's daughter, but she was twice the bulk of her mother – and it was not fat, it was muscle – and she had spiky orange hair and metal studs embedded in the corners of her eyebrows. Without saying a word, she grabbed Jimmy by the hair and *lifted* him out of the bed with one hand, and dropped him like a sack. While he rolled around the floor, trying to get out of the way, she aimed vicious kicks at his testes or his kidneys, depending on which way he was facing. Finally, he found temporary refuge by squeezing under the bed and she lay down on the floor beside him and said, *Listen, you do what my mother says or I'll suck your lungs out through your nose.*

'That was enough for Jimmy,' says Crawford. 'He grabbed his clothes and bolted; didn't trouble to dress. And guess what?' The effort of telling the story has clearly exhausted him and Flint leads them to a bench. When he's got his breath back Crawford adds, 'Jimmy doesn't go jogging no more. Leastways, not on South Beach.'

Flint examines his tired face and the half-smile, which is all he can manage, and says, 'Let's go back to Cutter's place. You need to rest.'

'I'll rest on the plane. We've got a flight to catch,' Crawford glances at his watch, 'in a little less than four hours.'

'We?' She doesn't need to ask where the plane is going.

'Grace, this is Friday, right? Come Monday morning, Cutter has to quit stalling and tell the bureau about Courtney, and they'll go in there with a SWAT team and all of their usual finesse, and she'll either get shot in the process or, if she's got any sense, clam up like an oyster and sit in jail until some fancy lawyer gets her bond and she vanishes into the night – and we won't know who hired her. You and me and Blade, we've got two days to find a way to make her talk.'

Flint feels as though she's lost her bearings. 'This is crazy. You don't even know she's there.'

'She's there. Blade's had her under surveillance since yesterday morning.'

'No, Jerry, I can't. I have to get back to Jack.'

'For what? So you can watch him through a glass wall and beat yourself up for what happened?'

An intense rush of anger makes her cheeks flush, but something stops her from saying the first spiteful thing that comes into her mind. 'Jerry, I have to—'

'Jack doesn't need you, Grace, because there's nothing you can do for him; not right now. But the case needs you, *I* need you. Cutter can't send anybody officially to Miami because, officially, it's not a strike force case. Whereas you and me, we're both on leave and if we, acting on our own volition, choose to follow up a slender lead, well, there'll be shit flying all over us if it all goes wrong but we're *deniable*, Grace; we're the only ones who are. You have to come with me.'

She sees the logic of Crawford's argument, feels the tug of his appeal. And the truth is she wants nothing more than to be outside the shooter's villa off 3rd Street preparing to make a hard entry, as hard as it needs to be. In any other circumstances. If it wasn't for Jack.

'Sorry,' she says, announcing her decision. She pats Crawford on one knee and stands up from the bench and starts to walk away.

'Where are you going?'

'DC,' she says without turning round.

'Suit yourself,' Crawford calls after her, 'but you need to know that Jack's not there.'

It takes a moment for the meaning of his words to register. Then she stops in her tracks and swivels on her heels. 'What did you say?'

Crawford is still sitting on the bench, now with his legs crossed, examining the fingernails of his left hand. 'Cutter can't shake this feeling that the bad guys are going to bring in another shooter to have a crack at Jack, and it's making him edgy. So this morning he and Rocco flew down to DC to have your boy moved to a different hospital: a hospital within a military facility; a facility with a perimeter that's guarded by kick-ass marines armed with real scary guns.'

She can't believe what she's hearing. 'Where?' she asks incredulously.

'I don't know, Grace – and if I did I wouldn't tell you. You get to know on Monday. After we've spoken with Courtney.'

Miami

Thirty-Five

Al Singleton was indelibly labelled 'Blade' by the more irreverent members of the Metro-Dade Homicide unit he ran for twenty years because, they said, he was so skinny he could dress up in green and go to a fancy-dress party as a blade of grass. Now retired from Homicide, he's spinning out his days as a private investigator while he waits for his wife to finish her own stint with Homicide – and the day she does they will flee Florida and build themselves a home in the Blue Ridge Mountains of Tennessee. To Flint he still looks impossibly thin. She and Crawford emerge from the terminal at Miami International into the swampy heat of the night to find him leaning against the side of his Mustang with his arms folded on the roof. He's parked in the tow-away zone chatting to a female uniformed cop who's showing no intention of moving him on.

'Officer, you should arrest this man,' says Flint and that gets her a boyish grin from Blade.

There are worry lines at the corner of his eyes and his hair is greying at the temples, and as he comes from behind the car to embrace her, she can see the first evidence of an expanding midriff. Otherwise he looks as fit and youthful as he does in the photographs she's seen of him, taken when he was a marine sniper in Vietnam. When Flint was still working for the Metropolitan Police and assigned to the British Consulate in Miami as a liaison officer, it was Blade who taught her how to shoot.

'Arrest him for what?' asks the cop, joining in the joke. The badge on her uniform blouse says her name is Díaz and she's clearly young enough to be Blade's daughter.

'For pretending to be an old man. Obtaining retirement and a full pension under false pretences.'

'Well, I'd need to see some evidence,' says Díaz.

'Evidence? Just look at him!'

Díaz cocks her head and looks Blade up and down, and then she slowly circles him, pretending she's giving him a really thorough once-over and Flint, who's doing the same, says, 'Look at that butt,' and Díaz comments on his thighs and adds dubiously, 'Could have been a case of *early* retirement, I suppose.' Or mistaken identity, Flint suggests, and they keep on ribbing him until he finally begs them, 'Come on, girls, cut it out!'

Flint, laughing, puts her hands on his shoulders and kisses him on the cheek and tells him, 'It's really, *really* good to see you.'

Her mood doesn't last. In the car, heading for downtown Miami, Flint assumes they will take the MacArthur Causeway and cross the bay to South Beach. Instead of which, when they reach the edge of the city, Blade turns due south on I-95 in the direction of Coconut Grove and Flint instantly knows that their confrontation with the probable shooter of her son will not take place tonight. *Why?* she asks grumpily from the back seat. Because what they're set on doing isn't exactly official, Blade explains, and on Friday nights the Beach is especially well patrolled – on account of all the visitors the bars and clubs and restaurants attract – and, if it's all the same to her, he'd rather not get stopped at one of the random checkpoints set up by the Miami Beach cops and have them look in the trunk of the car.

'Because?'

'Because Jerry said you wouldn't be carrying weapons on the plane, since neither of you are active federal agents at the present time. So, I've got a bag in the trunk, the contents of which I can't easily explain.'

'Besides which,' says Crawford who's riding in the front passenger seat, watching Flint in the driver's mirror, 'Blade needs to brief us.'

'Right. We'll get something to eat, I'll tell you what I've found out about Courtney, and then we'll get some rest and go see her first thing in the morning.'

'Real early,' says Crawford.

'When there are no police checkpoints to worry about,' says Blade – and Flint sees the two of them exchange a glance that hints to her of a conspiracy.

'Terrific!' she says. 'And while we're *eating* and *resting*, what if Courtney runs?'

Crawford twists in his seat to look at her. 'No way, Grace. It's not going to happen, not without us knowing.'

'Really? And you know this because?'

'Because Blade's got a tap on her phone, and a tracking device on her car, and three of his people watching her house. Right, Blade?'

'Four people, in fact. Front and back. She's going nowhere.'

'So you see, Grace . . .'

Flint's sense of frustration, the sense that she's been outmanoeuvred, is becoming hard for her to bear. She wants to ask them, *Did you guys rehearse this routine, or are you just making it up as you go along?* But what's the point in arguing? She falls silent, turns in her seat to look out of the side window; watches with disinterest the rapid passing of the familiar landmarks of the Miami skyline.

In Coconut Grove they check into the Buccaneer Hotel where Crawford has secured three rooms at the discounted government rate. They agree to meet in twenty minutes in Le Café on the ground floor where the food is both pretentious and exorbitantly priced. Still, the place holds potent memories for Flint, for the second-last time she was there she held a semi-automatic pistol under the table, aimed rock-steady at the groin of a Russian mafioso named Alexei Rykov, while Cutter blithely informed him that they were not, as he thought, husband and wife and his fellow conspirators in a scheme to launder counterfeit one-hundred-dollar bills, but federal agents – 'And you, you sonofabitch, are under arrest.' The look of sheer astonishment on Rykov's face is an image that Flint both keeps and treasures.

But there are other images of that same operation in the Buccaneer that are much darker: images she does not wish to keep but which, in the familiar surroundings of her room, return to haunt her; send her to the minibar in search of liquid comfort. She arrives in the restaurant fifteen minutes late, mildly embarrassed to learn that Crawford and Blade have been too polite to order in her absence. She says she doesn't want much to eat but that she'll take her share of the wine.

While they eat heartily she plays with her food, pushing it

around the plate. They tell each other war stories of past operations while she remains silent. She feels apart from them, excluded by their air of joviality which is at such sharp odds with her own sour frame of mind.

Finally, 'Guys, can we get on with this? I really need to go to bed.'

Sure, they agree, hastily pushing their plates aside. Two waiters appear to remove the debris of the meal and offer coffee, which all three of them decline. Blade delays until the waiters are out of earshot and then begins, 'I'll give you the short version because, given the time constraints, that's all I've got.' He doesn't have a file to refer to. Everything he tells them about the shooter is in his head.

Courtney Mary Morrison, he says. Born Tacoma, Washington, 17 October 1966. Parents, Frank and Velma Morrison; Courtney was their only child. Frank sold sewing machines for the Singer company door-to-door, travelled a lot around the state. Velma was a seamstress and, after Courtney was born, she worked part-time from home making and mending clothes to order. They were decent enough folks but Frank worked mainly on commission and they struggled financially, Velma doubtless pinching and scraping on the household bills to get by. Maybe that's why she bailed out. On the morning of 26 November 1977, not long after Courtney turned eleven, Velma went out to deliver some completed orders and never came home. Maybe she'd met another man. More likely, she met foul play. In any event, she vanished. On the FBI website, she's still listed as missing, as is her car: a white Buick Nevada, 1969 model; almost two hundred thousand miles on the clock; dents on the fenders, left and right, front and rear. Velma, says Blade, was notorious for her parking.

'So, Blade' – Crawford, grinning – 'you're somewhat lacking in the detail.'

Flint, whose mother also vanished when she was a child, listens white-faced. The idea she could have anything so profound in common with the shooter seems to her obscene. She forces herself to concentrate while Blade continues his account.

For a couple of months after Velma disappeared – over the Christmas holidays and into the new year – Frank Morrison tried to juggle the conflicting demands of looking after his child and being on the road to pursue his trade. It couldn't be done and, in mid-January 1978, custody of Courtney passed informally to her aunt and uncle: Velma's sister, Vera, and her husband, Hans, who lived some one hundred and twenty miles south of Tacoma in Portland, Oregon. Hans Petersen worked as a security supervisor at Portland Airport and before that he was in the military for twenty years – which is maybe where Courtney got the idea. For, right after graduating from high school in Portland, without even considering college, she enlisted in the US Army.

Blade pauses his monologue to straighten a crease in the pink linen tablecloth. 'Now you're right, Crawdaddy, I am somewhat lacking in the details. I don't know shit about her army career, except for a couple of things. During her basic combat training she qualified as an expert marksman, meaning that after training she was able to hit at least thirty-six out of forty fleeting and pop-up targets at ranges between fifty and three hundred yards in simulated battle conditions. That's exceptional for anyone, never mind a young woman fresh out of high school who'd never handled a weapon before, because those targets appear simultaneously, two or more at a time, and you've got a split second to decide the correct order of engagement.'

'How did you do on your BCT?' Crawford asks.

'Nowhere close, yet I got selected for sniper training. She didn't because our government, in its wisdom, doesn't allow female soldiers into combat or to go to sniper school, so she opted for the next best thing: got herself selected as a small arms repairer, and went on a thirteen-week AIT course – advanced individual training. Then, so far as I know, she worked with weapons every single duty day for the next three years: stripped them down; repaired them; put them back together and test-fired them repeatedly on the range until she was sure they were fixed. This lady, she *knows* guns.'

'She's no lady, Al,' Crawford says quickly. 'Ladies don't shoot babies.'

Blade seems puzzled by the intervention. Then he catches the brittle look on Flint's face and says, 'Right, let me rephrase that. This *fucking bitch*, she knows guns.'

'Better,' says Flint, and she forms a slight smile with her mouth to ease the tension. 'Fucking bitch doesn't quite describe her adequately, not for me, Al, but you're definitely headed in the right direction.'

The men smile while Crawford shares out the last of the wine.

Blade's cell phone vibrates on the table top and he takes the call. 'Yes,' he says, and then he listens in silence. One of his watchers reporting in, Flint supposes.

'The FB, she's tucked up in her bed,' Blade says when the call is over. 'No sign of Melinda.'

'And Melinda is?'

'I was coming to that,' he says.

Private First Class Courtney Morrison was honourably discharged from the army in July of 1987, at the age of twenty. What happened after that, Blade confesses he doesn't know. Except that, thirteen months later, Morrison gave birth to a daughter, Melinda, in a public hospital in New Orleans. The birth certificate stated that the identity of the father was 'undetermined'.

And then they vanish, Courtney and Melinda, and no amount of scouring of public records has so far produced any trace of them. Until, that is, May 2001, when Courtney signed a one-year rental lease on the house in South Beach, and made an application for a Florida driving permit, and Melinda was enrolled in school. On every official document she signed, Courtney stated her occupation as 'freelance designer' – of what, she didn't say. In June 2002, Courtney purchased the house for $550,000.

'Which was a month after the Tucson shooting,' Flint states.

'Twenty-seven days, to be precise.'

'Did she pay cash?'

'Two hundred thousand in cash. For the rest she got a loan, based on her assertion that she made close to one hundred thousand dollars a year, supported by certified accounts and her last tax return.'

'That's nice to know,' says Crawford. 'That she pays her taxes, I mean.'

'Oh, absolutely, she pays her taxes, she donates to charity, she votes – she's a registered Democrat, by the way. On paper, she's an exemplary citizen in every way. There's nothing against her in any public record, not so much as an overdue bill or an unpaid parking ticket.'

'Well, of course she pays her bloody parking tickets.' Flint finishes her wine in one angry swallow. 'If you shoot people for a living, you don't shit on your own doorstep, do you? You don't attract attention to yourself in any way at all.'

'Unless you have a daughter like Melinda,' says Blade.

Melinda is trouble, he explains; a simmering volcano that regularly erupts. Four times in four years Melinda has been sent home from school for getting into fights in which she used what the school deemed to be excessive violence. And twice in the past year the police have had occasion to call on Courtney because of her daughter's involvement in violent affrays that occurred off school premises. The last time, four months ago, she came *this close* – Blade's thumb and forefinger are half an inch apart – to being arrested and charged with aggravated assault. Only her agreement to submit to mandatory counselling saved her.

'Then Melinda is our lever, isn't she?' says Flint after a pause. 'Certainly our way to get through the front door without breaking it down.'

'It's a thought,' says Crawford and Blade smiles.

Flint is in her room lying fully dressed on the bed, in that twilight state that is halfway between sleep and wakefulness. Against her will, she is reliving the worst moments of the Rykov operation in the Buccaneer Hotel when one of Rykov's thugs, a goon named Vladimir, had pointed a MAC-10 submachine gun at her head and said *Come here*, and she had gone to him because she had no choice – and she'd thought there was a chance she might distract him. He'd reached for her crotch, bitten her breasts, would have raped her, no doubt about it, but for the explosive arrival of the rescue squad. Vladimir never knew what hit him; actually, a bullet in the head. Flint survived physically unscathed but she bears deep scars.

She cannot sleep. She has the sudden urge to call someone who isn't a cop, to talk about things unconnected to her work. She would call her father – she really believes she would – but she has no idea where the British police have him hidden or how to reach him. She would call Dr P, but it's coming up to 4 a.m. and she doesn't have the nerve. She has no girlfriends, or at least none she feels she can call; no partner, not even an occasional lover. She feels utterly alone.

The passage of time seems deadly slow. The digital clock on the bedside table tells her it is 3:58 and she closes her eyes and imagines the passing of five minutes, and looks again – and the clock says it's 3:59. She gets up from the bed, goes to the bathroom and turns on the shower. She lets it run at the hottest setting until the room is filled with steam and then strips off her tired clothes and hangs them from the towel rails to ease the creases.

Naked, she returns to the bedroom and sits down at the writing desk to compose a note that she will slip under Jerry Crawford's door as she leaves the Buccaneer.

As someone once said, time spent on reconnaissance is seldom wasted. See you guys at South Beach.

Thirty-Six

The cab driver shrugs and says, 'Okay, lady, if you know what you're doing,' and drops her off at the deserted corner of 6th Street and Ocean Drive. There are still a good thirty minutes to go before sunrise and the sky is the colour of asbestos. There is no one on the beach – no one she can see. She's wearing a pair of white satin running shorts, a pink T-shirt and a matching baseball cap, all of them emblazoned with the Buccaneer's motif. *You could do me a huge favour* she'd said to the night manager at the hotel and, with not much resistance, he'd opened up the fitness centre and allowed her to rummage for clothes. But there were no trainers she could borrow so she crosses the beach in bare feet. She reaches the waterline and sits down on the sand to wait. The waves barely lap at her toes, as though the sea has been drained of all of its energy – which is rather how Flint feels. This will not do, not if she is to survive what is to come. She needs to get the adrenaline pumping by focusing on the enemy.

Is this where you got your sand, Courtney, the sand for your sock? Is this where you thought, well, the target's going to be tiny so I'll need to be pretty bloody precise? Because babies do make tiny targets, don't they, Courtney, when the range is more than one thousand feet and you don't know the strength of the wind? Did they give you baby targets to shoot at when you did your basic training, when you qualified as an expert? Or is shooting at babies a new career move for you, a new page added to your portfolio? Did you see his body jerk, Courtney, through your scope? How did that make you feel? Good? Bad? Indifferent because of your professional detachment? Or, Courtney, do you have any fucking feelings at all?

Her rage mounting, Flint gets up from the sand and begins to run, heading south along the beach. She's not exactly fit, for she seldom exercises, but this morning, fuelled by epinephrine, she feels as though she could complete a marathon. She keeps her thoughts focused on Courtney and her speed builds. Before she knows it, she's reached the southern extremity of the beach and she turns to head north. Which is when she sees the shooter.

Actually what she sees is a distant figure also running north along the beach, too far away to distinguish. But she *knows* it is Courtney, knows it in her bones, and that certainty drives her to pick up her pace. For every two strides Courtney takes, Flint is determined she will take three.

She's breathing pretty easily and the pain in her legs is so far endurable. She's catching up, overhauling.

How does it feel, Courtney? Now that I've found you?

A minute after Crawford called to say that Flint had gone AWOL, told him about her note, Blade was on the phone to Brendan Glees, head of the watch team on South Beach, demanding to know if anyone had been seen approaching the house. No, Glees said; the place was as quiet as a tomb. Then Blade confirmed the physical description of Flint, and said who she was and why he was worried, and asked if she'd been spotted anywhere in the vicinity and again Glees responded in the negative, and Blade felt a huge sense of relief – until Glees added, 'Maybe she's at the beach.'

'Why would she be at the beach, Brendan?'

'Because that's where Hotshot is' – Hotshot being their code name for Courtney Morrison. 'Left her place in jogging gear about forty minutes ago.'

In his Homicide days Al Singleton was renowned for his imperturbability but even he can lose it. 'Then, Brendan,' he began calmly enough though his voice had a certain edge, 'that's where you should be, isn't it? Don't you think? *For fuck's sake.* Leave one pair of eyes on the house and, the rest of you, move it and do it *now*. Find Redwing.'

'And do what, exactly?'

'Watch her, watch her back. Stop her if you have to.'

'Stop her from what?'

'Committing mayhem in a public place. And,' a last thought, 'when you find her, call me.'

Then Blade hurriedly pulled on his clothes, yanked Crawford

out of his room. They took the elevator to the ground floor and ran through the lobby as though the hotel was on fire. Now they're in the Mustang crossing MacArthur Causeway, Crawford doing the driving while Singleton waits for his phone to ring.

'Jerry, you don't really think Grace would bushwhack Hotshot in broad daylight?' This is Blade seeking reassurance.

'In her present mood,' says Crawford, 'I wouldn't rule it out.'

'Then maybe you should hurry?'

Crawford glances at the speedometer which tells him that the car is already travelling at 80mph. A reflex makes him check the mirror where he half expects to see the flash of pursuing lights, but the mirror is clear. He nudges the accelerator. Blade's phone warbles and he answers on the first ring. 'Brendan, what you got?' he says and then he listens intently, the expression on his face giving nothing away.

What Glees has, in uninterrupted sight, is two women on an otherwise deserted stretch of beach, running in parallel. Hotshot is close to the waterline. Redwing – Flint's code name for the purposes of this operation – is twenty yards to her left, exactly in line. Whenever Hotshot accelerates her pace or slows it down, so does Redwing. If Hotshot comes to a halt and just stands there with her hands on her hips staring out to sea, so does Redwing. If Hotshot turns her back to the sea and stares at Redwing, Redwing stands and returns the stare. In Brendan Glees' opinion, Redwing may as well be carrying a sign that says *I'm stalking you* – and Hotshot is clearly spooked; she's giving every impression that she doesn't know what to do next.

'But Redwing's staying clear, is she? Not making any approach?'

'Correct.'

'Outstanding,' says Blade, as he frequently does when he's pleased. 'With you shortly,' he adds with a meaningful look at Crawford who checks the mirror once more and, against his better judgement, nudges the accelerator another couple of degrees.

So, what's your plan? Flint is thinking when the shooter makes her move. Without another glance in Flint's direction she turns and walks into the ocean and keeps on walking until she's waist deep in the slight swells. Now she's swimming with an effortless crawl, heading out to sea, and Flint stands at the water's edge watching, waiting for the shooter to make her turn; left or right, north or south? But the shooter doesn't make a turn. She maintains a stubborn easterly course, as though she's heading for the Bahamas, and she's becoming harder to spot from the shore with every stroke. *What's your game?* is now the edgy question in Flint's mind and for a moment she worries that she might have pushed too far; that, since the nearest landfall to the east is the Bimini islands – which, Flint happens to know, are a good fifty miles away – what she's witnessing is a suicidal swim; that Courtney would rather drown than be captured and interrogated.

Then, *No, you're bluffing*, Flint decides, and pulls off the Buccaneer's T-shirt – because it will only get waterlogged and drag her down – and wades into the water, flinching as she feels its sudden chill. She still wears the Buccaneer's baseball cap in the hope that it will act as a beacon that Courtney will spot; tell her that her bluff has failed.

Flint's out of her depth and swimming now, also heading east, her crawl also effortless. She's gratified by the speed with which she is moving through the water, and by the illusion that she can keep this up for hours.

Right, says her nagging inner voice, *and what's the furthest you've ever swum?* One hundred lengths of a mid-sized pool, is the answer; when she was twelve and earning her silver medal for swimming endurance.

Right, and what's the longest time you've ever been in the water? The answer is no more convincing. When she was a rookie cop with the Met she'd gone into the Thames, without much thought, to save a jumper off Chelsea Bridge, and she'd caught up with him in mid-stream – and he didn't fight because he'd decided he no longer wanted to die – but the tide was running upstream and they were carried helplessly most of the way to Barnes before the police launch arrived and they were pulled half-dead from the river. And Flint had sworn to herself, *never, never again*.

Right, and when was the next and last time you swam? In Australia, off Hayman Island, on her honeymoon, when Mandrake – *fucking* Mandrake – had persuaded her to go scuba diving, despite all of her protestations – and she'd given in because she thought she loved the jerk and had wanted not to disappoint him – and, thirty feet down, her mask had slipped. In her next breath she'd filled her lungs with sea water, and Mandrake was nowhere around – of course – and she'd barely made it to the surface. And Flint had sworn – and this time she'd *really* meant it – she would never, ever swim beyond her depth or, if she did, only within five strokes of the poolside.

My point exactly.

Shuddup!

So, what are we doing in the middle of the ocean?

SHUDDUP!

Her inner voice aside, she's doing okay, she thinks; keeping her rhythm, swimming well.

Brendan Glees, watching through binoculars from his position on Ocean Drive, calls Al Singleton. 'Blade, where are you? Because if Redwing can't fly like a bird, I hope she can swim like a fish. Otherwise, we need a boat.'

Flint has stopped swimming. She is conserving all of her energy and her concentration for the task of staying afloat. She has no idea where the shooter is, no idea how far she is from the shore. All she knows for certain is that the current is carrying her inexorably out to sea and that the swells are getting stronger. She tells herself to ignore the creatures that occasionally brush against her legs, to keep her panic at bay.

So, pilgrim, what's Plan B? as Cutter would surely say.

She doesn't have one. She hopes for the luck of being spotted by a passing pleasure yacht but each time a swell lifts her she searches the horizon and sees nothing, nothing at all. She tries to convince herself that, sooner or later – *sooner, please God* – someone will find the Buccaneer T-shirt she abandoned on the beach and put two and two together and alert the Coast Guard. Or that, even now, Jerry and Blade are canvassing Ocean Drive for anyone who might have seen her, and someone will remember a half-naked woman in a baseball cap entering the water.

Oh, really? She has no idea what Jerry had in mind when he'd promised a 'real early' start. Has he found her note yet? Is he even awake?

To distract herself from such negative thoughts – before the panic becomes irresistible and she starts to hyperventilate – she tries to picture herself in another place, somewhere on dry land. She sees herself in Dr P's airless office on Broadway, sitting in that over-stuffed chair with its broken springs, and scripts the dialogue of their next session.

If there ever is one.

Shuddup!

She can see Dr P's intense eyes boring into her and that riot of silver hair.

So, do you think it is interesting that you subconsciously chose to drown at sea, in the same way that Mandrake drowned? Do you think there was an association in your mind?

I didn't choose to drown, Dr P. I fought for my life. Which is why, incidentally, I'm able to be here.

Of course. But I wonder what you were thinking when you entered the ocean.

Plain and simple: I was following a perp, the shooter of my child.

Even though you fear water?

I don't fear water, Dr P. I just don't like it filling my lungs.

Yet you were going to swim to Bimini if you had to? Fifty miles? Ridiculous!

No! All I was doing was letting her know that there was no place she could go where I wouldn't follow. I thought – I hoped – that when she saw me coming after her, she'd turn around.

But she did not turn around?

Not so far as I know.

And yet you kept on going. Until you were, what? Two miles, three miles from the shore?

I hadn't reckoned on the current. I didn't realise how far out I was.

Really? But when you did realise, when you knew you were being carried away by the current, when you thought you would die, did you think of Mandrake? Did you wonder how it was for him in the moments before he drowned? Did you feel an affinity?

No. Not really.

But this is not true. As her future conversation with Dr Przewalskii fades from her imagination, it is thoughts of Mandrake's last moments that dominate her consciousness. She can see him now in vivid hues. Him in the water, her on the boat; him bobbing in a trough like a cork, waving with his arms, begging for help. She does not immediately go to him because half of her wants him to die. The boat drifts, rising and falling in the swells, as Mandrake rises and falls, his mouth frozen open in fear. He is lying on his back trying to stay afloat, trying to keep an arm raised, his time running out. And then she does go to help, pushing the throttle forward, pulling on the tiller to bring the boat around, closing the gap, taking a life jacket from the locker, attaching it to a line. Getting closer, adjusting her course so that she doesn't run him down, trying to judge the moment to put the throttle into neutral – and she gets it wrong and the boat's momentum takes her careening past the spot where she meant to stop and when she throws the life jacket over the stern it lands far short of Mandrake's reach. She rams the throttle forward and hauls on the tiller and the bow pitches and catches the crest of a wave and she is temporarily blinded by the spray. When she can see again she's on a sweeping turn that should bring the boat to Mandrake, but Mandrake is no longer there.

She wants to think of Jack coming out of his coma; of her father's forgiveness; of taking Jack home to Mid Compton, where she knows he really belongs. But thoughts of Mandrake keep intruding.

How does it feel when the ocean finally claims you? When you lose your battle, or simply surrender, and slip beneath the surface?

Flint also swallows water, feels herself going under; panics, thrashes with her arms and legs. For an awful moment she doesn't think she's going to make it and then her head breaks the surface and she gasps for air.

Bloody concentrate!

She shakes her head to try to clear the water from her eyes and ears, tastes the salt-stained vomit streaming from her nostrils. Turning on her back she wills herself to think of her arms as slow propellers that can keep her afloat indefinitely.

The sun is rising, bolder by the moment, and the surface reflection is dazzling. This gives her new hope because surely it means that Jerry and Blade must be awake, will have found her stupid note, will be searching the beach for her, raising the alarm. Her body no longer feels so cold and she wonders if this signals she has reached the warmer waters of the Gulf Stream. Her only notion of the passage of time comes from the increasing height of the sun

which, from her varying positions, is difficult to judge. An hour
passes, maybe two. There comes a point when she believes she
hears, through waterlogged ears, the gradual approach of an engine
– a boat or a plane, she can't be sure. The sound increases until it's
right on top of her, practically inside her head, and then it vanishes,
like an auditory illusion.

Thirty-Seven

Courtney Morrison walks along 3rd Street towards her house with the weary gait of a jogger who's run too far, giving herself time to look for the surveillance vehicle she is certain will be there. By returning to her house she knows she is taking a risk, but a calculated one. If they meant to arrest her on sight they would have done so on the beach where she was unarmed, totally isolated with nowhere to run, and they'd have sent in a team, maybe even a SWAT team; not a lone agent in a baggy T-shirt who was clearly there to try to unnerve her. It is Courtney's calculation that they want her to run, to see where she goes. *Well, be careful what you wish for, fellers*, she thinks. If they're giving her time, that's all she needs.

She spots an unmarked white van with tinted windows parked on the opposite side of the street some thirty feet from her driveway and reckons she's located the opposition, or part of it. She has no doubt there'll be others parked elsewhere, in vehicles or in the windows of convenient buildings. They'll be watching the back of the house for sure.

When she reaches the driveway where her car is parked, she cuts across the small lawn to collect her copy of the *Miami Herald* and then climbs the four steps that lead to the front porch. She opens the security screen, punches in the code to disable the alarm, unlocks the front door and then pauses to reach up with her hand and test the earth of a basket of pale pink geraniums hanging from the gable. *Too dry,* she seems to conclude. She goes inside, leaving the front door open, goes directly to the kitchen to fill a pitcher with water and returns to the porch to refresh her plant.

This is a woman who is unconcerned about possible surveillance, who doesn't have a care in the world is the impression she wishes to convey.

She latches the security screen but leaves the front door ajar. She opens the living-room windows, front and rear. She assumes they will have planted listening devices, or will be using parabolic microphones, so it is very casually that she calls out, 'Melinda, honey, are you home?'

If there are listening devices what they now pick up is a Bobby Darin compilation playing on the stereo, coffee beans being ground, other preparations for Courtney's breakfast; Courtney calling out again, 'Honey, are you there?'

Will there be cameras, fibre optic lenses embedded in the walls? Possibly, even probably, she decides. So for their benefit and as a further demonstration of her nonchalance, Courtney goes to the utility room behind the kitchen, strips off her running clothes and drops them in the washing-machine. She adds other items she selects from the laundry basket, adds a detergent capsule and fabric softener, selects the programme she wants and starts the machine. Bobby is crooning 'Beyond The Sea', one of her favourites, and Courtney sings along.

Naked except for her underpants, she returns to the kitchen and turns on the coffee maker. She takes two oranges from the fruit bowl on the counter, cuts them into halves, presses them into the juicer. Watching her, you could not possibly believe that this is a woman who knows that the day she has always anticipated – endured the expectation like chronic, nagging pain – has finally come. While she sips the juice she checks her answering machine for messages, takes the *Herald* from its protective wrapper and scans the headlines. It occurs to her that if this goes wrong, if she has miscalculated, then she will be among them tomorrow: SUSPECTED SNIPER ARRESTED ON SOUTH BEACH; something like that.

Actually, it's more likely to read SUSPECTED SNIPER SHOT ON SOUTH BEACH for she will not go quietly – not if Melinda hasn't come home. Melinda is not supposed to be home, she's staying with her best – her only – friend, but Melinda is . . . Courtney ponders on the best way to describe her daughter and settles on *unpredictable*. Yes, you can never be sure what Melinda is going to do, which is one of the two reasons why Courtney has taken the calculated risk of returning to the house; of walking into a potential trap.

Time to find out, she tells herself and, now whistling to Bobby's tune, she unhurriedly climbs the oakwood open staircase to the second floor. *She's going to take a shower*, the watchers are meant to believe.

There are three bedrooms on the second floor, all with bathrooms en suite, and although Melinda's room overlooks the street, and gets the most traffic noise, it is by far the largest. It is also unlike any other teenager's bedroom Courtney can imagine. There is no clutter, no disorder; no clothes on the floor, no unmade bed. The walls are off-white, not painted some hideous colour, nor are they adorned with posters of rock stars or movie idols. There is no TV set, no hi-fi system, no guitar, no set of drums. Melinda's computer is the smallest iBook available and it sits beside a bamboo matchstick lamp on an otherwise empty table. There are no photographs or trinkets anywhere in the room except for a kakejiku scroll hanging in an alcove alongside an arrangement of delicate white paper flowers and just seven books – the complete works of Yukio Mishima, not in translation but in the original Japanese.

It is Melinda's friend, Unagi Shinoda – a young woman so delicate she seems to have no bones – who is responsible for the stark aesthetic and for enticing Melinda with Yukio Mishima's bleak and often gruesome vision. Sitting cross-legged on the tatami mats that cover the floor, in an elaborate pattern that ensures good fortune, Unagi read aloud and then translated for Melinda each and every page of Mishima's *The Sailor Who Fell From Grace With the Sea*, drawing her into the disturbing world of Noboru, the book's adolescent misfit hero and the clandestine fraternity of his classmates in which he is known only as 'number three'. Melinda says that what fascinates her about Noboru and the fraternity is not their random violence but what she describes as their quest to understand the intrinsic order of the universe through the deconstruction of the status quo. Her mother is not so sure. Courtney worries that what fascinates Melinda and Unagi is the despairing fate of Noboru's creator. Having set himself impossibly high standards of physical fitness and moral rectitude, and having failed to inspire a Japanese renaissance of the samurai code, in 1970 Yukio Mishima committed seppuku – ritual suicide. A replica of the sword on which he impaled himself hangs beneath Mishima's framed portrait on Melinda's wall.

Glancing at the sword, Courtney feels a familiar shiver of uneasiness, backs out of the room into the hallway. She goes to her own bedroom, leaves the door open; still portraying a woman with nothing to hide. She has one thing left to do before she leaves.

First she chooses the clothes she will wear: her underwear, a pair of casual beige shorts, a matching linen top with short sleeves, white lace-up trainers and socks. She carries them into the bathroom, closes and locks the door. *Are there cameras in here?* she wonders. On balance she doubts it: Even the FBI or ATF, or whoever the opposition is, wouldn't stoop that low, not if they think they're going to have to justify the tapes in court. A microphone, maybe, she thinks. Just in case they are listening, she pulls down her panties, sits on the lavatory to urinate and flushes the bowl.

Now she goes to the large sash window and opens the lower half, lifting it up to its fullest extent. The window overlooks her neighbour's yard but she can barely see it because of the thick branches of a silver birch tree that overhang the dividing fence. By barely reaching out of the window she can touch the dense clusters of tiny flowers.

'I got to do something about that tree,' her neighbour had said last fall. 'Fell it, or prune it back.'

'Why on earth would you do that, Mr Jenkins?' had been her reply.

'Well, some of those branches are getting awful close to your property and they've got to be blocking your light.'

'Mr Jenkins, I just *love* that tree and the way it diffuses the light. I love the smell, I love the chirping of the birds that nest in it. Please don't harm it.'

'Well, if you're sure,' he'd said doubtfully.

Oh, she was sure all right. A dozen times in her head and once in actuality – making a dry run in the middle of a sleepless night – she has climbed out onto the window sill and leaned into the branches as though they were welcoming arms. As she has always seen it, Mr Jenkins' birch is much, much more than just an unruly tree.

She remains standing where she is, apparently gazing out at the branches, while her fingers feel the underside of the window frame to find the strip of plywood covering the two-inch deep recess that she made with a chisel. The strip is held in place only with Blu-Tak and she peels it away. Now her fingers find and tug and finally liberate the nylon pouch she concealed in this hidey-hole in June 2001, a month after she and Melinda moved in.

The pouch doesn't contain much – an ordinary-looking key and five hundred dollars in twenty-dollar bills – but Courtney thinks of it as her escape kit; all that she needs, more than she needs, to get away.

She turns on the shower and sets the automatic timer to run for fifteen minutes before it closes the valve. Not that she intends to take a shower; she's had more than enough water for one day.

Quickly she dresses, secures the pouch in the pocket of her shorts and climbs out onto the window sill, leans forward to take firm hold of the sturdiest branch and swings her feet onto the one below; drops into a crouch, rolls under the second bough, hangs from it for a moment with her arms fully extended and then lets go. The drop is no more than eight feet and she knows how to break her fall; child's play for a graduate of basic combat training.

There is no sign of Mr Jenkins in the yard or watching her from his kitchen window. Wouldn't have mattered if he was there because she would have given him her biggest grin and said something like, *Just had to see if I could do it*, and he'd have shaken his head as if to wonder if she was crazy.

Now that I'm down here, mind if I go this way, Mr Jenkins? she imagines herself saying as she crosses his yard and climbs the wooden fence. She drops into the narrow passageway on the other side and walks to the end, which brings her to 4th Street and then she's on Alton Road heading for the causeway – and on the shower timer there are still nine minutes to run.

'Mrs Shinoda?'

'Yes.'

'This is Melinda's mother.'

'Ah, yes, Miss Morrison, a pleasure.'

Courtney Morrison is outside a convenience store on Le Jeune Road, talking on a payphone, keeping a sharp eye on her taxi driver who is holding a thirty-dollar deposit for the ride to the airport.

'Is Melinda still with you?'

'Sure, she here. Sleep, like Unagi. You want I send her home?'

Mrs Shinoda has a soft undulating voice that seems to flutter down the phone line.

'No. In fact, I want you to keep her.'

'Keep her?'

'For a few days, maybe a week. Listen, I'm sorry it's such short notice but I've had a call from a client and I have to go to New York for a meeting as soon as possible. In fact, I'm on my way to the airport right now.'

'Okay.'

'Is this a problem for you, Mrs Shinoda?'

'No problem.'

'Terrific, I'm really grateful. One more thing: I don't want Melinda going back to the house while I'm away. No need to alarm her but in the last couple of days I've seen some strange characters hanging around the neighbourhood and I don't want her being in the house alone.'

'Okay.'

'If she needs anything – extra clothes, cosmetics, toiletries – just buy them for her, please, and I'll pay you back as soon as I get home. Or I can wire you some money when I get to New York. Should I do that?'

'No. Money no problem.'

'If you're sure?'

'Sure.'

'And, of course, our normal arrangement applies,' says Courtney, referring to the two hundred dollars a day she pays Mrs Shinoda for minding her daughter whenever she travels on business. 'Tell Melinda I'll call her as soon as I can.'

'I tell.'

'And, thank you again, Mrs Shinoda,' Courtney says while giving the taxi driver a hand signal to say she'll be there in just another moment.

'You go. You miss your plane.'

'Right.'

'I take care Melinda very good, no problem. You go,' she adds, and hangs up the phone.

Courtney completes the ride to the airport, tells the driver to keep the change, enters the terminal at Concourse E. Then she walks to Concourse H, exits the terminal, hires another cab.

'Where are we going?' asks the driver, watching her in the mirror, sizing her up.

'Fort Lauderdale.'

'You want to narrow that down?'

'I'll tell you when I've made up my mind.'

The driver shrugs and starts the engine. 'It's on your dime.'

'Right.'

'You got no bags?'

'The airline lost them, like they always do.'

'Ain't that the truth.'

'Drive,' says Courtney, slumping back in her seat, wishing to indicate that she feels no need for further conversation.

Courtney gets the driver to drop her off a good mile short of her final destination on the western outskirts of Fort Lauderdale. She thinks it is wise to assume that by now the opposition will have worked out that she has fled the coop. They will have issued an all-points bulletin, checked with the cab companies, established that a woman fitting her description took a ride from downtown Miami to the airport. They will now be wasting time establishing from the one hundred airlines flying out of Miami International that she did not take a flight. Sooner or later, they will realise that her trip to the airport was merely a blind and will be re-checking with the cab companies and, sooner or later, they will learn that a woman of the same description travelled from the airport to west Fort Lauderdale. No reason for them to know exactly where she is headed.

When she is sure the cab has departed, she walks briskly the remaining distance to what a towering sign mounted on stilts proclaims as 'Broward County's Safest Lock & Leave': six low cinderblock buildings, each the length of a football field, set in parallel rows behind a ten-foot-high hurricane fence that is topped with spools of razor wire. There is no guard on the entry gate and to open it Courtney enters her PIN code on the keypad, conscious of the white-on-red notice that warns: SECURITY CAMERAS ARE IN OPERATION 24 HOURS A DAY!

All of the storage units are identical, each the size of a one-car garage with width to spare, each protected by a solid roll-up door and an individual alarm system that requires a second PIN code.

Courtney's unit is number 216, at the distant end of the furthest building from the gate, which makes it the most isolated and therefore private – not that there is anyone around. She feels as though she is walking through a barracks that an army has long since abandoned; locked up and left.

Reaching her unit she disables the alarm and kneels down on the ground to examine the heavy brass padlock that secures the door to a hasp set in cement and reinforced by four six-inch bolts. The last time she was here she sealed the lock with a thin coating of green candle wax so that she would know if it had been tampered with. She finds the seal still intact and picks at it with a fingernail. She inserts the key from her escape kit, removes the padlock from the hasp and lifts the door just sufficiently to allow her to duck inside. After closing the door she stands for several moments in the darkness, listening to the gentle hum of the extractor fan, all of her senses alert. When she is satisfied that she's alone she feels her way to the left wall, finds the switch, turns on the light, closes her eyes while the overhead fluorescent tubes flicker into life. Now she looks and cannot help but smile at what she sees, and what she feels like saying is *Abracadabra!*

Contained in Unit 216 of the Safest Lock & Leave is Courtney Morrison's treasure trove; her real escape kit, the one that will take her as far as she wishes to go. At the rear of the unit is a stand-alone safe that holds ten thousand dollars in cash and two complete sets of identity in different names: two passports; two matching social security cards; two driver's licences; six credit cards, three for each name. At her choice she can become Allison Elizabeth Berlin – whose documents are entirely genuine, albeit issued some thirty years after the real Allison died in infancy – or Rosemary Alice Broughton, whose documents are forged, but immaculately so. The credit cards are genuine and valid, billed to two different accommodation addresses in Orlando, and at regular intervals over the past two years both Allison and Rosemary have made small purchases over the internet to establish convincing patterns of existence – but she will not use them any more, except to bolster her bogus identities. For all of her future financial needs Courtney will rely on another card she takes from the safe, this one a brash yellow; her Postcard, issued by the Swiss post office – an ingenious cash card that allows her to withdraw funds from almost one million ATMs around the world, leaving barely a trace. So long as her Swiss Post account is in credit (topped up as necessary by cash deposits from her client), Courtney can move money around the world practically anonymously; no international bank transfers, no messy audit trails. *Clever, the Swiss*, Courtney thinks.

And she has another reason to be grateful to the Swiss for their innate discretion. Also in the safe are other pre-paid cards obtained on her behalf by her client. Issued by Swisscom, these are SIM cards for mobile telephones and although SIM is an acronym for subscriber identity module, in this case the term is misleading for in Switzerland you can buy a pre-paid SIM card and a telephone number to go with it without providing any proof of identity. It's like a numbered Swiss bank account, entirely anonymous. You pay cash to credit the card with any amount you like, from one hundred dollars up. And, until your credit runs out, you can make and receive calls almost anywhere in the world without any risk of being identified; you're not a name, you're simply a number. And there's an outfit in Geneva that sells these cards in bulk. Courtney has one hundred of them.

More items are retrieved from the safe: two new cell phones still in their original packaging, the second one for back-up, just in case; her laptop computer on which all of the sensitive data is heavily encrypted on a hidden drive that requires an intricate password to open; a thick manila envelope, addressed to her lawyer, containing legal documents prepared and notarised more than two years ago that will transfer the ownership of her South Beach house to Melinda; the keys to her other house, one that cannot be connected to Courtney Morrison; the keys to her car.

It is a Volvo sports wagon, two years old but with barely one thousand miles on the clock, and it occupies most of the space in unit 216. In the garish overhead light it seems black, or maybe blue, though it is actually dark green, and it is Courtney's belief that the federal agents who eventually watch the murky tapes from the security cameras will not be certain of its colour. Though the Volvo is registered to a Delaware corporation, its licence plates are presently obscured by fake Florida tags. These are camouflage to further confuse the Lock & Leave security cameras and once she is clear of the place she will remove them. In the trunk her three suitcases are already loaded, ready to go.

A change of clothes into a smart business suit and then Courtney is also ready to go, almost. Her final chore is to start the timer that, five minutes after she closes the door to unit 216, will arm the detonator of a Semtex bomb. Anyone who subsequently forces the padlock and opens the door will trigger an explosion: nothing too lethal, she intends, but sufficient to ignite the two hundred gallons of kerosene she has stored in the unit in plastic containers and create an inferno that will erase from this place most if not all of Courtney Morrison's physical traces.

Fewer than fifteen minutes after Courtney arrived at the Lock & Leave – fewer than three hours after her unnerving encounter on South Beach – Allison Berlin leaves, heading due west on I-75, free and clear for now.

Thirty-Eight

The Miami Beach police have sealed off the front of Courtney Morrison's house with yellow scene-of-crime tape, though it is not yet clear what kind of crime has been committed, if any. Alerted by a 911 call from Blade, two patrol units had responded and now detectives from the Criminal Investigations Unit have arrived to ponder the mystery of what Courtney left behind. Doors and windows open, the alarm unset – and yet Morrison's wallet containing cash and credit cards and her driver's licence, her cell phone, her watch, a pair of diamond earrings, her house and car keys, they all lie undisturbed on the kitchen counter. No part of the house has been ransacked, nothing obviously missing or disturbed, and there is no sign of violence. Still, there is ample evidence of a domestic routine abruptly interrupted: an untouched bowl of muesli and fruit on the counter, coffee stewing in the pot, damp clothes waiting to be removed from the washing-machine.

'Beats me,' says Lieutenant Manny Lucca who cultivates the impression that he's familiar with defeat but who Blade knows to be an exceptionally cunning investigator. 'It's like she stepped out onto the porch for a moment and forgot to come back.'

'Or got herself abducted by aliens.'

Lucca smiles.

'Anyone see her go?'

'Not so far, though we're still asking around the neighbourhood.' Lucca, who is slowly working his way through the contents of Morrison's wallet, finds a picture of Melinda looking far less fearsome than she does today and shows it to Blade. 'Who's she?' he asks. 'Any ideas?'

'Maybe the daughter?'

'Right, you said.'

'Said what?'

'When you called nine one one. You said this Morrison woman hired you because her daughter was in trouble.'

This is not entirely accurate. Straining to stay just onside of an outright lie, Blade had merely *implied* to the 911 operator that Courtney Morrison was a prospective client who had a problem with her daughter, and that when he'd turned up at her house to discuss it he'd found the place open and abandoned.

'What kind of trouble?'

'She never said,' replies Blade, honestly enough.

'Do you know the kid's name?'

'Melinda.'

'Okay, Hoskins' – this to one of his investigators who's picking through the kitchen cupboards with no idea what he's looking for – 'run a check on a Melinda Morrison. Let's see if the trouble she's got is official.'

'Got a DoB?' asks Hoskins.

Of course Blade knows Melinda's date of birth but he can't think of any plausible reason why her mother would have told him that in an initial telephone call. 'Sorry,' he says with a shake of his head. 'We never got to talk about the details.'

Lucca sends Hoskins to the car to radio in a demand for an immediate criminal record check of Melinda Morrison. While they wait for the result, he and Blade find a shaded spot on the front porch where Lucca lights the stub of a fat Cuban cigar.

'Tell me, Blade, this private investigator shit you're into, it suits you?'

'Well, the hours are what you make them, the pay's better and nobody shoots at you – leastways, not so far. Anyway, it's temporary. Soon as June finishes her time with Homicide, we're out of here.'

'Really? To do what?'

'Build a house in Tennessee, maybe write a book. Wait for the kids to give us some grandchildren.'

'Do their duty, right?' Lucca smiles and lets some moments tick away. Then, 'So, how do you find your clients?'

'They find me. Word of mouth.'

'Best way, I'd think. And which particular mouth whispered into Mrs Morrison's ear, I'm wondering?'

Blade says he doesn't know, and Lucca parodies *She never said*, and they both laugh, and Lucca blows gently on the end of the cigar until the ash glows a brilliant red. 'You're not holding back on me, are you, Blade? Not jerking me around?'

'Can't imagine why I would.'

'That's what I thought,' says Lucca.

'So, you didn't need to ask.'

'But then, Blade, I've got this itch I need to scratch; this feeling that something's not quite right. You know how it is?'

Blade watches Hoskins coming out of his car with the purposefulness of a man who has important news to impart. 'I surely do, Manny. That itch you've got, it's called paranoia, and the longer you serve, the worse it gets. How long have you got to go?'

'Couple of years.'

'And then?'

'I don't know. Maybe I'll start a PI business like yours; you know, one that gets the customers through word of mouth.' Lucca looks around as though he is trying to find somewhere to dispose of his cigar butt. Then, 'So, when she called your office, was it from her landline or her cell? I mean, when we check her phone records, what will we find?'

'Nothing,' says Blade while Hoskins mounts the steps to the porch.

'I figured.'

'Because she called me from a payphone.'

Lucca puckers his mouth, blows a ring of smoke. 'You sure about that, Blade?'

'As I recall.'

At Opa-Locka airport, thirty minutes north of Courtney Morrison's house, Jerry Crawford sits fretfully on board a Coast Guard HU-25 Guardian jet that is poised at the end of runway 9L, about to join the already extensive air/sea search for Grace Flint – or, more likely, her body. It is now more than four hours since Brendan Glees observed her entering the water and the search coordinator has warned Crawford that he is not optimistic about her chances of survival. 'Frankly', he'd said, 'if the sharks haven't taken her then it's more than likely that hypothermia has.'

'It's eighty degrees and rising,' Crawford had protested.

'Not in the ocean, it isn't.'

'Listen, you need to know, Flint doesn't know when to quit.'

'Agent Crawford, this is a reality check. I'm only telling you like it is. Doesn't mean we're going to stop looking. Doesn't mean we're not doing everything we can.'

True enough. There are already two Coast Guard cutters and two RB-S small response boats scouring the Straits of Florida, and an HC-130 surveillance plane is on its way from the Coast Guard's Clearwater base. What the Guardian will bring to the search effort is its thermal imaging cameras which can scan vast areas of the ocean and locate a warm body as small as a puppy's from a mile high.

If she's still warm, Crawford is thinking.

'Crawdaddy, you always this nervous about flying?' Glees asks. He's strapped into the seat next to Crawford, directly behind the flight deck from where the crew is still doggedly negotiating take-off clearance with Miami Center. The problem is the crew's requested departure route will take them dangerously close to the flight paths leading into and out of Miami International and air traffic control is trying to find a slot that won't bring the Guardian into mid-air conflict with a passenger jet.

'Omaha One-one, that's a negative, hold your position,' commands a voice on the radio.

'Are you hearing this shit?' says Crawford, who is a nervous flyer at the best of times.

Glees pretends it is nothing more than routine. To distract Crawford he tells the story of the time he and Blade were in a Metro-Dade PD chopper in all-out pursuit of a homicide suspect, and the asshole had driven his car through the perimeter fence at MIA and set off down the taxi-way, and the chopper pilot – who must have thought he was Tom Cruise – had gone after him, and the next thing they knew, they were head to head with an incoming Boeing 747 . . .

Crawford isn't listening; his attention is rigidly fixed on proceedings on the flight deck.

'One-one, you are cleared for take-off. Fly heading one zero five and maintain one thousand feet and do not deviate. Go well, gentlemen, and go now.'

'Roger,' says the co-pilot. 'Heading one zero five and maintain one thousand feet. Have a good day.'

The sudden acceleration of the Guardian pushes Crawford back in his seat. His stomach, he feels, is somewhere near his throat.

The knowledge that Melinda Morrison has twice been cautioned for violent behaviour seems highly relevant to Detective Hoskins. Maybe she threatened her mother, he says. Maybe the mother got scared and just ran out of the house; didn't even have time to grab her things. Maybe, continues Hoskins, warming to his hypothesis, there was a history of threats or even fights and that's why the mother called Blade.

'It's Mr Singleton to you,' says Lucca. 'And, if she was being threatened, why didn't she call us?'

'Because if she'd called the police we'd have taken Melinda down; with her priors we'd have had no choice. Maybe she didn't want that. Maybe she just wanted somebody to read her kid the riot act; somebody who would know how to scare the shit out her, but not a real cop – no offence, Mr Singleton; not a real cop who would have put her kid in jail.'

'Blade,' says Lucca, 'this make any sense to you?'

Blade's thoughts are on what Melinda said to Jimmy: *Listen, you do what my mother says or I'll suck your lungs out through your nose.* 'Wasn't my impression,' he says carefully. 'I got the feeling they were pretty close, that Mrs Morrison was concerned about Melinda, not scared of her.'

Lucca glares at Hoskins who holds up his hands in surrender. 'Hey, it was just a theory.'

'Yeah, well, let's leave theory to the scientists and get ourselves some facts. Like, where's Melinda now?'

'School?'

'It's Saturday, Hoskins.'

'I meant to say, maybe she's with her school friends.'

'If she's got any. You know which school, Blade?'

'Miami Beach Senior High, I believe.'

'Okay, Hoskins, we'll go and make ourselves popular with the principal by spoiling her weekend. You better leave one of the patrol officers here to mind the house.'

'No need,' says Blade a little too swiftly and that gets him a knowing look from Lucca. Blade fidgets with his shoulders, looks at his watch. 'I figure that since I'm here, and the clock is running,

I may as well stick around for a while. Maybe she'll come back, her or Melinda. Either way, I'll call you. If not,' another shrug of the shoulder, 'I'll lock up the house and bring you the keys.'

Lucca is as watchful as a cat. '*Prospective* client is what you said.'

'Right, because I hadn't decided to take the case – and now I have, because she's got me intrigued. And, in any event, when I leave my office the meter starts running, and on weekends I charge double time.'

Lucca nods, not because he believes a word he has heard but because he is also intrigued. *Let's see where this goes*, he seems to be saying as he punches Blade lightly on the arm and heads towards the door.

Thirty-Nine

Flint is riding the swells on a cushion of air, or that's the way it feels. She has no idea where it came from, no recollection of climbing on board, but she seems to be lying on a thick wedge of polystyrene that is about as large as a queen-size mattress. Or perhaps she is hallucinating. She has certainly experienced some very strange dreams.

Dr P has paid a visit, sitting on the end of the makeshift raft wearing a scarlet robe, glowering at Flint like a stern judge about to pass sentence. Jack has been there, looking even more like a miniature version of Mandrake, mouthing the same lies. Aldus Cutter has appeared to her naked, speaking to her in Jerry Crawford's voice, saying that she looks as pink as a lobster, and she's made long languid love to a man in London she knows called Harry Cohen – and that is really weird because, nice guy though he is, Harry has never figured in her sexual fantasies.

The sun is merciless, spearing her with its heat. Whenever she drifts into consciousness she splashes herself with handfuls of sea water, trying to keep her body temperature down. The temptation to drink a few drops of the water is overwhelming and the sharp taste of salt in her mouth is her rebuke; a mocking reminder that amidst all this water there is nothing she can drink.

But the worst thing, the hardest to bear, is the replay of the auditory illusions. Yet again she is certain she hears the sound of approaching engines, feels a flutter of hope, lifts her head to scan the horizon, sees nothing but water, nothing at all.

At three thousand feet above sea level the Guardian is making parallel sweeps over an imaginary grid that covers one section of the fourteen-thousand-square-mile search area designated by the coordinator at Opa-Locka. Further north the HC-130 is flying similar patterns while the four Coast Guard vessels are searching the colder waters closer to the Florida coast. The relentless drone of the two Guardian's engines is soporific and Crawford catches himself drifting off to sleep. *Maybe for a minute*, he thinks and closes his eyes and the next thing he knows Glees is tugging urgently at his arm. 'Put your headset on,' he says. 'They think they've found something.'

Sitting in the rear of the Guardian, hemmed in by electronic hardware, is the avionics operator, a petty officer 3rd class named Popovic, and Crawford cranes his neck to look at him. Popovic's gaunt face glows white in the light of the monitor he is studying intently while, with the tips of two fingers, he works the joystick of a small transmitter to adjust the position of the primary thermal imaging camera that hangs underneath the nose of the Guardian. Popovic's prominent Adam's apple bobs as he begins speaking into an intercom microphone and Crawford grabs his headset to listen in.

'Target locked on, sir. Checking the coordinates.'

'In your own time, Mr Popovic.'

There is a pause and then, 'Skipper, the heading is three zero niner and the range is seven miles.'

'Okay, Mr Norbury' – this from the commander to the co-pilot – 'confirming: three zero niner and seven miles. Take her down.'

Almost instantly the aircraft tips steeply on its side until the wings must be practically vertical, makes a tight left turn, falls towards the sea at dash speed. The rate of descent is unlike anything Crawford has experienced, and terrifying, and he takes no comfort from the fact that even Glees looks distinctly uneasy. At the very last moment – or so it seems to Crawford – the plane pulls out of the dive and slows dramatically, and now they're flying no more than two hundred feet above the swells at very close to stall speed and Crawford is thinking, *How much do you people get paid?* However much it is, it's not enough to justify the risk; not in Crawford's strongly held opinion.

There are two observers on the Guardian, one on each side of the aircraft, scanning the sea with high-powered binoculars through panoramic windows, and it is the left-hand observer who says, 'Contact, Skip. At eleven o'clock from your position, range eight hundred yards.'

'I see the target. Let's take a closer look, Mr Norbury.'

The aircraft banks gently to the left, drops even closer to the waves, and Crawford and Glees, sharing the same window, strain to get their first glimpse.

'What the hell is that?' asks the commander.

The observer says, 'Some kind of rigid foam. Looks like packaging from a crate that got washed overboard.'

'Must have been one mighty big crate.'

'Okay, sir, I see a subject on board. Looks to be female . . . No, strike that. The subject is half naked and definitely female. No movement.'

'Can you see her, Agent Crawford?'

'No,' he says, struggling to focus his binoculars. Then, 'Yes! Now I see her.'

No more than one hundred feet away, Flint is sprawled on her back, her legs outstretched, her bare arms folded across her breasts. Crawford can't see her face because it is covered by a baseball cap but he can just make out what he believes to be the distinctive motif of the Buccaneer Hotel. He gives a loud whoop of delight.

'I gather we've found your friend, Agent Crawford.'

'You surely have.'

'She's still not moving, Skip,' says the observer. 'She's either asleep or unconscious, or she's . . .' He does not complete the sentence.

'Well, let's see if we can wake her up. Mr Norbury, take us up to five hundred feet and then make a pass directly over the subject, and when you do, hit those throttles. Mr Popovic, get yourself a rear view. See if she responds.'

'Yes, sir.'

'Okay, gentlemen, take your seats and strap yourselves in. This could get a little bumpy.'

To distract herself from the sound of phantom engines Flint has moved to another zone. In her imagination she is no longer adrift on the ocean but sitting comfortably and safely in her spiritual home: the apple orchard at Glebe Farm, in a shaded spot, sipping homemade lemonade, talking with Jack. Dr P is also present, mute for now, acting as observer. To all appearances Jack is still a baby, but he seems to have gained remarkable linguistic skills.

So, Mummy, tell me about my father.

He died, darling, before you were born. But, had he lived, he would have loved you enormously.

No, he wouldn't. Because you made him promise that he would never try to see me.

Only to protect you, my darling.

Why was he so bad? Why did you hate him so much?

Jack's face is red, mottled with uncertainty.

I didn't hate him, or not until the end. He was weak, Jack, and bad people exploited his weaknesses; drug dealers initially, and then spooks. The dealers made him vulnerable to pressure and the spooks applied it. Specifically, Nigel bloody Ridout of MI bloody six recruited your father to seduce me. Nigel bloody Ridout recruited your father to spy on the covert operation I was running.

Oblivious to the conversation, Flint's father – who is wearing a Panama hat and khaki shorts that expose his bony knees – cheerfully refills their glasses with lemonade. Flint's scenario does not permit Sally to be present, but in her mind's eye her father's lover hovers in the near distance, on the fringes of the orchard, like a spectre.

I love Sally, says Jack as though he's privy to his mother's thoughts.

And so you should.

But you took me away from her.

I know I did, and that was wrong. I should never have taken you away from Sally or Grandpa or here. This is your home, it's where you belong.

And you. It's your home, too.

One day it will be.

When?

Soon, Jack. Very soon, I promise.

Dr Przewalskii coughs in protest and Flint turns to face her. *Oh, I know what you're thinking, Dr P, but believe me . . .*

Whatever Flint was going to declare is lost, consumed in the tumultuous roar of two turbo-fan engines delivering some ten thousand pounds of thrust directly above her head.

'Mr Popovic, what do you see?'

The Guardian, having almost touched the waves, is now in a

steep spiralling climb; the sort of climb that spreads the lips, exposes the gums.

'The subject is definitely alive, sir. She sat up like she'd been hit with a cattle prod.'

'Take us back down, Mr Norbury, and depressurize the aircraft. And, Mr Cooper, prepare a sustenance pack, if you will.'

Cooper is the left-hand observer who doubles as the drop master. Into a gunny sack that is attached to two life jackets he places a bright orange position-indicating radio beacon, a jumpsuit that is also orange, a tube of sunscreen, bottled water, six Isotar high-energy candy bars and then he says, 'Do you want to scribble a note, Agent Crawford? Tell her to hold on? That help is on the way?'

Crawford pulls a pen and a notebook from his jacket pocket, begins writing, is still writing when the implication of Cooper's question strikes him. 'What do you mean, help is on the way? We're here!'

'Yeah, but right after I make the drop, we're leaving.'

'*Leaving?*' Crawford's tone is incredulous.

Over the intercom the commander interjects, 'Mr Crawford, we're running out of time – or, more precisely, out of endurance; meaning we're running out of fuel. Unless you want me to ditch this sucker in the sea, we've got no choice. We have to return to base.'

'What? You can't just leave her . . .'

'Please, just listen.' The commander's voice is loaded with an air of finality. 'As we speak there are two rescue choppers lifting off from Opa-Locka and the SRBs are on their way, and in the prevailing conditions they can make forty knots. The C-130 is also on its way and its got the endurance to babysit your friend for as long as it takes. Once that gunny sack hits the water, the radio beacon will be transmitting a signal that everybody can home in on. Within one hour, give or take, your friend is going to have so much company she's gonna need a dance card. Now, you've told us that Miss Flint is no quitter. Well, she doesn't need to fight, not any more. All she needs is the common sense to use what we're sending her: to protect herself from the sun, take in water and nourishment, stay exactly where she is and remain patient – and that's what you might tell her in your note. Are we clear about the situation, Agent Crawford?'

'Clear,' says Crawford as he resumes scribbling.

From about one mile away the Guardian begins a slow, low run towards Flint's precarious position and drop master Cooper opens the hatch.

Lackland AFB Texas

Forty

Seven miles west of the city of San Antonio, on seven thousand sprawling acres, Lackland Air Force Base hosts Wilford Hall, the largest Air Force medical facility in the United States, which specialises in the treatment of penetrating trauma injuries – such as those resulting from gunfire – and moderate to severe brain damage, which are two reasons why Jack Flint now lies within its care. Another reason, equally important to Aldus Cutter, is that the base no longer welcomes visitors. In the more edgy world of post-9/11, Lackland today is a strictly 'closed facility', efficiently guarded and very secure. For example – and Cutter knows this to be true because Rocco Morales has tried and failed – obtaining an up-to-date detailed map of the base is almost impossible, even on the internet.

Jack was transferred from Washington to Lackland by air-ambulance thirty hours ago to undergo a fresh battery of exhaustive diagnostic tests. In the case manager's office at Wilford Hall, where the window blinds are drawn and it's difficult to know if it's day or night, Cutter patiently awaits the results; waits also to learn the fate of Jack's mother.

'Rocco, quit your damn pacing, will you?' he grumbles from his supine position on the sofa. 'You're making me dizzy.'

Morales sighs heavily and slumps into a chair but even seated he can't keep his legs from fidgeting. It has been more than four hours since Blade last reported in from a payphone with his latest update: that Flint had been found alive, that rescue helicopters were on their way to her location and that Jerry Crawford was on top of the situation. Since then, not a word.

'Should I call Al on his cell, or Opa-Locka?'

'Are you kidding me?' Cutter raises himself into a sitting position, flexes his head to stretch his neck. 'You call either, you're gonna leave an audit trail that says we know Jerry and Grace are down there in Miami on some kind of operation – which we don't, right? So far as we're concerned, they've wandered off the reservation and wherever they are, whatever they're doing, we know nothing about it. And we don't want to know about it. Right?'

'Oh, sure,' says Morales, resuming his relentless pacing.

From his portfolio of stock reactions, Cutter pulls out the look that says he is bemused. 'You know, Rocco, you puzzle me. For a former cold-eyed killer, you're acting pretty friggin' flaky.'

This stops Morales in his tracks. 'Hey, Mr Cutter, I resent that. I was a *soldier*.'

'Sure you were, but you shot people; that was your job, right? My point being, when you were a shooter – in Afghanistan, in Iraq, in wherever – you'd lie in some fly-blown shit-hole for hours on end, days if you had to, waiting for your moment, and not move a muscle; ice cool. Now look at you. Blade hasn't called in for a couple of hours and you're as twitchy as a virgin on a first date. You're behaving out of character, Rocco. See what I'm saying? Question is, why?'

'Because I have this gut feeling, sir.'

'That says what?'

'That finally – and it was bound to happen – Grace has pushed her luck too far.'

'Naw,' drawls Cutter getting to his feet, heading for the coffee pot. 'I've also got a gut feeling, and my gut's bigger than yours, so let me tell you what's happening. You want some coffee? No, strike that; state you're in, the last thing you need is caffeine.' Cutter pours himself a cup, loads it with Sweet 'N Low. 'Rocco, I've got one hundred dollars that says that when the rescue choppers reached Flint's location the only thing wrong with her was her attitude. Winch man went down, or they dropped a diver in the sea, however they did it, and the first thing he hears is, *What took you so long?* My hundred dollars says they flew her back to Opa-Locka and insisted that she go to hospital, bitching all the way, and Jerry and Blade are with her – which is why Al's not answering his cell. Can't be heard talking to you, can he? Not if their operation is to remain deniable. Soon as he can get to a payphone with no one noticing, he'll call again.'

Cutter doesn't pace the room, he struts.

'Know what else my gut tells me? Round about now or anytime soon, Flint is gonna discharge herself from hospital – because with any luck the worst she's got is a mild case of sunstroke – and head for the shooter's house, because she's gonna figure out that the best way to find the shooter is to find the daughter, and somewhere in that house there will be leads.'

'How's she going to get in? Blade said he gave the keys to the cops.'

'Yeah, he did, didn't he.' Cutter winks. 'Rocco, I've got another hundred dollars that says Blade neglected to mention to you one tiny detail.'

'He had copies made?'

Cutter beams.

Miami Beach

Forty-One

At her daughter's request Mrs Shinoda has prepared gomaae for this evening's meal: spinach dressed with a sauce made of soya bean paste, ground sesame and just a tablespoon of sake. Unagi and Melinda are eating from finely decorated bowls in Unagi's bedroom – which is a carbon copy of Melinda's – sitting cross-legged on the floor, when Melinda's cell phone rings. She looks at the screen, sees that her mother is calling.

'Hi, Mom. Where are you?'

Silence on the line.

'Hello?'

'Hello, Melinda.' Flint makes no effort to impersonate Courtney Morrison's voice and Unagi sees the sudden tightening of her friend's face.

'Who is this?'

'A friend.'

Melinda is getting to her feet. 'You're a friend of Mom's?'

'No, a friend of yours – or I could be. In the days to come you're going to need a friend, Melinda.'

'What are you talking about? Who are you?' Melinda's puzzlement is turning swiftly into anger. 'How did you get my mother's phone?'

'She left it behind. I think she wanted me to have it, so I would know how to find you. Do you know where she's gone, Melinda?'

'New . . .' slips out before she can stop herself.

'New where, Melinda?'

'I don't know.'

'Oh, come on, Melinda. New York? New England? New Haven?'

'Fuck off, bitch!' Melinda shouts this down the line with sudden, explosive venom and Unagi's dark eyes register her alarm.

Doushita no? she whispers – *What's the matter?*

Flint asks with unnatural calm, 'Do you mean go away? You know I can't do that, Melinda. You know that's not going to happen.'

And then Flint ends the call.

Flint is in Courtney Morrison's bedroom, picking through her things, working with the ambient light coming through the windows. No lamps are on in the house. From the street the impression you get is that the Morrison residence has been abandoned; locked up and left in a powerful hurry.

Through the radio earpiece that Blade has supplied – state-of-the-art equipment is what he'd promised – Flint hears a crackle of static and snatches of a disembodied voice. *Visitors* is the only word she thinks she makes out. 'Come back,' she quietly demands, her mouth close to the microphone that is clipped to the collar of the Coast Guard's bright orange jumpsuit. 'I didn't copy that. Say again.'

More static is the only acknowledgement she receives. So much for state of the art, she thinks, moving swiftly from Courtney's bedroom to the top of the stairs where she hides in deep shadow, listening for the slightest sound. Blade and Brendan Glees are in separate cars parked one hundred yards apart at the front of the house while Jerry Crawford has found a concealed spot in the backyard, all on lookout duty and all linked to her by radio; a radio that *doesn't bloody work*, apparently. On her feet Flint wears a pair of trainers liberated from Courtney's wardrobe that are almost a perfect fit. The handgun Blade has loaned her is a nine-shot .45 semi-automatic with a rosewood grip and a frame made of lightweight scandium alloy. State of the art, no doubt; it feels like a feather in her hand.

There is no auditory evidence of an intrusion but Flint's instincts tell her that she has to make sure. One step at a time, pausing on each step to re-examine her surroundings, she descends the staircase. A sound from below and Flint freezes, analyses what she's heard. Her senses decide it was nothing more than the faint report of a door shifting on its hinges – but moved by what? The brushing of a human body? It has already occurred to Flint that, even in the half-light, the luminescent jumpsuit makes her a glowing target but her working assumption is that if and when Melinda returns to the house, she will not come armed. If it's Melinda's mother who's come home, then Flint's working assumption is the opposite.

Through continuing interference she hears Blade say, '. . . what's your status?' *Distinctly dodgy* is the answer but she can't afford to say it. Instead, with her left forefinger, she lightly scratches the face of the microphone twice, then once, then twice again – an improvised code that says she is uncertain. She hears three sharp taps in reply – *Message received and understood* – and that bolsters her resolve to continue the descent.

Now she's standing at the foot of the stairs, examining every part of the living room over the foresight of the semi-automatic. To her left, the kitchen door is half ajar; not how it was, she's pretty sure.

Flint edges away from the kitchen, moving across the living room until her back is pressed against the wall. With her left hand she reaches behind to unlock and open the front door and says loudly to nobody – because no one is there – 'Okay, gentleman, I need back-up. Intruders on the premises.'

And then to the kitchen she calls in minatory terms, 'You in there, we're armed federal agents and we will open fire if necessary. If you have weapons, place them on the floor. Then step away and show yourselves, and keep your hands where we can see them.'

The silence mocks her.

Now what? Flint asks herself, feeling the dead weight of indecision. She knows she has to act but she also knows that in the prefrontal cortex, just above her eyes, the stress has activated an enzyme which is clouding her judgement. Should she advance towards the kitchen, or escape through the front door, or just stay put? She can't make up her mind.

Frozen, she's staring at the kitchen door when it swings towards her; not by much, a couple of inches or so, and then it settles. Now it swings back on its hinges, settles again and then the pattern repeats – and she's thinking that the cause has to be the ebb and flow of a current of air. But how can there be a draught passing through the kitchen when, before she went upstairs, she'd made absolutely sure that the back door was locked, the window firmly closed?

Because that was then and this is now.

'Okay.' Flint snaps the slide of the .45, a distinctive warning if ever there was one. 'For the last time, put your hands in the air and show yourself AND DO IT NOW.'

Nothing, and the glob of grey brain matter that is Flint's amygdale is working overtime, spewing unwanted adrenaline into her bloodstream, disrupting rational thought. And then, mercifully, her training kicks in and she no longer needs to think. She's crossing the living room on the silent soles of Courtney's trainers, reaching the doorway, no hesitation, making her entry fast and low, slamming the door against the wall with her shoulder as she passes through, finding cover. In a low crouch behind one of the cabinets she listens, hears only the sound of her heart pumping and the slow tattoo of a dripping tap.

In circumstances like this, Flint was taught not to wait. A soundless count of one and she steps out from behind the cabinet and stands with her legs apart, the knees slightly bent, arms extended and braced, the .45 in the approved two-handed grip held just below her line of vision, swivelling her head and upper body in an arc across the target zone like the gun turret of a tank. There is no target to fire at.

She makes another hard entry, this one into the utility room. Empty, and nowhere for even a child to hide. She returns to the kitchen, the gun now by her side pointing at the floor, is about to speak into the microphone – *Crawdaddy, Blade, Glees? Do any of you bloody copy?* – when she feels a breath of wind on her face, suddenly knows the source of the draught.

The back door is no longer locked or closed, it's shifting in the breeze.

Instantly Flint resumes what the instructors at Quantico call the ready position – ready to kill, that is – one searing thought on her mind. This was Jerry Crawford's door to watch and guard from his concealed position in the yard and nobody could have reached it without him seeing. He would have called out a challenge, fired a warning shot if he'd had to, and Flint would have heard it, or that was the plan. As Flint sees it she must make the assumption that there's only one explanation for the eerie silence, represented by the last words any cop wants to say or hear said: *Officer down!*

Five fast strides take Flint to the threshold where she uses the toe of one of Courtney's trainers to fully open the back door. She steps into the yard, peering into the darkness, resisting the temptation to call out Crawford's name.

'Hello, bitch.'

The voice comes from her right and Flint pivots towards the sound, dropping to one knee, raising the gun, the trigger half pulled. She barely has time to register her first look at Melinda before she senses the fast approach of something – someone – from behind; half turns, takes two stunning blows, one to her left shoulder, the other to the left side of her head. The blows send her sprawling and, as her right elbow hits the ground, the gun discharges far too close to her face. She is deafened by the blast, feels the sting of powder burns on her cheeks.

Two more blows, a heavy one to the back of the head, a lighter one to the kidneys. Her instinct is to protect her head with her arms. Instead she rolls onto her left side and blindly lashes out with the hand that is still holding the gun; feels the solid impact of the rosewood stock on bone, hears a yelp of pain. Flint strikes again with all of the force she can find and this time she thinks she hears the sound of breaking bone.

'YOU FUCKING SHIT . . .'

Melinda is lying on the ground, clutching her ankles, screaming obscenities.

Which leaves the other one, a whirling dervish of a girl who dances around Flint delivering painful kicks. She looks like a child, so small and thin-boned you might think you could snap her like a twig but she's fast on her feet and she knows how to hurt. Twisting, rolling, Flint does her best to dodge the kicks, tries to counter-attack with her own feet. It is more by luck than judgement that she finally lands a decent blow to the midriff, takes her tormentor's breath away, buys herself the time to scramble to her feet. The gun is still in her right hand. She takes two steps back, takes aim at the child's head, changes her mind, lowers her arm.

'Listen,' she says, 'just stop it. I don't want to have to hurt you.'

Unagi, motionless, watches Flint with blank eyes. Perhaps she also hears the approach of the cavalry.

'Out here in the yard,' Flint calls.

Blade comes charging through the back door, takes in the scene.

'Who's she?'

'Melinda's friend.'

'And where's Melinda?'

There, Flint is on the point of saying, but Melinda is no longer lying on the ground. She's vanished, nowhere to be seen.

Melinda's right ankle may or may not be broken but it hurts like hell and it can't bear her weight. Holding on to the banister with both hands she has to hop up the stairs on one foot to reach her bedroom, retrieve what she needs. Her return journey is even more difficult because now she has only one hand free. Flint is waiting for her by the switch at the foot of the stairs; snaps on the lights, tells her to stop.

'Is that a real sword, Melinda?'

'What do you think, bitch?'

'I think you should put it down.'

'Right.' Melinda grins, makes two scything motions with the sword as though she's cutting grass. She is stranded on the seventh step from the bottom, too high to make a leap. 'So, what? You're going to shoot a kid?'

'If I have to,' says Flint.

'That's really fucking brave.' Melinda is five foot five, maybe five six, but Flint reckons she must weigh one hundred and ninety pounds. From this angle of view she has no visible neck. She's wearing jeans that are cut off just below the knee and a black tank top that shows off the bulk of her deltoids and biceps. The colour of her hair is as vivid an orange as Flint's jumpsuit.

'Put the sword down, Melinda.' Flint is aware that Brendan Glees has entered through the open front door, that he's standing to her left slightly behind her, that he's holding a handgun that is pointed vaguely in Melinda's direction.

Melinda pays him no attention. 'Make me,' she says to Flint.

'Okay,' and Flint fires one shot that is aimed at the banister just below the point where Melinda is holding on. The wood splinters, and Melinda snatches her hand away, and the momentum of the movement causes her to wobble. Trying instinctively to regain her balance, she slams her right foot on the stair and the stab of pain in her ankle makes her shriek. She lifts her right foot to relieve the pain and now her balance is totally lost and she's falling forward, her head coming down, and as she falls, Flint – watching in slow motion – sees Melinda turn the sword so that the point is pressed against her stomach, sees her take the handle in both hands.

Melinda's final scream is of words that Flint does not comprehend. They sound Japanese: a cry of defiance or triumph, perhaps; maybe a curse.

Forty-Two

There is hell to pay, of course. Even as Blade called in the incident, asking for paramedics, the first patrol car was pulling up outside Courtney Morrison's house in response to reports of shots fired. Now there are half a dozen marked and unmarked cars parked haphazardly in the street, two ambulances, a crime scene truck. Beyond the police cordon, TV news crews are setting up their lights.

Inside the house a triage team is working on Melinda who lies where she fell at the foot of the stairs, still impaled on the sword, while out in the backyard a second team attends to Jerry Crawford. He is suffering from severe concussion and maybe worse, caused by a blow to the back of his head, but at least he's regained consciousness.

'We're getting too damn old for this,' he says blearily to Flint who is squatting on the ground beside him.

'Speak for yourself.' With her fingers she touches his lips. 'On the other hand, you could be right.'

'That her?' Crawford can't move his head because of the neck brace but his eyes find the spot where Unagi stands motionless as a pillar in a pool of light spilling from the kitchen window, her hands and her ankles restrained by plastic ties. 'Doesn't look like she could make a ripple in a pond.'

'Yeah? Well, I've got bruises all over my body that say otherwise. Trust me, Crawdaddy, she's a hellcat.'

'Know what she bushwhacked me with?'

'A slab of concrete that weighs almost as much as she does. She and Melinda hauled it up to the top of the fence and tried to drop it on your head. Lucky for you, they mainly missed. You took a glancing blow.'

The medics tell Flint she's getting in the way. She leaves

Crawford to their care and wanders past Unagi into the kitchen where Blade and Manny Lucca are in animated conversation. Actually, considering the circumstances, Lieutenant Lucca seems surprisingly relaxed. Approaching them, Flint hears him laugh as though Blade has told a joke.

'You were being *circumambulatory*? That's a mighty big word, Blade. What the fuck do you mean?'

'I was walking around the truth.'

'Right! Walking, Blade? I'd say you were more like *running* around the truth.' He winks at Flint. 'How are you doing?'

'I don't really know. Okay I think, but it's been a long day. I've got a question: the reporters outside, is there any way to keep them in the dark about Melinda?'

'Hell, I don't see how. You get a seventeen-year-old kid committing hara-kiri in South Beach, people are liable to talk, don't you think?'

'Sure, but I need a little time.'

Lucca looks amused. 'That prick behind me' – he jerks his head to indicate the man standing in the doorway of the living room – 'he gets his way, you don't have *any* time.'

His name is Seth Deaver, a special agent with the Miami field office of the FBI, and he turned up twenty minutes ago claiming federal jurisdiction. Flint told him no, that the jurisdiction was hers, and since she outranks him by several grades in the federal hierarchy, the ring remains hers. But Deaver hasn't given up. He's been on the phone to his boss and his boss has been lighting up the lines to Washington and now the justice department is involved, and it all depends on how Cutter plays the game. Will he deny the operation or belatedly claim it? So far Cutter hasn't responded to her urgent messages and Flint is beginning to think that his silence could be ominous. She gives no hint of this to Lucca.

'The prick's still on the phone, I expect,' he says, not turning round to look.

'Glued to his ear.'

'Then it doesn't seem like he's going to quit.'

'Manny, he's a Feeb. He thinks he walks on water. What else do you expect?' She touches Lucca on the shoulder, smiles at Blade, passes on. 'Coming through,' she barks at Deaver and he hurriedly steps aside.

The living room looks like a slaughterhouse. Though the triage team has stemmed the flow, Melinda is still losing blood through the exit wound and it's spreading around her like a lake that has breached its banks. They are transfusing her with O negative, giving her oxygen, applying defibrillation paddles to the chest wall to normalize her heartbeat but they can't decide what to do about the sword. Removing it entails enormous risk. So does moving Melinda with the sword still in place.

Flint looks down on Melinda's pallid face and feels the pull of pity. Then it's Jack's frozen face she sees and the pity drains. The leader of the triage team tells her that the call is impossible to make; that an ER surgical unit with some experience of impalement injuries is on its way. 'Let's hope,' Flint says vaguely and drifts away, skirting the lake, careful not to get blood on Courtney's trainers.

Two uniformed cops who are guarding the front door let her through with respectful nods. They may not know precisely who she is but in a curious way the vivid orange jumpsuit seems to imply her authority. The sergeant commanding the cordon approaches her and asks, 'Anything you need?'

'Air,' she says. 'And then I ought to feed the animals.'

She means the reporters who are baying at her from behind the tape, pointing their microphones, pleading for snippets of information. She seems to hesitate and then flutters towards them like a moth drawn by their lights.

Courtney, are you watching this on live TV? is what she's thinking.

'Ma'am, ma'am, can you tell us what's going on?'

She stands before the cameras waiting for the clamour to subside. Eventually she begins, 'Earlier this evening a federal officer was attacked at this location and seriously injured. The paramedics are still assessing the agent's medical condition prior to moving him to hospital. One of the perpetrators ... excuse me, one of the *alleged* perpetrators of the attack is in custody. We have reason to believe that more than one perpetrator was involved but, so far, only one arrest has been made. Obviously, the investigation is continuing. We anticipate further arrests in due course.'

Flint stops, as though she's said all that needs to be said. When the barrage of questions erupts she feigns to look surprised.

Walk the fine line, girl. This is going out live, and it's on tape, so send a message to Courtney but do not tell a single lie.

'Whoa! Hey, one at a time!' Flint holds out her palms to calm then. 'I'll answer your questions as best I can. No, the injured officer is not an FBI agent, though the FBI is fully participating in the investigation into the attack. As to what the injured agent was investigating, I can't tell you that, not right now, except to say that it was a federal crime. Yes, the suspect in custody is a female. No, she did not attempt to disembowel herself, whatever you may have heard. In fact the last time I saw her, which was a couple of moments ago, she looked . . . well, I guess the word is serene. No, the suspect in custody has no known connection with this location. No, she was not the subject of the agent's investigation. Were other federal agents involved? Yes, me. That's all I've got, folks.'

Flint turns her back on the cameras, walks away; ignores the shouted further questions and a strident demand: *And who the hell are you?*

Still no word from Cutter but before he left the scene Special Agent Deaver said, with suprising good grace, 'Well, ma'am, it's all yours, apparently, and I wish you luck.' So Flint assumes Cutter has worked his customary magic in Washington and somehow persuaded Justice that the strike force should retain control of an operation that was never officially sanctioned; that – for the record – never even existed. One of these days she'll ask him how he pulled it off and all he'll offer up is one of his honeyed Texan homilies: *When serving up bullshit to a sweet-toothed crowd, be sure to mix in a little molasses.* Some such nonsense. She mentally shrugs. What does it matter how he did it? She's never doubted that Cutter's talent for dissimulation is almost as ripe as hers.

The ER surgical unit has arrived and decreed that the sword should be removed from Melinda's abdomen in situ and even now the living room is being converted into a makeshift operating theatre. Flint goes to check on Crawford who is still in the backyard. The chief paramedic, wearing a tag that says his name is Barney Wallace, tells her they are ready to move Jerry to hospital but Flint says no, not yet. And then, before she knows it, events are spiralling out of control.

Wallace, who towers over her, says, 'Hey, lady, it's not your call.'

'Yes it is, that's exactly what it is. Tell me about his vital signs. Is he stable?'

'That's not the point. The point is—'

'The point is, Mr Wallace, unless you're telling me that your patient's life is in immediate danger, he and you are going nowhere.'

'I'm calling my supervisor.'

'No, you're not.'

Wallace's radio is in a holster clipped to his lapel and all he needs to do is press the transmit button and talk, but something in Flint's mien makes him hesitate. Over the top of her head, he sees Lucca checking on Unagi and calls out to him, 'Hey, Lieutenant, you got a minute?'

So here comes the acid test of Flint's dubious authority for there is no doubt in her mind that when it comes to managing events at the crime scene, Manny Lucca is the one in charge. She turns to watch his approach, gives him a pleading smile.

'Hey, Barney, what's up?'

'Whoever this woman is—'

'*Deputy Director* Flint is who she is,' Lucca interrupts, stressing her title in a manner that suggests Barney should show a little respect.

'Yeah, well, whatever. *She* says I can't take my patient to hospital, which is where he needs to be, and I'm not accepting responsibility for what might happen if we delay. Now, either you let me do my job or you give me a goddamned order to put my patient's life at risk.' Barney Wallace has protruding eyes that now bulge with righteousness.

'Right,' says Lucca.

'What the hell does that mean? We move him or we don't?'

'You can't move him,' says Flint. 'Until I tell you.'

'I wasn't asking you.'

'The answer's the same,' says Lucca, and Wallace has a look on his face that suggests he's ready to explode.

For a moment he stands glowering at Flint and Lucca as though there is nothing to choose between them. Then, 'Okay, I'm out of here.' He turns and makes a circular motion with an upheld hand that says to his team, *Let's wrap this up*.

'WALLACE!' His name explodes from Flint's mouth like an unexpected thunderclap. 'Stay where you are' – said with such menace that Wallace freezes on the spot. 'Turn around,' she demands and reluctantly he does. 'Listen to me,' her voice much softer now. 'We're trying to apprehend a professional killer, some-one who shoots people for a living, someone who's taken money to murder a child. And I can't afford to have you leave here right now because, if you do, you will compromise this operation, and more innocent civilians could end up being killed. Do you understand? You're not just attending a crime scene, Mr Wallace, you're a vital part of a mission to save lives. And, just for the record, your patient is both a colleague and a really close friend of mine, and if I thought for one minute that—'

'Question is, does he take sugar?' says Crawford quietly from his supine position on the stretcher.

'What?' – this from Wallace.

'Hell, you're all talking about me like I'm not even here. Don't I get a say in any of this? Barney,' Crawford continues quickly, 'I appreciate your concern and your professionalism, I surely do. But, like you, I'm a public servant working at the sharp end, and we all know the rules: when the shit's flying we're first in, last out, right? And, right now, the priority is catching the killer and if that means I have to lie here for a while . . . well, that's just the way it is.'

Wallace says, 'Do you understand what an untreated sub-dural haemorrhage can do to you?'

'You think my brain is bleeding?'

'I don't know. Given the injury you sustained, it could be. I do know that we need to get you to the hospital to find out. I do know that if you are haemorrhaging, and we don't do something about it pretty damn quick, you're likely gonna to die.'

Flint shudders inside. Rough count, there are seven people watching her – eight if you include Unagi – and she feels like an executioner with one hand on the switch.

'Grace?' asks Lucca uncertainly, shifting on his feet.

Move him out is what she wants to say – what she might say unless Jerry intervenes. Restrained by the neck brace, he's watching her like a bear caught in a trap.

'Give it one hour,' he finally says.

'No, thirty minutes max,' is what she replies. 'Then, come what may, you go to hospital.'

The people around Flint look away as though they want no part of her decision. Wallace says, 'I'll tell you something, lady. I'm mighty glad I'm not your friend.'

Flint is in Melinda's room, lying on her bed. She has her eyes closed, Melinda's cell phone in her hands, willing it to ring.

'Knock, knock,' says Blade from the doorway. 'Do you mind a little company?'

'Hey, I was wondering where you were.'

He closes the door. 'I thought I'd slip away and give Cutter a call.'

'And?' asks Flint, getting to her feet.

'Couldn't reach him because he's on his way to Washington. Some kind of flap.' Blade smiles and adds, 'Can't imagine what. Anyway, I got Rocco instead and I've got good news for you about Jack. The doctors at Lackland are optimistic that there's no permanent brain damage. Actually, officially they are *guardedly optimistic* but that's doctors for you. Rocco said that when they gave him the news they had grins on their faces about a mile wide.'

She can't take this in; too much information arriving too quickly. Staring at Blade as though she's trying to recall who he is, all she can manage to say is, 'Lackland?'

'Lackland Air Force Base. In Texas . . . where Jack is. You didn't know?'

She nods her head but Blade knows she means *No*. Her knees are beginning to buckle when Blade reaches her, wraps her in his arms. 'Grace, what I'm saying is, Jack's going to be okay.'

Flint's arbitrary deadline for moving Crawford to hospital has five minutes to run. She and Blade are sitting side by side on a tatami mat, their backs against the wall, when they are startled by the trill of a mockingbird's song. It takes a moment for them both to realise that Melinda's phone is ringing. Flint grabs the phone, Blade is on his feet heading for the door. 'Don't answer it, not yet,' he reminds her. On the phone's bright tiny screen there is an announcement that says that the identity of the caller is UNKNOWN.

Blade wrenches open the door, yells down the stairs, 'Manny, we have contact.'

It seems to take forever for Lieutenant Lucca to arrive in the doorway, gabbling into his radio; another age before he makes the thumbs-up sign giving Flint the go-ahead to take the call.

'Oh, Courtney,' she says into the phone. 'What have we done to our children?'

In South Beach, Flint stands at the top of Courtney Morrison's staircase looking down on the surreal scene where ER surgeons are fighting for Melinda's life. On Sanibel island, some one hundred and sixty miles to the north-west, Courtney stands in the kitchen of a small cottage that is lit only by flickering images on a television screen – live images of the exterior of her South Beach house. She is holding a cell phone into which she declines to say a single word. Not that her silence will affect the outcome. In Jacksonville, Florida, constantly encouraged by Manny Lucca, engineers for T-Mobile are relentlessly honing in on the location of her signal.

'Courtney, shall I tell you what I can see?'

Lucca is making frantic hand signals: *Keep her on the line.*

'In your living room, on your dining table, they've laid sheets and towels, anything they could find in your linen cupboard, to make Melinda as comfortable as possible; all ruined, I'm afraid, because of the blood. They're working to remove the sword – the one she had on her wall, the one she stuck into her belly – without causing a fatal haemorrhage. Because that's the risk, you see: that when they remove the sword they'll sever an artery and she'll bleed to death before they can stop it. So, they're being *very* careful, taking their time – though I'm not sure that time is on Melinda's side. I won't lie to you, Courtney. Melinda is in a very, very bad way. All I can promise you is that they're doing everything they can to save her. You'd know that, if you were here.'

Keep talking, Lucca is signalling.

'Jesus, Courtney, what a bloody mess. My baby's in a coma and Melinda's at death's door. Even if she makes it, she's likely to be wearing a colostomy bag for the rest of her life – and, as things stand, she's going to be wearing it in jail. Because she tried to kill a federal agent, you see, and that means she's looking at thirty years to life and, if he dies – and that's a real possibility, Courtney, because he's still out in your backyard with a possible sub-dural haemorrhage – then we're talking about a capital murder charge. Maybe her age will save her from the chair, but I have to tell you, Courtney, one way and another, Melinda's prospects are looking pretty bloody grim.'

Flint pauses for two beats. Then, 'Unless you help her.'

Lucca scribbles on a notepad, shows it to Flint: *She's in Lee County, somewhere near Fort Myers Beach. Sanibel island, maybe.*

'You can help her, Courtney. Shall I tell you how? Wait, hold on a second, I think the doctors are about to . . . I'm going to try and get a better view. She's got so many tubes and trauma lines coming out of her, just like my baby did after you shot him . . . Okay, I can see more clearly now. Yes, I was right, they're about to remove the sword. Courtney, if you've got a god, this would be a good moment to pray.'

Coming from Melinda's phone Flint hears what she thinks is a stifled sob. Whispering now, she continues her running commentary.

'Easy does it, guys, e-a-s-y does it. Hell, what am I talking about? They know what they're doing, of course they do. You should appreciate, Courtney, that since you came into my life – actually, shot into my life – I've seen more emergency doctors at work than I care to count and I can tell you that these guys are good, *really* good. Amazing, isn't it, if you think about it? You and me, it takes us – what? – a fraction of a second to pull the trigger and take a life? And if we're slightly off target and there's still a life that might be saved, these doctors come out of nowhere and they spend hours trying to undo what we've done. Yet we're the ones who get the money. I know I do. I know that I'm better paid than any of the doctors who kept my baby alive, got him to the hospital; for that matter, I'm better paid than any of those guys down there in your living room right now who are trying to save Melinda . . . Another matter of interest, Courtney, what did Gröber and Çarçani pay you to shoot my son? More than . . . wait, wait . . .'

Lieutenant Lucca has passed his phone and his notepad to Blade and he's running down the stairs. Blade scribbles, shows it to Flint: *It's Sanibel. The bitch is trapped. Manny's gone to get the causeway closed.*

'Okay, Courtney, the sword is out . . . They're working on the exit wound . . . So far, so good . . . It's . . .'

Sounds of a commotion, insistent shouts of *Move it* come barging from below.

'Did you hear that, Courtney? They're moving her out. If you're watching this on TV then, any second now, you're going to see Melinda on a gurney come flying out of your front door. Wait, they're moving my guy too . . . Christ, he looks pale. We've got two very poorly people here, Courtney, but at least they're on their way to hospital . . . I don't know which one yet. I'll try to find out.'

Blade has scribbled another message: *In the vicinity of Rabbit Road and West Gulf Drive.*

Lucca is coming back up the stairs, out of breath, mouthing a message of his own: *Sanibel's being sealed.* He thrusts into Flint's hand a street map of the island. *SWAT team on its way. Maybe you should tell her?*

Flint waits; waits until she hears the keening sirens of the convoy that is leaving Courtney's house.

'Okay, can you see that, are you watching? Melinda and the guy she tried to kill – his name is Jerry, incidentally – they're on their way, sharing the same ambulance. Which is ironic if you think about it, victim and perpetrator lying side by side. But then, I suppose Melinda is also a victim, in a way.' Flint coughs into the phone. 'Excuse me, I need to take a drink of water.' *Now?* she mouths to Lucca. *Yes.* 'Courtney, can you hear the other sirens yet? The ones that are much, much closer to you. Maybe not. Give it a moment . . .' Flint is urgently scanning the map, trying to locate Rabbit Road. 'They should be crossing the causeway by now . . . entering Periwinkle Way, I guess. It won't be long before they get to where you are so you need to decide what you're going to do. Fight or flight, is that what you're thinking, Courtney? Well, frankly I don't think either is a real option, do you? I mean, you're trapped on an island that is now totally sealed off and, if you decide to fight, you'll be going up against at least a dozen guns; guns with laser sights and guys with CS gas canisters and stun grenades – all the usual paraphernalia. Oh, I know you're a great shot, Courtney, of course I do, but this time your targets will be shooting back and that makes a whole lot of difference. Believe it, I've been there . . . Courtney, you don't have a chance – and neither does Melinda –

unless you come in. I hate your guts, Courtney, but I'll make you this promise: if you come in, if you cooperate, I'll do everything I can for you; you and Melinda.'

'Go to fucking hell!' – the first and only words that Courtney Morrison speaks.

When Flint looks, the message on the screen of Melinda's phone says, CALLER HAS HUNG UP.

Sanibel Island

Forty-Three

In a corner of the terminal at Opa-Locka airport, waiting for the Metro-Dade police helicopter to arrive to take them to Sanibel, Lieutenant Lucca proposed to Blade that it might be better for Flint if they left her behind. She'd had a long, traumatic day, he said, and she could do with some rest. Anyway, she wasn't needed for the end game and, frankly, there were people – at FDLE, at the State Police and especially at the FBI – who thought she would be more of a liability than an asset when it came to securing the arrest of Courtney Morrison.

'Just promise me one thing,' Blade said. 'If that's what you plan on telling her then before you do just give me the heads-up, will you?'

'Why?'

'So I can take adequate cover.'

'Which is exactly my point, Al. Hey, don't get me wrong, I like Flint. I like her spirit, and there's no question she's one gutsy lady. But she's reckless, out of control.'

'And you say that because?'

'Look at the stunt she pulled this morning. You had your prime suspect under surveillance, corralled. All you had to do was call me. Instead of which, Flint—'

'And if I had called you you'd have done what, Manny? Arrested Morrison on the grounds that she was one of about half a million people who live close to the beach from where the sand came? That she might, or might not, resemble the shooter in the pictures? Except we can't prove that the woman in the pictures *was* the shooter. And then what? Round about now, I reckon, Morrison's lawyer *and* the State Attorney would be asking you what exactly was your probable cause, and since you didn't have any, except for our say-so, Morrison would be walking. Instead of which Flint spooked her. I don't know what Grace said or did on the beach but, whatever it was, it worked – even if she did get herself half-drowned in the process. And then she spooked Morrison's kid – and, okay, the kid hurt herself but that wasn't Flint's fault – and, as a result, we know where Morrison is and she's not just a suspect any more. She's a fugitive, probably armed, and she won't obey lawful instructions to surrender – then suddenly, entirely due to Flint, you *do* have probable cause. Okay, you're right, Flint's a wild card, no question about it; not a conventional cop and not a good example to any of your fledgling detectives. On the other hand, being conventional, going by the book, doesn't always get the job done.'

'Al, like I said, she's got to be exhausted, dead on her feet' – Lieutenant Lucca's last throw of the dice.

'Flint? You're kidding me. Manny, you and me, *we're* exhausted – I know I am. Grace, with the target in her sights? Believe me, she doesn't really need a ride in your chopper. In her mind she's already halfway to Sanibel, flying at twenty thousand feet.'

Her second helicopter ride of the day and Flint has grown almost nonchalant. She did notice with some alarm that this helicopter had just one pilot, a single engine, only two rotor blades instead of four. *But, hey, it flies.* They've been in the air just about an hour and already she can see Sanibel below them blinking like a discotheque with the blue and red lights of emergency vehicles. Flint is on a bench seat, squeezed between Blade and Lieutenant Lucca, listening through headphones to updates from the ground as the noose tightens around Courtney Morrison.

She's holed up in some place called Dogwood – not a typical Sanibel low-rise condominium, apparently, but a collection of twelve free-standing cottages set back from West Gulf Drive in lush tropical vegetation. Courtney's property is a simple wooden A-frame on the northern edge of Dogwood that is bordered on three sides by water. The only entry leads into a small kitchen and then the formal living room. There is one bedroom with a bathroom en suite, and that's it. They know this because an enterprising Sanibel cop, one of the island's nineteen sworn officers, tracked down a local realtor who still owned a promotional video showing every detail of the interior from the days when it was rented out as 'the perfect honeymoon cottage'. In the back of a command truck the police SWAT team from Fort Myers is studying the video now.

Half a mile away the headlights of four state trooper patrol cars are illuminating the patch of ground where the helicopter will land.

'Mainly,' says Lieutenant Lucca to Flint apropos of nothing, 'the major crime problem on Sanibel is alligator attacks.'

'Really?'

'Yeah, and gators feed at night. So, if you're planning on going snooping anywhere near the lakes around Courtney's property, you might want to keep that in mind.'

'I thought I'd just walk in through the front door.'

'Right,' says Lucca as though she's making a joke.

But that's exactly what Flint has in mind.

Standing ten feet away from the four steps leading to Courtney's cottage, highly visible in her bright orange jumpsuit, Flint calls out into the darkness, 'Courtney, we need to talk, so I'm coming in through your front door. I'm unarmed and I'm coming in alone – and you do whatever you think is in your best interests. But before you shoot me, if that's your intention, you need to know that there's sufficient firepower out here to re-invade Iraq. Courtney, you shoot me, you die; it's as simple as that.'

No! the FBI hostage negotiator insisted when, ten minutes ago, on the fringes of Dogwood, Flint hastily outlined her intended strategy. The cardinal rule of negotiation, he said, was never make threats. 'What you're making is a sale, and what you're selling, however tenuous, is hope.'

And Flint said, 'It's Lance Agnew, right? We've met. I attended two of your lectures at Quantico and the last time, afterwards, we talked about your analogy between a car salesman and a negotiator and about, in both cases, the critical establishment of trust. As you said, sell the customer a lemon, they're never going to trust you again.'

'I remember.'

'Okay, I transcribed my notes of your lecture and that's now mandatory reading at the strike force and I've been following your advice all day. I very deliberately have *not* sold the subject a lemon; everything I've told her is true, and she knows it – or she ought to. So I'm suggesting I've established at least some basis for trust, enough for her to believe that what I tell her is for her potential benefit. And when I tell her that she's facing overwhelming force, that's not a threat, that's a caution, prudent advice.'

'Everything you've told her is true?'

'I think so. Why the raised eyebrows?'

'Because I've listened to the tape of your telephone conversation with Morrison and you implied – hell, more than implied, you practically promised her that if she comes in, her daughter won't be charged with attempted murder, or worse.'

'So?'

'You know that's not your call. What Melinda gets charged with is down to the States Attorney's office, or maybe the District Attorney.'

'Sure it is, but I also know that I'm going to be a primary witness at Melinda's trial, and no prosecutor in their right mind is going to press a charge that I won't support on the stand. *If* her mother comes in, *if* she cooperates, *if* she agrees to testify against her co-conspirators, then my opinion will be that the worst Melinda should be looking at is a charge of aggravated assault.'

'And if she doesn't come in? Or if Jerry Crawford dies from his injuries?'

Flint doesn't have answers except to say, 'In my experience, Mr Agnew, worst-case scenarios are self-defeating if not a counsel of despair. Let's see what happens, shall we?'

Do not make threats. Do not provoke. Do not bluff. Do not make promises she knows you can't keep. On the other hand, give her reason to believe that she can save Melinda, if not herself. Don't force it. So long as the negotiations are going in the right direction, go with the flow.

Agent Agnew's advice to the forefront of her mind, Flint takes a deep breath and calls, 'Okay, Courtney, this is it; here I come.'

The front door is not locked or barricaded. Flint pushes it open, enters the kitchen area, moves to the threshold of the living room, pauses to make a panoramic scan. To her immediate left she sees an unframed canvas hanging on the wall – a striking portrayal of a lighthouse reaching up into towering storm clouds – and, beyond that, a closed louvre door that she knows leads to the bedroom. On the wall she is facing there is a circular mirror with a swirling wrought-iron frame in which the only light – the flashes of light from the emergency vehicles – is reflected like shell bursts. Beneath the mirror is a small wooden dining table with one folded leaf and two padded upright chairs. To the right of that, from Flint's perspective, is a matching low coffee table and a plump sofa covered in a floral fabric. Courtney Morrison stands behind the sofa, the barrel of her rifle resting on one of the cushions. It looks to Flint like a Russian Dragunov SLR, so single shot and ten rounds in the magazine. *Is that what you used to shoot Jack?* she would like to know.

'Take it off.'

'Take what off?'

'Whatever that is you're wearing.'

Flint hesitates but only for a moment. She tugs on the zipper of the jumpsuit, shrugs it from her shoulders, rolls it down over her hips and thighs, wonders if she can step out of it without first removing her trainers – Courtney's trainers, actually; wonders if Courtney will notice that she's been the victim of petty larceny.

It can't be done. Flint pulls off the shoes without troubling to undo the laces, gets out of the suit, stands there naked except for her underpants.

Now what?

'Raise your arms and turn around, all the way around.'

Flint pirouettes like a ballet dancer to prove she's not concealing a weapon or a microphone.

'Jackson Memorial,' she says as she completes the turn.

'What?'

'I told you on the phone I'd find out where Melinda is. Well, it's Jackson Memorial in Miami, the Ryder Trauma Center, one of the best there is, apparently. The last I heard she's doing okay. She's lost a lot of blood but by some miracle the sword missed the iliac artery and there is no serious organ damage or damage to the spinal cord. She did slice through the small intestine and there is a risk of peritonitis but they're dealing with that. Chances are, she'll live. As far as Jerry is concerned – that's Jerry Crawford, by the way – he's also at the Ryder Trauma—'

'I don't give a damn.'

'Well, you should, because—'

'SHUT THE HELL UP!' Courtney suddenly furious, shouting at

the top of her voice, the sound bouncing off the walls; passing through the walls, tweaking the nerves of the waiting men outside. 'I'll tell you when to open your mouth. Now, sit down on the floor and put your hands on your knees and don't even . . .'

Do not provoke.

On the other hand, if Flint submits to Morrison's tyranny, this is going to be a long, long night and she doesn't have the will to drag this out.

'Courtney, you know what? Screw you,' says Flint, turning her back, picking up the jumpsuit, beginning to dress. 'You're not worth the bother.'

'What do you think you're doing?'

Do not bluff.

'I'm out of here, Courtney. I've got better things to do.'

Courtney Morrison raises the rifle to her shoulder, takes a bead on the back of Flint's head. Flint ignores the click of the safety catch shifting to off, continues to dress, pulls up the zipper, won't turn her head when Courtney asks, 'You think I'm kidding?'

'I think you've lost the plot. I think you're a hair's breadth away from condemning Melinda to a life in prison – and for what? So you can go out in a blaze of glory?' Now, slowly, Flint does swivel to look down the snout of the gun barrel. 'Except it won't be glorious, Courtney. It will be sad and stupid and an utter waste of both your life and Melinda's.'

In the intermittent light reflecting from the mirror, Courtney's eyes are unnaturally bright and there are dark stains beneath them as though she's been crying blood. Her mouth is pinched. There is a sheen to her skin, a patina of sweat.

'I'm dead anyway,' she says flatly. 'As good as.'

'If you think so, Courtney.' Flint is watching the finger on the trigger, waiting for the pressure to increase, deciding which way she will move. 'If you don't have the guts.'

So this is it: the moment when Courtney will probably squeeze the trigger and, in the course of that moment, before the hammer hits, Flint will have a millisecond to jerk her head out of the way and then another moment to launch herself at Courtney before she can fire a second shot. *Fat chance.* And anyway, at the sound of the first shot the charged-up cavalry outside will be smashing its way in through Courtney's thin walls, spewing hellfire. Flint can

imagine the chaos of the entry, one very likely outcome of the
confusion, the subsequent headline: FED KILLED BY FRIENDLY
FIRE.

Do not provoke.

'If you're too much of a coward, Courtney, to do the right
thing.'

The stock of the Dragunov is still pressed into Courtney's right
shoulder, and the barrel points unwaveringly at the target, but
Courtney has lifted her head from alongside the sight to look at Flint
in astonishment. 'What the hell are you talking about?' she asks.

'I'm talking about Gröber and Çarçani and the Gup brothers
and whoever else it is you think is coming after you, putting out
their contracts to silence you, to stop you from talking. You think
that if we don't kill you, they will, and there's not a jail we can put
you where they can't reach inside. Or, if there is, they'll reach you
through Melinda; you say one word, she dies. And you're right in
your thinking, dead right. Let me tell you something about Gröber.'
Flint looks at her watch as though she's concerned about the time.
'The last person that I know for certain he murdered – *personally*
killed, that is, with his own hand – was a harmless little lady called
Ilse. She was shrivelled up like a dried prune and she lived in a
wheelchair in a rambling broken-down old house in Leipzig,
Germany, a house with a garden that was full of ornamental
gnomes, and she couldn't have hurt a fly. But Gröber believed that
Ilse had betrayed him, that she'd told me something about his
whereabouts and, about a year later, when he was still on the run,
Gröber crept back into Leipzig in the middle of the night and broke
into Ilse's house. He dressed her in some freaky diaphanous robe,
put her to bed, lit the room with votive candles, surrounded her
with gnomes from the garden, put a drip in her arm and pumped
her full of morphine until she died.' Flint pauses, reliving the
memory, and then she adds softly, 'Courtney, Ilse was Gröber's
sister, his only living relative.'

Outside the cottage the SWAT team is maintaining radio silence
but squawks of static punctuate the chirping of the crickets.

'Listen, Courtney, it's been a long day and I want to sit down,
and not on the floor. So I'm going over there to sit at the table and
if you want to shoot me you'll do it anyway.'

'And did she?'

'Did she what?'

'Did Ilse betray her brother?'

'No, not really. In her house, among her things, I found a lead to Gröber but she knew nothing about it. I was undercover, her lodger, she thought. She had no idea I was a cop.'

Courtney considers for a while; nods towards the dining table, lowers the rifle so that it's now pointing at Flint's midriff. 'Go ahead,' she says and then when Flint is moving, as though it's an afterthought, she adds, 'so, you and Karl have something in common. You both like killing family. He said you murdered your husband. That right?'

Courtney has clammed up, nothing more to say. But she's come out from behind the sofa to perch on one of its arms and the rifle is now resting on her bare knees, the barrel pointing at the floor. And, as Flint sees it, her tacit acknowledgement that she knows Gröber – well enough to call him Karl – has cracked open the door. With her admission, and her adoption of a less threatening posture, Courtney seems to be saying it is not impossible there's a deal to be made if the terms are right.

Everything Courtney is wearing – the singlet, the shorts, the Nike Shox on her feet, the chronometer with an oversize dial that emphasises the thinness of her wrist – appears in this light to be black. So is the Ka-Bar combat knife that is strapped to her left calf. *Do you know how to use it, Courtney?*

Seated at the dining table, Flint says impassively, 'I didn't murder my husband. I was there when he fell off a boat into the ocean and drowned, and there was nothing I could do to save him. End of story.'

Courtney wrinkles her mouth as if to say she doesn't care.

'Maybe I could have saved Ilse . . .' Flint breaks off as though she is reflecting on the possibility. 'I could certainly have arranged for her to get protection, but then I didn't see the threat. I didn't really comprehend what a sick-minded son-of-a-bitch Gröber is.'

'You know now.'

'I surely do. Listen, Courtney, I *can* protect—'

A hand held up to shush her. 'How long have we got? How long before that fucking cowboy army you brought here starts kicking down my door?'

I don't know is the truthful answer but what Flint replies is, 'If you don't fire that gun or pull that knife then,' a casual lifting of the shoulders, 'as long as it takes for you to decide what you're going to do.'

In response Courtney says something so unexpected, so surreal, that Flint can't believe her ears. 'So, do you want a drink? You certainly look like you could use a drink.'

Oh, absolutely, Courtney! Let's have a drink together, shall we, like we're a couple of moms on an evening out. Like we're friends, bosom pals. What shall we talk about while we sip our cocktails? Our children, perhaps?

'Sure, I'll join you,' she manages to say.

'Middle wall unit above the sink.' Courtney is pointing with the rifle towards the kitchen. 'There's tumblers and a bottle of Jack D. Ice in the fridge if you want it.'

So tell me, Courtney – yes, cheers, good health – so tell me, when you lined up the cross hairs on little Jack's head, what were you thinking?

Target acquired.

Well, of course, but didn't you think he looked cute? Such a pretty boy, he certainly has his father's looks . . . Yes, yes – chin, chin – his father is the husband who drowned.

On her return from the kitchen carrying the bourbon, two tumblers, ice cubes in a dish, Flint passes the front window and glances through a slight gap in the curtains. She thinks she's being watched, a black masked face pressed up against the glass, but she can't be sure. It doesn't matter. From the input of the parabolic microphones aimed at every window, the watchers outside will already know that Flint is Drinking With the Enemy.

Afterwards – if there is an afterwards – Flint will have to justify her extraordinary decision.

I followed your advice, Mr Agnew. Remember what you said? Go with the flow . . .

It has occurred to Flint that the Jack Daniels or the water to make the ice may have been spiked with Rohypnol or GHB or some other incapacitating drug. So, when Courtney says she will take her bourbon neat, no ice, Flint elects to do the same. She pours two measures, places Courtney's glass on the coffee table, withdraws;

only pretends to sip her drink until she is convinced that Courtney has actually swallowed a mouthful of the liquor.

'Do you drink a lot?' Courtney asks, the question coming out of nowhere. 'Only when I was searching your apartment, before I found the videotapes, I couldn't help but notice you were well supplied.'

Surprise, bewilderment then a dawning perception of what Courtney is admitting to and, with that, a rush of anger so intense it is like an electric shock – but none of this clamour of emotions registers on Flint's face.

'Courtney, I don't think we're sufficiently acquainted to be discussing my personal habits.'

'My, my, *sufficiently acquainted*,' says Courtney in an awful imitation of an English accent. 'You sound like one of those prissy English novelists – but then you are a prissy Brit, aren't you? From middle England, Karl told me; from someplace called – what? – Mid Compton.'

'Karl's got a big mouth.'

'Where your father still lives?'

'Not right now.'

'But, like you implied, Karl's got patience.'

This is getting out of hand. Courtney's physiology has changed; the muscles in her face have relaxed and she's no longer sweating, and her present demeanour is far too brash for Flint's liking. She's not even bothering to hold the rifle any more, though it is propped against the cushion only a hand's reach away. Flint is beginning to suspect that she's walked into a trap.

Courtney now mimics Sally's Melbourne accent – *Give that to me, give that to me* – and the resemblance is spot on. 'And he did throw the ball, didn't he? And then he looked at the camera and called you Mama.' Courtney giggles. 'The Jack Flint Show! Wow, what a fuck-up that was.'

'Your point being, Courtney?'

'That you set up your own kid, made him the target. Your Kathy McCarry cover was too good to crack. I took your place apart and didn't find anything that said you weren't McCarry, nothing I could take to the bank – until I found the tapes. It was the tapes that told me who you were. I'd bet Karl had orgasms when he watched them.'

In Flint's neck there is a vein that's throbbing so hard she fears it's going to rupture. 'Gröber was in my apartment?' – asked with studied calm.

'Karl? Never. Karl is totally allergic to the States, won't come anywhere near it, because of you.'

'So?'

'Before I put your tapes back where I found them, I had them copied onto a DVD, took it to him in . . . Well,' Courtney makes a wry smile, 'that's for me to know and you to wonder and one day we'll talk about it . . . maybe.'

Courtney has just made her opening bid.

Flint rubs her neck in the place where it hurts, takes a sip of bourbon, grimaces at the sour taste, apologises. 'I'm more of whisky girl myself.'

'I noticed.'

'Courtney, do you have a pen and something I can write on? And I need a candle so I can see, because I want to put in writing what I'm about to say; make it official, for your protection.'

No response, just a blank stare.

'Because if that *one day* is ever going to arrive then you and I need to have a very clear understanding, a contract, a written contract, that specifies what I can and cannot do for you – for you and Melinda – and what you must do in return. Let me write it down.'

Courtney points at the table where Flint is sitting and Flint searches the underside, finds a drawer. Inside are two half-burned cathedral candles, a book of matches with Lola's Café printed in gold lettering on the cover, a roller-ball pen and a box of expensive handmade Milanese writing paper.

Milan!

Flint lights both candles, withdraws half a dozen sheets of paper from the box, places them on the table, begins to write.

'Courtney,' she says, 'what I'm offering you here is a deal that most people would find bizarre, given that you shot my son. But as I see it, you're just the low-hanging fruit on the tree – no offence intended – and what I care about are the rotten apples further up, the vermin that sent you to shoot my son. So while what I'd really like to do is jerk your spine out through your chest, I'm prepared to forgo that satisfaction if you give me Gröber, Çarçani and—'

'I don't know any Çarçani.'

'But you were in Milan, right?' says Flint holding up a sheet of the notepaper as though it is evidence.

'It's a big city.'

'Yeah, well, we'll get to that. First and foremost I want Gröber and then the Gups—'

'Just one Gup' – Courtney enjoying herself.

'I want Gröber and any and every asshole connected to Gröber that you know about and this is the way, the only way, it's going to work.' There is an intermission while Flint finishes writing the first page. Then, 'First, you will give up all of your weapons and surrender to me. When we step outside you will be arrested and taken into local custody but, I guarantee, within twelve hours, twenty-four at the most, you will be released into witness protection—'

'This is a joke?' Courtney asks scornfully.

'Not the US Marshals' programme,' Flint continues as though there has been no interruption. 'We, the Financial Strike Force, have our own programme; much more exclusive and *much* more secure. You will be transferred to a safe place – not a prison, more like house arrest – where, as soon as it's feasible to move her, Melinda will join you. You will be kept in reasonable comfort, you will be guarded around the clock by strike force protection agents, and, if you wish, you can have telephone access to an attorney of your choice.'

In the candlelight Flint scans the page to make sure she's covered all the points and then slips it onto the coffee table within Courtney's reach. Courtney makes no move to read it. Ignoring the snub, Flint settles down to writing the second page, careful to keep the lines neat and parallel, not saying a word until she's finished.

'After and not until Melinda has joined you, your debriefing will begin. I say debriefing rather than interrogation because, the way we do things, we aim to understand the context as well as the facts. We want to know not only who you've shot but how you became a shooter, the wherefores and the whys. In other words, Courtney, you will be coaxed to compile your autobiography; no good-cop bad-cop routines, no bright lights, no sleep deprivation. Now, when I say *we* . . .' Flint puts down the page she is consulting to signal a time-out. 'It's not *we* because I won't be there. My boss, not to mention the Department of Justice, won't want me anywhere near your debriefing because I'm, well, how shall I put this? Compromised? Too close to the case? I have a vested interest – or perhaps that should be a *conflict* of interest? The fact you shot my son, you see?'

Courtney does not acknowledge the question. She watches Flint's face intently but as though she's a bystander; a member of the audience, not part of the cast.

'Your principal debriefer will be Rocco Morales. That's because you and Rocco have things in common. Like you, he's ex-military, Special Forces in his case, and he was also a sniper. He killed for his country, not for profit of course, but he still got paid to pull the trigger and I'm sure there are people who would say it makes little difference. Anyway' – Flint uses the back of one hand to brush the spot on her right cheek where the powder burn is itching – 'if I can swing it, and I think I can, Rocco will be working with Alan Singleton, also ex-military, a marine, also a sniper. Do you see the symmetry? Three of you with a similar understanding of what it's like to look through a scope. I hope you will find some empathy, that Rocco and Al will make it easier for you to confront what you've done.'

For all the response she's getting, Flint might as well be talking to the wall but stubbornly she presses on. 'Finally, I'm going to recommend that your third debriefer is a Dr Marina Przewalskii, who's a psychotherapist and . . .'

Now she's got a reaction, a look on Courtney's face that says, *Are you for real?*

'Oh, I know, Courtney, I've got no time for shrinks either. But Dr P is, well, different. She's a Russian dissident who went head to head with the KGB and if she didn't win, neither did she lose. She's as smart as she is tough and I believe that she can help you to understand and describe your life – and, when you finally go to court, that's going to be important. By the way, she loves to cycle. So, when you go for one of your runs – yes, you will be permitted to run, though you'll be wearing an electronic tag and they'll be tracking you every step of the way and if you step outside the prescribed boundaries they'll be all over you like a rash – but my point is, if you feel like some company on your runs, Dr P will ride along.'

'Terrific,' says Courtney, rolling her eyes.

Presently impervious to sarcasm, Flint picks up the second page to signal a return to the agenda.

'When your debriefing is complete you will be required to make a formal statement, what we call a proffer, describing all of the offences you've committed and naming any and all of your co-conspirators. Courtney, listen to me because this is important, probably the most important piece of advice you've ever been given. When you make your proffer, do not omit or dissimulate or prevaricate. You need to admit to the murder of Rexhep Kastrioti in Tucson, you need to admit to the attempted murder of my son, and you need to admit to everything else you've done. Because if you don't, if there are illegal acts you fail to identify in your proffer that subsequently come to light, then this whole deal collapses and there is nothing I can do to help you. Err on the safe side, Courtney. If you've ever so much as driven through a red light, put it in your proffer.'

'Crawford,' she says.

'Excuse me?'

'You said that the guy Melinda tangled with is called Crawford. Is that the same Crawford that got all messed up by the bomb that went off in, where was it? Kissimmee?' she tentatively suggests. Then, 'Yeah, that's right, Kissimmee.'

Flint has gone very still, watching Courtney watching her, willing herself to show no response. She asks her question casually. 'Are you saying that was you, Courtney?'

'I heard about it.'

'What did you *hear*, Courtney?'

'That your friend Crawford was lucky. Now he's back in the hospital, I'm thinking he's careless.'

'Cute, Courtney.'

With a distinctive slap the second page joins the first on the coffee table and is similarly ignored. Courtney stifles a yawn and says, 'I think I'll take one last shot – this time with some ice.'

Forty-Four

Beside a clump of stunted palms on the beach side of West Gulf Drive a conference has been convened to consider a conundrum. Courtney Morrison's gratuitous reference to the Kissimmee explosion, with its alarming implication that the shooter might also be a bomber, has caused the SWAT commander to withdraw his men to an imaginary perimeter fully one hundred yards from the cottage. And there they will stay, he says, until he knows for sure there is no bomb; that there will be no repeat of the searing scenes at Kissimmee.

This unilateral decision has thrown the operation into chaos but there is no one to countermand the order, for the lines of command at Dogwood are very unclear. Strategically speaking, Chief Pete Hendy of the Sanibel police is the senior officer at the scene but he has no tactical authority over SWAT – or, for that matter, over any of the disparate forces of law and order that are gathered in groups along the shoreline – and no experience of a 'hostile hostage situation' which is what the stand-off has now officially become. Blade and Brendan Glees do have experience of such situations but they are mere civilian observers, permitted to be present only as a courtesy and, much as he would like to, Lieutenant Lucca cannot call the shots on Sanibel. Lance Agnew of the FBI has vast experience, of course, but his presence is entirely fortuitous: taking his vacation on Sanibel, as he does every summer, he just happened to be enjoying a cordial beverage at Chief Hendy's home when the call came in.

Here's the conundrum. In so far as this hotchpotch of an operation has any owner, it is the FSF and the only representative of the strike force on site is Flint – who is also, technically, the hostage; certainly in no position to assume command. The strike force Go Team is en route from New York, and Rocco Morales will be on his way from Lackland AFB just as soon as an intense electrical storm has cleared the area, but that leaves a vacuum for at least the next three hours. In the huddle under the palms, Chief Hendy is attempting to fill it.

From the head of the Fort Myers K9 unit he wants to know, 'Any of your hounds trained to sniff out explosives?'

'Sure, all of them. But if she's rigged a bomb inside the cottage then, in order to locate it, we're going to need access and I don't see how . . .'

Chief Hendy nods his acceptance of an obvious truth. 'Lieutenant, you got any thoughts?'

Manny Lucca picks a stray shred of cigar leaf from his lower lip and says, 'Question is, assuming there is a bomb, how's it set to detonate? Kissimmee was remote control – cell phone to cell phone I was told – and if that was Morrison's work she's likely to use the same method again because most bombers are creatures of habit. In which case, you put a couple of stun grenades through the window and maybe some smoke or CS gas, she's not going to have time to make the call, even on auto-dialler. On the other hand, if Kissimmee wasn't her work – or maybe she's an exception to the rule – she could have rigged a bomb half a dozen different ways, all of them bad. Worse case would be she's got a wireless transmitter in her hand with what they call a dead man's trigger. In that case, she's already pulled the trigger. The problem comes if she lets go.' Lucca blows on the ash of his cigar. 'That happens . . . BOOM.'

'Or,' says Blade, 'second worse-case scenario, she's got a transmitter with a positive push button taped to her midriff. All she has to do when the window breaks is slap herself on the belly.'

Chief Hendy gave up smoking twenty years ago but right now he has a powerful urge to ask Lieutenant Lucca for one of his cigars. 'So, no frontal assault?'

'That would be my advice, at least for the time being.'

Lance Agnew has said nothing so far. He's been squatting on his haunches, using the fingers of one hand to draw random patterns in the sand, apparently distracted, only half listening to the conversation. Now he stands up, brushes his hand against his shorts and says, 'Gentlemen, ask yourselves: what's her game, what does she want? Is she a suicide bomber, intent on killing herself and as many of us as she can? In which case, why did she so much as breathe the word Kissimmee; why tip us off that she has a bomb, or bombs? That makes no sense to me. More likely, I think, she was issuing a warning that any assault will result in mutually assured destruction – or there is no bomb and she's bluffing. Either way, she's playing for time; time to achieve the best deal she can get, and you have to say she's doing pretty well so far. The longer this thing goes on, the more extravagant Flint's promises become. Not that they matter a damn.'

'Really?' asks Chief Hendy. 'How do you figure that?'

'Flint's under duress, being held at gunpoint by an assumed killer who may also be armed with explosives. In those circumstances, who wouldn't make extravagant promises? No, I don't think any prosecutor or any judge is going to be bound by undertakings given in such circumstances – even if any of us can actually remember what it was Flint said. Chief, is their conversation being taped?'

'No. We don't have the means, not immediately to hand.'

'So,' a flutter of a smile crosses Agnew's mouth, 'I don't see any harm in letting this run. When she's extorted all she wants from Flint – including a suite at the Ritz-Carlton on Palm Beach I shouldn't wonder – then they'll both come out, nobody gets hurt and we can all go home . . . except Morrison, of course. She's never going home.'

'Lance, Flint is giving her a goddamned written contract!'

'I know she is and that could complicate things' – and Agnew frowns before he brightens. 'But, look, even a written contract is surely invalid if it's obtained through coercion, or at least subject to . . . renegotiation. Considerable renegotiation.' There are nods in the huddle, grunts of agreement, and Agnew brings his hands together as though the matter is settled and then he adds an after-thought, 'Yes, well, when it all gets confused during the surrender, we better make sure Flint's contract doesn't get mislaid . . . right?'

Page three of the contract is almost finished, Flint's hand flying across the paper, Courtney watching silently with what could be amusement in her eyes. Her drink has been refreshed. Now slumped in the sofa, she holds it in both hands, the bottom of the glass resting on her tank top in the region of her navel.

'Okay,' says Flint, putting down the pen. 'When you have

completed your proffer a grand jury will be convened. Actually, more than one' – and she retrieves the pen to make amendments. 'Tucson for sure, and wherever the grand jury sits in Maryland . . . Orlando, I guess, covers Kissimmee,' Flint now taking Courtney's involvement in the bombing as a given. 'Then there's Manhattan where the DA is certain to press for a racketeering indictment, and . . . well, Courtney' – Flint's turn to look amused – 'you tell me. Everywhere else you've plied your trade.'

Courtney does not rise to the bait.

'In each case you will be required to testify truthfully about your involvement and about the role of any and all of your co-conspirators. It is very likely that all of the various grand juries will hand down indictments against your co-conspirators – and, of course, against you. It's possible that some states attorneys will also file charges against you. But you won't be prosecuted or sent to jail, not yet. You will remain in strike-force-protected custody, and with Melinda, until your co-conspirators have been apprehended, extradited to the US if necessary, and put on trial – trials at which you will also be required to testify truthfully. Now, Courtney, truthfully is the key word here . . .' Flint pauses to underline it twice with the pen, 'because, I'll say it again: if you lie, even by omission, at any stage in these proceedings, then the deal is off. Is that clear, Courtney?'

Courtney says facetiously, 'What about the guy who parks my car on South Beach? Is he a *co-conspirator*?'

Flint hears a creak on the front steps and, judging by the way her eyes move to watch the door, so does Courtney. But Courtney doesn't reach for the rifle or make any other defensive move. She remains relaxed on the sofa still holding the glass in both hands (the refill of bourbon untouched and the ice now in the final stages of melting), displaying a casual confidence that Flint finds unnerving. A long minute passes while they both wait for something to happen.

'Maybe a racoon?' Flint suggests.

'Yeah, with size twelve boots, perfect abs and a tiny pecker.'

Not for the first time today Flint feels as though she's swimming against the tide.

'You know, Courtney, you really are something.'

'Something else,' she says, her face tightening. 'Shall I tell you what your problem is? You think you know me, know how to manipulate me – all this bullshit you're giving me. Do you really think—'

'What bullshit is that, Courtney?'

'There you go again! Blah-blah this, *Courtney*. And blah-blah that, *Courtney*. Do you really think that if you use my name a hundred times a minute I'm going to *empathise* with you like I'm going to *empathise* with your mythical Rocco and Al; like I'm going to *empathise* with your mythical commie shrink when I go for *one of my runs* – and isn't that a fucking joke – and she *comes along for the ride*. P-u-r-l-ease!'

'What would you like me to call you, Courtney?'

'Ms Morrison will do for a start; until we're *sufficiently acquainted*.'

'Okay. Let me ask you something. Why do you think I'm here? I mean *here* as opposed to on the other side of that door with the guys with the perfect abs and the little peckers who are just itching to squander your life? Why do you think I'm in here making commitments, *written* commitments, that provide you with the only possibility of not dying in this room, or in one of several electric chairs? Why would I do that, *Ms Morrison*?'

'Ever heard the phrase, *not worth the paper . . .*?'

'Oh, I see,' says Flint. 'You believe that what I'm telling you is worthless because if and when you give yourself up I'm just going to tear up the contract, right? You believe that I'm not serious about securing your co-operation; that all I really want to do is put you in jail and throw away the key. Because, after all, it was you who shot my son; you, not Karl Gröber, who pulled the trigger. You think this is about personal revenge, that I'll tell you any lie I have to, promise anything you want, just to nail your sorry hide. Is that it, Courtney – excuse me, *Ms Morrison*? Is that what you think?'

Without waiting for an answer Flint is on her feet, searching the living room with her eyes; not finding what she's looking for she heads with purpose to the kitchen, renews her search there.

'Hey, what the hell are you doing?' – Courtney halfway off the sofa, slamming the glass on the coffee table to free her hands.

'I'm looking for your . . .' Flint breaks off. She's found Courtney's cell phone alongside the muted counter-top TV but it's what she sees on the screen that distracts her: captured from the air, unsteady images of West Gulf Drive where the lights of clusters of vehicles flicker like encampment fires. The chatter of the rotor blades is only a distant echo but as she watches, the camera zooms in on Dogwood and then, inexorably, the very cottage in which she is standing until the front siding and the front portion of the roof fill the screen. The caption at the bottom of the screen says SANIBEL SIEGE. No sign of SWAT, Flint observes. *Guess what, girl, we're on TV*, she might have remarked if Courtney wasn't in such a pissy mood.

'GET BACK IN HERE!'

Flint returns to the living room holding up the cell phone as though it's a trophy and asks, 'Do you have a lawyer, someone you trust? Because if you do I want you to call their office, get their answer machine, make sure the message tape is running. Then, Courtney . . . I'm sorry, I can't go on calling you Ms Morrison; it makes you sound like my school teacher. Then, Courtney, when you're sure the tape is running, you give me the phone and I'll identify myself indisputably. I'll describe the situation we're in and then I'll record into that machine every commitment and condition I've written down, word for word. When I'm done, you should call your lawyer at home – and if you don't have the number I can get it – and tell them to go to their office immediately and retrieve the tape and put it in a place of safe-keeping. And they should call you back to tell you when it's been done. Then and only then will we walk out of here, if that's what you want to do.'

Courtney doesn't respond immediately. To buy thinking time she busies herself using a handkerchief to mop up splashes of bourbon from the coffee table. Flint watches in nervous silence, thinking maybe she has turned the tide, determined not to break the spell.

Eventually, 'Melinda doesn't get jail time.'

'Not if I can help it. Not if Jerry Crawford survives.'

'And what happens to me?'

'Courtney, certainly you'll do time, though it will be in a federal facility that's exclusively reserved for protected witnesses; not a holiday camp for sure but neither is it like any other maximum security prison you've ever heard of.' Flint smiles to soften her face. 'The security, you see, is primarily designed to keep the bad guys out; to keep you safe.'

'Where?'

'I can't tell you that. Not until we've made your . . . reservation.'

'How long?'

This is the crunch point when it can all go wrong. Flint is acutely aware that what she says in the next thirty seconds, and even how she says it, may decide the outcome of the 'Sanibel siege' and settle the prospects for her own survival. *That's up to the judge*, she could rightly say, the cop-out answer she has considered giving during her long anticipation of this moment. But Courtney Morrison is unlikely to buy that hollow fact, and anyway, Flint for once refuses to hide behind the familiar cloak of dissimulation. There is an obvious paradox here: that a woman who practises deception for a living now feels compelled to tell the unvarnished truth, whatever the cost. They stand eight feet apart, one dressed all in orange, the other all in black; two women of roughly the same age and similar physical characteristics who both lost their mothers when they were young; both now single mothers of children who lie critically ill in hospital because of what each has done.

'On the basis of what I know so far, I would say you're looking at a minimum of three to four life sentences plus one hundred, maybe two hundred years. Frankly, the actual length of the sentences becomes irrelevant. As things stand, you're looking at life without any prospect of parole. Which is better than a death sentence – or maybe not, depending on how you feel.'

Nothing more from Flint, nothing to soften the blow – or not yet; not until Courtney has had time to absorb the implications. Then, when she judges the moment to be right, Flint adds an addendum, 'Except.'

Courtney hesitates before she feels compelled to ask, 'Except what?'

'Except our judicial system is, or can be, extremely pragmatic. It does deals with the devil if the terms are right. If you offer up all the information you have – *all of it*, mind you – the government will still ask the judge for multiple life sentences but they could be concurrent, not consecutive, and "life" could mean twenty years of prison time, minus however long you will have spent in protective custody. And,' Flint continues with barely a pause for breath, 'you have one other exceptional thing going for you. Before you're sentenced, the victims will get to have their say in court and, since my son is too young to speak, I'll be one of those doing the talking.

And if you redeem yourself in my eyes – which means, if you do your level best to give me Gröber – I'll be forgiving. If it's true, if you play the game, I will testify to your exemplary cooperation and argue that you should be given a minimum as well as a maximum sentence; a minimum of, say, ten years. And, when your first opportunity to go before the parole board comes around, I'll be at the hearing to support you. I can't guarantee the outcome because it's not within my power, but . . .'

Another long pause while Courtney makes her calculations.

'So, Courtney, the bottom line. You're, what, thirty-nine? Okay, before you're fifty, if you do what you should and I get my way, you'll be out of jail, relocated to wherever you want to go and living under a new identity.' Flint offers up the cell phone to indicate that she's reached the end of her pitch. 'It's the deal of the century, Courtney, and all I've got to offer. Take it or don't; it's up to you.'

Flint seems calm, even tranquil, but this is an entirely misleading impression. While Courtney remains mute, just stands and stares, Flint tots up her grievances: Crawford, bombed; Jack, shot; herself, almost shot, and almost drowned; Crawford, crushed; herself, repeatedly kicked by some Japanese mutant, threatened with a sword, and now a Dragunov SLR. The truth is she's had it with Courtney – *had it up to here*. Ten more seconds and then she will move, close the gap between them, go for her eyes, grapple for the knife. *However hard you are, Courtney, you don't have my rage.*

She is silently counting down the seconds, – and she's counted down to four – when Courtney says, 'Give me the phone.'

Forty-Five

Flint is standing on the top step of Courtney's cottage, keeping her hands where they can be seen, her face bleached white in the sudden unremitting glare of a battery of klieg lights. She can make out nothing beyond them. 'Blade,' she calls out into the darkness for the second time, and still gets no response. She feels as if she's exposed on a stage, denied feedback from a hostile audience; an audience that has also snatched away her victory. She was *this close* to bringing Courtney in when they pulled their stupid bloody stunt. Furious is not a word that adequately describes Flint's current frame of mind.

'Okay, all of you officers out there, listen up. In case you've forgotten, I'm Deputy Director Grace Flint of the Financial Strike Force and this is a strike force operation that you're here to support – and one or more of you is obstructing it. As you well know, the suspect has agreed to surrender her weapons and place herself in my custody once she's spoken to her lawyer. That's her legal right, gentlemen. But she can't speak to her lawyer because the landline's been cut and some moron out here has had her cell phone blocked.' Flint slowly turns her head from left to right scanning the invisible crowd with her look of scathing disdain. 'This is entirely unacceptable and if I get out of here alive I'm going to find out who was responsible and ruin their brilliant career, unless they fix the problem. Now, whoever you are, get Courtney's SIM card unblocked or send me up another cell phone – and damn well do it before she changes her mind.'

Flint turns towards the door, then turns back. 'And, gentlemen, in case any of you have something even more stupid in mind, copy this. Behind you, in front of you, within a few feet of wherever you are, there is an improvised explosive device that the suspect can detonate with the touch of a button . . .'

Courtney had rolled up her tank top, shown Flint the transmitter taped just below her sternum.

In a whisper Flint had asked, *Where's the bomb?*

Bombs, plural. In here, out there.

How many bombs, Courtney?

Twenty-four.

Jesus, Courtney!

'If you are in a position to hear my voice then you are likely to be standing in the middle of a minefield. Tread very carefully, gentlemen.'

Pages four and five of Flint's contract describe what will happen when Courtney Morrison has served her minimum sentence: refuge in a temporary safe haven; the offer of plastic surgery to alter her appearance; the elaborate construction of a personal history that will be the foundation of her new identity; the documents that will be provided to bring that new identity to life.

Then Flint addresses the matter of Courtney's relocation: the choice of friendly countries that are available where the strike force has reciprocal agreements; the degree of protection she can expect; the conditions by which she must abide; finally, the tricky question of how her new life will be funded.

'Normally we would provide limited financial support for the first few months, until you get a job, because you won't have any resources when you come out of prison – because, once you're convicted, the first thing we will do is seize your assets: your houses, your cars, the contents of your bank accounts, your secret slush funds, anything you own. And, Courtney,' Flint looks up from the page, 'you will have an obligation to declare *all* of your assets wherever they are located; that's part of the deal.'

There has been a curious shift in the relationship between Flint and Morrison, at least in its ambience. Courtney still has the transmitter taped to her belly but she has abandoned the combat knife and the rifle. She is sitting with her elbows resting on the dining table opposite Flint, following what she writes as though they are working on this together; not allies exactly but collaborators.

Flint yawns, stretches her arms above her head. 'You've probably got at least one numbered account in some offshore bank that you're certain we won't find, and you wouldn't be the first protected witness to think that. But I have to tell you, the forensic accountants who will trawl through your affairs, they're like maggots on a corpse; if there's flesh to find they'll find it. Trust me, it's not worth the risk. And, anyway, I'm going to recommend that in light of what I'm sure will be your exemplary cooperation' – a sharp glance from Flint to stress the conditional point – 'we don't seize all of your assets. You get to keep a portion which we'll hold in escrow until your release. Knowing the treasury department, which has a large say in these things, it won't be a fifty-fifty split but I think I can get you enough of a share to set you on your feet.'

Courtney nods her understanding as though she accepts that in difficult times the cost of doing business is expensive.

'Which leaves the question of Melinda and what happens to her while you're doing your time. What I've written down here,' Flint pushes page five of the contract across the table, 'is not very much, which is all that I can promise. Certainly, we'll make sure she gets whatever medical treatment she needs, we'll give her new ID and then we'll relocate her. But I think you know that Melinda's problems extend far beyond her basic safety. She has a lot of issues that require professional help and she has to recognise that.'

The last entry on page five says only this: *For Melinda, we'll do as much as she allows us to do.*

'Can your commie shrink help, if she really exists?'

'Oh, she exists, all right – and, by the way, she was never a communist; that's what made her a dissident . . . Yes, I think she can help, but only if Melinda plays ball.'

'Will I be able to see her?'

'While you're in prison? No, it would be much too dangerous for both of you. Melinda can't know where you are and vice versa. Exchanges of letters we can arrange, voice tapes, photographs, maybe a phone call on a secure line once in a while. Courtney, I will promise you this—'

The cell phone comes alive, vibrating on the table. By unspoken agreement made with a glance, it is Flint who answers the call.

'This is Lance Agnew. The SIM card is unblocked.'

'Thank you.'

'Flint?'

'Yes, sir.'

'I hope to hell you know what you're doing.'
Me too, thinks Flint.

Flint encounters no difficulty in dictating the contract into the telephone answer machine of the New York law firm Martin, MacRae & Beauregard. It is when the night-watch supervisor at strike force headquarters attempts to find Ms Beauregard that the problems begin and then rapidly escalate. Her home number is unlisted and, anyway, it turns out she's not at home and when a strike force agent finally tracks her down to the Museum of Modern Art where she is attending a reception she is not at all inclined to leave the party. Ms Beauregard is not a criminal lawyer; her specialities are wills and probate and the management of complex trusts, and her clients rarely if ever call upon her services during unsocial hours.

'She says she won't do it.'

'Then have her dragged out of there, in handcuffs if necessary,' says Flint, her frustration overwhelming her common sense.

'Oh, right! And the probable cause would be?'

'Damn it, Watch, that tape has to be secured. Listen, see if you can find one or other of her partners, get them to talk some sense into her. The point is, Beauregard has to do it herself, she has to personally fetch the tape, and she's the one who has to call here when she has, because she's the only one the subject knows and trusts.'

'I'll get back to you.'

While they wait, Flint and Courtney move from the table to a position beneath the main living-room window where they sit on the floor with their backs against the wall. Flint is concerned there may now be sharpshooters hiding in the trees with orders – counter-orders to hers – to end the siege with a single shot if they get the chance.

'If you were out there, how would you set up a kill?'

'If it was me out there you wouldn't know it, so you wouldn't . . .' *be hiding under the window* is what Courtney is about to say until Flint shushes her with a finger to her lips; cups her hands behind her ears to say, *Assume they're listening*. 'So you wouldn't have any reason to feel afraid, and sooner or later you'd show yourself.'

'Yes, well, I'm the living proof of that, aren't I, Courtney? How long did you wait for me to show myself?'

'I didn't.'

'Right, excuse me. How long did you wait for me to show you my son?'

No verbal answer from Courtney. In a parody of Flint's mime she cups her own ears, shakes her head, uses her fingers to make a zipping motion across her mouth.

'Courtney, there are things you shouldn't talk about and things that you must. You need to understand the difference.'

'Has my lawyer called?'

'You know she hasn't.'

'So, let's wait until she does.'

There is no answer to that, none that Flint can think of. She rests the back of her head against the wall and watches the candles slowly burning down. The starburst light reflecting in the mirror is also diminishing as the emergency vehicles strategically retreat.

'What happened this morning?' – Courtney asking the question to pass the time. 'How far did you swim out?'

'You saw me coming after you?'

'Sure I did. I was under the water holding my breath when you went by, practically on top of me. Last I saw, you looked like you were heading for Bimini. I thought, *I hope she knows about the current out there*. I guess you didn't. Is that Coast Guard issue?' – Courtney nodding her head to indicate Flint's jumpsuit.

'Yeah. It comes with the standard rescue kit, the kind they drop from a search plane,' Flint replies coolly, refusing to be riled. 'And you?'

'I just swam south for a while, parallel to the beach, and then I went home. No point in both of us getting drowned, I thought.'

'Right. Sensible decision.'

They lapse into an uneasy silence, waiting for the phone to ring.

Courtney says that after she arrived in Sanibel she didn't have time to shop but there are hurricane emergency supplies in one of the cupboards if Flint wants something to eat, and for want of something better to do Flint goes to explore the kitchen. The television is now showing an ancient episode of *ER* and she flicks through the channels in search of further coverage of her own situation. In vain; the Sanibel siege has had its moment in the live news spotlight, apparently.

In the third cupboard she opens Flint finds a first-aid kit, a flashlight, a transistor radio and six blister packs of spare batteries, rolls of duct tape, a Swiss Army knife (that she instinctively steals and slips into her pocket), bottled water, a roll of toilet tissue, Wet Wipes and a dozen silver foil packages that are labelled MRE – meals ready to eat.

'Okay, Courtney,' she calls from the kitchen, 'on the menu tonight we have soda crackers and peanut butter followed by a choice of beef steak, chicken and noodles or turkey breast. The steak comes with potatoes and the turkey breast with rice. What's your preference? Courtney?'

Getting no response, Flint returns to the living room. Courtney seems to be asleep; her eyes closed, her mouth slack, her hands by her sides nowhere near the transmitter button. It occurs to Flint that with one well-aimed kick to the side of Courtney's head she could end the siege right now, but that thought only briefly dances in her mind. Back in the kitchen she chooses a package of chicken and noodles for Courtney, and with the aid of the flashlight reads the instructions on how to heat it.

'Can I ask you a question?'
  'Let me guess: how did a nice girl like me get into this mess?'
  'Something like that.'
  'It's a long story.'
  'Courtney, you know, we've probably got the time.'

Forty-Six

In July of 1987 Private First Class Courtney Morrison, expert marksman and small arms repairer, having been honourably discharged from the US Army, headed for southern Florida with her accumulated savings and Private Holly York, her soul mate for the last three years. Though both were veterans in army terms they were not yet twenty-one years old.

In Fort Lauderdale, on Ocean Boulevard, they rented a 'comfort suite' in a cheap hotel, paying one month's rent in advance. They shared a largish bedroom with two twin beds, a bathroom and a kitchenette where they thought they would enjoy some serious R&R while they figured out what to do with their lives, meaning the next few months. Holly was also known as Hope, because of her disposition.

Eleven days after their arrival in Fort Lauderdale Holly went out for the evening and never came home. The next morning Courtney called the police to report her friend missing. Six days later Holly was found stuffed into a trash can, all hope extinguished.

'Do you know what the cops asked me, their very first question?' Courtney has barely touched her food and now she shoves the plate away. 'The first thing they wanted to know: was Holly a party girl? Meaning did she fool around? What kind of a question is that? She'd been raped, she'd been beaten, her throat was cut. That's really *fooling around*, don't you think?'

Flint, as calm as she can be, asks, 'Did they ever find who did it?'

'Nope. And, to tell you the truth, I don't think they really tried. On the night she was killed she was seen in some bar dancing with a couple of guys. *Lewd* dancing, the cops said, whatever that means. So, the way they figured it, she was *asking for it*, you see? Asking to have her face turned into hamburger meat. I couldn't recognise her. The only way I could ID her was because of the rings she was wearing.'

Courtney's eyes have lost their brilliance. They are trained on Flint's face but their dull focus is on somewhere in the far distance.

'What did you do?'

'Got the hell out of there. Hope didn't have any close family, none she ever spoke about, so I packed up her things, took them to a homeless shelter, took the first Greyhound bus that was headed out of state. Didn't really matter where it was going.'

Flint wants to know if Courtney had thought of going home, to her uncle and aunt in Portland or maybe her father in Tacoma. No, is the flat response delivered with a vehement shake of the head and no further explanation. Instead, she says, she drifted: first to Atlanta and then to Jackson and, finally, to Ocean Springs on the Mississippi coast where she found a room to rent and, her savings depleted, a casual job waiting tables at Aunt Jenny's Catfish Shack.

'It was fine, just what I needed; the kind of place where you can forget what you've seen.'

'Until?' asks Flint, because she has a pretty good idea where this is headed.

'I'd been there about four months. It was pretty quiet – not much happens in Ocean Springs between the festival in early November and Christmas – but I still had my job at the restaurant, working a shift five nights a week. One night in early December . . .' Courtney makes a mirthless laugh. 'One night? Shit, as if I don't remember. It was a Friday, December eleven. About eight o'clock these two guys walk in; young white bucks, good looking, expensive clothes. I do my routine – *Hi, I'm Courtney and I'll be your waitress tonight* – and they get a little playful with me but nothing out of line. Said they'd come down from Jackson to do some fishing. They eat, they leave, they leave a decent tip; twenty bucks, as I recall. When Aunt Jenny's closes I head for the Long Lane Bar, which is what I usually did on a Friday night because Soledad, one of the cocktail waitresses, was the closest thing I had to a friend in Ocean Springs. Anyway, these two young bucks, Mac and Larry they said their names were, they were sitting at the bar. *Buy you a drink, Courtney?* Sure, why not? I took a beer off them, went to chat with Soledad – and the next thing I know my insides are on fire. I don't know what they put in that beer but it was really,

really evil. I'm rolling on the floor, literally, and Mac and Larry, they're acting *so* concerned. *This woman needs to get to the hospital! We're gonna take her there right now!* Sure they were. They carried me out of the bar and put me in the back of their car and they asked me where I lived – and do you know what? I not only gave them my address, I gave them the fucking keys to my fucking front door. How dumb was that?'

Flint stays silent.

'You can guess the rest. They took me to my place, they carried me to my bed as gently as you like and then they raped me. They took it in turns and then they did it together, and then they did it again and again and again. I don't know how long it went on for; maybe twenty-four hours. I do know that they stuck their dicks into . . . well, I'll spare you the details, spare *me* the details. I suppose I'm lucky – I'm *supposed* to be lucky – that they didn't beat me to a pulp or cut my throat.' Courtney's eyes are still focused on some unfathomable place. 'You ever been raped?'

'Nearly.'

'What does that mean?'

'When I was a young cop in London – in prissy England, as you call it – I volunteered to act as bait for a serial rapist. Late at night I'd walk around the areas where he liked to hunt, in a short skirt and apparently alone. I had a back-up team, of course, and a radio to call for help, but one night the radio didn't work. He got me, beat the shit out of me, did his best to penetrate; would have done if the back-up team hadn't realised that something was wrong.'

'And, afterwards, how did you feel?'

Flint recalls a bewildering array of colliding emotions.

'I mean, did you want to kill the retard that did that to you?'

'Yes.'

'But you didn't?'

'No, because—'

'I did,' says Courtney.

As Courtney tells it, in the aftermath of her rape she withdrew into her shell. And, no, she didn't go to the police.

'Right, and have some jerk ask me if I like to *party*? Do I like to *fuck around*? Was I *asking* for it?'

'Courtney, most cops don't think that way.'

'Really? Well, I'm pleased to hear that. Maybe we can dig up Hope and tell her that she's not a slut after all.'

'Courtney . . .'

Two days after the rape she'd crossed the causeway to Biloxi and on the street bought an unregistered Smith & Wesson five-shot revolver, a 'Lady Smith', that she had no legal right to possess. For the next two weeks she remained curled up on her bed like a wounded animal with the gun under her pillow. Two days after Christmas she left Ocean Springs for New Orleans where, towards the end of January, she found out she was pregnant.

'I couldn't get my head around it. First I was in denial, then I went into shock. Then I'm thinking, *So, which one of those assholes is the father? Whose putrid sperm got there first?* Then I begin to get mad – I mean really, *really* mad.'

'Did you think about getting an abortion?'

'Sure. Exactly what I planned to do – after they'd paid their dues. I figured I'd go to Jackson and find them and say, *Okay, guys, one of you is the father of my child and since we won't know which one until the kid is born both of you are gonna pay – and I'm not talking about a twenty-dollar tip. This is big time. This is gonna be the most expensive fuck you've ever had.* So that's what I did, went to Jackson to extract every cent I could. I hadn't planned on killing them. I only took the Lady Smith along in case they got violent.'

In Jackson's central public library Courtney had spent days – the best part of a week, she thinks – trawling through back copies of the *Clarion-Ledger* newspaper. It was in the *Celebrations* monthly supplement of September 1987, on one of the many pages devoted to engagement announcements, that she finally found a photograph of Mac and his lovely bride-to-be. The announcement said that Tammy Jay Laurent and Charles 'Mac' Hazlip Jr. would be married at the First Baptist Church.

'Want to guess the date of their nuptials?'

'Oh, I'd guess about a week after he raped you?'

'Eight days.'

'It figures. One last boys' night out before he entered into holy matrimony. I expect Tammy Jay was having the final fitting for her wedding gown that weekend. Probably glad to see him out of the way.'

'Can you believe that?'

Flint, dwelling on her own two marriages, thinks that she can.

The *Celebrations* announcement was a paid-for advertisement and Tammy Jay's parents had purchased almost a full page in order to record the distinguished lineages of the prospective bride and groom. To Courtney the names and provenances of the respective grandparents, the great-grandparents, even the great-great-grandparents, reeked of privilege and old Southern money. Mac, she learned, was a graduate of Mississippi State University, and a three-year football letterman, and now a junior partner in the prestigious law firm that his grandfather founded, and a keen sailor. After a honeymoon cruise aboard the family yacht, the final paragraph said, the couple would reside in Jackson.

It took Courtney no time at all to find Mac. That same evening when he left his downtown office Courtney was waiting for him, sitting on the bonnet of his BMW sports coupe – MAC ONE was the licence plate – as though it was hers.

'He did a double take, like he was trying to remember who I was, and then, the sonofabitch, you know what he did? He *smiled*, like he was pleased to see me, like we were old friends who hadn't been in touch for a while. *Hey, Courtney, is that you? Well, goddamn. How are you doing?* I swear he would have kissed me if I'd let him . . . Fuckhead . . . piece of garbage . . . piece of shit . . .'

Flint waits for Courtney to regain her composure.

'I told him that we needed to talk. He said, *Fine, why don't we drive someplace and get ourselves a beverage?* I don't know where we went, somewhere near water, a river or a lake. All the time we're driving, he's got one hand on my thigh. I know what he's going to do so when he stops the car somewhere dark – somewhere under a bridge or a flyover – I said, *By the way, congratulations on your marriage to Tammy Jay*, and he said, *Well, thank you, Courtney, but every time I fuck her I think of you.* And that did it. Up to that point I was only thinking about the money, how much it was going to cost him. Now I'm thinking, *I don't want your money, I don't want you alive!* He grabbed my head, tried to force me to go down on him. I had the Lady Smith in my pocket. I shot him in the balls. Boy, was he surprised. He's got his pretty lips wide open – like he's asking, *why?* – so I put the barrel in his mouth and fired again. Took off the back of his head; I mean, *really*. I've never seen that amount of gore. I'm thinking, *Shit, this is a nice car; I could have had this car as part of my down payment.* But, you know, even if you have it valet cleaned you can never get rid of all of the traces . . .'

'Courtney, you have to stop right there because I need to read you your rights.'

'A bit late for that, isn't it?'

'Even so. You have the right to remain silent. If you give up that right—'

'So, I torched them, the car and Mac. Seemed like the best thing to do.'

Finding Larry was easy. Courtney reckoned it was close to certain he would turn up for Mac's funeral so she did too, slipping into a pew at the rear of the First Baptist Church on North State Street just as the service was coming to an end. Courtney had cut her hair and dyed it to black, matching her outfit, so it would have been hard for Larry to recognise her, not that he was paying much attention. He came down the aisle directly behind the coffin holding on to Tammy Jay as though he feared that she might collapse at any moment. They both looked awful, Courtney says, like a couple of the walking dead.

'Well, they would, wouldn't they? I mean, it was hardly two months since she'd walked down that same aisle in her wedding gown – strapless, diamond-white with a beaded bodice; I saw a picture in the paper – and he was Mac's best man and now they're in their mourning clothes.'

'How did that make you feel?'

'Like I really ought to tell her how I'd done her a *huge* favour.'

Afterwards, after the funeral party had left for the cemetery, Courtney approached an assistant pastor at the church, claimed to be a friend of Tammy Jay from college – *We were members of the same sorority* – and politely inquired, *Who was that young man helping her out?* Laurence Goodall was the answer. Senator Goodall's son.

'Senator Goodall! *The* Senator Goodall? Wow, was this my lucky day. Because, you see, I'd met Senator Goodall when I was stationed at Fort Bragg and he came out on a visit and I was one of those who got to shake his hand, talk with him for a while. And I'm thinking, *Larry, you really fucked up this time because you shouldn't go around raping army vets – not when your daddy is the ranking member of the Senate Armed Services Committee.* Can you believe that? I'm thinking, *Courtney, girl, you're rich for life.*'

In her hotel room, paid for with some of the six hundred dollars she had taken from Mac's wallet, Courtney settled down to write a letter to Larry Goodall. She thinks she must have made a dozen drafts before she was satisfied she'd got the balance right: the balance between scaring him half to death while not opening herself up to an accusation of extortion. She did not threaten him, or not directly. She wrote to him as a desperate young woman who, after one night of unprotected sex – *to which, Larry, you know I did not consent* – found herself pregnant and virtually destitute. *I feel no great anger towards you*, she lied. *I'm simply asking you to accept responsibility for what you did, and for your help.* Then came the kicker. *Larry, I want you to know that I have the greatest respect for your father, who, as a serving soldier, I had the honour to meet. I do not want to bring shame to his name, or shame the name of his future grandchild.* No mention in the letter of Mac. Let Larry make of that what he might.

Courtney is cruising as though she is on verbal auto-pilot. Flint couldn't stop her from talking even if she wanted to.

'I mailed it to Larry care of the senator's office in Jackson. I put *Private and Personal* all over the envelope so it wouldn't get opened in error but I wanted to put it in Larry's mind that if he didn't respond, the next letter might be addressed to his father. I gave him the number of the payphone in the lobby of my hotel. I told him I'd be there waiting for his call at five in the evening for the next two days, and *only* the next two days. Big fucking mistake. Gave them too much time to—'

Courtney's explanation is interrupted by the insistent vibrating of her cell phone; the night-watch supervisor at the Marscheider Building calling to report that, albeit with ill grace, Ms Beauregard is finally en route to her office to retrieve the tape. He is beginning to describe how this achievement was secured when Flint cuts him off with an abrupt, 'Watch, this isn't the time,' and ends the call. Seemingly lost in her own world, Courtney takes no interest in these proceedings. She is staring at her fingers as she picks at the cuticles and Flint worries that whatever engine was driving her to talk has run out of gas. 'Go ahead,' she says encouragingly, with much more confidence than she feels.

'What?'

'You said you made a big mistake.'

'Huh?'

'You said you gave Larry the number of the payphone in the hotel lobby and told him when to call. Why was that a big mistake?'

Courtney is struggling to remember.

'What happened, Courtney? Did Larry call?'

No, not the first evening, nor the second. On the second evening, having waited in the hotel lobby for almost an hour, Courtney returned to her room as confused as she was angry. She had been certain that her strategy would work, didn't understand why it had failed, and now she was suddenly determined to take her case directly to the senator. *Okay, Larry, you think I'm not serious? Watch.*

'I was so mad I didn't pay attention. The door wasn't double-locked, not like I had left it, and that didn't register. I saw the blinds were drawn, and not by me. I've got a pretty good sense of smell and I smelt his cologne but that didn't register either. I marched straight into that room and locked the door behind me and turned around – and there he was.'

'Larry was in your room?'

'No, definitely *not* Larry. This guy was a dead ringer for Hannibal Lecter, except his shoulders were about five feet wide, and he spoke in the same creepy way: *Good evening, Courtney*. The clothes he was wearing, he looked like a mortician and I thought, *Courtney, this is where you're gonna die*. I didn't have the Lady Smith any more 'cause after I shot Mac I'd dumped it in the river and I was trying to figure out what else I could fight him with when he opened up this bag he was carrying and emptied the contents onto the bed. First thing I saw was bundles of dollar bills.'

Twenty-dollar bills in fact, one hundred to a bundle, ten bundles in all; twenty thousand dollars and Courtney was thinking, *Larry, it's not enough, but it's definitely a start*. And then he'd disabused her.

'Sit down,' he said, taking her arm and forcing her down onto the bed. 'Courtney, I guess you know you're in trouble, you just have no idea how big that trouble is.'

I don't know what you're talking about. Let go of me . . . She struggled to free her arm but he was too strong for her.

'I'm talking about this,' and with his free hand he held close up to her eyes a photograph of Mac's burnt-out BMW, his charred carcass still inside – and that stopped her struggling. 'You've annoyed some very powerful people, Courtney, people you really don't want to be upsetting.'

She was about to say, *What's this got to do with me?* but before she could he let go of her arm and from the inside breast pocket of his black jacket produced a wallet of more photographs. He showed them to her one by one: the parking lot where she'd found Mac's car; her looking around the car; her sitting on the bonnet; her watching as Mac approaches; her and Mac standing together, him leaning towards her; the pair of them getting into the car; the car at the top of the exit ramp waiting to turn onto Court Street; the car en route through the city; the car parked under a flyover; her getting out of the car with some kind of white rag in her hand, opening the cap of the gas tank, pushing all but the last few inches of the rag into the tank, lighting the fuse . . .

'These you can keep,' Dr Lecter's double said, dropping the photographs into her lap. 'We'll keep the negatives.'

'Who *are* you?' was all she could think of to say.

It was a question that was never answered, not on that bright winter's day in 1988 nor on the half dozen or so later occasions over the next ten years when she'd met Dr Hellecter – 'Hell plus Lecter, that's what I took to calling him,' says Courtney, 'even to his face.' But *what* he was became immediately clear to Courtney when he told her what she had to do to prevent the negatives reaching the police: *You killed Mac Hazlip Jr., now you're going to kill his father. Oh, and you leave Larry Goodall and the senator alone.*

'Wait a minute,' says Flint, the shock of Courtney's words hitting her like a slap. 'Are you saying this guy worked for Senator Goodall?'

'Nope, because I don't know that for sure. But whoever he worked for they were surely protective of the Goodall family. Hellecter told me that if I ever wrote so much as a postcard to Larry or his daddy or called them or went within a mile if them, or if I

ever told a living soul that Larry had raped me or that he was the
father of my child, I'd be dead within the day.'

'How did he know that Larry raped you?'

'Beats me.' Courtney smiles. 'I guess he must have read my
letter.'

'Jesus!'

'Your witness protection set-up, I really hope it's as good as you
say.'

Hellecter knew that Courtney was an expert marksman, knew her
entire military record – or every part of it that was written down. He
showed her Private First Class Courtney Morrison's official file and
she was pretty certain that she was looking at the original, not a
photocopy. He even knew something that wasn't in the record: that
while she was stationed at Fort Bragg and messing around with
some guys from the 82nd Airborne, they had given her a Dragunov
sniper's rifle they'd brought back from Afghanistan to test fire and
that, at a range of one thousand feet, she'd scored a perfect ten.

'That's what you'll be firing on Sunday,' Hellecter said, 'or one
just like it. Do you play golf?' She'd shaken her head in confusion.
'Well, on Sunday you do. Shady Oaks Country Club, Clinton
Boulevard, the West Course. Mac Hazlip Sr. has a tee-off time of
ten o'clock sharp, playing in a foursome. This is your target,' he
said, handing her four photographs of a silver-haired man with
strong facial features uncannily similar to those of his dead son.
Good genes, Courtney thought. *This is how Mac would have
looked in forty years' time, if he hadn't been such an asshole.*

Then Dr Hellecter had given her the key to a car, told her how
to find the secure lot where it would be parked on Saturday night,
told her that the rifle would be in a golf bag in the trunk. 'When
they named the club Shady Oaks they weren't kidding,' he said, and
for the first time she had seen him smile, albeit it in a creepy Dr
Lecter-ish way. 'The course is littered with oaks a hundred years
old, and pines as tall as steeples. When it comes to picking your
spot, you'll be spoilt for choice.'

True. In fact, everything he'd said was true. Before dawn on
Sunday she left the hotel and walked half a mile to the lot and
found a nearly new Buick parked where it was supposed to be; in
the trunk, a lady's golf bag containing the Dragunov, a silencer, an

optical sight, a cheek plate, two magazines of ammunition.

'That Dragunov?' Flint asks, nodding in the direction of the sofa as though this is an entirely casual inquiry.

'No. He told me the weapon was clean and untraceable so just to leave it at the scene. In fact, since then I've never used the same rifle more than once. Always a Dragunov but ... I guess I'm superstitious.'

And cunning, thinks Flint, because no two of Courtney's killings could ever have been connected by ballistic evidence.

Still pre-dawn and she'd driven out to Shady Oaks and parked the car in one of the surrounding residential streets no more than a five-iron from the course. In ample time she found her ideal spot in a thick cluster of oaks bordering a fairway and waited. Her only chance of being detected, she thought, was if someone hit a wayward shot close to where she was lying and came looking for the ball, but no one did. Watched through her scope came a procession of foursomes – all male, mostly white, expensively clad – and a pattern emerged. She came to realise that almost all of them played their tee shots to within one hundred yards beyond where she was lying and were then obliged to hang around while they waited for the green ahead to clear. If the pattern held, Mac Hazlip Sr. would not be a moving target.

He came into her view, into the cross hairs of her scope, striding down the fairway like he was Tiger Woods while his playing partner drove the cart. His clothes were all a matching maroon, the colour of the flesh of uncooked salmon. He'd hit the longest drive of the foursome, which meant he would be the last to hit his second shot – which meant he would be a virtually stationary target for about a hundred times longer than she needed. When he reached his ball he was eighty to ninety yards away from her.

'He was already as good as dead,' Courtney says. 'I mean, from that range and with that much time, I could have shot him with my eyes shut and one hand tied behind my back.'

'No first-night nerves?'

Flint's query comes with a sardonic edge because the tone of Courtney's guileless admissions is starting to irritate her, but Courtney doesn't seem to notice. She takes the question at face value.

'No, not a single one. I've thought about that, and do you know why? Because for the best part of three years I'd test fired at I don't

know how many thousand cardboard targets, and that can get to
be pretty tedious. So, to make it more interesting, I used to imagine
that I was shooting at real people in hostile situations that I'd
invent. For instance, in the next second this guy is going to
assassinate the President of the United States unless I put a bullet
through his brain. It worked, at least for me. It was why I could
almost always shoot a perfect ten. And, I don't know, I guess the
mind can play funny tricks. The reverse happened. When I was
lining up the shot on Mac's daddy I didn't see a real person, just
another cardboard target.'

And Jack? Flint wants to know. *Was he just another piece of
cardboard in your sight, another assassin that you imagined?* But
this is a question she chooses not to ask.

Courtney says that a silencer robs a bullet of velocity but since
the Dragunov has an effective killing range of almost four thousand
yards, and she was shooting ninety yards maximum, that was not
a factor she needed to consider. She'd fitted the silencer to the
barrel, waited until one of the foursome had taken his second shot
and all attention was focused on the green, and nailed Mac Hazlip
Sr. through the heart. Because she shot him from behind he pitched
forward and lay sprawled face down and Courtney rightly figured
it would be a while before his playing partners would notice the
entry wound. In that while she abandoned the Dragunov – with
some reluctance, she admits – took off the surgical gloves she was
wearing and walked calmly through the trees to the road where she
had parked the car. She must have been already back on Clinton
Boulevard, she reckons, heading into Jackson, when Hazlip's
companions comprehended he had not been stricken by a heart
attack.

She returned the car to its bay in the secured lot, left the key
under the driver's seat, as per her instructions. She ate lunch in a
Denny's restaurant and then returned to the hotel where she
resisted the impulse to watch the local news on television; also
resisted the impulse to flee. *Stay put*, Dr Hellecter had insisted,
*because the second thing the police will do, after they've set up their
checkpoints, is canvass the hotels to establish who's left in a hurry.
Relax. Treat yourself to a couple of decent meals and maybe a little
shopping. Go to the movies. Only check out of the hotel when you
are scheduled to check out, and then take a bus back to New*

Orleans. And Courtney, he had added though not in an overtly menacing tone, *if something goes wrong, if you get arrested for any reason, you say nothing. You don't talk to anyone about anything. You don't answer any questions or agree to perform any test or allow your property to be searched or participate in any line-up. You sign nothing and you don't waive a single one of your constitutional rights. You demand your right to an attorney and your right to make a phone call, and this is the number you call –* and he'd given her a slip of paper, his final gift.

Well, actually, not his final gift, Courtney admits. Three days after arriving back in New Orleans she had found in her mailbox a hand-delivered envelope containing ten thousand dollars in one-hundred dollar bills and a printed note from Dr Hellecter that said, *You did well, and you'll do well again, I'm sure. I'll be in touch.*

And some four weeks after that she had found in her mailbox another hand-delivered envelope containing twenty-five thousand dollars in cash, photographs of a middle-aged woman, her address in Las Vegas and a summary of her daily routine; precise instructions as to where and when a car would be left in a secured downtown lot with an untraceable Dragunov in the trunk. Courtney had counted the money and made a series of seminal decisions: that she would embrace the career imposed on her by Dr Hellecter, and the wealth it offered; that she would not abort the child growing in her womb; that one day, however far away – and despite Hellecter's dire warning – she *would* call on Larry.

'And did you?' asks Flint.

'Not yet,' says Courtney teasingly. 'Not ever, I guess, not now.'

'You got that right.'

After the Las Vegas hit, for which she also received a bonus of ten thousand dollars, Courtney did not hear from Dr Hellecter again, not for almost three years. She gave birth to Melinda at the Charity Hospital and then drifted away from the sweltering heat of New Orleans to the Gulf coast, first to Fairhope in Alabama because she liked the sound of the name and then, in the late fall, to Mobile because she'd read somewhere that it was the politest city in America. Of the money she had received from Hellecter she still had almost sixty thousand dollars left – 'And we're talking nineteen eighty-eight dollars, so I was close to being rich' – and she could

easily afford to rent a furnished apartment in a pleasant neighbourhood using the identity of Carol Styles, a fake ID she had created
for her trip to Las Vegas but never used. She bought herself a small
car, invested cautiously in government bonds and learned the art of
motherhood. Then, when Melinda was eighteen months old and
day care was a practical possibility, she enrolled in a part-time
course at Remington College – 'Just to give myself something to
do.'

'Studying what?' Flint asks.

'Criminal justice,' replies Courtney without a hint of irony.

In posing as Carol Styles was Courtney trying to hide from
Hellecter? Not really, she thinks. She always had this feeling that he
could find her whenever he wanted; wasn't really surprised when in
early May 1991 he'd turned up at her door bearing a gift for
Melinda, saying, *Private Morrison, you're looking good.* This time
the job came with a down payment of fifty thousand dollars; infla-
tion, she supposed, and because the assignment involved foreign
travel. Her destination was the Caribbean island of St Kitts, her
target the eldest son of the deputy prime minister.

'Courtney, did you ever ask *why* you should murder these
people?'

'No.'

'Weren't you ever just the tiniest bit curious?'

'You know what they say about curiosity.'

'Oh, don't be so bloody glib' – Flint's exasperation boiling over
like milk. 'You killed people you didn't know, people you'd never
heard of, without knowing why? Just because some asshole told
you to?'

'Yeah, and for nearly three years before that I fixed weapons,
hundreds of weapons, so that people I didn't know, people I'd never
heard of, could get shot. Just because some assholes told me to.'

'Come on, Courtney, there is a difference!'

'Sure there is' – Courtney's anger also building. 'Dr Hellecter
wore fancy suits and those other assholes, they wore combat
fatigues and they all took orders from people I didn't vote for.
Listen, I know for a fact that some of the weapons I fixed for the
army were sold to Iran, in direct violation of US law, and the money
the government got from those sales went to the Contras in
Nicaragua, also in direct violation of US law, so that they could buy

weapons to shoot at the Sandinistas. I never did ask why, or how many hundreds of people I was helping to kill. I just did my job. Yes, you're damn right there's a difference. When the government breaks the law and people get murdered and I'm part of it, I get to walk away with an honourable discharge and my veteran's benefits. This time, because the asshole giving the orders wore a suit, I go to jail. Perhaps I should have written to President Reagan and asked him why, but I didn't, not then and not later. I never, ever asked.'

'Forget I mentioned it,' says Flint who feels she is sinking into the quicksand of an untenable argument.

'Your friend Rocco, I expect he got medals for shooting people he didn't—'

'I said, *forget it*!'

Courtney accepts her small victory with a quick glance. 'Okay. Just spare me your prissy lectures, will you?' And then, with barely a pause, she reaches even deeper into her bag of surprises and says, 'I *do* know why Karl wanted your son shot.'

Flint can't bring herself to speak.

'He wanted you off his case of course but, more than that, he wanted to fuck with your mind. He wanted you to be in a permanent state of hurting, to drive you mad if he could. You know what he said to me? *Before and after the autopsy I want pictures of the body, lots and lots of pictures.* He didn't care how I got them or how much it cost. He was going to send them to you, a few at a time, on each anniversary of your kid's death. That's how much he hates you – no, more than that. The last time I spoke to him he said, *Perhaps you can get me some body parts? A finger, an ear? Perhaps the genitalia? Yes, the genitalia would be excellent . . .* He's another one with a real scary way of talking.' Courtney feigns a shiver and then she adds, 'I wasn't going to do it, by the way. I may seem like the bitch from hell to you but I'm not a pervert.'

Numbed by ghastly images that assault her mind, Flint struggles to remain focused. 'You've missed a step,' she says as though all that matters is establishing a faithful chronology.

'More than one.'

August 1991, St Kitts: mission accomplished and another bonus paid. In 1992 – July, as best as she remembers – FedEx delivered a package from Hellecter, containing a laptop computer and instructions to familiarise herself with the internet and how to establish connections and set up email addresses that could not easily be traced, and the art of making messages virtually invisible through unbreakable encryption. Courtney enrolled in a second part-time study course and towards the end of that year, just before Christmas, when Dr Hellecter had come calling with another present for Melinda, she had felt sufficiently confident to say she was ready. Ready for what? The answer was in the thick envelope Hellecter handed her as he left: step-by-step instructions on how to obtain and safely assemble the components of an improvised explosive device – 'In other words, a bomb,' says Courtney unnecessarily. 'If I told you how easy it was I'd scare you half to death.'

You already have, thinks Flint; *more than you will ever know.* 'And just as easy to get it wrong and blow yourself up, and Melinda. Courtney, is that what you did?' she asks in a tone that sounds a little too prim. 'Expose your child to that kind of risk?'

No, she'd drawn the line at that. Having absorbed the theory of improvised bomb-making, and having accepted yet another ten thousand dollars from Hellecter – *to cover your expenses* – Courtney had declared herself to be a painter and rented a studio in downtown Mobile; an artist's studio where many types of chemical solvent could be unremarkably stored. She had experimented cautiously. The first IEDs she made and then tested – in uninhabited areas of wetland along the Mississippi coast – were not much more powerful than firecrackers. Only when she had perfected her technique did she build one on an industrial scale and then make the eight-hour trek to Memphis, Tennessee, where she planted it in the crawl space under a substantial Colonial house that, four hours after she left the scene, when the timer triggered the detonator, was reduced to so much smouldering lumber. Two dead, Courtney learned from Hellecter when she was back in Mobile; an unintended result since the house was supposed to be empty and the explosion nothing more than a warning.

'Who died?'

'I don't know. He never said.'

Flint can't help herself. 'And you never tried to find out? Never got hold of a Memphis newspaper or went onto the internet? I mean, how hard would that have been?'

'And why would I do that?' Courtney has a defiant glare on her face that says, *You just don't get it, do you?* True enough. Empathising with the enemy is supposed to be one of Flint's great strengths; to get inside their heads, to be able to think as they do is what makes her such a formidable opponent. But with Courtney she feels as though she is staring into a bottomless pit or is lost on an endless sea without any horizon to fix on. The longer they are together the less she understands. 'It doesn't matter,' she says, wishing she hadn't asked.

'No, really, I'm interested why you think I should care. I was trained to shoot by the army and making sure you identify the people you kill wasn't part of the course. Never came up in basic training, not that I recall.'

'Okay, Courtney, I get the point.'

'But *do you*? Do you really get the *fucking* point?' Her right index finger is tapping lightly on the button of the transmitter.

Flint holds up her hands in mock surrender. 'Can we leave it? Can we just move on?' And to make very clear that is her own intention she doesn't wait for a response. Without asking for permission she picks up Courtney's phone and dials the number of the night desk at the Marscheider Building and says, 'Watch, what's taking so long?'

Ms Beauregard has had a change of heart, apparently. She no longer thinks the tape is unimportant, not worth the disruption to her evening. She now wants it fully transcribed and immediately typed up as a legal document and counter-signed by a strike force lawyer or, failing that, at least two senior agents. She is adamant she will not make the call to her client until that has been done.

'So do it,' says Flint.

'We already are.'

The call over, she tells Courtney, 'We've still got some time.'

In the spring of 1994 Courtney and Melinda moved to a larger apartment in Mobile, a converted loft with soaring ceilings and exposed beams, windows that reached down to the floor and even a rooftop garden. Melinda was now five and a half and doing well at school and Courtney had a baccalaureate degree in criminal justice. She'd never had any intention of pursuing a career within the justice system – 'I only wanted to know how it works,' she says with mischief in her eyes – and with too much time on her hands she'd looked around for something to do; to fill the uncertain gaps between her assignments for Dr Hellecter. She still rented the artist's studio, 'Just in case,' and she thought she might as well use it and teach herself to paint. Landscapes, oils on canvas, became her first métier and if she lacked talent she did not lack enthusiasm. The striking painting on the living room wall is one of her early works, she admits.

'What do you think?'

'It's . . . original,' Flint suggests, because the lighthouse looks like a Saturn rocket just after lift-off.

'It's crap,' says Courtney. 'I only leave it there to remind myself how bad I was.'

'Well, it has energy . . . a sense of drama.'

'It's utter, total garbage, and you know it is, but take a look at these.' On her knees Courtney moves to the sideboard and retrieves from the bottom drawer a portfolio that contains her more recent work, as a copyist. These are reproductions of Saul Steinberg drawings that first appeared as classic covers of *The New Yorker* magazine. To Flint's eye – examined in the beam of the flashlight – they are indistinguishable from the originals. At Glebe Farm lithographic prints of four of them decorate her bedroom walls.

There is more. Courtney has also created her own images drawn in the style of Steinberg; for example, to complement his 'View of the World from 9th Avenue' she has drawn 'View of the World from Downtown Barranquilla', in which the port side of that Colombian city is intricately drawn, and in the background there is a brilliant blue Caribbean Sea across which small boats and light planes race towards a line on the distant horizon that is marked in childlike capitals 'AMERICA'.

It is not lost on Flint that the skills that must have been required to make these faithful copies and imitations – an extraordinary eye and a steadiness of hand – are also the essential skills of a professional sniper.

'Barranquilla was where I did my first job for Karl,' says Courtney. 'Not that I knew him as Karl, not then.'

'Whoa! Hold up.' Flint feels as if she's been ambushed. 'Haven't you missed a couple of steps?'

Not really, says Courtney. After the bombing in Memphis, which occurred in the mid-summer of 1993, she heard nothing more from Dr Hellecter for eighteen months, not that she cared. Her investments were doing well, providing more than enough income to live on, and she was becoming more and more absorbed in her art. Then he turned up at her studio like the proverbial bad penny to announce that her services were urgently required by *an overseas associate of ours who will be in touch with you very shortly.* Courtney took strong objection to this. *Hey, what do you think I am? Some kind of whore you can pass on to your friends?* And Hellecter said, *That's exactly what you are, because we own you, Courtney, and we always will,* and from his jacket pocket he produced the photograph of Mac in his burnt-out BMW and reminded her that when it comes to murder there is no statute of limitations. The next day she received an encrypted email, and various coded attachments, signed Krups, with details of her assignment and the target in Barranquilla but no mention of the fee or her expenses. Still furious with Hellecter, she emailed back, *Sorry, this whore doesn't fuck for free.* And that night Hellecter practically kicked down the door of her apartment, scaring Melinda out of her wits, and took Courtney up to the rooftop garden, to the very edge, and showed her the drop, and swore that if she ever did that again, or anything like it, he would personally throw her *and* Melinda from this very spot – and that was the moment she knew that one of these days she would have to kill Dr Hellecter.

'And did you?'

Courtney is still reliving the moment on the rooftop, doesn't really comprehend Flint's question.

'Barranquilla was a bitch,' she says in a monotone, 'most difficult assignment I've ever had. Still, after two weeks I finally nailed the sucker, I got paid by Krups, one hundred thousand dollars, and I went back to my life. For the next two years all I did was paint and draw and raise Melinda. Had a couple of exhibitions, even sold some drawings. Heard nothing from Hellecter, or from Krups, and I was thinking that I might be free of them when . . .'

In the mail, special delivery, had come an elaborate invitation for Courtney – or rather for Carol Styles, the pseudonym she still used – to visit Italy: a first-class airline ticket to Milan and confirmation of her reservation at the Four Seasons hotel. There was an accompanying note that said *Please do not disappoint me*, which was signed Krups. She went. There was a limousine waiting for her at Malpensa airport, flowers and champagne in her superior room. There was also a note suggesting that the next morning, when she was rested, she might go to church to confess.

Flint feels her heart shiver. 'Any particular church?'

'Yeah, and that was one of the things that gave you away; that was way too cute, if you don't mind me saying. When they asked me to check you out – or rather, when they asked me to check out Kathy McCarry – they told me you were proposing a real estate project to the Gup brothers called San Ambrogio, and that you'd come up with the name, and I thought, that sounds familiar, and finally I remembered that was the church where I'd first met Karl – or Krups, as he was calling himself at the time. I thought, is that one hell of a coincidence or what? Which was why I decided to take a look around your apartment – which is how I found the videotapes of your kid. If you'd picked another name for the project, I might not have bothered. You see?'

Of course she does.

Courtney says that the concierge at the Four Seasons gave her a map with the route marked and that she walked from the hotel to San Ambrogio. As she entered the courtyard, which was deserted except for a couple of Japanese tourists, a young man intercepted her, led her into the church and to one of the confessionals. She entered the stall and waited in the semi-darkness until a voice coming from the other side of the partition told her to kneel down, to move closer to the screen.

Why was it difficult for you in Barranquilla? Why did it take so long?

You forgot to mention the bodyguards and the fact he never showed himself in public.

But eventually he did, yes?

No, he didn't. I had to climb a ten-foot wall and avoid the dogs and the surveillance cameras and bury myself in a stinking pit of manure and lie there for six hours until I got clear sight of him – and even then the range was over one thousand feet and I had just one shot.

Which tells me that you are very resourceful.

Thanks.

I need you to be very resourceful once more. Do you think you can make a plane disappear?

Flint is halfway to her feet. 'Courtney, *stop*, stop right there. If you're about to tell me that you brought down a plane then our deal is off. There's no way on earth I can—'

'That's what I said. *No fucking way, José.* I told him, *I think you're confusing me with a terrorist, Herr Krups – or whatever your real name is. Blowing up a plane, that's way out of my league.* And he laughed, in this really freaky way – and, trust me, that's not something you ever want to hear in the dark – and then he said, *It is only a very small plane, Miss Styles.*

A single-engine Cessna Skyhawk as it turned out, with only the pilot on board. On 21 April 1997 the plane was en route from Tampa, Florida, to Jackson, Mississippi, when it disappeared from the radar twenty miles short of Pensacola. Minor pieces of aircraft debris were subsequently recovered from the Gulf of Mexico by the US Coast Guard and some of them were scorched, indicating the possibility of an in-flight fire or explosion. But the bulk of the wreckage, and the body of the pilot, remained and remain somewhere deep on the ocean floor.

Yes, says Courtney, this time she did check the newspapers and found in the Jackson *Clarion-Ledger* a respectful obituary for a prominent state political lobbyist, one Herman Hicks. The name meant nothing to her but she instantly recognised the accompanying photograph.

'Let me guess,' says Flint though what she is about to say is closer to a certainty. 'Dr Hellecter?'

Forty-Seven

Beware a lawyer who is fuelled by self-righteous indignation. Ms Beauregard is *outraged* at the treatment of her client, *appalled* by the denial of her fundamental rights. Flint should keep in mind that her *blatant disregard* of the law, first and foremost Courtney Morrison's right to have a lawyer present, will *loom large* in any subsequent proceedings. In Ms Beauregard's opinion, it is by no means certain that it is her client who will be the one standing trial.

'You know what?' says Flint wearily, her voice thick with fatigue. 'The only thing I'm concerned about is getting your client out of here alive and then keeping her alive for the foreseeable future and, to be frank with you, counsellor, I couldn't care less what you think or do. But for the record, just so you know, I *did* read Courtney her Miranda rights – or tried to – and she chose to waive them and I could no more stop her from talking than I could stop the tide from coming in. So don't threaten me – or, if you think that's a sensible strategy then you need to get in line because your client is way ahead of you. She's threatening to detonate numerous explosive devices and I believe she means it, and what I want you to do is help me defend the only right that matters for now, which is her right, and mine, not to die in the next few minutes. Get off whatever trip you're on, counsellor, and just tell her what she wants to know.'

Without waiting for a response Flint passes the phone to Courtney and goes to the kitchen with the debris of their MREs, the tumblers she intends to wash, what's left of the Jack Daniels. She tidies things away, wipes down the counter tops. She removes the garbage sack from the pail beneath the sink and places it by the front door. *Soon as you're finished with your phone call, Courtney, we're out of here*, she wishes to imply.

Courtney comes into the kitchen with an amused *can-you-*

believe-this look on her face, holding out the phone. 'She wants to talk with you.'

'What's so funny?'

'She thinks there could be a book deal, even a movie.'

'Really? Well, always count on a lawyer to fix on the priorities. Yes?' she says tersely into the phone.

'I have advised my client that the contract you've offered her is binding, irrevocable.' Despite the exotic promise of her name, Ms Beauregard speaks with a Brooklyn accent that is pitched irritatingly high on the diatonic scale. 'I want to be sure that you also understand.'

'So long as Courtney abides by the terms.'

'I've also advised her that she is to say nothing, nothing at all. I'm recording this call and I'm giving you formal notice that my client declines to answer any further questions unless and until I'm present. Is that clear?'

'Absolutely,' says Flint. 'When can you get here?' And then she quickly adds, 'Well, actually not *here*, not anywhere near Sanibel, because Courtney's present whereabouts have been broadcast on live TV, and that's like declaring open season on her. So what you need to do is get to your apartment as quickly as you can and pack enough things for, I don't know, maybe six months, maybe a year? And do you have a husband or a partner, any children, any pets? Because if you do, we need to get them out of there—'

'Are you *threatening* me?' Ms Beauregard, as angry as she's ever been.

'Last thing on my mind, counsellor. It's Courtney's clients you need to worry about, not me. You see, counsellor, at this less rarefied end of the law we play by different rules and if you're going to publicly stand up for Courtney – and I think that's admirable – you need to understand that when the psychopaths she's been working for can't find her – and I aim to make sure of that – they'll come after you and anybody else who might know where she is; anyone they can put pressure on, and by pressure I mean they'll kidnap your partner or your kids or your siblings, poison your pets, put a bomb in your car. They'll do anything, absolutely anything, to get to your client and silence her because, from their point of view, she is the witness from hell. So, once you know where we're holding Courtney – and you'll have to know if you intend to be present whenever she's asked a question – you will become both a potential risk to her security and *at* risk yourself, and that means I also have to arrange for your full-time protection at a secret location. This is not a nine-to-five case, not one you can leave at the office. This is a case you will have to live twenty-four hours a day until, with Courtney's help, we can find these creatures and extract them from under whichever slimy rock they're hiding – and that means weeks and maybe months of your time. So I need to know: how quickly can you pack and who else do we need to move?'

Flint waits, and so does Courtney.

'Hello? Ms Beauregard? Hello? Counsellor, are you there?'

The phone is dead, the call ended, and Flint stares at the screen in mock disbelief. 'Courtney,' she says, 'I think your lawyer just quit.'

'To concentrate on the movie deal, right?'

'Is that what you think?'

'I think she's a flake and I think you frightened the shit out of her and I think that's exactly what you meant to do.'

'You want to share a house with Ms Beauregard for the indefinite future?'

Courtney grins, shakes her head.

'There are thousands of lawyers better qualified than she is to handle your case, when that time comes. The important thing for now is that our deal is in writing and secure. Do you believe that?'

Courtney nods her head.

'Then I think it's time to go' – and Flint reaches out her hand, and Courtney knows why but she hesitates and her body stiffens, and there is still a chance that she could change her mind. 'We'll call the hospital, find out how Melinda's doing, and then we'll go . . . Courtney, please?'

Afterwards, in her after-action report, Flint will state that only seconds passed before Courtney responded but right now the waiting seems endless, as though time has been frozen. Each of their faces is also frozen, expressionless, as Courtney struggles with her basic instinct.

'Please' – Flint's hand still outstretched.

Eventually – after who knows how long – Courtney lifts her tank top, reaches for the transmitter, tugs at the adhesive tape.

Flint says, 'Carefully, Courtney ... Courtney, can I help you with that?'

Blade suggests to Lieutenant Lucca, 'Manny, I think they're coming out, and when they do there are some pretty pumped-up folks here who might get jumpy and there could be – well, you know – an accident. So I think it might be a good idea if I drift over there, insert myself in the line of fire; as a deterrent, if you get my meaning.'

'Blade, you're a fucking civilian; you have no status, no right to be here.'

'You've got a point.'

'So I better come with you.'

'That's what I thought.'

'Courtney, one last thing before we step outside. I need to know if you're aware of any other imminent threat to life. Meaning, aside from the devices that you've planted here, is there anything else I should be concerned about? Any more bombs?'

A shake of the head but then Courtney reconsiders. 'Unit two one six at Broward County's Safest Lock and Leave,' she says.

'What about it?'

'Don't open the door.'

'Can't be defused?'

'Not from the outside. Tell them they'll have to knock through the wall from the adjoining unit.'

'Is that what you were going to do when you went back?'

'I was never going back.'

Forty-Eight

Not knowing where she is, Flint can't find the light switch. She stumbles from the bed and gropes her way towards the faint glow that tells her the position of the window, her hands outstretched, searching for obstacles. She feels wrecked, as though she has been roused from the deepest of sleeps or almost no sleep at all. There is a dull ache in her right calf and a half-memory of cramp in the muscle. Maybe that's what woke her.

She makes it to the window unscathed and pulls open the curtains, blinking in the sudden light. She sees a wide manicured lawn dotted with beds of flowers of subtle hues and, beyond the reach of the grass, a tranquil sea on which a sailboat appears to be motionless, as though it has been painted. Painted by Courtney, perhaps.

Now it all comes rushing back to her.

The anti-climax of Courtney's surrender: no bright lights or strident commands or even hooded men with guns; just Blade and Manny Lucca waiting at the bottom of the steps and Chief Pete Hendy coming into frame saying to Courtney with elaborate courtesy, 'Ma'am, I'm afraid we need to restrain you for a while so if you'll just come on down and put your hands behind your back . . .'

Chief Hendy's protective hand on the top of Courtney's head as he guided her into the back seat of a patrol car. Blade's brief hug as he whispered his congratulations; Lieutenant Lucca's firm handshake; nothing more than a long hard stare from Agent Agnew.

The arrival of the bomb squad and the K9 dogs; their painstaking discovery that Courtney had exaggerated the threat since only eight of her twenty-four IEDs were wired for detonation.

Rocco Morales' belated arrival at the scene bringing news that Jerry Crawford would wake up in the morning with nothing worse than a severe headache; no skull fracture, no sub-dural haemorrhage.

'And Jack?' she'd hardly dared to ask and Rocco had given her a proper hug – this one lifting her off her feet – and his own impression of a mile-wide smile and said, 'Grace, I saw him, I held his hand, and do you want to guess how many tubes he's got coming out of him? One, and that's a glucose drip. Grace, another week, maybe two, and he's ready to come home.' (*And where exactly might that be?* she'd thought but she kept it to herself.)

The ride to Chief Hendy's house – this house – where, the chief had assured her, Mrs Hendy would be only too delighted to rise from her bed in the middle of the night in order to prepare the guestroom and provide a little sustenance. And so it had proved. Mrs Hendy – '*Now, you call me Louise*' – was a tall, fine-looking woman full of laughter and generosity and curious only as to Flint's immediate needs. Would she like scrambled eggs, a hot bath, a glass of warm milk?

Flint had accepted the milk and a couple of aspirin and gone gratefully to a freshly made bed – and that was how long ago? Judging by the height of the sun it is now late afternoon or early evening in Sanibel, so fifteen hours or more. No wonder her skin feels parched and her bladder demands to be relieved. She heads for the en suite bathroom trying to remember when she last had her watch. Another question intrudes: where is the orange jumpsuit and her underwear and Courtney's trainers, the only things she has to wear? She vaguely recalls washing her underpants in the sink, leaving them to dry on the edge of the bath, but they're not there now. She's naked and she can't find a robe and the only solution is to take the top sheet from the bed and wrap herself in it. She emerges from the bedroom tentatively calling, 'Hello?'

'Well, there you are, my dear' – Mrs Hendy hurrying from the kitchen, delight in her eyes. 'I was beginning to worry that you'd never wake up. You must be—' The sudden sight of Flint in her shroud causes her to pause. She looks confused, crestfallen. 'You didn't like the clothes?'

'The clothes?'

'I had to guess your size of course but I just knew you were no more than an eight.'

'Mrs Hendy . . . Louise, I have no idea what you're talking about.'

'You didn't see what I got for you?' A smile of relief and Mrs Hendy takes Flint's arm and leads her back into the guestroom and to the bedside table where there are three gift-wrapped packages from Ann Taylor waiting to be opened.

'Now,' says Mrs Hendy, 'I didn't know your tastes, and that awful orange thing you were wearing didn't offer any clues, so yesterday I took my daughter into Fort Myers and she picked out some things for you. Penny's about your age and I just hope—'

Yesterday!

Rocco Morales says that it's no big deal; that her system needed to shut down and that, in extremis, restorative sleep is the brain's most effective act of self-defence.

Flint is having none of it. 'Rocco, I was out of it for almost forty hours – and that's not sleep, that's a coma.'

'So? How do you feel now?'

'Fine, but that's not the point. Why didn't somebody wake me?'

'For why? Grace, if you've forgotten what you've been through in the last few days, never mind the last few weeks, we haven't, and Cutter said—'

'Cutter?'

'Your boss, and mine.'

'I know who he is, Rocco. What did he say?'

'Let her sleep for the duration. That way we avoid the aggravation.'

'Very funny, Rocco.'

'Also true.'

They are squabbling like petulant siblings in the Hendys' garden, seated at a table where Louise has served a feast of butter-fried crayfish and salad leaves picked from her garden, dressed with a lemon vinaigrette. They've opened two bottles of Chardonnay, the last of which Blade and the chief have taken with them to the bottom of the garden and the jetty where the chief's Sports Fisherman is moored. Louise is in the kitchen, fixing dessert.

Flint is fully aware that she and Rocco have been left alone for good reason and that their bickering is wasting precious time.

'Time out,' she declares giving the T sign and Rocco smiles his agreement. 'What's going on?'

'Courtney is secure. We've had all of the jurisdictional hassles you would expect – with the Feebs leading the way, as you would also expect – but Cutter butted heads and Courtney was finally released to us last night. She's been successfully relocated. There are four protection agents with her and two more on the way and Kate Barrymore is holding her hand until we get there which should be sometime tomorrow.'

'We?'

'Me and Blade; Cutter bought your proposal. He was also up for Dr Przewalskii coming on board but she can't give us more than a few days of her time because of her other patients, and that means she can't know where Courtney is located.' Rocco shrugs. 'Maybe later on, when Courtney's settled down, we can bring them together someplace else for a while.'

'How's she doing?

'Courtney? I'd say she's doing just fine. In fact I'd say she's enjoying herself. Like you said, you can't stop her from talking but she's being pretty selective as to what she talks about. This far she's given us the Gup brothers and not much else. She knows she's got our full attention so she's milking it for all she's worth.'

'She told me she only knew one of the Gups.'

'Right, Nathan was the one she talked to. But Cutter figures we've got enough to pin a RICO conspiracy on both Nathan and Joseph, and he wants them taken down, tonight.' Rocco glances at his watch. 'In about six hours their sleep is going to be mightily disturbed . . . Of course, what Cutter really wants is to join up the dots all the way to Senator Goodall and he's going to be our first priority.'

'NO!' Flint doesn't mean to shout; the word just erupts from her throat like spume. 'No,' she says again at a more reasonable volume though no less adamantly. 'Gröber is our *first priority*.'

Rocco holds up his hands as if to say *What can I do?* 'Grace, if we have an informant – actually, a prime witness – who can implicate the ranking member of the Senate Armed Services Committee, who also happens to be one of our most senior and respected senators, in at least one contract killing . . . You don't think that Cutter's having wet dreams?'

'Courtney can't implicate him. That's what she said.'

'Yeah, well, Cutter doesn't buy that. He believes that Senator Goodall is Courtney's greatest prize, the one she'll hold on to until the end.'

'I don't give a damn about Senator bloody Goodall, not until Gröber's taken down.'

'Grace, I know you don't, and maybe that's the problem.'

Flint knows she should be having this argument with Cutter – and she will; believe it, she will. But she is livid with Morales – her protégé, for Christ's sake! – for taking Cutter's side. 'Just remember who made you, Rocco,' she says, half under her breath.

'Excuse me?'

'You heard. And also remember who brought the witness in.'

'And you think that gives you bragging rights?'

'I think you should do what you're told.'

'Which is exactly what I am doing, *Deputy* Director.'

Glaring, they slip into a sullen silence, each stubbornly holding to their ground. Blade and Chief Hendy are slowly returning from the jetty, the chief's hand resting on Blade's shoulder, chatting like old friends. Louise, who has been waiting for her cue, emerges from the kitchen bearing a deep-dish apple pie.

'By the way . . .'

'What?'

'Dr Przewalskii wants you to call her; wants to talk about Jack and where he should go.'

'Oh, really? And do you think that's any of her business? Or maybe you think that Cutter should make the call?'

'Grace—'

'Get lost, Rocco' – and Flint is out of her chair, striding down the lawn towards the tranquil sea.

At the bottom of the Hendys' garden Flint sits cross-legged on a thin strip of white sand while the light fades and the colour of the water darkens from blue-green to inky black. She is mesmerised by the birds – swifts or swallows, she isn't sure. Anyway, countless flocks of birds that sweep and swirl in miraculous formations above her head, feeding on the evening bugs. In her restless state of mind she feels she could watch their ballet forever if only they would stay.

'That's really something.'

She turns her head to find Blade behind her, gazing at the sky.

'Am-az-ing,' he says as though he's star-struck.

'Isn't it just.'

'If we could fly like that, we'd rule the world.'

'I thought we did.'

'No, we just act like we do and then we do our level best to screw it up. They got here before us and they'll still be here long after we're gone.'

'I hope so.'

'Yes, well . . .' Blade holds out both hands, offering Flint a turquoise-coloured cashmere sweater that is part of the haul from Ann Taylor. 'I thought you might want this. In case you're cold.'

She takes the sweater but she doesn't put it on. 'Pissed is what I am, Blade. Pissed at Courtney because she never, ever said she was sorry for what she's done. Pissed at Rocco because he's an ingrate. Pissed, *really* pissed at Cutter because he thinks that nailing some crummy senator will get the strike force on the front page of the *New York Times*, and that's somehow more important than stopping Gröber. Pissed at myself for being pissed at Rocco because it's not totally his fault that I will now wreck his career as surely as I made it.' She smiles, gets to her feet. 'Pissed at you for letting me rant on like a bloody lunatic. Come on, shape up, Detective Sergeant Singleton! Tell me it's never supposed to get personal.' She links her arm in his. 'Walk with me, Al.'

Without exchanging words they meander along the waterline for a mile or so until Blade halts their progress, frees his arm, takes her shoulders and turns her towards him. 'Grace, it's always personal. If you don't detest shitheels like Gröber, if your hatred for them doesn't keep you awake at night, then all you're doing is a job and, if that's the case, Cutter's right: go for the targets that'll get the strike force on the front page of the *Times*, because that's the way you keep your budget. But you don't see it that way, and neither do I, and Rocco's not the only one who's talking with Courtney . . .'

She's not sure what he means. 'Al?'

Blade lets go of her shoulders, turns to look at the Hendys' house which now shimmers like a beacon in the twilight. The birds have vanished. 'We should go back,' he states.

'*Al?* What are you saying?'

'I'm saying, I'm on your team. I'm saying that you and I have the same priority . . . I'm saying that I'll give you what you want.'

'When?'

'Let's get you home.'

On the bed in the Hendys' guestroom, propped against the pillows, there is a plain white envelope, letter size, waiting to be opened. There are four words written on it in neat capital letters: FLINT and, underneath, MY EXEMPLARY COOPERATION. Inside the envelope there is a single sheet of paper, unfolded, on which Courtney has created in pencil and crayon a new drawing in the style of Saul Steinberg. It portrays in the foreground the streets and buildings of a city and, beyond that, an expanse of water that is coloured a vivid blue and, beyond that, at the very top of the page, a vague, far-distant skyline represented by nothing more than pencilled squiggles. Except there is one building on that skyline that Courtney has picked out and exaggerated in a cartoon bubble: a drawing made with a draughtsman's care of a distinctive four-storey house set under gable roofs. Beyond the house is a glimpse of a street that Courtney has labelled 'Via Matteo da Campione'.

Courtney's latest drawing bears a caption that might have been written in Steinberg's hand: 'View of Karl's World from Lugano'.

Lugano

Forty-Nine

Route 2 leaves the outskirts of the city squeezed between the western shore of Lake Lugano and the outer spurs of the Alps. The road is narrow, cut into the rock and in places vertiginous and Flint is driving much too fast for the conditions. There was a thunderstorm in the night and the surface is still slick and three-quarters of the way round a blind curve she is confronted by a pair of cyclists riding abreast and swerves and, just for a moment, feels the Lexus skitter. Then the car is back in her control and she misses them, though not by much, and her companion chuckles and says, 'Nigel warned me about your driving.'

She waits until her composure has returned. 'Meaning?'

'He said you once butted your way through two lines of traffic, knocking them aside like skittles. In the Turkish bit of Cyprus, wasn't it? You wrote off fifty vehicles, he said.'

'Did he also tell you that I was taking fire from the Turkish army at the time? And it wasn't fifty vehicles, it was twenty-three, including the Jeep I was driving, and they weren't written off; some of them were barely scratched.'

'Yes, well, Nigel has been known to exaggerate.'

Flint grunts. 'Nigel Ridout lies through his teeth is what he does, and *most* of the time.'

His name is Crispin Mallory, or so his MI6 credentials claim. *Really?* Flint had asked and he'd replied, *Does it matter?* He is the Secret Intelligence Service's representative to what he irritatingly called *Your grouse shoot*: a multinational, multi-agency task force hastily assembled to monitor the capture of Karl Gröber and Alexander Çarçani – and afterwards, no doubt, to squabble among themselves over the spoils. The carabinieri or the Polizia Cantonale will make the arrests, depending on which side of the haphazard Italian-Swiss border Gröber and Çarçani are found. But

Rome's interests are also represented by a posse of agents from SISDE, the Italian security service – all of whom, it seems to Flint, follow the same rakish dress code – and the Swiss contingent is bolstered by more soberly attired agents from both Fedpol, the national police, and Strategischer Nachrichtendienst, the strategic intelligence service. The foreign intelligence agencies of Germany, France and Albania have all dispatched observers and the FBI has sent two legal attachés from Washington. A third attaché has arrived from the American embassy in Bern, though to Flint's suspicious eye he bears the hallmark of the CIA. Then there is the sizeable British delegation that Commander Tom Glenning has assembled from his National Criminal Intelligence Service, Scotland Yard, the Immigration Service and – to Flint's huge chagrin – MI6. As soon as she knew that Six would have any part of this she'd called Tom Glenning in London to loudly complain, and run into a brick wall.

'Six have a perfectly legitimate stake in this operation and you know they do.'

'When you say Six, does that mean Ridout?'

'Of course it does.'

'Nothing about Nigel Ridout is legitimate. Anything he touches he contaminates.'

'Oh, come on, Grace, act your age. He's not paid to be bloody Snow White but neither is he the complete maverick you make him out to be. And, in case you've forgotten, Ridout's people were the first to identify Gröber as a target – and a threat to British and US interests – long before you even knew the man existed. Six has every right to be represented.'

'Tom, I don't believe this,' Flint said and then commenced to list her grievances against Ridout; the long list of ways in which he had disrupted her operations against Gröber over the years. 'And have you forgotten that it was Ridout, or one of his people, who ran the TIPOFF checks for that creep Billy Goodheart and . . .' She broke off her litany, knowing that Glenning was no longer listening.

After a silence, 'Have you finished? Hear me, Grace, this is not your decision. You can't dictate to HMG who it sends to the party.'

'Fine, Tom. I just want Her Majesty's Government to know that if Ridout does anything to interfere with this operation, I will expose him and his rotten outfit. I have a dossier that details every dirty trick he's pulled to protect Gröber and I'll go public with it, I swear . . . and you can tell Ridout that.'

'Tell him yourself.' Commander Glenning, losing patience with her, put down the phone.

So she had. On an insecure line from Lugano she'd called the main number at 85 Albert Embankment – the not-so-secret London HQ of the Secret Intelligence Service – and asked to speak to Nigel Ridout. When the operator prevaricated, claiming to have no knowledge of anyone by that name, Flint said: 'Nigel Ridout is director of the East European Controllerate of your service, and my name is Grace Flint of the US Financial Strike Force, and this is urgent. If you can't find Mr Ridout then I'm going to have to ask you to take a message for him, which needs to be very explicit – though I should warn you this is an open line. Now, do you want to have one more go at trying to locate him?'

Sounding amused, Ridout had come on the line and said, 'Grace, is this wise?'

'Nigel, I just wanted you to know . . .' and she'd launched into her diatribe; her choice of words careful, her accusations coded but the underlying threat unambiguous.

'My, we do like to cross our i's and dot our t's, don't we, Grace – or have I got that the wrong way round?' She could imagine Ridout in his office, turning in his swivel leather chair, changing his perspective from the sweeping panorama out over the River Thames – from the Palace of Westminster to the dome of St Paul's Cathedral – to the view through the glass wall that divides him from his controllerate: his kingdom in which many of his brightest subjects are young, fit and invariably shapely women; *my virgins*, as he'd once described them to Flint, knowing he would get a rise. She could also imagine his eyes pausing to glance at the computer monitor on which the trace of her call was undoubtedly being reported. 'In any event, you're quite wrong: I don't have the slightest wish to disrupt your operation. In fact, my dear, the opposite is true. I'm *willing* you to succeed, to bring the wretched Gröber to account, and Çarçani, and I really don't care in which particular jurisdiction their feet are nailed to the cross, just so long as the nails go deep. Grace, whatever differences we've had in the past over friend Gröber, well, they no longer apply. We can discuss this over lunch one day if you like and I expect that some if not many of your criticisms will turn out to be justified. I don't doubt that we've erred, Grace, which is why we are now committed to assisting you in any way we can. That's why I'm sending you one of my brightest.'

Oh, Nigel, if you could only hear yourself. 'One of your virgins?' she'd asked wrily.

'Actually, yes, in a manner of speaking, though this one's a boy. Go easy on him, Grace. That's all I ask.'

Crispin. Late twenties, she guessed. A little over six feet tall, trim, a mop of dark hair flopping over his forehead; a rather bland face made interesting by a lazy left eye and a thin white scar running from the corner of the eye down towards his mouth. He'd found her last evening in the hotel lobby and introduced himself and they'd walked together to the conference room, him doing most of the talking because she'd had little to say. He had taken it for granted that he would sit next to her during the briefing and she hadn't objected. From his accent and his urbanity she thought he was a product of one of the more exclusive English schools – Winchester or Eton, at a guess – but as the evening wore on, and the talk had turned to tactics and strategy, she'd listened to his occasional contributions and detected a sharper edge to him, one that suggested he'd also received more specialised training: further education, as it were, in one of the clandestine branches of Special Forces.

The briefing was in Italian and he hadn't needed to put on earphones to listen to the simultaneous translation. And later on in the evening, during the group dinner, she'd heard him speaking German and French and what she took to be Albanian, all with impressive fluency. He ate sparingly and nothing that contained saturated fat and he didn't drink alcohol, either at the table or when – together with twenty or so other diehards – they had retired to the hotel bar. During the hour they spent there she'd noticed that he was constantly watchful of his surroundings and that, whenever possible, he'd kept his hands free.

She was at the bar alone, thinking of slipping away, of going to her room, when he'd come up behind her and asked quietly, 'Do you like crowds? Only, I thought we might . . .'

'Might what?'

'Go off on our own?'

She'd got down from the bar stool and pushed by him with a parting glance of disdain.

'I meant in the morning,' he called after her. 'Do you know this part of the world?'

He followed her out of the bar and into the lobby, catching up with her by the elevators, taking her arm. 'Because I know it rather well. Two months ago I spent days scouting the lake for the best vantage points of Campione and—'

Flint yanked her arm free. 'And why would you do that, Crispin?' – hard suspicion in her tone.

'It was nothing to do with Gröber,' he said quickly. 'It couldn't have been, could it? We had no idea he was here . . .' He was not sure she believed him. 'Honestly, Grace, until you found Gröber we didn't have a clue where he was.'

'So?'

'So . . .' He hesitated and Flint turned her back on him to step into the elevator and Crispin's explanation came tumbling out. Gröber was not the only money launderer who'd set up shop in Campione d'Italia, apparently. And at least two of the others were working on an industrial scale, allegedly. They were a Pakistani and his wife who occupied a villa on Via Posero, supposedly. And Via Posero was just up the hill, only a rock fall away from Via Matteo, Gröber's haven, and because of that coincidence he knew of a perfect spot from where he was certain they could observe what would happen in the morning.

'We're not going to see much from here; in fact, bugger all,' he said. 'And, to be frank, I was surprised that Pacelli didn't invite you to go along on the raid, and even more surprised when you didn't kick up a fuss.' General Pacelli is the SISDE executive in overall command of the Italian contingent and at the briefing he had 'requested' that all the foreign observers should stay away from Campione and remain at the hotel in Lugano until Gröber and Çarçani had been taken into custody. Flint had also been surprised; indeed, livid. She didn't kick up a fuss because she had no intention of complying with Pacelli's 'request'.

'Do you have a car?'

She didn't reply immediately because she was still weighing up the options, still making up her mind. On the one hand, she did not want Crispin's company; on the other, during her reconnaissance the previous day she'd found only one road leading into and out of Campione which the carabinieri were certain to block before the arrests and with no local knowledge, and no time to acquire it, she had no idea how she was going to get close.

Somewhat against her better judgement she'd said, 'I'll see you in the lobby at six.'

'Okay, coming up in about four hundred yards, around this next bend, there's a lay-by. Pull in.'

But she can't. As they round the curve they see that the parking area is entirely occupied by three motor caravans, all bearing Dutch number plates.

'Pull over anyway,' he says.

'Where?'

'Just stop.'

Flint manages to squeeze the front wheels onto the lay-by but most of the Lexus is still on the highway. 'Crispin, you better hope that the next thing that comes around that bend behind us isn't an articulated lorry doing sixty miles an hour, because, if it is, we're going to need another rental car – and I'm not paying for the damage.'

'Nobody's going to hit your car, Grace' – Crispin exiting the vehicle, pulling his MI6 credentials out of his shirt pocket. 'They wouldn't dare.'

Very funny, Crispin.

God knows what he's telling them but it must be truly alarming for the Dutch are preparing to leave the lay-by in a hurry, frantically clearing the picnic table of the remainder of their breakfast. Everything Crispin is wearing – the desert boots, the cargo pants with many pockets, the shirt with epaulets – is olive green, suggesting a military provenance, and he approached them with his credentials held high like a badge of authority. Flint waits impatiently behind the wheel of the Lexus with a wary eye on the rear-view mirror. Finally the lay-by is cleared – Crispin directing the departure of the Dutch convoy like an imperious traffic cop – and she is able to get off the highway.

'What on earth did you say to them?'

'I lied.'

'Of course. And?'

'I said that they must have missed the warning signs. That the lay-by is closed because we are about to conduct a controlled explosion in the mountain that could bring down tons of rocks on their caravans, not to mention their heads. Actually,' he feigns to look concerned, 'I'm not sure they fully understood because my grasp of Dutch is no more than adequate. How do you say controlled explosion in Dutch?'

'I think they got the message, Crispin.'

All business now, he opens the fifth door of the Lexus and removes two heavy-looking navy-blue holdalls. He was waiting with them in the hotel lobby when she'd arrived forty minutes early for their rendezvous with the half-formed intention of slipping away before he got there. 'I guess you couldn't sleep either,' he had said pleasantly, as if he hadn't guessed what she'd had in mind.

He declines her offer of help, slips the straps of the holdalls onto his shoulders. 'Can you manoeuvre in those?' he asks, meaning Courtney's trainers which she is still wearing in the entirely irrational hope that so long as she does, her luck will hold. 'Because to get to where we're going we have to go down a pretty steep bank and then there's a fence to get over, maybe six feet high, and then we'll cross a railway track – and don't touch any of the rails, because one or more of them may be live – and then there's another bank, and that one we have to climb. It's about twenty feet and it's practically vertical. What I'm suggesting is, I could go first, get shot of these' – he means the holdalls – 'and then come back and help you.'

She's ignoring him, already halfway across the road.

Their vantage point is on a small promontory above the lake directly opposite the original Casino Municipale of Campione d'Italia, a long squat building set on the water's edge. Directly behind it rises a futuristic complex with a central tower ten storeys high: the new municipal casino, designed by Mario Botta, which cost sixty-five million dollars to build, Crispin tells her. At this point, he says, the lake is almost exactly one mile wide – sixteen hundred metres, to be precise – and up to nine hundred feet deep.

'You're a mine of useless information, Crispin.'

'Look.'

From one holdall he has unpacked a field tripod and from the other a Meade high-resolution telescope; one that can track planets in the far solar system, or show you in exquisite detail the craters on the moon.

'What can you see?'

Doubtfully she says, 'It looks like the head of a rivet.'

'Okay, the magnification is too powerful. Let me change the eyepiece . . . Now what can you see?'

'Wow!'

From a mile away Flint can see the face of a man so clearly she would know what he was saying if she could lip-read Italian.

'Now pan left,' says Crispin, giving her the handbox which controls the Meade's worm gears. 'What do you see?'

'At a guess, algae . . . Crispin, this is a truly impressive piece of kit but don't you think you're overdoing it? How about a pair of binoculars?'

'One more try,' he says, substituting another eyepiece. 'And?'

Now this is truly extraordinary. The magnification is no longer extreme but the streets and houses of Campione appear to be so close she might be strolling along the waterfront in the early morning sunlight.

'Find the marina if you can; there's a sign that says La Fornace, Porto Comunale . . . Got it? Now pan right, slowly, just a couple of degrees. You should see a lido and then, just beyond it, a house with a red-brick face, a balcony on each of the top two storeys.'

'Got it.' The house that Courtney had drawn.

Flint is scrutinising the windows, hoping for a glimpse of Gröber's face, and she is so engaged by the possibility that she doesn't pay immediate attention to her subconscious sense that something is erroneous, seriously out of place. *What's wrong?* She continues watching through the telescope as the question grows louder in her head until the inner voice is practically screaming *WHAT'S WRONG?* And suddenly she knows the answer – or at least the part of it that matters – and she raises her head from the eyepiece and looks at Crispin and feels a surge of anger so intense she has to do something to vent it. Without warning, without thinking, she drops her head and charges him like a bull, butting him in the groin, grabbing with her hands for the back of his knees, pulling him off balance, bringing him down. Before he knows what's happening she's on top of him, straddling his chest, trying to get her hands round his neck, and it's only because he's very quick and far too strong that he manages to seize and hold on to her wrists and twist her onto her back and hold her down, and now he's the one doing the straddling.

He's winded and breathing hard. 'What on earth's the matter with you?'

'How do you know?' She spits out the words. 'How do you know that's Gröber's house?'

She's stopped struggling because she realises it's useless but sooner or later he'll make a mistake and then . . .

'What do you mean?'

'How did you know that Gröber's house has a red-brick face, balconies, whatever? How do you know anything about it?'

'Pacelli described it at the briefing.'

'No he didn't, not that precisely; nothing like it, you double-crossing bastard.'

'Then it must have been your informant's drawing.'

'NO!' – screaming at his face. 'You've never seen the drawing – or, if you have, you better tell me how. You lying . . .' She brings up her knees to jab his kidneys. She can't get sufficient force to elicit more than a grunt from him but he lets go of her arms and climbs off her anyway.

'Grace, please . . .' There is blood on his neck where she's scratched him.

She's still lying on her back, looking up at him, considering her next means of attack. She has a Swiss Army knife in her pocket – the one she stole from Courtney's kitchen – and she's thinking she may use it.

'Believe me, I'm not here to double-cross you.'

'Really? Then I'll ask you again: how do you know Gröber's house?'

'Because . . .' he says, and then, 'I'll show you,' and cautiously he offers his hand to help her up. She won't let him touch her but she agrees to get to her feet and follow him back to the Meade. 'Take a look, please. Go up from Gröber's house, three or four degrees. Now, pan right, slowly. Do you see an abandoned block of flats? The walls are painted white, most of the windows boarded up. Now come down just a fraction, just a touch, and you should be looking at a large villa half hidden in the trees. Got it? Okay, that's the European arm of the ZSK Trading Company of Dubai, or so our American cousins would have us believe.'

The top floor of the villa is walled entirely in glass, like the observation deck of a luxury liner.

'Cousins? You mean Langley?'

'Actually it was the US Treasury that came up with the Via Posero address but, yes. Nigel heard that the CIA had been sniffing around ZSK in Campione and asked me to bring over a team to take a look.'

'ZSK?'

'The Z stands for Zahid, as in Zahid Khan,' says Crispin. 'His wife's name is Safiya, which gives us the S; born in Tripoli but now a Tunisian national. The K comes from their son, Karim, who seems to have access to more passports than I do. He's the courier; he moves the money.'

Flint waits for Crispin to tell her why this is relevant to Gröber and while she waits she watches the observation deck and a figure appears in the lens. Male, otherwise she can't make out much detail. 'That him?' she asks, stepping aside from the Meade.

Crispin takes her place, changes the eyepiece, fine-tunes the focus. 'That's Zahid,' he confirms, inviting her to take a fresh look.

Now the lens is filled by Khan's commanding face. He is standing behind the glass staring out over the rooftops of Campione like a potentate surveying his kingdom, and not necessarily with pleasure. His mouth is down-turned, his nostrils are splayed and his dark eyes are wide and fixed on a distant point, as though he is watching the approach of something that concerns him.

'There were four of us,' says Crispin. 'I put two spotters on the roof of the abandoned flats. From their position they couldn't see much more than the rooftops of the villa but there is only one way out of Khan's place, via a steep driveway, and, in terms of observing the exit, they had the best seats in the house. Once I'd found this spot, I camped out here for the duration and I used the fourth spotter as a floater. We established their routine pretty quickly. The Khans have a live-in maid who does all of the shopping and runs the errands, and a FedEx van calls every weekday to deliver and collect packages. Otherwise, nobody goes to the villa and nobody leaves it. Except on the second day we were watching, Karim, the son, came out of the driveway in a dark blue Fiat with Swiss number plates, and the floater picked him up at the bottom of the hill and followed him out of Campione and to Lugano airport where he took a flight to Bern with an onward connection to London. But Zahid and Safiya never showed themselves. Oh, a couple of times I spotted Zahid on the top floor, looking at the lake through a pair of binoculars. Other than that, nothing. As far as we could tell, Zahid and Safiya never so much as stepped outside of their front door.'

Crispin speaks in a flat monotone as if he is reliving the boredom of that tedious vigil.

'Until, that is, just after nine hundred hours on the sixth day the spotters on the roof of the flats reported that a black Mercedes had left the driveway. They couldn't get a proper look at the sole occupant but they were pretty sure it was a man. I caught glimpses of the car as it came down the hill and I alerted the floater; instructed her to wait in a car park beyond the one-way system. Since after that point Campione is essentially a one-road town, I didn't imagine she could possibly have any problems in picking him up and following him to wherever he was going. Elementary, nothing more than basic training.'

Flint looks up from the Meade, rubs her right eye to relieve the strain. '*She*, Crispin? One of Nigel's virgins?'

'Precisely. Except they're not, of course, not most of them; not in the literal sense.'

'He told me you were also a virgin.'

Crispin smiles, refusing to take the bait. 'I think he means *unbloodied*, Grace. In Nigel's terms we're all virgins until we've shed blood for the service – or drawn it. And by that definition I'm no longer a virgin since ...' He rubs the small wound her fingernails have left on his neck.

'Get on with it,' she says impatiently.

Flint resumes her observation of Khan's villa and, after an interval, Crispin resumes his narrative. The Mercedes never appeared in the floater's rear-view mirror, he says. Somewhere between the bottom of the hill and the casino, a distance of less than a kilometre, it simply vanished.

'I left the floater in place, just in case, and told one of the spotters to walk the route from Via Posero to the casino. Along that route there are very few places where you can park a bicycle, let alone a Mercedes, and she didn't find the car. So she planted herself at a picnic table on the lido and waited and, some two hours later, she saw a man fitting the description we had of Khan walking past her towards the porto comunale. She followed him and saw that he had parked the Mercedes in the municipal parking garage. He drove directly back to Via Posero. During the debrief that night we asked ourselves two obvious questions: where had he been while we lost him, and why did he need a car to accomplish a round trip of less than a mile?'

Khan hasn't moved and Flint knows she won't learn anything more by watching him. So she's using the Meade to retrace his short journey from Via Posero to Via Matteo and the house with the red-brick facing which, she calculates, is no more than five hundred yards from the parking garage in the porto comunale.

'He went to meet someone in Via Matteo and he was transporting something heavy,' she says as if the answers are obvious. 'Tell me, Crispin, what exactly does the ZSK Trading Company trade in? No, don't tell me, let me guess: gold bullion?'

'You're very quick, Grace.'

'Thank you. And you still haven't answered my question: how do you know? How do you know that's Gröber's house?'

'I'll get to it,' says Crispin, refusing to be rushed.

He had re-deployed his meagre forces so that when, on the

seventh day, the Mercedes once again left the driveway on Via Posero, the floater was parked in the porto comunale and one of the spotters was keeping out of sight in a cemetery with an uninterrupted view of Via Matteo.

'Khan didn't park the car in the garage as we'd expected. Instead he drove partway along Via Matteo and then pulled over to the side of the road, turned on the hazard lights and honked the horn. Instantly, or so it seemed to the spotter, two men – young, tough-looking characters – emerged from a house – the house you're looking at now – and removed two suitcases from the boot; nothing special about the cases except they were obviously heavy. Then Khan drove off, followed by my floater, did a loop round the one-way system and went home. I doubt he was away from his villa for more than five minutes.'

The light is getting stronger and, conversely, the image through the telescope is deteriorating, taking on a slightly fuzzy quality. Turbulence caused by the increasing heat, Crispin tells her when Flint grumbles. He changes the eyepiece to one of lower power and asks, 'Better?' Clearer, she says, and even at this reduced level of magnification she can still make out each individual brick.

'So, I was now in something of a dilemma. I barely had the resources to maintain surveillance on one house, let alone two – and Nigel wasn't up for sending reinforcements. The best I could do was keep the spotters on the roof of the flats to watch Khan – and hope he didn't do anything unexpected – while the floater and I concentrated on chummy's house – whoever chummy might be. That was down to London to resolve, because we could hardly ask the Campione authorities, could we?'

'You weren't running an official operation then, Crispin? Not one the Italians knew anything about?'

'Perish the thought' – and he chuckles. 'Anyway, London came up trumps within twenty-four hours, meaning they established that the Via Matteo house was owned by one Oskar von Klimt, Austrian national born in Salzburg, July the eighteenth, nineteen forty-nine – for what that was worth. Because, you see, London checked further, and an Oskar von Klimt was indeed born in that very town on that very day and lived there for the next fifty-odd years where he became a banker of faultless reputation. It was after his wife died that he sold his shares in the bank and moved to Campione to enjoy his not inconsiderable fortune. There was nothing against him, nothing that London could find . . . Anything happening?'

'It's as quiet as a graveyard,' says Flint, lifting her head from the eyepiece like a swimmer coming up for air. 'Either they're sleeping late, or they make it their business to go nowhere near the windows – or there's nobody there.'

'No, Pacelli was adamant at the briefing that Gröber and Çarçani are in the house.'

'Yeah, but that was last night.' Flint's feeling jaded, wishing she'd thought to ask the hotel for a Thermos flask of coffee. She yawns, stretches her arms. 'Trust me, I've been here before, metaphorically speaking, and Gröber has an uncanny knack of knowing when to slip away.'

Talking of uncanny: 'I'm sure you could do with a cup of coffee,' Crispin says, reaching into the side pocket of one of his holdalls.

'And?' Flint is relentless, still demanding the answer to her question: *how do you know?*

'I was sitting here pondering why a blameless Austrian banker would be mixed up with the likes of Zahid Khan: greed or boredom, I supposed. Then it occurred to me that the Oskar von Klimt whose house I was watching could be an imposter; a fanciful idea, I agree, but not beyond the realms of possibility. The real Oskar could have been eliminated and his identity stolen, I thought. I was rather struck by the fact that London said he still kept in touch with old friends and colleagues in Salzburg, but only by means of the occasional postcard from Campione; no visits, no telephone calls. No one in Austria had set eyes on Oskar for the last three years. I called Nigel and suggested that, if the opportunity arose, we might try to gain entry to the house while Oskar was away and obtain his fingerprints, or samples of his DNA. Nigel was not opposed to the idea – until the shit hit the proverbial fan.'

Crispin continues, 'I expect you've noticed the jetty at the end of Oskar's garden? Well, the day after Khan's second delivery I was watching two burly chaps loading heavy suitcases into the cabin of a small motor boat – nothing more than a day cruiser – when one of the spotters called to tell me that Khan had visitors; that a chauffeur-driven limousine had just disgorged three men, unmistakably from the East, on Khan's doorstep. I wanted to know where the boat was going but Nigel's absolute priority was that we establish the identity of Khan's visitors – understandably, given the purpose of our original mission. So, I'm afraid from that moment we abandoned all interest in poor Oskar; put him very firmly on the back burner and more or less forgot about him. It wasn't until we heard that your informant had placed Karl Gröber in Campione *and* in a house on Via Matteo that we put two and two together: Oskar had to be Karl, didn't he? I mean, there is a limit to how far coincidence can credibly be stretched, isn't there?'

Flint doesn't answer. She's still sifting through Crispin's explanation, looking for the flaws.

'Which means, I fear, that the real Oskar is no longer with us,' he says. 'In the lake, I wouldn't be surprised; in nine hundred feet of water.'

She knows he's deceiving her, if only by omission. Because she says nothing he has a need to fill the silence.

'Nigel was furious with himself, I must say, when he realised that we'd missed the chance to grab Gröber.'

'Grab him? How?'

'Send in the bodysnatchers.'

'And Nigel would have done that?'

'In a moment. Gröber would have gone to sleep in Campione and woken up in London and known nothing about what had happened in between. But we missed—'

'C-r-i-s-p-i-n?' Flint says slowly, stretching his name so that it sounds like an accusation.

'What?'

'These bodysnatchers of yours, they're not here now, are they?'

He laughs as if she's told a joke. 'Not yet,' he says. 'I can't say we didn't consider snatching Gröber but, on balance, Nigel thought that would be going a bit too far and, anyway . . .' He wavers, as if he's uncertain whether he should tell her.

Here it comes, Flint thinks; *finally the truth – or the biggest of his lies.*

'As Nigel would put it, we have other fish to fry. Khan's visitors, the three chaps in the limousine, we've identified them. Two are unimportant; just minders, muscle. The third is a Saudi national who goes by a dozen different aliases. We believe he's Osama bin Laden's brother-in-law and his principal money man. Do you see?'

'No. What are you saying, that Zahid Khan launders money for al Qaeda?'

'That's why I'm here,' says Crispin. 'Once Gröber's safely in the bag, that's precisely what we intend to ask him.'

Fifty

It's coming up to nine o'clock and the start of the raid is almost an hour overdue and Crispin says he's going back to the car to get his mobile phone and call the hotel, see if he can get hold of one of the detectives from Scotland Yard, find out if they know what's going on.

Flint resumes her vigil, methodically scanning Campione's waterfront from Gröber's house on Via Matteo to the border, a distance she knows to be less than one mile. It all looks terribly normal – or what she imagines to be normality in Campione. A ferry arriving from Lugano, the first tourists of the day spilling onto the dockside as the shopkeepers raise their shutters, open their doors; people lazing in outdoor cafés; a modest but steady flow of vehicles crossing from Italian to Swiss territory, unimpeded by any formalities. No sign, not a hint, of carabinieri units massing offstage to begin their assault and, even more disturbing, no sign of covert surveillance on or near Via Matteo. She searches the lake, from Gandria in the north to Bissone in the south, and does not find a single police launch.

Something's wrong: the message coming from her gut as well as her eyes. She waits impatiently for Crispin's return.

And while she waits she refocuses the Meade on Gröber's house and thinks that she catches a glimpse of a face in the right-hand window of the top floor. She stays fixed on that window for the next few minutes, switches the lens to increase the magnification, sees nothing more. During her surveillance training she was warned to understand that in a state of acute tedium the mind can play tricks; that in the absence of any real evidence we may see what we want to see. Even so, her instincts tell her that she was not imagining things; that the house has not yet been abandoned. She searches Crispin's holdalls, looking for something to clean her sweat from the eyepiece; finds a packet of optical wipes.

She begins again, re-examining every inch of Gröber's lair from the satellite dish on top of the roof down the façade to the garden and then on to the jetty and the lake. Nothing is moving: nothing, except for a water taxi approaching the porto comunale.

Crispin announces his return by dislodging a shower of shale as he clambers to the top of the bank. She turns to look at him and sees that his expression is gloomy, as if he wishes to warn her that he's the reluctant bearer of bad news. Sure enough, 'You're not going to like this,' is the first thing he says.

There are problems with the arrest warrant, he tells her. A senior magistrate in Milan has decided that it doesn't meet the legal requirements posed by Campione's peculiar status as an exclave of Italy. There are irregularities in the wording and it needs to be re-drafted, re-submitted to the magistrate, re-approved. The bottom line: the arrest operation has been cancelled, Crispin tells her; or, rather, put on hold for at least twenty-four hours.

'Grace, there's no point in blaming the messenger,' he insists because she's staring at him as though he's the one who's made the decision.

'Which magistrate? What's his name?'

'I don't know, I didn't ask. Does it matter?'

'Yes, I think it matters and I'll tell you why.' Her voice is frigid, her tone laced with sarcasm. 'Because I swore the information for that warrant, and then I spent the best part of two days in Milan going through it, line by line, word by word, with Carlo Colonna, the magistrate who signed it. There are no irregularities in the warrant, Crispin. It's watertight, because Colonna put me through hoops to make it so, and whoever's overridden him is either a fool or a charlatan. He's been got at, bribed or blackmailed – and I'll give you one guess who got to him.'

After a moment, 'You mean Nigel?' Crispin sounds genuinely astonished by the idea. 'Come on, Grace! How on earth can you believe that Nigel could *get at* a magistrate in Milan. I mean, I know you have reason to doubt his motives but this is perfectly ridiculous.'

'Oh, bugger off.' She bends down to pick up a small rock, hurls it as far as she can into the lake. She picks up another rock, swings round as though she's looking for a target. 'Nigel could get at the Pope, if he had to. That's what he does, that's his talent: Nigel will corrupt anyone, anything, to get what he wants.'

There is no arguing with her, though Crispin tries. He says the warrant *could* be legally deficient, despite her best efforts and the best efforts of Magistrate Colonna, but she simply won't listen. She wants to know if he's brought his phone back from the car and he says that he has and she holds out her hand for it.

Commander Glenning's direct line is one of the numbers she keeps in her head.

'Tom, the operation's been canned.'

'I heard.'

'And there's no surveillance on the target.'

There is the slightest of pauses before Glenning responds. 'That I hadn't heard. How do you know?'

'Because I've spent the morning looking at the target area through a telescope and I can see into every doorway and every window and every car, and I know how surveillance is done, Tom, and there's nothing in place; absolutely zero.'

'Do you know why?'

'I can guess – can't you?' She waits for him to work it out and when he doesn't respond she adds, 'Nigel.'

This time there is a longer pause. 'I don't see how that could be,' he says carefully.

'I'll find out how he did it, but that's for later. Right now I need your help.'

What she wants is Glenning's permission to use all the members of the British contingent now cooling their heels in the Hotel Lugano to set up a perimeter around Campione. She's got the lakeside more or less covered, she tells Glenning, but no one is watching the street. 'They can walk out of there through the front door any time they like, and we'd have no way of knowing. In fact, they could have a moving van parked outside and be loading up the furniture right this moment and we wouldn't have a clue. I need bodies on the ground, Tom; every warm body you've got.'

No hesitation from Glenning this time: 'No, Grace.'

No! She can't believe it.

'Tom, I don't understand' – remaining as calm as she can, trying to keep the panic out of her voice. 'I haven't come this far just to let these bastards walk away.'

'I can't help you, Grace.'

'Why, for God's sake?'

'Because this is Europe, not the Wild West. Because you're not a sheriff, or some global supercop, and I can't give you a posse to detain whoever you want without a warrant and outside your jurisdiction – and outside mine, for that matter – just because you think that you should.'

'I'm not talking about detaining anybody. I just want to keep tabs on them, to know where they go.'

'Even so,' says Glenning, his mind made up. 'What I will do is call Milan and find out why there's no surveillance – if, indeed, you're right. Call me back in a couple of hours.'

And with that he says a terse goodbye and Flint, incredulous and fuming, struggles against the urge to hurl Crispin's phone into the lake.

So this is Flint's Plan B, the only one she's got: Crispin has agreed to continue surveillance of the house through the telescope while she drives the Lexus to Campione and finds a suitable spot from where she can covertly watch Via Matteo and still be in a position to follow Gröber and Çarçani if they take off. She and Crispin will keep in contact by mobile phone and if anything happens . . . well, Flint says, they'll have to make it up as they go along. She is acutely aware that she has no reason to trust Crispin, and no other choice. As she scrambles down the bank towards the railway track, more often on her buttocks than her feet, the memory of a cartoon she saw recently in *The New Yorker* slips into her mind: two men looking at a folder that's labelled PLAN Z; one saying to the other, *Of course, if this one flops we're done.*

Reaching the car she retrieves her phone from under the driver's seat and turns it on and the screen tells her she's missed two calls from 'Unknown'; two calls received within five minutes of each other about two hours ago, no message left on her voicemail. Only Cutter, Rocco Morales and the strike force watch supervisor in New York – and now, of course, Crispin – know the number of the SIM card she's using. She calls the Marscheider Building.

'Has anyone been trying to reach me?'

'Not that I know of, DD, but let me check.'

While she waits on the line she studies the map, looking for the fastest route to Campione. Some two kilometres to the south of the lay-by, at a town called Melide, Route 2 meets the N2 autostrada as it turns sharp left to cross the lake. That will take her to Bissone and from there the Campione border is only one kilometre to the north. So the entire U-shaped loop from where she is now to Via Matteo can't be more than six kilometres – and how long can that take? It strikes her as the first item of cheery news she has received all morning.

'That's affirmative,' says the watch supervisor. 'Magpie.'

Magpie is Rocco Morales' current code name, the only name he will be known by at the Marscheider Building for as long as the interrogation of Courtney Morrison continues. Blade is Blackbird, Courtney is Thrush.

'I can't patch you through because the line is not secure. Magpie will get back to you in thirty – that's three zero – minutes.'

'Got it,' she says and ends the conversation, anxious to be on her way.

But there are dawdlers on the road to Melide, gawkers delayed by the spectacular views, and the carriageway is too twisting and too narrow for her to overtake more than most of them, and when she finally reaches Melide – the palms of her hands sticky on the steering wheel – she misses the turning that would have taken her across the lake and has to make a hard U-turn at the next junction – where there are prominent signs specifically forbidding any such a manoeuvre – and for one heart-stopping moment, filled with a cacophony of blaring horns, she fears she has cut it too fine. Waving a hand in apology, she accelerates away from the chaos she has caused, retraces her route, finds the road to Bissone. She has barely made it to the Campione border – marked by flags and flowers and a decorative arch – when Magpie calls. She continues driving, only one hand on the wheel.

'Hey, how's it going in Netherland?'

'It could be better. How about you?'

'Good . . . better than good. Thrush seems to have taken a shine to Blackbird and she's singing like a . . .' Morales chuckles. 'Well, I

guess you'd say like a bird.' Then abruptly he drops his bantering
tone. 'There's something you need to know.'

'Wait.' Flint is entering Campione's one-way traffic system
which, travelling in this direction, takes her away from the lakefront, and she needs both hands to make a sharp right curve. 'Okay,
go ahead.'

'Thrush met Hustler three times.' Hustler is the strike force's
code name for Karl Gröber.

'The first time you know about – in the church, in the con-
fessional, though she never saw his face. Neither did she meet
Romeo on that occasion.' It was Flint who chose Alexander
Çarçani's soubriquet to ironically reflect the fact that he trades in
female flesh.

'Okay.'

'The second time she met Hustler and Romeo but *not* in
Netherland' – the code for Campione. 'That meeting took place in
a café on the opposite shore, from where the ferries run. You with
me?'

'Yes. But then how does she know—'

'I'm getting to that. Same location on the opposite shore for the
third meeting, the one when she was given her final contract.' He
means the contract to murder Flint's son. 'Now, here's the
important part. At that meeting Hustler and Romeo tried to give
the impression that they'd flown in especially to meet her; that
they'd come from the place where the church is. Are you still
following this?'

'Yes – *shit!*'

'What?'

'Wait one.'

There are two uniformed cops standing in the roadway blocking
her path, their palms raised in the air to tell her to stop. She pulls
over to the side of the road. 'Magpie,' she says, 'don't go away,' and
then she drops the phone into her lap.

They only speak Italian, a language she pretends not to
understand, but she can't not understand the universal hand signals
they make demanding to see her papers. She could show them her
strike force credentials, in the hope that the fraternal brotherhood of
law enforcement holds sway even in Campione, but the Lexus is
rented in the name of Kathy McCarry – and that's a complication

she doesn't want to get into – so it's Kathy's ID that she chooses to show them, together with the rental contract. She has been stopped, she is made to understand through mime, for operating a mobile phone whilst driving; an offence punishable by an on-the-spot fine of six hundred euros or, if she prefers, the equivalent in Swiss francs.

She shows them that she doesn't have that kind of money in her purse.

In which case, they indicate, they can either escort her to the nearest ATM to withdraw the necessary funds or the car will be confiscated until she pays the fine. They are enjoying themselves now: swaggering but also ingratiating, mildly flirtatious; getting off on their petty power to make her helpless. It takes another twenty minutes for her to get the money, for them to fill out their wretched forms and inspect the Lexus for any further offences she may have committed, before they let her go.

She grabs the phone. 'Magpie?'

The line is dead.

Bloody, sodding, bloody rotten hell!

Flint calls New York, says she needs to speak again to Magpie urgently. The watch supervisor, sounding slightly surprised, is non-committal; only agrees to pass on her message. She calls London and Glenning's personal assistant says he's been called away from the office unexpectedly and won't be back for the rest of the day. She calls Crispin and gets his voicemail; the line engaged, she suspects, because he's talking to bloody Nigel.

The Lexus is beginning to feel like a trap and she has to get out. She slams the driver's door harder than she needs to, crosses the lido, walks along Via Matteo until she is standing on the pavement opposite Gröber's house searching each pair of windows with her eyes. Hardly covert surveillance but she no longer cares. She has half a mind to cross the street, knock on the door, to kick it down if she has to.

And then do what, exactly?

Out of the sun, it's cold and all she has on is a polo shirt and jeans. She needs her jacket, she decides. She's returning to the car to get it, crossing the lido, when Magpie calls back.

'What was all that about?' he asks sounding irritated, mildly pissed off.

'Nothing, just a little difficulty with the local constabulary.'

'Yeah, well, if you're planning on putting me on hold for the duration again just keep in mind that it's well past my middle of the night.'

'Sorry.' She's found a spot on the pebble beach that's in the sun and gives her a three-quarter view of the house.

'Okay, you're forgiven. Where was I?'

'You were saying that Thrush didn't buy it; didn't believe they'd flown in for the meeting.'

'Right. So when the meet was over and they went off in their limo heading for the airport, supposedly, she had them tailed. Sure enough, they were driven straight to Netherland; had themselves dropped off outside a fancy house on the lakeside, and Hustler had the key to the front door. That's how Thrush found out where he lives. But it's the next part that's important. Starling and her friend decided to hang around—'

'What!' Starling is code for Courtney's daughter.

'I should have said, Thrush likes to keep her business in the family, apparently. When she needed a little help from time to time she used Starling and her young Japanese friend – who turns out not to be so young, by the way. She's almost twenty-five.'

Flint grasps Magpie's every word but she can't seem to take in their meaning. She has trouble forming her thoughts and also her next question.

'Roc—' she begins and has to stop herself and start again. 'Magpie, are you saying that Mel— that Starling was part of this; that she knew what her mother did?'

'Thrush says no, that Starling never knew the nature of the business – but Thrush would say that, wouldn't she? Me, I'm keeping an open mind.'

Flint's eyes are fixed on Hustler's silent house but what she's seeing in her mind is a replay of Starling on the stairs.

Is that a real sword, Melinda?

What do you think, bitch?

'Did Starling go on any of her mother's . . . Christ, I don't know what to call them. Any of her mother's . . .'

'Missions?' he suggests.

'That'll do.'

There is a pause before Rocco answers, 'Once.' And then he tells her what she already suspects. 'Starling was your shadow for three days before . . .' Now he also struggles to find a way to express himself in neutral terms. 'Before the business was done. Starling and her friend tailed you when you left your office each evening to establish your pattern. According to Thrush, when the actual deed was done, Starling was in a movie theatre in Bethesda, blissfully unaware – but, like I said, I'm keeping an open mind.'

Flint has nothing to say. Afterwards, in her analysis of what happened, Dr Przewalskii will conclude that this was probably the moment when Flint reached the tipping point; when she completely lost her facility to make rational judgements, to abide by any rules.

'One more thing: this is what you need to know,' Rocco says hastily, sensing that she's about to end the call. 'Romeo has a boat on the lake. Starling hung around in Netherland for a couple of hours, taking photos for her mom, and she saw Romeo leaving Hustler's house by the back door, meaning lakeside, in a dinghy. There was a vessel waiting for him which we've identified from Starling's pictures as a Ferretti 53 – and I'm not talking about your average family cruiser. You want me to give you a description?'

There is no need because Flint can see it floating like a mini ocean liner about five hundred yards offshore, its stern turned towards Gröber's house, puffs of white smoke rising from the engine exhausts. A water taxi is pulling away from it, only the driver on board.

'Rocco, we can talk later, get some sleep,' she says, already running across the lido towards the car.

Even though the engines are running, the Ferretti is still idle. Through the telescope Crispin can count the links of the anchor chain running up from the surface of the lake to the bow. He reduces the power of the lens and refocuses on the flying bridge. Çarçani and the boat's skipper are leaning on the rail, chatting, drinking coffee, Çarçani smoking a cigarette. Gröber's not with them – not yet.

'Taking their time, aren't they?' Nigel says laconically when Crispin reports in. 'Mediterranean time, I suppose. And where is Grace, if you know? Pressing the enemy? A little too close for Herr Gröber's comfort, I expect.'

Inside Gröber's house is the answer. Searching it from top to bottom, no doubt – with a tyre iron in her hand, the only weapon she has. Crispin spotted her coming into view from the left-hand side of the house, from his perspective; saw her smash a pane of glass in the French windows, reach inside, let herself in.

'It's too late. There's nothing she can do,' says Crispin.

Nigel Ridout laughs. 'Really? We should write her off, you think? Game, set and match? And your considered opinion is based on, what, precisely? You think you know her?' Ridout leaves his challenge hanging for a moment and then, 'Do something for me will you, dear boy; *indulge* me.'

'Sir?'

'Stop thinking like a cunt.'

This is the closest Flint has ever been to Karl Gröber; touching the things that he's touched, learning about a side of him she's never known. As she searches the house for him – recklessly so, all of her training abandoned as she barges from room to room without taking any precautions – she sees ample evidence of how he spends his leisure time in Campione. There are books everywhere, not only on the shelves but scattered on every table: contemporary histories; biographies of artists, writers, composers; anthologies of poetry and short stories; lavishly illustrated coffee-table books about art, sculpture, Roman artefacts, classical architecture; encyclopaedia, dictionaries of philosophy and literature. Then there is his music collection: scores, perhaps hundreds of CDs, also scattered throughout the house; Mozart, Bach, Brahms, Handel, Puccini. It strikes her as perverse, even obscene, that while Gröber washes the profits of the sex slave trade he might choose to listen to, say, an aria from *Madame Butterfly*.

She's on the top floor of the house in what seems to be the master bedroom. There are binoculars on the bedside table and she takes them to the window to study the Ferretti. She sees some activity on the lower deck, opens the window to get a better view. Three of Çarçani's men dressed identically in dark trousers and white shirts are tidying the cushions on the banquettes, wiping dew from the rails. She is sure they are Çarçani's men because they have the same look, the same arrogant strut, as the three reptiles who tormented the mythical Frau Fischer with their sexual innuendo in rooms above a pasticceria in Milan. In fact, they could be the same three men. If Flint could hear them speak she would instantly know, because it is their mocking voices that stay with her.

Now Çarçani himself comes into her view, appearing on deck from the main salon. He seems to be entirely at ease, nothing in his body language to suggest he fears surveillance or imminent arrest. He banters with his minions and the faint sound of their laughter reaches her. She imagines herself as Courtney, looking through the cross hairs. *From this range, with this much time, I could shoot you with my eyes shut . . .*

No sign of Gröber.

She dials Crispin's number again, fully expecting to get his voicemail. Instead: 'Hello? Grace? I've been calling you for—'

'Crispin, listen to me. Çarçani has a boat the size of a gin palace that's moored about five hundred—'

'I know. That's why I've been trying to reach you for what seems like an eternity, and—'

'Is Gröber on the boat?'

'I'm not sure. I didn't see who went on board.'

What? She feels she's losing touch with reality. 'Crispin, how could you *not* see?'

'Because the Meade was focused on the house, not the boat. In fact, I didn't know the boat was there until I took a break – looked up from the lens to rest my eyes; took in the wider view. And then I spotted her – well, hard to miss, really – and something about her caught my eye. So then I did take a look through the Meade and saw there was a water taxi alongside, and then I scanned the bridge and, bingo, there was chummy, as bold as you like. Which was when I started trying to call you.'

It all sounds perfectly plausible – except: 'But, Crispin, if you were focused on the house then you *must* have seen them leave.' *Unless you were too busy talking to bloody Nigel,* she thinks but doesn't say.

'No,' he answers with studied patience, 'because they didn't leave from the house. I haven't seen a living soul – not until you showed up with your tyre lever. And, by the way, Grace, before you went into burglar mode, did it occur to you that you might set off an alarm?'

Yes is the answer but she doesn't bother to give it. 'Crispin, what are you looking at now?'

'You.'

'Well, stop it. Watch the boat. Stay on the line and tell me if it moves.'

Flint the recidivist is breaking the law again: steering through Campione with only one hand on the wheel, exceeding the speed limit, crossing solid lines to overtake as though she owns the road. The police have every reason to stop her but this time, she has decided, it will take more than their upraised palms.

'Talk to me,' she says.

'Where are you?'

'On my way to you. What's happening?'

'Nothing. Çarçani's gone below, I think. Still no sign of Gröber . . . No, strike that; I see him – at least I think I do. He's on the lower deck talking to Çarçani's goons . . . Wait . . .'

Flint is safely across the border into Switzerland – not that any Swiss traffic cop is likely to be more tolerant of the way she's driving.

'Wait,' he says again.

'Wait for what? Come on, Crispin, stop—'

'I just wanted to be sure . . . Okay, it's Gröber, no doubt about it. And the anchor's being raised. They're underway.'

'Going where?'

'Well, their present heading would take them to Lugano but I doubt they'll be that obliging. I'm waiting to see which way they turn.'

Now on the A2 crossing the lake, Flint risks taking her eyes off the road to glance over her right shoulder. The Ferretti is too far away for her to detect any motion.

'Where could they go?' she wants to know.

'They're spoilt for choice, really. There must be twenty, even twenty-five landings where they can dock. Mind you . . . hold on, they're turning to starboard, they're heading north.'

'CHRIST!' Just ahead of her a truck she was about to overtake has pulled into her lane. She drops the phone, brakes hard, knows instantly that even so she will run out of road; swerves to her right, the only thing she can do. Just inches measure the margin by which she misses the nearside tail of the truck – and now she's in the inside lane bearing down on a dawdling white van that she is certain to ram. There is nothing she can do except accelerate, overtake the truck on the inside then swerve left to avoid the van, try to squeeze between a gap that is constantly narrowing. Go for it!

Nigel warned me about your driving.

Fifty-One

Lake Lugano meanders – serpentinely, vaguely in the shape of an inverted human colon – from Porlezza in the north-east to Lavena Ponte Tresa in the south-west, both of which are in Lombardy, Italian territory. But for most of its length of approximately nineteen miles its waters are in Switzerland, which is why Flint continues to push the Lexus hard. As far as she knows – and whatever chicanery has been accomplished in Milan – the Swiss arrest warrants for Karl Gröber and Alexander Çarçani are still valid, still in place. And if the Ferretti can be intercepted in Swiss waters . . .

She is driving north from Melide on Route 2, a mile or so short of the lay-by, when she sees Crispin jogging along the road towards her and pulls over to pick him up.

'What's happening?'

'Give me a second,' he says breathlessly because he's been running with the weighty holdalls containing the Meade and the tripod. HMG property, he explains defensively, seeing the look on her face. And does she have any idea how much a Meade telescope costs?

'*Crispin?*'

'Okay, you need to turn round. They're heading south.'

'What? You said north on the phone.'

'They did go north. Then I saw them coming back. I was about to tell you when you . . . what on earth happened, by the way?'

Flint waves a hand to say it doesn't matter. 'Going where?' she asks, grabbing for the map.

'Assuming they want to be in Italy then the most likely bet is here,' showing her what looks like an appendix at the bottom of the colon and, at its southernmost point, Porto Ceresio. 'Or, after they've crossed into Italian waters – which is here, about a mile short of Ceresio – they can turn north-west and run parallel with the border up to Lavena Ponte Tresa, which is here.'

'And then?'

Crispin shrugs. 'If they've got transport waiting, just about anywhere they please. Listen, if we want to know where they're going we don't have much time.'

'Then drive,' says Flint, scrambling across to the front passenger seat.

Swiss banking secrecy is one of the banes of Flint's professional life. On the other hand, Dr Adel Rentsch, head of the anti-money laundering section of the Swiss Federal Police, has been a solid ally of Flint in her pursuit of Gröber's money, identifying in various Swiss accounts nearly two million dollars that she has deemed to be of 'suspected criminal origin' and caused to be blocked, at least for the time being. For a Swiss cop she is irreverent and not overly concerned with protocol. She is also remarkably quick-witted.

Dr Rentsch is a breath of fresh air, a no-nonsense woman – and Flint's last hope.

Reached on her direct line at Fedpol headquarters in Bern she says in her customary cheerful way, 'Ah, Grace, a little bird told me that you were in Lugano. Your colleagues missed your company at breakfast – though, unlike them, I doubt that you overslept. How are you, my dear?'

'I'm fine. Did your little bird also tell you what's going on?'

'I have heard of problems with the Italian warrants; that the carabinieri has been obliged to delay its operation.'

'The carabinieri was mugged by a bent magistrate, Adel, if you want my opinion. But listen, Gröber and Çarçani have left Campione by boat, heading south. We think they're trying to get to Lombardy.'

Rentsch grasps the point immediately. 'Indeed? And where are they now?'

'They've just passed through the channel between Melide and Bissone, where the road crosses the lake.'

'Then there is no time, Grace.'

'But there could be,' Flint insists. 'Adel, they're going very slowly, no more than . . .' she looks at Crispin who holds up the fingers of one hand, 'no more than four knots. We don't know why and it makes no sense . . . Maybe there's something wrong with the engine?'

'Moment.' There is a brief pause before Flint hears Rentsch talking rapidly in German on another line. Then, 'Can you see the boat?'

'Yes,' says Flint. Through the telescope it looks larger than life. 'Describe it to me, please.'

'Let me put you on to a colleague who can do that better than me.' Flint passes the phone to Crispin and, listening to the precise description of the Ferretti he gives Adel – its height, its length, its beam, even the depth of its keel – is not at all surprised that he knows so much. *Been on board one, have you, Crispin?* she might ask in other circumstances. *Been on board that particular Ferretti, by any chance?*

When he hands back the phone he must see something in her eyes for his face adopts a wounded expression, as if to say, *What did I do?*

'Grace, if anything changes with the boat please call me at once.'

'I will. Good luck.'

'Where are you, by the way?'

'In church,' says Flint. 'Praying.'

To be more precise, they are on the terrace of a church – Chiesa di Santa Maria del Sasso – which perches on the slope of a sugarloaf mountain at the southern tip of the Swiss peninsula around which the Ferretti must pass if it is to reach Lombardy. Crispin had driven as fast as the road would allow to Morcote – once a fishing village, now a tourist trap crowded with tacky shops – where they had abandoned the Lexus and run through the stepped lanes leading up the slope. There are signs warning that the climb up to the church is steep and takes fifteen minutes but they'd done it in less than half that time. Crispin had insisted on lugging both the telescope and the tripod. Even so, when they reached the church it was Flint who felt as though her lungs were about to burst.

'Let me guess,' she said when she could at last get her breath, 'you never take the lift at Ceauşescu Towers, do you?' – Ceauşescu Towers being the mocking name used by critics of MI6 to describe the hubristic architecture of its headquarters. 'I'll bet you run all the way up the stairs two at a time.'

'I try to keep in decent shape,' he said, po-faced.

'Tell me, what were you before Nigel got his grubby hands on you? A soldier? Special Forces?'

'Unborn – according to Nigel, that is.'

The views of the lake from the bell tower of Santa Maria are truly spectacular – and, for Flint's purposes, superlative. Through the telescope she can see the Ferretti and almost anywhere it might go. She can't see the maritime border between Switzerland and Italy because it is unmarked but Crispin knows where it is. 'There,' he says after setting up the Meade to scan an imaginary dotted line.

But the Ferretti is making very little progress towards the line. Against the prevailing wind – which on this part of the lake blows from the south, according to Flint's map – it is barely making way. Yet she sees no sign of concern on the face of the skipper who is at the helm on the flying bridge or on the sullen countenance of the young man who leans idly against the rail on the lower deck – the only living souls in sight. For the third time today her gut tells her that something is wrong.

She excuses herself, moves away from Crispin until she is beyond his hearing and calls Dr Rentsch.

'Adel, they're hardly moving, and they don't seem to care, and I've got a nasty feeling that what I'm watching is a set-up.'

'Where is the boat?'

'About two kilometres from the end of the peninsula, so maybe three kilometres from the border.'

'Then perhaps we do have time – and then we will know.'

'Meaning?'

'Ten minutes from now. Watch.'

While they wait, Crispin says to Flint, 'Shall I tell you what puzzles me? The access to the engine compartment is below deck so if there is a problem with the fuel supply or the electrics or the cooling system, whatever, then what on earth is the skipper doing lolling around on the bridge? I mean, when it comes to the mechanics of the boat, you'd expect him to be the keeper of all knowledge – or I would – so why isn't he below? What do you think?'

'I think you seem to know an awful lot about Ferrettis; *that* Ferretti in particular. How is that, Crispin?'

He looks puzzled for a moment and then his face relaxes, as

though he's solved a riddle. 'Oh, I see what you've been thinking
. . . No, not that Ferretti, Grace; that *model*.'

'Because?'

'Because my brother owns one; *drives* one, as he likes to say, and
it amuses him to invite me to cruise the Caribbean with him every
few months. That allows him to remind me, and whichever luscious
girlfriend he presently has in tow, that while his kid brother is a
mere *minion of the state* – his words – he, at the age of thirty-six,
is officially retired and *driving* a boat that cost the best part of a
million pounds and otherwise living in considerable luxury; in
Antigua, at the moment.' Crispin's tone has taken on a brittle edge.
'When I go out to the Caribbean for my jollies he even insists on
paying my air fare; first class, of course – and I let him.'

'Retired from what?'

'Grand larceny, or that's what Nigel calls it. Giles – my dear
brother – worked in the City for a private bank that was quick to
recognise the financial opportunities in some of the territories of
the former Soviet Union, especially those that had oil and other
mineral reserves. Giles was sent out there by his employers in a
missionary role to preach the gospel of privatisation, and he found
many believers among the oligarchy – and I seriously doubt there is
anyone who matters who he doesn't know on first-name terms. He
was sufficiently clever to make sure the bank did very well out of
his machinations while, behind their backs, Giles did even better.
One hundred million dollars is our most cautious estimate of how
much he received in what he describes to me as his *commissions*,
his backhanders, how much he stole.'

Flint is not yet sure she is hearing the truth. 'And Six knew this
when they recruited you, that your brother was a crook?'

'Oh, Grace,' and Crispin laughs as if she's teasing him. 'You
know Nigel, it's the main reason *why* they recruited me, of course.
To spy on my brother – who *is* a crook, not was. After his successes
he could walk away from the bank but the Moscow mafiosi don't
have a retirement plan as such: in their eyes you're either useful or
you're dead. Since Giles very much enjoys life, not to mention his
lifestyle, he prefers to remain useful. Which is why his kid brother
– who works for the Foreign Office, Russian desk, so Giles believes,
and who is not always discreet when the whisky flows and he's in
his cups – has more air miles to his credit than you can imagine.

Which is why I know at least part of what the mafiosi is up to, because my brother is also indiscreet in his cups. And which is also why I could bore you to death with a recitation of the finer features of a Ferretti, if you have the time. Satisfied?'

She doesn't answer the question. Instead she asks, 'Are your parents still alive?'

'Yes, they are, and they rather agree with Giles that, in career and financial terms, their younger son has so far underperformed.'

His resentment is transparent, and Flint is almost half convinced, nearly half prepared to believe that Crispin could be genuine: not a total conniving shit of Nigel's creation; that while he swims in Nigel's swamp he somehow contrives to keep his head above the slime. 'Well,' she offers in a mollifying tone, 'what do parents know?'

'Grace, it bothers me that you think I'm your enemy.'

She walks away from him, returns to the Meade, refocuses on the Ferretti. 'Let's see what happens,' she says.

She is watching the sullen one on the rear deck, sees his body tense, when Crispin shouts, 'Grace, look!' She lifts her head from the telescope to look where he's pointing; sees a launch coming around the peninsula from the west at ski-boat speed, the word POLIZEI emblazoned on its side. 'And there!' – Crispin now pointing to the east from where a second launch is coming, this one with a flashing blue light on the cabin roof. And then it's Flint's turn to point and shout because when she swings her head to look back at the Ferretti she can see two more launches fast approaching its stern from the north. Crispin lets out a whoop of delight. 'Who says the Swiss don't have a navy?'

Then the superstructure of the Ferretti shudders and Crispin's grin is eclipsed. 'I don't think there's anything wrong with the engines,' he says. And, right on cue, the water around the boat seems to boil and it surges forward, the bow rising as though to meet a challenge. The rate of acceleration is not flashy but inexorable, measured by the steadily increasing span of her milky-white wake.

The police launches on her port and starboard beams are adjusting course to take account of the new interception point, describing gentle arcs.

'Can she outrun them?'

'I doubt it,' says Crispin. 'But she can make more than thirty knots and if they get in the way of thirty-six tonnes of boat doing anything like that speed she'll turn them into matchwood, or shreds of fibreglass.'

The Ferretti is drawing level with Morcote, approaching the end of the peninsula; not much more than a mile to the Italian border, no more than two or three minutes to go. All the launches are now alongside her, like outriders, two on each beam. If they're going to do something they need to do it now.

'They have to shoot him,' says Flint, thinking out loud, talking to herself as much as to Crispin.

'What! Shoot who?'

'Whoever's driving the bloody thing.'

'A bit extreme, don't you think?'

'No' – said emphatically.

And she thinks she might just get her wish, for as the flotilla passes beneath their position, they can see men in black combat gear crouched on the decks of the two lead launches with automatic weapons pointed at the Ferretti. *Do it, do it*, Flint is willing them when the boat seems to stagger, as though it's run aground, and the deceleration is so abrupt, all four launches overtake it before they also seem to stagger and slow. Now the Ferretti is picking up speed again and turning in a tight circle until it is heading north – and Flint has no idea what's happened or why, until Crispin tells her.

'He took all the power off and caught them napping.'

'Why?'

'Because he wanted them ahead of his bow.'

'Why?'

'So he could turn and get them behind his stern.'

'*Crispin, WHY?*'

'That's why,' he says, pointing to the Ferretti's rear deck. 'Çarçani's goons.' The three of them are lying down, spread in a line across the deck, taking cover behind the transom. They also have automatic weapons but these look to be of a larger calibre. 'They've set up an ambush. Call your friend, Grace, tell her to warn the police.'

Flint has already dialled Dr Rentsch's number. There is no reply. Helpless, they can only watch as the launches race four abreast across the glittering surface, overhauling the Ferretti. They are within fifty yards of its stern, skipping through its wake, when Çarçani's goons spring their trap and the sound of heavy automatic fire rises up from the lake. The two centre launches – the initial targets, presumably – veer away from the line of fire like wounded animals but towards each other and the gap between them is so narrow their collision is inevitable. They ram almost bow to bow and climb into the air together, like a pair of dolphins leaping out of the sea, and then twist and turn and fall back into the water, raining debris and shattered bodies. There is no explosion but on the church terrace Flint can still hear the echo of the impact.

She looks at Crispin who stands as though he's paralysed, deprived of the power to move or speak. His face is expressionless. 'What now?' she asks but he doesn't reply – not immediately. She lets him take his time, waits for him to say what she already knows to be true.

'Well, they have well and truly fucked themselves now, haven't they? No way are they getting off the lake. Not after that, not alive.'

But the outcome is not yet inevitable for while the two surviving launches have abandoned pursuit and turned back to the site of the collision, their crews frantically probing the debris for survivors, the Ferretti has also turned and is once more speeding south towards the border. It is beyond Morcote, beyond the tip of the peninsula, just a few hundred yards to go.

Now it is into Italian waters, safely across the imaginary line, entering the inlet that leads to Porto Ceresio less than a mile away.

Flint is watching through the Meade as it settles in the water and its wake lessens. Two of Çarçani's men are going forward on the upper deck while the third is standing by the transom with a coil of thick rope in his hands. No sign of their weaponry.

Then her vision goes blurred and Crispin gasps and says, 'My God!' and a split second after that a sound like thunder reaches her and she looks up from the telescope to see a dense black fog streaked with orange spume rising up from the Ferretti – or rather, from where the Ferretti was. It seems to have vanished, or been obliterated.

Crispin pushes past her to get to the telescope.

'What happened?'

'She just blew up,' he says as he changes the lens, strives to get focus. 'As if she was hit by a missile, some kind of warhead.' Now he can see properly. 'Jesus! The entire superstructure has gone. There's nothing left except the hull. Here, take a look.'

'That's unbelievable!' What she can see looks to her like the skeleton of a boat, nothing more than a smoking shell that is barely above water. 'How could that . . . I mean, what could do that? Did the fuel tank blow up?'

'No. The engines are diesel and diesel doesn't blow like that. If it wasn't a warhead then either they were carrying high explosives on board – and why would they do that? – or . . .'

When he doesn't continue, Flint turns her head to look at him. 'Or?'

'Or it was an IED, a bomb. Looking at that kind of damage, it's the only explanation that makes sense to me.'

'You mean someone planted a bomb on Çarçani's boat?'

'That, or . . .' he hesitates again, and since she already knows what he's going to say, she says it for him.

'Or Çarçani did.'

Crispin is on the phone again, talking to London – to Nigel, of course; talking also to the British contingent at the Lugano Hotel. She still can't reach Adel Rentsch and she's already called the Marscheider Building, left a message for Cutter, and while she waits for Crispin to finish she climbs the wooded slope behind the church until she is above the bell tower and finds a spot in the sun to sit and think: to filter the suspicions and questions that are crowding her mind; to see if she can add to the few certainties she holds.

From where she sits she can see a host of boats around what's left of the Ferretti. Many if not most of them are flying the Swiss flag so, she supposes, the technicality that it blew up in Italian waters is just that: a detail that the Swiss have ignored. Can't blame them, not after what Çarçani's goons did. She's glad they're dead. She only regrets that they must have died instantly, without even a split second of pre-recognition.

So, she wants to know of herself, does that make her glad that Gröber and Çarçani were not on board the Ferretti when the bomb went off? That after it left Campione and headed north, and before it altered course to head south, they got off – for that is now her absolute certainty. Is she pleased they are still alive, still subject to her retribution, or would she rather they had been killed instantaneously? She doesn't know. She can't make up her mind.

She feels suddenly chilled, as though a cloud has blotted out the sun. It has been four years since Gröber became her prime target – her *obsession*, Dr P would say – and now she has to start again; four wasted years, and her half-dead child in the hospital, not to mention Jerry Crawford, is all she has to show for it.

She sees Crispin leaving the church, looking for her. She doesn't call out to him. She wants more time with herself.

Come on, girl! Self-pity is crap. Count up the pluses.

Well, there are some, she admits. Gröber and Çarçani on the run, their safe havens gone; Courtney singing like a songbird – and, who knows, Cutter may yet get to cuff the ranking member of the Senate Armed Services Committee; the motherload of intelligence about any number of criminal conspiracies that the terriers have extracted – are still extracting – from the Gup brothers' most secret files.

Yeah, her inner voice reminds her, *and Nigel's sitting in his office with a smile this wide because he's fucked you again – and you don't have a thing to prove it.*

Yeah? Well, we'll see about that because, believe it, Nigel's on my list.

Crispin has spotted her and he's climbing the hill. She can't make up her mind about him: Nigel's accomplice or only his dupe? For now he remains on her mental list of suspects: guilty until proven innocent – not that he will know that, not until she's sure.

When he reaches her he has the grace to appear mildly out of breath.

'Crispin, I can't believe you've left HMG's property unattended. Do you know how much those telescopes cost?'

He grins, acknowledging her tease. 'Frankly, I no longer care. But just in case you think a leopard can ever change its spots, they're down there,' pointing to the bottom of the hill, 'where I can keep my eye on them. Now, I have some news which—'

Flint groans. 'Which I'm not going to like, right?'

'Yes and no,' he says, sitting down beside her. 'Shall I tell you?' She nods. 'The carabinieri have established that at just after ten this morning, two men fitting the descriptions of Gröber and Çarçani were collected by water taxi from a boat – almost certainly the Ferretti – that was anchored about half a mile across the northern Italian border. The boat had engine problems, or that's the story they gave the taxi driver. He took them, and four pieces of luggage, to Porlezza, which is the main Italian port at the northern tip of the lake. There was a car and a driver waiting for them; no real description of either, except that the car was large and black. They reached Porlezza at about ten thirty, which means they have, what?' He glances at his watch. 'They have about a six-hour start. Nigel has been assured by the Italian authorities at the highest level that the arrest warrants are no longer considered flawed – and, indeed, that additional warrants are being added as we speak – and that the carabinieri is now conducting a manhunt the length and breadth of Italy. Arrest on sight is the order; shoot on sight if necessary.'

Flint waits until she's sure he's finished. 'And, Crispin, tell me, when you said *yes* and *no*, which particular bit of your news did you think I'd like?'

'Well, at least the Italians have got off their arses. At least there's a hue and cry.'

'Terrific,' says Flint, getting to her feet. 'And are they searching the skies, Crispin, because there's no point now in searching the airfields, is there? What do you think: say an hour to get to an airfield, then five hours in a plane. How far could they have got? Spain? North Africa? Greece? Turkey? Sodding *Albania*?'

'All right, Grace, you've made your point. At least you have the certainty that they're not in pieces at the bottom of the lake; that they're out there somewhere, somewhere to be found.'

'Found by who?'

'You, who else? I don't imagine for a moment that you're going to give up. Are you? Of course you're not. This is a setback, a very bad day at the office, I grant you. But it's not the end of the bloody world . . . Grace? *Grace?* Where on earth are you going?'

Further up the slope is the answer, as high as she can climb in Courtney's trainers. Suddenly she has this compulsive urge to see the lake all the way from Porlezza to Porto Ceresio – as though that panorama might reveal some hidden insights, clarify her suspicions – and she can only do that from the top of the mountain. She ignores Crispin's appeals for her to stop. She hears him coming after her and still she presses on until she is above the treeline, confronted by a sheer rock face she has no idea how to climb. Nevertheless she tries, finds one handhold then another, places for her feet.

Crispin catches up with her, takes hold of her calves, tugs her from the rock. She falls on him and he grabs her around the waist and he slips on the shale and they end up on the ground, he on top of her. Trying to make a joke of it, he says, 'Grace, we must stop meeting like this.'

'Get off me!'

'I will but you've got to promise to stop this. It's stupid and it's bloody dangerous, and I don't see how you breaking your neck is going to help you get Gröber. *Please*. Please stop punishing yourself.'

Is that what she's doing? Blaming herself for the whole debacle? Or is she just so angry, so out of control, that she no longer cares if she falls off a rock face and breaks her neck?

'Where are you when I need you, Dr P?' she says without meaning to.

'Sorry?'

'Get off me.'

He allows her to push him away, rolling from her onto his back. She gets to her feet and stands looking down at him, the expression on her face blank, unreadable.

'Tell me what really happened,' she says.

'I don't know what happened. I can only tell you what I think.'

'Then tell me, Crispin, tell me what you *think* happened.'

He also gets to his feet, notices a tear in the sleeve of his shirt, is distracted by a scrape of blood on his elbow.

'*Tell me!*'

'I think Gröber and Çarçani were tipped off about the warrants you obtained. Bound to have been, really, because too many people in too many places knew. I mean, I find it difficult to believe that Çarçani doesn't have at least one informant in the Albanian police or NIS, the intelligence service, probably both, and they knew you were about to pounce. And all the time he was running his disgusting rackets out of Milan he was being feted like a fashion designer, which means he must have had Italian connections, protection, call it what you will. So, yes, I think it is safe to assume they were warned about the warrants and, yes, I think you're right in believing that the magistrate who cancelled them was nobbled. Got at, as you said.'

'By Nigel' – not a question.

'Grace . . .' Crispin sighs. 'I know that nothing I can say will convince you otherwise but, please, ask yourself a simple question: if Çarçani was so well connected in Milan, then why would he need help to fix a magistrate? Leave aside your opinion of Nigel. Why?'

She has no immediate answer to that question so she ignores it. 'Go on,' she says.

'I think Gröber and Çarçani bought themselves some time, but not so much time – maybe a day or two – to arrange their escape. They would have been certain that whatever any magistrate in Milan decided, you would not be deterred, and the Swiss were an unknown factor. So they needed a ruse to get themselves out of Campione and back into Italian territory proper, and keep you – us – occupied watching the Ferretti while they escaped. It was practically foolproof because even if we'd guessed, even if we'd had the means to follow them from Campione into Italian waters, seen them transfer to the water taxi, what could we have done, Grace?'

'Bugger all.'

'Exactly. The only chance to grab them – if we'd known in advance, if the Swiss had been up for it – was when they left Campione and headed north, while they were still in Swiss waters. If they were at any risk at all, it was only for those three miles until they reached the Italian border; five or six minutes at the most.'

She can see the simplicity of the escape plan – and it worked. So why, she wants to know, did Çarçani's goons go to war with the Swiss police? Why did Çarçani blow up a million-pound boat?

'Well, I doubt the Ferretti was his – or, at least, it wasn't in his name. It will have been leased from some dummy corporation in which Çarçani may or may not have had an interest – we'll never know, I suspect. And it will have been insured. As for the goons, frankly, your guess is as good as mine.'

'So what's yours?'

He smiles at her persistence. 'I guess the idea was to give you the impression that Gröber and Çarçani were enjoying a lazy day out on the lake. I guess the skipper was ordered to cruise around until the evening, going nowhere in any hurry, and then dock in Porto Ceresio – by which time Gröber and Çarçani would be long, long gone and you would be none the wiser unless and until the Italian warrant was re-issued. The plan fell apart, of course, when the Swiss police intervened. Whether the goons had been instructed to put up a fight or whether that was madness of their own invention, I have no idea.'

'And the bomb? What's your *guess* about the bomb, Crispin?'

He studies her face for what seems like a very long time. Then, 'The same as yours, I imagine.'

'Go on.'

'I guess it was meant for you.'

He may as well have slapped her. '*What?*'

'You mean you hadn't guessed?'

'What are you talking about?'

'Grace, I think Gröber and Çarçani knew that whatever happened today, sooner or later the Ferretti would be boarded by the police, and that you were almost certain to be with them. Maybe not with the first raiding party but, sooner or later, you would want to see for yourself, go on board. I think the bomb was armed with a remote control detonator, probably attached to a mobile phone, and that they had spotters on the shore waiting for you to do just that.'

She's having trouble concentrating on what he's saying because memories of Kissimmee are flooding back, getting in the way: Cutter telling her, *The creeps who did this rigged a remote control detonator attached to a cell phone – or that's the way the crime scene folks are reading it. Likely as not they had a button man on a hilltop half a mile away watching through a night scope, waiting for his moment . . .*

'Grace, are you all right? Only you look—'

She coughs to clear her throat. 'So what changed their minds?'

'The ambush, I imagine. Gröber and Çarçani couldn't allow the goons to fall into police hands, not after what happened. Because the goons would have been *made* to talk, no doubt about it. You don't kill nine police—'

'Nine?'

'Yes. There were only three survivors, I'm afraid.' He wants to comfort her – take her in his arms, or something – but he doesn't quite have the nerve. 'Anyway, after the ambush I think the spotters called them, told them what had happened, and Gröber and

Çarçani had to make an instant choice: you or the goons. Since the goons posed the more immediate threat to their escape . . .' He shrugs. 'I expect Gröber and Çarçani told each other that if they did succeed in escaping there would always be another day.'

He doesn't need to say for what.

'Want me to drive?' Crispin asks when they are back at the Lexus.

'Sure,' and she hands him the keys. 'I just need to get my bag.'

It takes him a moment to understand what she means. 'You're not coming back?'

'No. The last thing I want right now is to be with a bunch of coppers getting wasted and playing Monday-morning quarterback. I want some time *not* to think.'

'But what about your things back at the hotel? Where will you stay?'

She surprises herself by bursting into laughter. 'Crispin, you sound exactly like my father – and you're not old enough to do that. This is a tourist town full of shops and hotels' – she gestures with her arms to point to the evidence that is all around them – 'and a tourist is exactly what I want to be, just for now. I've got money and that's all I need. I'll be fine.'

He doesn't look so sure. 'Shall I come back for you in the morning?'

'No, I'll take a ferry. They run like buses. Crispin, will you please stop fussing and just go?'

'Right.' He looks embarrassed. 'Well, I'll be off . . . Grace, one last thing. You know what I said about too many people knowing? Next time you find Gröber you might think of not telling anyone except me – if you need some help, I mean.'

'You mean Nigel's bodysnatchers?'

'Mine, actually. It's my unit, I'm in charge. Nigel doesn't have to know the details, not until it's over.'

'Are you kidding me, or is this another set-up?'

'Neither. I mean it.'

She picks up her bag. 'I'll keep you in mind.'

In the pharmacy where she buys a toothbrush and a bottle of skin cleanser Flint asks the assistant who serves her for advice about hotels and, on a whim, does as she is bidden and takes a steep track heading north out of Morcote that brings her, after a kilometre, to the tinier village of Vico Morcote and the Bellavista – and immediately decides that no hotel has ever been more aptly named. The only room available is a huge suite on the top floor which is flooded with evening light and the scent of camellias, and is half the price she's paying in Lugano. Actually, she doesn't care what it costs; after the events of the day the tranquillity provided by the Bellavista is priceless. She eats an early supper in the hotel's excellent restaurant and then retires to the private terrace of her suite with what remains of a bottle of wine. She phones Cutter again and finds herself talking to the watch supervisor at the Marscheider Building who says that the Director will get back to her first thing in the morning, her time. On another whim she calls Dr Przewalskii's office, intending to leave a message on the answer machine. To her surprise, the phone rings only once before it's answered.

'Hello?'

'Dr P? It's Grace Flint. Is this a bad time?'

'Time is never bad, I think.'

'I meant, are you with a patient?'

'Yes.'

'Then maybe I can call you later, when you're free?'

'I am free now, for you. You are the patient.'

'I am?'

'Do you want to tell me what happened today?'

'I can't. Not on an open line.'

'Ah, yes, the leaks into the bucket. Tell me, do you think these leaks matter any more?'

Flint probes and Dr Przewalskii acknowledges that she has received a call – 'a head up' – from Human Resources.

'A heads up,' Flint corrects her. 'What did they say?'

'Only that today has been very stressful for you because your operation blew up. That you might want to talk to me; that I was please to keep myself available for you. So, I am here.'

'Blew up? I suppose that's one way of putting it.'

'In your face. The operation blew up in your face. This was to do with the man Gröber, I expect.'

'Yes, Gröber and another degenerate, a perp called Çarçani. Nine policemen died today because of them, Dr P, and it was probably my fault.'

'Only *probably*, you think? So is it also possible you are not to blame?'

'I placed them in harm's way – not directly but because of what I did to try to apprehend Gröber and Çarçani. And it was a total waste of those cops' lives because Gröber and Çarçani weren't even there. They'd gone, bolted, and I was too bloody dim to realise it.' Flint hears the whine of self-pity creeping into her voice, tells herself to stop it. 'Listen, Dr P, I'm not calling you to moan about another lousy day at the office. I want to talk to you about Jack.'

'Good. He is much, much better, I hear. *Fantastic* news.'

'Yes, and it seems to me like a miracle. He's going to be ready to leave hospital in two or three days' time and I have to decide what to do. What I'm thinking is, I should take him back to my father . . . my father and Sally. Ask them to take care of him again – if they can forgive me.'

'Forgive you?'

'For being such a cow. For being jealous of them. For taking Jack away from them and putting my father through sheer bloody hell. For putting their lives at risk as well as Jack's . . . For asking them to take him back – because I can't take care of him myself; not yet. You do see that, don't you, Dr P? That I can't stop now; that I have to start again?'

Dr Przewalskii says nothing.

'Can I tell you what Thrush told me?'

'Thrush?'

'The shooter – what she told me about Gröber, what he feels about me, what he said about Jack?'

Courtney's recollection of Gröber's chilling words are playing through her mind like a tape.

Before and after the autopsy I want pictures of the body, lots and lots of pictures . . . Perhaps you can get me some body parts? A finger, an ear? Perhaps the genitalia? Yes, the genitalia would be excellent . . .

'I know, she has spoken of it again during her debriefing. I have read the disgusting things he said about your child. I know how much he hates you.'

'Okay, and that was a while ago when I was merely a threat to him; a persistent irritant but actually no more than a thorn in his side. Now that I've hurt him, really, *really* caused him damage, do you think he's going to change his sick mind? I don't. I think that as long as Gröber's out there he's a direct and constant threat to me, to Jack, to my father – to anyone I care about. Even you, Dr P. I *have* to find him. This won't stop until I do.'

There is another prolonged silence on the line until Dr Przewalskii asks, 'You have a victory, you think? Even though they escaped?'

'Oh, for sure. They're free and clear for now but Gröber's safe haven is gone and his operation is in ruins – and so is Çarçani's shitty empire. They'll have a bolt-hole somewhere, I'm sure, but there's nowhere they can go where they won't be at the top of the most wanted list – not after today. And with Thrush singing, and with the intel we're extracting from the files, we should be able to trace and seize assets worth hundreds of millions of dollars and take down who knows how many of their associates. And some of those scumbags will talk to save themselves and the investigation will grow exponentially. I'm pretty certain that as far as their criminal enterprises go, they're finished. We'll roll up Gröber and Çarçani like a rug.'

The scale of what she has achieved is only now dawning on Flint.

'So, what do you think, Dr P?'

Dr Przewalskii delays before she says what is obviously true: 'I might be completely wrong but maybe it was not such a lousy day at the office, do you think?'

Coda

Vlorë, Albania

Into a mobile phone that is equipped with one of Swisscom's untraceable prepaid SIM cards, Crispin Mallory of MI6 says laconically, 'Teardrop, tonight's your lucky night. Finally, Prince Charming is coming to the ball.'

'My place?'

'Exactly. And, by the by, he's bringing friends, three in a row, all SUVs.'

'Then you'll spread the news?'

'Already done. You'll have company before you know it – and I thought I might also join you.'

'Understood.'

'And, Teardrop.'

'Yes?'

'Remember, please, go gently into this dark night.'

'Sorry?'

'We want him alive.'

'Of course. And his friends?'

'If there is collateral damage, then so be it. I don't really mind what happens to his friends.'

From her observation post on the rooftop of a nightclub called Armando's, Teardrop – whose real name is Stephanie – scans the seafront through night vision goggles. This is the third night she has spent on the roof, and the coldest by far. She huddles inside her parka, waiting for the infantry, the dark figures who will shortly arrive one by one and merge into the shadows in the street beneath her. The snatch team numbers twelve, not including Crispin, nor the four crew members of the fast patrol launch that waits a mile off shore, masquerading under the colours of the Italian navy. This is the largest force Nigel Ridout has ever authorised for an 'overseas collection'; his euphemism for an abduction carried out on foreign soil.

Stephanie shivers, exercises her fingers and her toes to keep the blood circulating.

This is the way it will go down, according to Crispin's plan.

As the target approaches Armando's, Stephanie will drop two grenades from the roof; one smoke, one incendiary. To add to the confusion the explosions will cause, Stephanie will then fire continuous short bursts of blanks from the automatic machine pistol with which she is also armed. Any live fire that may be necessary to deal with the target's friends will come from her colleagues on the ground.

Four members of the team will seize the target, hold him down while a potent mix of pentobarbital and fentanyl is injected into a vein in his neck. By the count of five he will be unconscious, hooded, his wrists and ankles restrained by plastic ties. Then he will be carried like a corpse to the sea wall, no more than fifty metres from the entrance to Armando's, and dumped into a rigid-hull inflatable boat that waits with its engine running. The RIB is capable of forty-five knots and should reach the patrol launch within two minutes.

By Crispin's calculations, from the moment Stephanie drops the first grenade to the moment the target begins his involuntary sea crossing to the Italian coastline fifty kilometres away (and from Italy, onward, by private plane, to England) no more than five minutes will have elapsed.

Stephanie hears a noise behind her but before she can turn Crispin whispers, 'It's only me.' He joins her at the edge of the roof.

'All present and correct?'

'I think so.'

'You *think*?'

Stephanie shrugs. 'I've spotted three, maybe four, but you wanted radio silence so I can't confirm.'

'Where?'

She points to the locations below where she is certain three of the body snatchers have concealed themselves. Crispin asks to borrow her night vision goggles and conducts a reconnaissance of his own.

'I count eight, and there are two with the RIB, and then there's you. So only one unaccounted for – no he's not. See there, that line of parked vehicles, just behind the white van, crouching down? What's he doing there, I wonder.'

'Can you see who it is?'

'Prentice.'

'You want me to ask him?'

Crispin hesitates. Then, 'No, no need. I can see why he's there. There's somebody in the van.'

'A lookout?'

'Perhaps. We'll know soon enough.'

Along the otherwise deserted seafront, three pairs of headlights in close formation are rapidly approaching.

'All right, give everybody a heads up,' says Crispin and Stephanie presses the transmit button on the throat mike she is wearing.

'Target approaching. Stand by.'

Now she is removing the parka and taking from her backpack two grenades and two spares, the machine pistol and five clips of ammunition. Crispin edges away from her to give her room to work. He is still wearing the goggles, concentrating his attention on Prentice and the barely discernible figure who sits in the driver's seat of the white van.

What's your game, chum? he's thinking when the answer becomes apparent. The convoy of SUVs is only metres away when the van lurches into its path bringing it to a stop. The van door opens and the driver leaps out; hits the ground running, as though he's running for his life.

Crispin has one last glimpse of Prentice before the van explodes into a fireball.

Mid Compton

Today is Jack Flint's second birthday and at Glebe Farm there has been a party in the barn, a litter of abandoned kittens the principal guests.

To look at Jack you would think he has made a remarkable recovery from his awful injuries, though to John Flint he seems to be an unusually passive and pensive child; one who prefers the company of small animals to people. Whatever Sally or the specialists might say, Dr Flint is sure he can still detect a lingering wariness in his grandson's eyes.

Sally is pregnant and gloriously so. The more her belly and her breasts swell, the more she blossoms. Dr Flint seems bemused that she is carrying his child as though, beyond the obvious biological connection, he's not really sure how it came about. Given that he will need to survive well into his eighties to see his second child reach maturity, he has promised Sally he will take better care of his health and, somewhat to her alarm, a part of the barn at Glebe Farm is being converted into an exercise room to accommodate a fearsome-looking fitness machine he has ordered on the internet.

Grace did not react badly to the news, as he had feared – nor to the announcement that he and Sally are to be married in March. Just before Christmas, when he'd felt he could wait no longer and he'd told her on the phone – she was in Ukraine at the time – the pause she had allowed was barely perceptible. Then a soft laugh and, 'Do I get to be the maid of honour?'

What Grace did not react well to was her father's third piece of news: that he and Sally and Jack were moving back to Glebe Farm.

'Dad, you simply can't do that. There's still a risk. There always will be until we find him.'

'And how much longer before that happens?' – a question to which Flint had no truthful answer. 'I'm sorry, darling, I know you're doing your very best, of course you are, but we have to go home. We've got a practice to run, patients to take care of, and we desperately want to get on with our lives. My mind's made up, and Sally's absolutely on board, because if we have to stay in bloody Bexhill-on-Sea for a moment—'

'NO!' – cutting him off. '*Please*! Dad, you mustn't say that, say where you are. Nobody can know, including me.'

'Well, to tell you the truth, Gracie, I don't really care. I'm very grateful to Tom Glenning and his people for all that they've done but the life we have here is no life at all. I don't know what the median age of our neighbours is but I do know that I've never felt so old. Another week here and I fear Sally will be pushing me down to the seafront in a wheelchair while I drool onto my cardigan.'

'Listen, I'll get you moved, relocated to somewhere more—'

'We're going home, Gracie. I've spoken to Commander Glenning and told him that we're willing to take the risk, and he understands; even agrees, I think.'

And is Jack willing to take the risk?

She didn't say it. Given her own abysmal track record, this was something she could never ask.

Every day, at Commander Glenning's request, Oxfordshire Constabulary sends a patrol car to Glebe Farm at random intervals, and John Flint keeps his shotgun on a high shelf by the front door. There are also panic buttons installed on each floor of the house and in the barn, which will trigger a rapid police response, at least in theory.

Not much of a deterrent, Grace Flint thinks. She believes that the only way to protect her family – and, for that matter, the world at large – is to sustain unrelenting pressure on Gröber and Çarçani. She does that by travelling constantly, chivvying the authorities in the sixteen nations that are now part of Operation Payback to continue their ferocious assaults on the remnants of Çarçani's sex trade empire, and on the lawyers, bankers, accountants, crooked magistrates, cops and politicians who facilitate it. Whenever she detects a flagging of resolve she brings new evidence from the files and admissions of the Gup brothers and DVDs containing ever more harrowing filmed interviews with some of the women Çarçani enslaved. She no longer gives press conferences or appears on TV but, behind the scenes, she does her utmost to ensure that Gröber and Çarçani remain fixed in the public spotlight; among the world's most wanted criminals and permanently on the run.

The wear and tear on Flint has been considerable. When she arrived at Glebe Farm last night much later than she'd promised – a difficult journey from Budapest, she'd explained, including two missed connections – her father said, his face creased with concern, 'Darling, you look absolutely wiped out.'

'I'm all right, Dad, honestly. Just a bit tired.'

'More than that, I think.' He poured her a drink, made her sit down in an armchair in front of the living-room fire. 'Is it worth it, Gracie? Worth all this terrible strain you're putting yourself under?'

She thinks so. Since the Lugano debacle (and perhaps in part because of it) law enforcement agencies in the sixteen co-operating countries have arrested more than eight hundred associates of Gröber and Çarçani and seized assets valued in excess of one billion dollars, and at the most recent closed hearing of the Senate Permanent Subcommittee on Investigations – a hearing which Flint could not attend because she was once more travelling – Senator Coleman had wondered aloud if Operation Payback might not be the most productive international criminal investigation ever mounted by the United States.

'You keep this up, I wouldn't be surprised if they give you a medal,' Director Cutter had told Flint on the phone.

She'd laughed and said, 'What's second prize?' refusing to admit that she felt a tinge of pride.

Tonight, in the aftermath of Jack's birthday party, she is once more in the living room sitting before the fire, Jack cradled in her arms watching her face. He has nothing to say but his fingers are entwined with hers and he seems to be entirely content. Sally is in the kitchen preparing supper. Grace's father is in the barn settling down his patients, giving the kittens their last feed of the night.

She and Jack are both drifting towards sleep when she is suddenly aware of the sound of approaching car engines, the hard crunch of tyres on the gravel of the drive. Instantly she is alert, and so is Jack. She gets up from the armchair, places her son on the sofa and says, 'Darling, stay here. Mummy won't be long.' She leaves the living room and, once she is sure that Jack can no longer see her, runs down to the hallway to the front door. She can hear men's voices outside and even though they don't sound threatening she retrieves the shotgun from the high shelf, checks that both barrels are loaded; waits with her right ear pressed against the door.

There is a momentary silence until she hears her father say in an astonished tone, 'What on earth's going on?'

'John, it's Cutter, Aldus Cutter. Great to see you again.'

Not just Director Cutter. When Flint eases open the front door she also sees Commander Glenning, a dozen or more other men and four – no, five – unmarked cars parked in the driveway. The men are not in uniform but some of them are ostentatiously armed with automatic weapons and they bristle at the sight of Flint's shotgun. Cutter says quickly, 'Hey, Grace, what kind of welcome is that?'

She points the gun at the ground.

'And they are?'

'They're mine,' Glenning interjects. 'Specialist armed response unit. Let's get you both inside the house.'

Before she can ask why, Cutter tells her, 'You've got what you wanted, Grace. You've got your war.'

It was a huge explosion, says Cutter. Judging by the size of the crater left in the road, the forensic experts in Vlorë – who know a thing or two about improvised bombs – estimate that the van was packed with at least one thousand kilos of high explosive; most likely, trinitrotoleune. 'TNT to you and me,' Cutter adds.

Sally has taken Jack upstairs. John Flint is in the kitchen keeping out of the way.

'The assholes who planned this made one miscalculation – or that's the way I'm reading it.' Cutter is pacing the living room as he tells his story, more agitated than Flint has ever seen him. 'They assumed that Çarçani would be in the lead SUV.'

'Çarçani? This was his convoy? You're sure?'

'Yeah, and I'll get to that. Bear with me, Grace.'

'Sorry.'

He dismisses her apology with a wave of the hand but it takes him a moment to re-find the thread. 'Where was I? Okay. The blast was designed to take out the lead SUV, and that it surely did. They're still picking body parts off the rooftops. But Çarçani was riding in the back of the *third* SUV, which is why he's alive; just. He took a shrapnel wound to the head, and went into cardiac arrest. The paramedics who attended the scene pulled him through but they couldn't save his legs – both amputated above the knees.'

Flint couldn't care less about the extent of Çarçani's injuries.

'Didn't take off his hands, though – which is how we know. The blast stripped him, naked like a baby; obviously no ID on his person. So the locals printed him, got a ten-ten match with Çarçani and called Tirana, and Tirana called me. I was already on my way to London to meet up with Tom because five days ago we got a call on the tip line – anonymous, of course – saying that Gröber was in Ireland. Gave an address in a place called Blackrock which is about five miles south of Dublin, on the coast; even gave a description of his car, a blue Ford Mondeo. Didn't sound very likely but I asked the Garda Síochána to check it out and they put surveillance on the house. The guys were only just getting into position when the Ford came out of the garage like the house was on fire. No way they could follow it. The Garda put out an all-points and the Ford was found parked in the centre of Dublin about two hours later. It was a Hertz car rented at Dublin airport on New Year's Eve by a Margaret Funder out of Hudson, New York – same Margaret Funder who rented the house in Blackrock for one month.'

'Fake ID?' Flint asks.

'Nope. The passport, the driver's licence and the Amex card she used are all kosher. The problem is, she's not. The address she uses in Hudson is a mail drop and her mail gets forwarded to a law firm in London.'

'A firm of solicitors, in fact,' says Glenning. 'Want to guess which one, Grace?'

It takes Flint a moment to grasp what he means, until her episodic memory conjures up a picture of a pinched-faced receptionist and she hears herself asking, *Tell me something, do all the clients get treated this way, or are you being especially rude to me?*

'Marylebone? The grubby outfit the Gups used?'

'Spot on.'

'Cutting to the chase,' says Cutter, 'we asked the Garda to hold off for twenty-four hours, just keep the house and the car under surveillance, see what happened. Well, nothing happened. So the day before yesterday they gained entry to the premises, which is

another way of saying they opened the front door with an axe . . .'
Cutter waits until Flint smiles, 'and what they found told them that
the place had been abandoned in one hell of a hurry. The bed
unmade, items of clothing – men's and women's – scattered about,
toiletries in the bathroom, other personal items. Question is, why?'

Flint is sitting on the floor with her back against the sofa, her
arms folded, hugging her knees. Her eyes are brilliant, reflecting the
light of the fire.

'Oh, and I didn't say, more fingerprints than you could wish for;
two sets.'

'And?'

Cutter stares at her stone-faced.

'*Aldus?*'

'One set unidentified, so far. The other set belongs to . . .
Gröber.'

'For sure?'

'For certain. So?' Cutter waits, wanting to know if Flint has
figured it out.

She takes her time before she begins. 'The call to the tip line
came from Çarçani or one of his people. Çarçani gave us Gröber
because he blames Gröber for what's happened – well, let's be
frank, he blames Gröber for me.'

'No doubt about it.'

'Then, after I had had all the time I needed to arrange for a
raiding party, Çarçani warned Gröber, called him in Blackrock and
told him that he was about to be arrested, that he only had minutes
to get out of the house. He knew that Gröber would never
surrender and certainly not to me. He was probably hoping –
expecting – that Gröber would walk right into armed response; that
there would be a firefight, that he'd get himself killed.'

'Makes sense to me.'

'Except it didn't work because I didn't know about Blackrock
and you only asked the Garda for passive surveillance, not armed
response.'

'Right.'

'And having got away from Blackrock, Gröber found out, or
worked out what had happened, that Çarçani had set him up, and
he made some phone calls to Albania, to one of the rival clans – and
now Çarçani has stumps instead of legs. Is that your reading?'

'We're on the same page.'

'What I don't know, what I haven't figured out, is why was Gröber in Ireland? What was he doing?' She looks at her watch, gets to her feet.

'It's too late,' Glenning tells her. 'There are no more flights to Dublin, not tonight.'

'So, when?'

'The first flight out of Birmingham is at six twenty a.m. And you don't need to call because you're already booked.'

It is just after 4 a.m. and Flint is crossing the driveway towards her car, careful not to slip on the ice. The leader of Commander Glenning's armed response unit whispers into his throat microphone.

'Nectar's moving.'

'Isn't she just – and what a mover she is.'

'Hey, Badger Two! This is no fucking joke. You just make damn sure you stay with her.'

After a moment, 'Roger that.'

Acknowledgements

As wise publishers always roundly declare, all characters in this novel are fictitious and any resemblance to real persons is . . . well, in this case, not entirely coincidental. Jerry Crawford and Al Singleton, aka 'Blade', are veteran Homicide detectives and great friends, who have generously allowed me to borrow from some of their experiences. Most of what I say about them is, however, entirely made up. Blade said he knew he was reading pure fiction when I ascribed to his namesake greying temples and an expanding midriff.

And Dr Przewalskii does bear some resemblance to Marina Voikhanskaya, a wise and wonderful woman who, like Dr P, tangled with the KGB because she objected to the misuse of psychiatry in the former Soviet Union. Flint's sessions with Dr P are somewhat based on unnerving mock consultations I had with Marina, with me playing the role of her patient.

Len Gowland introduced me to the wonders of the Meade telescope by buying me one for my birthday. For that, and for our enduring friendship, I am profoundly grateful.

Olivia Hill was my adviser on all matters relating to pregnancy, childbirth and the rearing of infants – subjects which she knows a great deal about. Her help was simply invaluable.

Tamara Jones of *The Washington Post* wrote a superb article about the Bowie Health Center in Maryland where the youngest victim of a spate of random sniper attacks in the Washington DC area in 2002 received life-saving treatment. Some of the details of Jack Flint's treatment at the fictional North Bethesda Family Health Center are extrapolated from her article.

Ed Victor remains the best literary agent in the world not only because of the deals he negotiates but because of the unremitting care he holds for his authors; or, at least, this one. Gráinne Fox is following in his footsteps.

For various reasons, this book took far too long to write. For their patience, support and, above all, their understanding, I'm grateful to the Headline family, my publishers, and in particular Martin Neild, Kerr MacRae and Martin Fletcher.

Sara Walden was the first and last reader of every draft, and the reason for writing them.

This book is dedicated to Robert Ducas, his daughter, Annoushka, and Louise, his second wife.

Robert was my literary agent for twenty-five years. Even when that arrangement ceased he remained what he had always been: a towering, irreplaceable friend. Robert died of cancer, absurdly prematurely, in February 2004. Had he lived I'm certain he would have chided me for taking so long to write this book – and loudly defended me against anyone else who had the nerve to say so. He was loyal to a fault; an extraordinary man.

He died with religious faith in life beyond death. I hope he was right. I expect he's reading this book now saying, 'Not bad, Paul, not bad – but rather late?'